Heir to Govandhara

Heir to Govandhara

Saira Ramasastry

Writers Club Press
San Jose New York Lincoln Shanghai

Heir to Govandhara

Writers Club Press
an imprint of iUniverse.com, Inc.

For information address:
iUniverse.com, Inc.
620 North 48th Street, Suite 201
Lincoln, NE 68504-3467
www.iuniverse.com

ISBN: 0-595-13066-6

Printed in the United States of America

To my husband
Your love is my fantasy

Acknowledgements

I've been fortunate to have the kindness and support of many people in writing *Heir to Govandhara*. It's difficult to know exactly how to thank my family, because they've always done so much. My Mom and Dad—Petra and Jay—are the inspiration for Kasimi. I hope they will eventually get around to reading the book. My sister and her husband—Anita and Walter—are brilliant people who have provided constant encouragement.

Helen Spurling, my chum in Cambridge—thank you. Over how many pints did we hash out ideas and plots? Thanks for the mischief!

There are so many others: the Morace family, Bob and Marge Hedman, my editor Diana Kirk, Sachiyo Minegishi, the folks at Christ's College, and the Bro.

I will be forever grateful for the love and friendship of my husband, Chris Morace. He's the last of a dying breed of gentlemen.

To Kasimi!

For more information, please visit the
Heir to Govandhara website at
http://www.heirtogovandhara.com

Introduction

Prophecy On the Coming of the Third Miracle
~ Told by the Elders ~

The birth of Sri had been planned for three generations by the priests and scholars of the Kasimian lands. It was known that one of the sky powers would take on a masculine form exactly one thousand moons after Varuna, the sea god, slipped from the mortal realm to sit beside Kasimi. This new power would need a proper consort to create the next link from the Kasimians to the gods, and so Sri was intended.

She needed to be the exact combination of feminine components alongside spiritual purity achieved only through careful breeding. Varuna and his favored consort Sona had left behind a son, named Osra, who held the strength of his father in him. He was able to conquer the oceans to the lands beyond Kasimi to bring his good people slaves and fruits so they would not need to suffer as much. During one expedition, Osra received a vision from Varuna in the form of a storm. His boat was led by the powers of the sea god to a paradise whose only inhabitant was a beautiful woman with the voice that had been Osra's thoughts through his life. This woman, Putana, would be his match, and they would produce only one son.

ix

His name would be Varuna II, named after the grandfather who had prepared his parents' union. He had the power of his grandfather's storm in his soul, and was a successful warrior. Where Osra's voyages would take him, Varuna II was able to conquer the lands and spread the land of Kasimi further up into the mountains and to far off islands, protected by the sea power. He took many a slave to his bed, but his proper mate was determined by the Kasimian priests.

Varuna's favored had a grand niece through the bloodline of her brother, who was of proper breeding to attend to Varuna II. She had been raised to be a noble concubine just as her great aunt, and felt blessed to be given to the direct descendant of the sea god. She was united with the warrior and together they produced a male and female set. The boy child was Marici. The girl child was Sri. The gods sent Varuna II and his mistress two children because Sri had to be taken by the Kasimian noble priests at birth. She would be sheltered and hidden away from people until her bonding to the sky god.

Born from three generations of intended breeding, Sri was gifted with the blood of the Kasimians and the lineage of the divine. She would be the one worthy to entertain the sky god. On the fateful day, they would be united in a prayer of the third miracle, moved to embrace each other by the divine.

As a mortal female, Sri was simple and lovely. Her beauty was pronounced from an early age through features that promised to shape into the sharp, alluring lines of elegance. Her rounded black eyes lined with a thin border of red looked with scrutiny and passion on her small, sheltered world. Her paternal grandmother, Putana, had lent her rampantly curling tresses of blue black hair that looked best when free of constraints. Constantly sheltered from the sun, Sri's skin remained a light mocha with hints of yellow on her palms and feet.

Sri was trained to look delicate and docile, as a proper Kasimian woman. But a child of the sea energy would exhibit strength in her frame. Her height was a healthy compromise between that of a tall woman and an average man, with developed strength around her easy curves. The unusual combination of power and vulnerability in this child of Varuna was somehow appropriate.

As much as the priests would mold and form her, Sri had been given the blood of the divine. And yes—she was obedient. And yes—she was proper. The priests and scholars did not realize that Sri's blessed breeding could also be a curse; the tendencies for power were ingrained into her spirit. It would be dormant for years, but eventually Sri would come into her own.

On the night of Sri's birth, one thousand moons into the prophecy, the moon showed in two pieces over Kasimi. The full orange oval was divided by a lingering black cloud into three symmetric pieces which was the sign to the Kasimian priests that both the sky energy and his consort would be born that night. The child god would not avail himself until it was time; but his consort's birth was intended. The Grand Priest Ajan went to the house of Varuna II to await the coming of the girl child, saying prayers of thanks to the gods while Sri's mother screamed out in pain.

At dawn, as the moon slipped away into the morning, there were two children, brother and sister. Ajan did not allow the parents to touch the intended Sri, taking her immediately from her mother's womb into his arms. He cleaned the girl child himself and wrapped her in a special white blanket that had been made by the elder priests, and carried her in his arms out of her father's house.

The Grand Priest would be Sri's mentor and protector until she was of age. On the two week journey to the sacred temple on Govandhara, Ajan rocked the babe in his arms and made his

*promises to her. He would love her and nurture her, keep her pro-
tected from the rival gods who would wish to seduce her away
from the sky god. He would teach her and indulge her, yet keep
her humble and pure.*

*Ajan had been a warrior before he was chosen to be the Grand
Priest, and was far from a virtuous man. He was a member of the
Northern Kingdom, of one of the most influential noble houses in
Kasimi, thus raised in privilege and in wealth. Ajan grew to be a
powerful young man, taller and stronger than most of the accomplished warriors of the land. He was also charmed with the mysteri-
ously handsome face of the men of his family, with statuesque
features, and chocolate skin. His eyes were cerulean, as his mother
was touched by the far-north gods, and his voice took on a hypnotic
and calm quality that made him gifted in the verbal arts.*

*His parents thought that his calling was battle, and so he was
trained to be a warrior starting at the age of fourteen. His deft
fingers proved to be valuable with a bow and arrow and his rare
combination of grace and power made him easily accomplished
with the lethal tools of combat. With natural ability and the
name of his father, Ajan would quickly move to the position of
Protector in the Kasimian royal army. The reign of Ajan in the
high ranks would be a dark time of war, for the man would have
no respect for life that was not his own. This ruthlessness granted
him victory time and time again.*

*In one of the biggest battles in Kasimian history, the one that
would expand the land into the southern isles, Ajan brought the
army to victory. Ajan had told his soldiers to kill every man and
boy regardless of whether he came in peace—to conquer the
south isles meant extermination of all power there. He ordered
his soldiers to use whatever weapons they felt necessary to bring
pain and suffering in the deaths of these men. And when the battle was done, Ajan permitted his soldiers a night of feasting in the*

beds of the widowed women and fatherless girls. If a soldier grew fond of any of the women, he was permitted to claim her as a slave in his home.

But the gods would come to Ajan in a painful vision in the aftermath of this battle. He took a fifteen year old, red haired beauty to his bed that night to delight in her youth. The child seemed fresh and pure, trembling as he reached out to touch her at the first sign of night. When he woke after the first burst of love-making, the red haired youth was hovering over him, floating. The innocence of her youthful face was replaced with the horrors of the demons. Her eye sockets were hollow and her teeth pro-truded upward towards her eyes as sharp as the swords with which Ajan had killed the villages.

She spoke, only once in the ancient, scholarly language of the gods. "Protector and warrior of Kasimi," the voice screamed, "you have claimed the South Isles for us which is good. But you have passed thousands of innocent souls to our realm tonight that bring us anger and hatred, for their deaths were not in honor. You have angered us, Ajan. For this, you will dedicate your life to us. But you are a good son of the North, so you will rise quickly to power. Do as a priest what you did not do as a warrior. Serve us..." And then the vision disappeared.

Ajan led his soldiers back to the center of Kasimi to receive the nobles, priests and well wishers who would welcome them home from the victorious battlefield. Ajan would address the people and tell them this would be his last expedition with the army, for now, he would serve the gods with the priests. A most powerful warrior and nobleman, blessed with a handsome face and a piercing voice, would quickly rise to the rank of Grand Priest, as the demoness had predicted. Ajan was destined for power, but now he knew to use that blessing to serve the gods.

The Grand Priest would be the one to raise Sri, and prepare her to be the consort to the sky god. His purpose would be to create the Queen for his King, and then to serve them faithfully as they brought peace to Kasimi.

PART I

I

Kasimi had blessed *Govandhara* with another heartbreaking spring. The colors, always so vivid along the beaches of the Kingdom, were even more beautiful now. The priests of Kasimi would praise *Brahma* for blessing the land with the rays of the sun, and the plentiful fruit. But in truth, it was the people of *Govandhara* that made the spring so beautiful.

The people of the kingdom, mysterious and charming, made more use of the daylight than during the wet season. They chose silks with patterns hailing the flowers that bloomed, in colors that *Brahma* painted in the sky. They would make music with their laughter, and seek the beaches to praise Varuna. They would count another year gone by, waiting for the spring when their god and savior would come. Until that time, they had the spring—and Sri—to bring them hope.

At fifteen, Sri was truly lovely. Her skin, flawless in its mocha stain, was upstaged only by the tumultuous mass of waving, black hair that fell freely at her back. Her features were carved of the gods, sharp but feminine, and reflective of ancestors past. And her eyes. Black pools ringed with red, marked her as the Intended Queen. She was only one year away from marriage to the sky god, when he would emerge and bring Kasimi to glory once more.

Sri, like the other people of the temple, had gone for an afternoon stroll in the gardens. She had left her mentor behind, and wandered off in the endless mango trees that lined the forest path. She enjoyed the scent of ripening fruit, alongside the perfume of wildflowers. The thick heat made the smells stain on her skin and hair.

In the spring, Sri would travel without the weight of the heavier winter sarongs and wear cooler wraps. Her hair and feet could go unfettered, and without jewels. She enjoyed this free state, when her identity could fade away in *Govandhara*. Only in the spring.

It was unusual for Sri to wander off without Ajan, but today she felt compelled to go alone. She treasured him, but needed silence from his lessons and teachings. Lately, he had been asking too much of her. She needed the afternoon to herself.

The last thing Sri remembered before slipping from the border of mango trees, onto the sand was Ajan summoning her. His piercing baritone voice called out...

Sri, darling. Come to me. You have wandered too far.

Normally, this hypnotic tone would be enough to make Sri obey. But, this time—she did not listen. She wandered further through the bunches of wild flowers, and spread the thick overgrown branches of the last line of mango trees until she stood in her grandfather's garden.

Varuna, god of the ocean, was delighted to have this child come to relish his beauty. Rippling waves pulled at the girl's honey silk, kissing it gently and then releasing the material back at her side. Sri taunted back by running playfully towards the deeper parts of the ocean. Her great grandfather held his little Sri carefully and pulled her further into his tide making graceful waves for the child to glide in. Sri forgot the work of her hand maids, and let her honey silk wrap cling to her and the sea wash strands of her braided hair onto her face. After a few moments, Sri's elder parent pushed her back to the shore to gently place her on the hard packed sand. The Kasimian spring sun felt pleasing on wet skin.

Ajan found the dent in the mango trees that had brought Sri to the ocean and moved swiftly through so that his feet met the sand. His cerulean gaze met the vision of the beached Sri, softening the anger and disappointment at her disobedience. "Darling…" he murmured. Ajan quickly walked to Sri's side, kneeling in his white-silk pajama suit to whisper in her ear, "Darling…"

Sri looked up from her semi dry state to receive the chilling gaze of her mentor. She had disobeyed him and the subtle look of disappointment in his eyes shook her from her revelry. Sri pulled her honey wrap around her to keep warm. Delicate hands attempted to move the sea washed strands of hair back into the braids.

"Darling, do not wander off like that. You know how I worry." Ajan shed his disappointment for tenderness with his cherished ward. The girl had softened his warrior's heart long ago, though he often kept it hidden.

Sri nodded her head softly. The Kasimian sun was setting next to the ocean's edge. The sun's rays dimmed, a warning of sudden darkness. And, the lapping water that did occasionally drift up to Sri and Ajan's feet grew slightly colder in temperature.

Ajan picked up his beautiful ward in his arms as he stood. He held the precious child towards the view of the sunset and the ocean to enjoy it as his eyes would. He placed a chaste kiss on Sri's forehead and murmured tenderly to her, "Darling, shall we return to the temple for the evening?" Without waiting for a response, Ajan began his walk through the temple's forest. And as she had after many a long journey, Sri fell peacefully asleep in her mentor's arms.

The walk back to the temple was quiet and uneventful. The sweet scent of mangoes lingered in the air, while the sun went to sleep behind the blossoms. Ajan held Sri protectively through the path back towards their home, pausing only to admire the true beauty that was growing in his ward.

When his thoughts strayed to her sixteenth birthday, his arms would tighten slightly against the girl and his lips would seek the ocean stained taste of her cheeks. In truth, Ajan treasured these walks where he could truly cherish the child while she slept. He had made Sri—loved Sri—tended to the Intended since she had entered the Kasimian world. When he took her in his arms fifteen years ago, he could not have asked the gods for a more precious and pure gift. But, the gods had cursed his heart. As Ajan loved Sri, he would have to give her up in just eleven moons. This thought—made Ajan's lips find Sri's forehead.

Sri's mentor stepped out of the forest and began his proud strides towards the temple. The reflecting pools, one on either side of the path, were being decorated with large white candles on the marble edges as they were at every full moon. Ajan did not look at the image, as he usually would. His attention was completely on Sri—his only child—as he continued forward towards the temple.

At the first step in the main staircase to the temple entrance, Ajan collapsed with emotion and sank to a kneeling position with his ward in his arms. He felt so insignificant on his temple's grounds. The white marble structure was seven times Ajan's height, with intricate carvings of the gods etched in all sizes upon every inch of the temple. On the full moon, white candles were placed randomly in the carved crevices of the temple to comple-ment the natural light of the moon. The elders said that the temple was the mortal moon to match the gods' one up above.

The temple's inside was even more glorious than the outside. One grand room meant for worship, constructed of all white mar-ble dominated the place. Three levels of double balconies traced the borders of the worship room, where the temple's guests and inhabitants could watch the elder priests and scholars perform the rituals. The good people of the temple lived in small rooms on these levels, knowing that just outside, was a vision of the gods.

Ajan cradled his ward gently in his arms at the steps to his domain. He had many a servant, much influence and massive wealth as the Grand Priest. He was more powerful than all the heads of the noble houses—but to Ajan, there was only one jewel and one concern. He murmured to the child in his arms, "Sri, darling..."

~

The head priest from each of the four noble houses lived in Ajan's temple. Ajan was the representative of the Northern House, the most wealthy in Kasimi. He did not require the services of a scholar or an advisor, and chose to be the sole religious guide for his kingdom while also being the supreme spiritual ruler of the Kasimians. He could not trust anyone but himself in the dealings with the other priests.

"We need to find the sky power now, for we must prepare him for His Time in Kasimi. I have a few ideas as to how we may go about this task, my lords," said Ajan as he paced slowly about the meeting chamber. This secret space was built for private meetings of the priests and scholars, reached only by a narrow staircase descending from the back of the temple to an underground compartment. There was no furniture or marble to civilize the space. It stood bare and raw; its only purpose was for private and frank conversations. Ajan held the only source of light in the room, a staff of fire that served as his weapon of control during the debates. He held the light. The meeting began and ended with him.

Ajan paused, and looked at his advisors with curiosity. His cerulean gaze was chillingly calm and constantly shifting from annoyed to jovial through a slight tightening and widening of his eyelids. He trusted no one in this room. And, he knew the men despised him. The three advisors wanted his position and more importantly, his power. At any moment, Ajan's death could make that possible. He paced carefully, as to not pronounce or deny the long sword worn on his outer hip.

"Before I speak, I wish to know what thoughts each of you has regarding the emergence of the sky power. The prophecy said we would be guided by the moon and by our wisdom. His discovery, therefore, is in our hands. We must serve the gods with faith and trust." Ajan aimed the fire torch indirectly at each of the three priests' faces for a brief moment to better view their eyes, and humble them.

Sudha, the Priest from the South spoke first, as usual. He was a small man, shorter than most women, which made people see him as innocuous and unassuming. He had soft features and a rounded belly that folded gently over the belt around his tunic. He looked older than his age, with fine lines around his eyes and mouth and little hair to cover his head. Sudha had lived a comfortable life as a spiritual leader. His father was a minor land noble in the Southern House, and had two sons. Since Sudha was the younger of the two, with no prospects for marriage to a nobleman's daughter or for inheritance, the priesthood was a reasonable compromise for him. No one had ever connected Sudha to some of the political games that were played in the kingdoms, yet.

"We have all made lists of the boys born on the one thousandth moon in the prophecy from our respective houses. We should evaluate the bloodline and worthiness of each boy to determine who is the sky power," stated Sudha flatly. This was the obvious and neutral answer that everyone expected. It had to be said. Sudha could now relax for the rest of the meeting, having contributed words. He did not really know what to do about finding the sky god. He simply hoped that the power would be from his house.

Ajan circled behind Sudha and paused for a moment. He placed his strong hand on the southern priest's shoulder and squeezed it with some strength, in reassurance and warning. Ajan had little patience for words that were used to fill space without meaning. In his baritone, ice calm voice, Ajan responded, "Yes, Sudha. We all know that is one course of action and it is also the lengthiest. Do I need to remind you that we only have a short time now? Does anyone else have anything to say on this?" Ajan removed his grip on Sudha's shoulder slowly, letting his slender fingers touch the man's red silk tunic to the last.

The next man to speak was the Priest from The Isles. "We should watch and pray for a sign, Your Grace. We should look to this moon for a symbol of where the sky god could be found and then go there," said Vishal. His voice, was even deeper than Ajan's with a refined accent always bordering on arrogant. Vishal was more of a secular nobleman than a priest and more of a politician than a spiritual leader. He was the oldest son of the leader of The Isles and would inherit the Kingdom one day if he did not attain a more important position. His interests and goals were always questionable.

Ajan walked behind Vishal. But, he knew better than to try the same tactics with this man that he had used with Sudha. Vishal was smaller than Ajan; however, Vishal was a powerfully built man. His hard set features pronounced his strength by the clenched position of his jaw and the deep set nature of his coal black eyes. Vishal was also a very distant relative of Sri, which gave him weight in Kasimi. That fact made Ajan give Vishal some liberties in the meetings. "Yes, I have thought about that as well, Vishal," murmured Ajan flatly.

Ajan had thought about this, and also dismissed the notion not long ago. "Do you have anything to contribute, Devyn?"

The last to speak was always Devyn, the priest and scholar from the colony of Goane. Devyn was not respected by the Kasimians, for he was an outsider. Osra had colonized Goane for the fruits and slaves two generations ago. Osra also introduced the Goane people to the beliefs of Kasimi, and selected Said, his second in command, to be the leader of this new house along with some other Kasimians who wished to relocate. However, Said's heart fell upon a beautiful auburn haired, Goanian woman who he took as his only wife and lover. They had five girls, and Devyn was their only son. He was not a pure Kasimian, and his seat in Ajan's temple was highly controversial. This fed Devyn's need to prove himself, making him an ambitious and formidable adversary for Ajan. But, the Grand Priest had a strange admiration for this advisor. While he had been known for many an intrigue, Devyn had never double crossed Ajan. His work had been pure and in Ajan's best interests, always.

Devyn ran his hands through his salted red hair slowly, to match the rhythm of Ajan's pacing. Her rubbed his black eyes several times, pressing the blood from his pupils back into his mind. Then, he admitted, "No, I have nothing to contribute at this time."

Ajan's eyes looked over Devyn's modest frame a few times and gave him an efficient nod. "I can accept that," he replied, with a ring of appreciation in his otherwise dark tone. Ajan placed his torch against the wall, letting the fire beat precariously against the hard rock. It was a small room, and every gesture had a claustrophobic and precise effect. The Grand Priest pivoted on his barefoot heel, and took a seat in front of his advisors to speak to them of his plan.

"My worthy advisors," Ajan began, to soften the men to his plan, "I wish for Sri to lead us to the sky god." Ajan held out his elegant hand to motion for the three priests to stop and hear him out. He then closed the five fingers until only one stood, as he brought it to the center of his full lips in a quiet command for silence. He let his dark gaze look on each of the three men again. Their very first reaction to his idea would give him the most information. Ajan made sure to imprint those expressions into his memory, in perfect detail.

"Sri is the Intended. Who better to lead us to the sky god than his intended love? I believe it is in this woman, that we shall find our King." Ajan flicked his eyes across the men again, to watch them. All men appeared neutral and aloof at this time, so Ajan moved forward. "Soon, I will teach Sri the next level of meditation where she may commune with her divine ancestors. I saw her reach her great grandfather just the other day. I believe that she is the only one with purest gift to find our King. She will meditate, and then we will seek her vision out."

The first response to this idea would be from Vishal, who announced his disagreement with a round laughter, which eerily filled the deserted meeting space. He was seated on a rock, and decided to bring his posture to a ready alert by centering his balance in his feet—ready to stand at any moment. His thin lips twisted into a sneer as he opened one palm in the common gesture of counterargument. "She is not a woman, Ajan. She is a fifteen year old child. I do not think she has the strength of wit to lead us to our next King. She is not a divinity, Ajan. She is an intended wife—a woman. Nothing more. Your plan lacks sense!" At the end of the honest retort, Vishal was standing facing Ajan at his own level.

"Do not be so arrogant, Vishal, as to underestimate the power of youth. Sri is fifteen, yes. And we are much older. Our minds are clouded by the sins of politics and favoritism. In this Intended, we have something so pure and perfect. She is wise and well learned.

To insult her knowledge is to insult me for I have been the one to teach her," Ajan stated in a flat, calm voice. He walked in a tight circle around Vishal's spot, choosing to point the hip that held his sword towards the Priest from The Isles.

Vishal did not hide his feelings well. He was quick to anger, and took a sick kind of pride in his aggressive gestures. His clenched fists were a perfect complement to the loud voice he used to continue his argument against Ajan. "You act as if the wisdom of the real world is a bad thing, Ajan. You act as if our King will be some pure, innocent youth who can only be known by a pure, innocent woman. That is where I find fault with your reasoning. Our King will be strong, omnipotent and wise in the ways of the real world. In no way can an inexperienced soul like Sri be prepared to seek out one as mighty as the solar god. You ju..."

Sudha did have one good purpose. He often interrupted the other Priests before they went too far with Ajan. It was this Southern Priest who had prevented the temple from truly experiencing Ajan's wrath. "Vishal, if you are so certain that this plan will fail...then why not let us go forth with the plan until it fails?"

"Because we don't have time!" screamed Vishal. The tension in the man's fists had spread to his shoulders and jaw which were locked in place with anger. "I will not have the destiny of Kasimi...of our people...compromised by an infatuation with Sri. I do not know what is going on with you, Ajan. But I would advise you...in good conscience I must advise you to watch yourself."

"Is that a threat, Vishal?" asked Ajan with a low voice as he arched a defined brow. "Because, I do not take to threats kindly. In fact, I act on them." Ajan dared to take a deft hand and squeeze Vishal's shoulder from his position behind the Priest from the South Isles. He gripped tighter, ensuring a surgence of pain through Vishal's bone and took on an strangely affectionate tone.

"We are all friends here, *acha*? We should not argue like this, should we?"

Vishal's face was red. His charcoal gray eyes were not visible behind the tightly shut eyelids that had recently closed. His own, rough yet well cared for hand gripped Ajan's own in its place on his shoulder, and squeezed artfully with an equal amount of tension. "Yes, we are all friends here."

Devyn had not spoken. He remained sitting on his rock with his knees tucked casually under his chin. He watched, apathetic, as the priests quarreled. He laughed under his breath from time to time because the words coming out of the other nobles' mouths were so crafted. He knew the real meaning, the real desire of each house. Devyn knew what each priest really wanted. He was at an advantage because Goane had no chance of ever competing politically with the other houses. Goane's only option was to truly and purely worship the gods. The game of politics within worship, was both unattainable and unacceptable to Devyn.

Sudha retreated beside Devyn, knowing that whatever tension existed between Ajan and Vishal would have to exist with those two men alone. His rounded body, with some maneuvering, found a spot on Devyn's rock, as the priest took his place in the shadows.

Ajan remained in a deadlock with Vishal as the tension that had existed for some years between the men found itself in their grip. His fingers did not grip tighter, as to not exert more energy in the disagreement than was required. After a few moments of awkward silence, Ajan spoke with proud authority. "We will go forward with my plan. I shall prepare Sri personally for this most important task starting at dawn. From this point on, she will only have contact with me. Sri will not attend worship, and will not listen to anyone's teachings but my own as to not cloud her mind with other ideas. Is that understood, my lords?"

The question was meant for Vishal, though it was carefully addressed to all the priests. Sudha and Devyn nodded efficiently, not verbalizing answers. Vishal lifted Ajan's hand from his shoulder and placed it back by the Grand Priest's side in purposefully slow motion. The Priest from The Isles then pivoted and let his charcoal eyes gaze at Ajan's northern blue ones before responding. Vishal presented a smile that favored the right side of his mouth and said nothing. His response was in his stare.

Ajan stared back at Vishal, though his gaze did not take on the same amount of animosity. After a long pause, Ajan walked away from the three priests and went to reclaim his torch. He placed it just below his expressionless face, making his eyes glow about the desolate meeting chamber. "You may all go. I will speak with Sri in the morning and prepare her. We will meet again at the next moon."

Sudha and Devyn bowed at the waist towards Ajan, and turned to walk through the hallway that would lead them out of the meeting chamber. Vishal continued to stare with increasing anger at Ajan, and now the two were alone where they could share a more intimate conversation. The Grand Priest sat down, symbolically lowering himself before the noble, and asked, "What is it that you want, Vishal?"

Vishal took a deep breath, raising his muscled chest and then exhaling with tremendous force. He also sat down, in silent consent to converse. He took a few breaths to compose himself and to control his anger. Then, calmly but with a strained edge in his tone, Vishal asked, "I am trying to figure out what you want, Ajan. Do you really trust a child to find our King?"

Ajan answered without hesitation, "I trust no one else to find our King." He placed the torch down, to lean against the bare wall and continued. "I understand your hesitation, Vishal. I can also appreciate your goals for your Kingdom. But, this is the prophecy. This is the gods' intention for Kasimi. I have prayed on this, and now see that the only one who can show us the path, is the Intended."

Vishal placed his face in his callused hands and sighed. He then snapped his neck up and looked at Ajan with controlled yet present anger. "I am not threatening you, Ajan. It is not my way. But, this blind faith that you appear to exhibit will be the cause of your downfall."

Ajan answered with his hypnotic, calm voice, "Or the cause of yours." Ajan looked at Vishal with a mixed expression of sympathy and anger, and shook his head a few times. He grasped his torch with his right hand, and felt for his sword with his left one. After both men had left this chamber, Ajan knew that Vishal would have to be watched. Vishal had been honorable to state his grievances with Ajan's plan. He had also quietly announced the war that would exist between these two until the King was found.

"Go, now." Ajan dismissed Vishal with a brief waving of his hand.

Vishal stood up slowly, not breaking his locked gaze on Ajan. There was a sense of relief in his posture. Vishal had never agreed with The Grand Priest's politics. In his opinion, the South Isles had been ignored too long. Finally, the two men had stated their war and it would begin. Vishal turned his back on Ajan, without bowing, and walked out of the meeting chamber.

Ajan remained behind for a few moments. Things were going to happen now, that he had not prepared for. Sri would need to grow beyond her simple fifteen years into something more powerful. The coming of the King was near, and his emergence to Kasimi would not be without tension and uprising. The Grand Priest would need to play games now, to gain support to squash the impure goals of Vishal. There was much to do; but his first goal and love would remain Sri. The Grand Priest exited with his torch in his hand, to the only place in the temple that was meant just for him.

~

Jabala sat at her vanity table and brushed through her lustrous, dark brown hair in quiet meditation as she waited. She would stare at her image in the mirror while letting her hands trace through the ringlets that lingered at her neck. Large brown eyes dominated her still youthful face, followed by subtle and some-what common features. Her beauty was not obvious and grew in definition the longer one looked at her. She was not aristocratic or noble. It was the way she moved her eyes or placed her dark, bow-shaped lips that made Jabala an alluring woman.

Jabala came to the temple as a little girl, when her mother requested to be Sri's nurse. Her mother claimed that her husband had passed away and she wished to raise Jabala as a member of the temple. They were accepted as humble servants to The Grand Priest, devoting their lives to serving the spiritual leaders. Jabala's fate was sealed, and she would never be permitted to leave her duties. It was a good fate for a child whose father was nowhere to be found. Her mother died five years later, leaving the girl to take her place in mothering Sri.

Jabala's room was located behind Sri's, to be available to serve the Intended at any time of the night or day. It was small but adequate. There was a single bed, with a warm quilt that Jabala's mother had made for her out of left over silk from the tailoring of Sri's sarongs. The different colors had been woven together into the symbol of the god of love, in constant reminder of the mother-daughter bond. There was a chest of deep cherrywood next to the bed to hold Jabala's simple clothes. Then, there was the unusual presence of a vanity table that had been Sri's as a little girl later replaced by one more appropriate for a teenager. Jabala's tall body still fit comfortably at the table, with the use of a large pillow rather than a chair. There were a few items that did not seem appropriate for a servant to possess. Lazily placed around the vanity rested a few intricate pieces of jewelry. There was also a bottle of rose scented water in a tiny, crystal container placed discretely in the corner.

Jabala stood and walked to the window in her opaque, red silk wrap. Her body flowed freely in the loose material, with no effort made to hide the full bosom that poured over the folds or the glimpse of a soft hip that was so pronounced. The small window in her room allowed her the view of the reflecting pools over the temple, guarded by the lit candles. The full moon poured into the servant's chamber creating a mood for tenderness. Jabala reached for her moonlit brown hair and began to twist it up into a bun as she gazed out at the temple grounds.

The pillow at Jabala's vanity table moved slightly as the floorboards beneath it came undone. A small, square section of the floor moved itself beside the displaced pillow as the image of Ajan came to view through the passageway. The warrior pulled himself into the servant girl's room without effort, and looked about the space. His eyes were captured by the red image, and the blessed signs of femininity that it held. And the anger that had been in his eyes turned to desire for the woman before him.

Jabala knew that Ajan would seek her tonight, after his meeting with the other priests—he always did. His visits had been more frequent over the past few moons; but, Jabala did not question The Grand Priest. She stepped down from her nook at the window and walked with a natural seductive quality towards Ajan, and placed her firm arms around his shoulders. She leaned in by his ear, the scent of the rose water at her neck, and whispered, "I am here, Ajan."

Ajan grasped Jabala in his arms and ran his hands over her back as he looked hungrily over her form. He pressed his body against hers as both his hands grabbed to pull her head back, so that his lips could contact Jabala's light brown skin. Her hair fell from its knot to Jabala's shoulders and back. Hungrily, he traced the flesh until he realized he had not greeted his lover or looked her in the eyes this night. He stepped back, bringing his arms around the servant's rib cage, and gazed at the woman. "I need you tonight, my sweet friend," he whispered in his piercing baritone voice. Ajan leaned his lips down at her neck again and murmured between lustful kisses. "I must possess you, tonight."

Jabala had heard that desperate tone of desire in Ajan's voice before, and knew that often the warrior confused anger and passion and could translate one into the other. The woman's hands reached to cradle The Grand Priest's face as she whispered, "You shall, Ajan. But first you must rid yourself of this rage." She led Ajan with his hands in hers to sit at her bed and kneeled before him, still holding him. She placed her head in his lap, allowing her hair to spill over him.

In this state, Ajan was easily manipulated by the powers of femininity. Without protest or thought, Ajan was left to the bed and naturally, his hands stroked the servant's hair. He knew he had to be guarded in his words—what had happened in the meeting chamber was between him and Vishal only. It would involve others soon enough. The man remained quiet for a long time.

Jabala raised her chin to rest on the edge Ajan's knees. The moonlight hit her brown eyes making them shine, and emphasizing her quiet intelligence. "I do not know why it is you do not speak to me of your troubles, Ajan. Do you not think I already know what they are? I am certain that there is nothing that happened in that meeting chamber that has not existed for years. I can see by the rage hidden underneath your eyes that it has finally surfaced. Do not let your rage turn to fear, love."

Ajan nodded a few times, and then leaned in at his waist to place a kiss on Jabala's forehead. He lifted her up with his strong arms to place her body against his as he leaned back on the bed. She knew him so well—could read him better than he could read himself. For this loyalty, he held the beautiful servant against him. It was a shame that he could not formally take her as his concubine. This arrangement would have to do for now.

Jabala nuzzled her head in the soft space between the man's arm and his chest, and attempted to carve her body into Ajan's on the bed. A finger played up and down Ajan's chest, like a feather taunting untouched flesh, as she began to undo the fastenings on the tunic without haste. "Were the words said that finally needed to be said, Ajan? Is that what makes you so tense? Did you finally make your plan known? You should be relieved, Ajan. It may have led to more of these political games; but it also brings you closer to the truth that you seek. It would be foolish to let these silly games that the temple plays make you lose focus."

Ajan's hands moved with no particular direction through Jabala's hair, as he always did. His eyes focused up at the ceiling overhead, slipping occasionally to look out the window. "It is not as simple as that, Jabie. Yes, these tensions have existed for so long, as you say. But to actually see the anger come into physical form, to take on its own animal...Jabie...people could get hurt. Sri could get hurt. She is not ready for what I started tonight."

Jabala had finished undoing the tunic, and pulled the white material apart to expose the Grand Priest's hardened chest. She ran her nails down the skin a few times, leaning in to kiss the brown nipples on Ajan's chest. "Sri was ready for what you started the day she was born, Ajan. She is the Intended which you sometimes forget. In that position—in that meaning—is strength in its purest form. We…you…have raised her without the silliness of politics in her mind. She has a focus so pure that she will see past all the faces that the others put on. She is not the problem nor is she your worry, Ajan." Jabala traced her lips slowly up Ajan's chest to his chin. "It is simple, Ajan. Look past the games. Look past the faces you make at one another and look at your fear. You are afraid that you are wrong." Jabala's lips met Ajan's and before she claimed his completely, she murmured, "I know you are right."

Ajan kissed Jabala, a peck, with muted hunger. First, he wanted to explore this idea more. Anyone else who would dare make accusations against him would experience harsh words. But, Jabie—she was different. She was his oldest and most cherished companion. She was his first and only real friend. "There are consequences to being wrong, Jabala," Ajan stated flatly. He raised his head and turned his neck from the position on the bed to meet Jabala's eyes. "I have no right to be wrong about Sri."

Jabala stared back at Ajan, and slanted the corners of her mouth down in frustration of his stubbornness. She often felt like an old woman soothing a boy—though Jabala was more than twenty years younger than the Grand Priest. She responded back in a challenging tone, "You have every right, to be right about Sri."

Ajan laughed at the response. Time and time again, Jabala managed the one line that brought sanity to his gaming mind. His eyes dimmed and he looked softly on his beautiful moonlit servant. How he appreciated her—how he needed her. He took one kiss from her lips, as she playfully feigned annoyance. "Forgive me for being a fool?" he responded in a whisper. He took another kiss, his tongue tracing the line of Jabala's full mouth. "Forgive me for wanting you?" he asked, his desire for the woman growing again. The next kiss, more deep and searching, lasted a long moment. With his lips still upon Jabala's, he made a promise that he would never keep. And then the two friends searched for each other in the dark, to begin the comfortable lovemaking they had shared for years.

It hurt her when he would make promises of affection, as some kind of symbol in their lovemaking. She preferred silence rather than empty words that could never be claimed. How many times had she said, "Don't, Ajan…" when he would whisper his promises in her ear as she let him enter her. But tonight, she let him make the empty claims of affection. These words were meant for someone else.

The first time they made love was on the night of her mother's death. It was a small ceremony. Only the temple servants bothered to come for the blessing and cremation. She had felt so alone, watching her mother's beautiful face grow disfigured in the heated flames. For a moment, her mother looked like a demoness before melting into ashes. In the moment when Jabala wanted to scream out in terror at the image of her burning mother, Ajan walked into the ceremony carrying little Sri in his arms. His gaze was on the heartbroken child, who cried over the death of the only mother she had known. Ajan placed Sri in Jabala's fragile arms, and let the two girls find comfort in one another. Both had lost a mother. The Grand Priest stood back and guarded the two as their cherished mother burned to her final ashes.

Jabala led her sister and her child back to her room to let her rest. Both collapsed in Sri's bed, holding each other in their grief, sobbing loudly. The pain of a young woman and girl's combined cry has the eerie ring of a prayer of desperation. Slowly, the sobs turned to quiet tears that eventually led them to sleep. Ajan came to the room to check on Sri, and found the wilted form of Jabala next to his ward. He kissed Sri on the forehead, and then stroked Jabala's hair to wake her.

She opened her eyes, and saw the seemingly immortal form of the Grand Priest in the darkness, and sat up to look into his eyes. He offered her sympathy and comfort, and brought his warm hand down to cup her cheek and chin. The young woman leaned in to place her head underneath Ajan's chin, and hold on to him for support, while Sri rested next to them. It was so natural that the embrace turned into a kiss. Jabala's tears began again as Ajan held her. He picked her up, and carried her to her mother's room behind Sri's where the one kiss turned into a series of longing ones. Both were in need of comforting, and the lovemaking seemed so familiar between the two.

For ten years, the two people found a great source of comfort and friendship in one another. They never loved one another, but that did not matter. Their relationship was trusting and loving; but without the complications that Kasimian society seemed to place on companions of the two genders. There were times when they wished they could take their lovemaking outside of their private chambers, but the temple was not ready for such things. Jabala was a servant, not a concubine.

Ajan held his moan as he reached his climax, with Jabala's bare form over him. He reached his arms up and around Jabala to bring the woman to him to enjoy the closeness for a while longer. He ran his fingers through her hair and down her back and placed kisses on her cheeks and lips, still feeling the effects of their passion in his body. "Oh Jabie…" he sighed.

"Will you stay tonight, Ajan?" Jabala asked, without demand.

Ajan took the rose scent in Jabala's hair and exhaled. "Yes, love…" he whispered. His hands gripped his friend tightly around him. His body rejoiced in the thought of more lovemaking with Jabala through the night. His eyes strayed to the door that connected Jabala's room to Sri's chambers. His mind went there, too. Yes, he would stay. But, he would not be there.

2

Jabala came in to the Intended's room a little later than the usual dawn. She went about the morning rituals of opening curtains, and moving water from the already filled pitcher to a bowl by Sri's side table. Jabala was sure to make her movements very sharp, to make loud sounds at every surface. She hoped she would not have to resort to singing to remove the girl from her bed.

Sri was half asleep, taking refuge from the plentiful sunlight underneath her quilt. "I know you're there, Jabie...but I'm not really here. I'm still asleep." called Sri, from her woolen fortress. "It would be better if you checked back for me in a bit. I'm sure to be here, then." The Intended was not fond of early mornings, and had plenty of experience in protesting them.

Jabala smirked—spoiled, wicked girl. "How do you know that I am here, if you are not here, child?" Jabala pretended to take Sri's words very seriously, posing her question-response in a flat manner. These exchanges were as familiar as Sri was old, and so unnecessary in Jabala's opinion. "You have two choices. You can rise from your bed and be a good young lady, or I can find you and make you into one."

A heavy, exaggerated sigh from the top of Sri's vocal range to the bottom to signal defeat. "All right." Sri whipped off the red wool covers, spreading them every which way on her bed and placed her sunburned feet on the marble floor next to her bed. The cool against the stinging burn prompted an "Ouch!" from Sri, as she looked up helplessly into Jabala's eyes.

Jabala squinted on seeing the blistered skin, and inquired, "What did you do to yourself, child? Walking barefoot again?" The woman grabbed a container of some kind of oil from Sri's vanity and knelt down beside the intended. She began rubbing the emollient into Sri's feet, being careful not to press to hard into the skin. "You make more work for me when you do this, Sri."

"I'm sorry, Jabie." Sri sang out the required apology. "We went walking through the forest yesterday, and I went off too far by myself...went to the beach, actually. I didn't think I'd need the oils...didn't know I'd actually get to the..." Sri stopped to let out an "Ouch! Too hard, Jabie!" before continuing "...get to the water. It was so beautiful! But, Ajan got mad with me."

"Of course he did, child." Jabala finished with Jabala's feet, and stood up to wash the oils off her hands at the vanity table basin. "You have never gone that far on your own, child. You must never wander off alone. You know that, child." Jabala dried off her hands using her sarong, and then returned to Sri's side. She began to brush and braid Sri's hair, while she had the girl sitting still.

"You don't have to mother me on this, Jabie." Sri leaned her head back as Jabala tugged the strands of hair into a single, tight braid. "But, Jabie...it did feel good to be on my own for a little while. To just be without everyone watching me all the time."

Jabala smiled gently, while weaving the strands together towards the end of the braid. "Being watched and cared for, is much better than being alone and forgotten. I am certain you will find your own space, without putting yourself in danger." Jabala reached for the purple ribbon she had waiting around her wrist to tie the hair at its end. She then placed her arms over the front of the girl, and pulled her in for a gentle hug.

Sri crossed her arms over Jabala's and squeezed her nurse back. "Thank you for braiding my hair, Jabie. I think I can take care of getting dressed on my own. I'll wear the purple silks today, *acha?*"

Jabala kissed the top of Sri's head, and understood the girl's call for a few private moments. "Of course, child. You might even try some lip coloring today." Jabala released Sri, and stretched as she stood up. "Don't be long, you only have a few moments before Ajan expects you." Jabala watched her little one for a few moments, before walking the short distance to her own room. She hesitated for a moment, but closed the door behind her.

Sri stroked her braid, feeling the perfect knots that Jabala always managed to weave into her hopelessly thick, black hair. Her fingers twisted the unincluded tale of the braid, hopefully persuading it into a ringlet. Sri laid back in her bed and looked out the window through the sunlight, not really interpreting the temple grounds just outside. How she wished she could just hide underneath her blankets today—something was just not right. Sri looked around her room for something to provide visual curiosity, to give her reason to escape from the warm, molded place in her bed. Nothing.

Something was not right. Everything seemed a little different. Ajan's behavior yesterday when she wandered off was not unusual—he was a protective mentor. But the inflections of his voice were unsettling.

Sri was not ignorant to her fate. But she chose not to worry about the serious purpose of her existence while it was so far off. She had read the religious prophecies of how she was...the *Intended*...as everyone called her. She knew that she had been *"planned for three generations by the priests and scholars of the Kasimian lands."* She also knew that people liked to tell her that, over and over again, as if the words were a kind of mantra. Maybe she was intended. But, she had been born from a woman, just like everyone else. She preferred to think of the prophecy as a text, and of herself as Sri. Otherwise, she would cry.

And Jabala. She seemed a little strange, as well. That hug, from nowhere. It was an apology from her nurse. But, for what? Jabala's words echoed in her mind. *"Being watched and cared for, is much better than being alone and forgotten."* Like a prayer, the words repeated themselves in her mind. And then Jabie hugged her.

Besides Ajan and Jabala, the temple seemed to be really watching Sri. Servants would stop their activities and make smiles at her as she walked by, before returning to their tasks. Never before had they done this—always concentrating on their work above all. They would whisper as she walked away, in a language of slang that she barely understood.

And Vishal, the priest who had always talked at her rather than to her. Since her fifteenth birthday, Vishal had been making an attempt to be nice to her to the point where it was painful for both people. He would always seem to turn up at the end of her meditations or the end of her lessons, and happen to have her favorite sweets. Sri would prefer if he went back to talking at her. Then, she could at least understand him. These days he strained conversations about the weather, religion…hair ribbons.

Sri quickly stood up, gathering herself from her thoughts, and walked to the vanity table where her purple silks had been laid out for her. Jabala knew that Sri would match her dress to her hair ribbon as she always did. It was nice to have someone who knew her so well, without crowding her. Sri shred her short, white night dress to the ground and threw the simple, purple over her. It was a loose silk, with no tailoring—just arms, and two slits from her ankles to her knees. She did, however, place her gold sandals on today. This would please her Jabie.

Sri threw water on her face and rinsed her mouth to be clean and presentable. But, she wouldn't go near the colorings that Jabala and the other hand maids wanted her to wear if she didn't have to. The point of coloring was to attract attention—and Sri seemed get more than her fair share of attention without the stains.

Sri tugged at her silk wrap, and her braid to make sure everything was in place. One thing—she brought the braid around to rest on her shoulder. Now, she was ready for lessons.

She closed her eyes and took a moment to center herself, as Ajan had taught her. Even though she felt calm, that strange feeling lingered in the back of her mind and found a place in the pit of her stomach. It would just have to sit there for now.

Sri walked with careful and graceful footsteps out of her chamber into the hall of rooms overlooking the central chamber of the temple. The piercing light of sun breaking in to the structure through an overwhelming number of sources—some colored and some clear—blinded her for a moment as she reached the edge of the balcony. When her eyes finally adjusted to the illumination, the women servants who were polishing the white marble floor on their hands and knees craned their necks to look up at the Intended. Their eyes were wide with a combination of awe and fear, as they stared at Sri without attempting to hide this usually rude gesture. A few of mouths were agape, searching for words or appropriate vocal cues, to communicate something to her.

Sri's own eyes widened back at the servants who stared at her. Was there something wrong? She looked over her shoulder to see if someone was behind her, but she was alone. All Sri could do was smile and bow her head to the women, but they continued to aggressively stare. She stared back, her smile frozen on her unstained lips.

The Grand Priest emerged from the tiny doorway in the back of the worship area. His poetic red silk pajama suit and bare feet provided a fierce image against the newly polished marble. His light eyes directed themselves to behold Sri from the same angle as the servants while he walked with large strides towards the Intended. Ajan's diamond amulet flashed light around him, erasing his shadows. He gazed up at his beautiful ward, attention drawn to her, with no smile of greeting on his lips. Finally, the words came that would give Sri clarity to the stares, and the whispering, and the strangeness that she sensed around her. Ajan reached for his jeweled sword, drawing it in an elegant motion out of the sheath, and raised it up at Sri in a dramatic gesture. In a loud, booming voice, Ajan proclaimed, "Behold, The Intended Queen."

Sri's eyes looked blankly at Ajan—her mind not registering what he had just done. Her lips parted and a delicate, finely kept hand covered the sigh that followed soon after. The servants made themselves even more humble from their spots on the floor, lowering their heads to touch the ground. Ajan—her mentor and teacher—kneeled down on one knee with his intent gaze locked on Sri with sword in hand. *"May the gods be with me,"* she thought to herself, *"I have no idea who I am."*

She had been taught the proper response to the hail of royalty and had practiced it in the privacy of chambers. But for the Grand Priest, for Ajan, to do this. It was real. It was not for later anymore. Sri looked down at the people who bowed before her, and lowered her hands to her sides. She nodded her head to Ajan, a graceful dipping of her neck. In a much more mature tone than she was used to using, Sri spoke the proper response, "Good morning, my people of Kasimi. You may rise." Her voice lilted up and down, the cultured accent of a good upbringing.

On cue, the servants raised their heads from their positions, and took another look at Sri before returning to their tasks. She closed her eyes and breathed a private sigh of relief that this was done.

She knew that this was only part of the beginning, but did it have to be done now?

Ajan rose from his position and pointed to his private study off of the temple proper, and underneath Sri's chamber.

Sri nodded, and went about her way through the hallway to the spiral staircase. She was stopped in her path by a foreign voice nagging her inside her mind. This new voice—had surfaced when the temple began to feel odd to her—this voice that she could not identify. *"Queen? He told you to bow. Subject—not Queen!"* What? Sri shook her head and rubbed her eyes, trying to hear the voice again. *"I think not. You tell him to bow."* Sri's cheeks grew red as she blushed. She could not make out the pitch of the sound, but the tone was distinctly feminine and harsh. *"Go now. Subject."* There was no time for this—she was expected downstairs.

Sri made sure to hold on to the railing as she descended the steps. Though the voice was gone, the message had made sense to her bringing a look of defiance to her usually innocent black eyes. Her steps held extra weight in them as they brought her inside Ajan's study.

~

Ajan was seated on the ground, his eyes staring at the doorway expecting Sri to enter. "Darling..." he whispered, "I did not realize it until I saw you this morning. You are now a woman, and a Queen."

Sri looked around Ajan's office. This was the only thing in the temple that did not feel strange to her. It had never changed, except the bookshelves had managed to become full. The room was the only one in the temple that did not have windows. "A promise of secrecy..." Ajan would say. The floor was black marble, not white marble to differentiate the room from the others.

There were no chairs, just large, red silk pillows. The bookshelves were now overflowing with essays and books, arranged in no particular order—but the colors managed to spread themselves out on the different levels. No one except Sri and Ajan were allowed in here, not even servants. A poor caretaker, Ajan had let the smell of mold and age characterize his parlor.

Defiance was still working its way through her system. Sri was always more proper with Ajan than with her other teachers. He was, after all, The Grand Priest. He was her mentor; but, she was his Queen. She had never felt this way before. That strange feeling in her stomach had turned into a bitter feeling, that made her slightly nauseous. "Am I your Queen, Ajan?" Sri asked.

"Darling?" Ajan inquired with one arched brow. His smile grew. As much as he wanted to protect and care for Sri, she would need to come into her own in the next few months. Perhaps this stubbornness that he used to discipline her for would be useful in making her powerful. "Yes, Sri. You are my Queen and my mistress," he stated, locking blue eyes on black ones.

The defiance relaxed into curiosity. Ajan's response was...unexpected. "Yet, I am still guided by you. I...obey you, do what you tell me...am disciplined by you. What...how am I Queen?" Sri asked simply. She didn't understand the relationship anymore.

Ajan pointed to the pillow across from his, in silent invitation for Sri to sit. He waited for her to be seated before responding to her. He was pleased at her questions; it gave him hope for the tasks they had at hand. Ajan took the sword that had been neatly placed next to him and put it across his lap. He took Sri's delicate hands in his, and guided them to rest on the sword so that she was leaning towards him. "You are my Queen, my darling Sri. Yes. The gods—your ancestors—have made my purpose in this life to guide you and love you...to raise you to be Queen. I am your guardian. You obey me and listen to me so that you can be the proper companion to the King. We are bound by a common destiny, my darling."

Sri looked up at Ajan, and nodded a few times, hypnotized again by Ajan's voice and words. It made sense and she relaxed. Her hands curled around the sword as she lifted the heavy instrument into her own lap for the morning meditation. She would use the discomfort of the sword's weight in her meditations. At different points in the exercise, Ajan would cue her arms to hold the sword up at different levels. She would continue, trying to separate the physical discomfort of the sword from her mind's focus. She had always dropped the sword after a few minutes, which forced her eyes open and her meditation to end.

She began with the sword held gently in her hands at her lap, breathing deeply. Ajan rose silently from his place and went behind Sri to watch her and guide her through the exercise. He had not told her how to correct herself. After a while, Ajan brought his arms around Sri, and coaxed her arms upward to hold the sword in her open palms a small distance from her lap. This limbo position was hard for even the strongest warriors to hold for a long time.

Sri did not change her focus. She let Ajan move her to the next position, and continued her inward concentration. Sri just did not understand—to her, this was more a physical exercise than a mental exercise. If she lifted heavier objects around her room, she could perhaps hold the sword longer. But Ajan had sworn that physical strength had nothing to do with this. The weakest child with the strongest mind could complete this challenge. How was that possible?

After a few minutes, Ajan moved behind Sri and lifted the sword and straightened her arms so that she held the weapon as a serving tray. This required tremendous discipline for the sword was heavy, especially for the slight form of Sri. Her arms began to tremble, and it would not be long before her muscles surrendered to the weight of the weapon.

Ajan watched Sri carefully. The exercise was reaching its critical point. Either Sri would drop the weapon and break her meditation, or she would succeed. The truth was that Ajan did not know the answer to this exercise. There had been solutions with other scholars. But, for each person, the answer was different.

Sri's arms were shaking, but her face remained calm indicating that she was in her trance. Suddenly, it occurred to her—she had a choice. She had the right to let her body respond to the physical cues it was receiving, without having to interrupt her thoughts. Her arms were shaking, and for so long she had used her mind to force her arms to stay in their position. If her physical conscious had the choice, it would do otherwise. Separation of mental and physical. Sri simply placed the sword down when she could not hold it anymore. She then returned her arms to her side, without breaking the meditation. She had let her physical conscious make its choice, without being manipulated by a perception of rules that did not exist.

Ajan blinked. Had Sri figured out her solution? After all this time, she had discovered an original answer. The assumption that the sword had to do with concentration was false. The meditation had to do with inward focus alone and the rules of the physical world did not apply. In one gesture, Sri had impressed the very essence of inner concentration on Ajan. He had learned—he had been enlightened by the Intended.

Ajan let Sri continue in her meditation for a while longer, to round out the exercise. He then kneeled behind Sri, and placed his strong hands on her shoulders to gently wake her. Slowly, her black eyes opened to the mysterious dark room and she reoriented herself to the chamber. "Ajan?" she asked, wondering the outcome of the exercise.

"Tell me what you did, Sri." Ajan whispered as his hands kneaded Sri's shoulders.

"I...my mind has the choice to focus. My body should have the same choice. Holding the sword is not comfortable, so why should I? You never told me to hold the sword. It wasn't a rule." Sri strained her neck to make eye contact with him.

"That is correct, Sri. You have succeeded. And..." Ajan let go of Sri's shoulders and moved to sit in front of her. His blue eyes were intense in color and his gaze was dangerously serious. He gripped onto Sri's forearms with authority. "...and you have taught me something. I was wrong, Sri. There is nothing more I can teach you. Not only do you understand concentration, you have mastered it. Your training...everything I can give you...there is no more. Now you must help me, Sri. You must help Kasimi, my darling Sri. I have something to ask you."

Sri knit her brows together. This was all so odd. These strange vibes that she had been receiving were not the silly thoughts of a young girl. They were a sign that something important was going to happen. As her mentor gazed at her—needing her—Sri felt in control. Calmly, smoothly, Sri placed her hands on Ajan's own to soother her mentor. "What do you need, Ajan?" she whispered.

Ajan relaxed on to his pillow. There was no easy way to tell Sri what she must do. The Priest felt humbled somehow, as he asked this task of his Queen. "Sri, you are almost sixteen. The gods have decreed that you must ascend to the throne with the sky god, our King, on your sixteenth birthday. You are the only one who can find him, Sri."

"What?" Sri blurted out in response to Ajan. This was not a request—it was insanity. "I thought the priests would find him. I need to find him? How?" Sri shook her head in short twitches, in complete disbelief of the situation. She was supposed to head to lessons this morning, only to find out that her studies had ended and she was leading Kasimi on a crusade for their leader. "Are you well, Ajan?" Sri's hand instinctively went to feel her mentor's forehead for a temperature.

"I am quite well, Sri. I have never known anything to be so true since the day you were born. I knew you were the Intended. I know now that you are my Queen. I know that you must lead me, you must lead Kasimi, to its King. You are the Intended, Sri. It is so simple and so clear." Ajan's voice took on a great volume, and his eyes bulged as he spoke.

Sri's eyelids flickered in disbelief at Ajan. She scrunched her eyes to the center of her face and then released them from the contortion. She spread her hands out and shrugged her shoulders. "How am I supposed to do this, Ajan? Tell me?" Sri was filled with worry and anxiety at the thought of holding Kasimi's fate in her hands. It surfaced as frustration in her voice and gestures. "Tell me, Ajan. You pronounce me Queen in front of the temple this morning. You tell me you have nothing left to teach me in our lessons. And now, you tell me that I am the only one who can find the King—my husband—our savior?" Sri balled her open hands into fists and pounded her pillow in frustration. "How? Ajan! How in *Brahma's* voice am I supposed to do this!"

If it were any other day, or any other circumstance, Ajan would discipline Sri. But, she had every right to be nervous and upset. Her actions did not anger him—he knew that she was working through her own fear, as Jabie had put it. "I cannot tell you how to do it, Sri. The gods did not tell us how you would do it. But, you will. It will come to you, in time."

"In time? Time, Ajan!" Sri's voice was rising in both pitch and volume. She was definitely afraid, of not living up to her born role—of disappointing Ajan. "I have less than twelve moons to find this man. You want me to find him, and you offer me no way to do this. That's just grand, Ajan. Thank you." Sri stood up from her pillow, reaching to put her braid on her shoulder.

Ajan looked up at his ward and Queen from his place on the pillow. "You have never walked out on me in anger, Sri. Do not let today be the first time."

Sri took a deep breath to center herself, as Ajan had taught her. She did not intend to walk out until Ajan brought up the novelty of the action. Now that he mentioned it, a walk would probably be the best thing for her right now. Sri looked down on Ajan. It occurred to her now, for the first time, that Ajan was probably just as worried and scared as she was. He was Kasimi's Grand Priest and her appointed guardian. He would have to answer to the people if she failed. Sri pitied Ajan. She walked over the pillows where Ajan sat, and placed her hands on his shoulders. "I am not walking out on you, Ajan. But, I can't stay here right now. I need to walk...to think."

"Alone?" Ajan asked, looking up at his ward. "You cannot walk alone outside of the temple."

"You just asked me to, Ajan." Sri retorted. She had never been this bold or strong with her mentor before. "Before I start this...journey...I will begin with a walk of my own and will trust myself to stay out of danger. I think I can manage that." Sri walked to the door, without looking behind her to see Ajan's reaction.

"Sri, darling?" Ajan called out, but it was too late. Sri had already left the study.

~

Sri looked only at the temple door and walked to her destination. She didn't notice the guards at the entrance who most likely asked where she was going. She didn't hear them, and decided not to try. Sri would walk, alone, and no one would question her. Yes, she would find her own private space. She would choose to find it. These rules and boundaries about where she can and cannot go made sense to her yesterday. But today, in Ajan's study, she realized that nothing made sense. It was up to her to clarify her situation by herself without blindly following rules. She would choose what to do.

Sri walked down the stairs handling two at a time, her eyes still focused on a destination that had not been decided upon. Her posture was tall, strong, fully feeling her height with each stride. There was a determination in her eyes that aged her quickly. Servants picking at their particular spots on the lawn, or attending to their areas at the reflecting pools stopped and looked at Sri in that mixture of awe and fear that was spreading through the temple. Someone must have yelled out her hail, as the hundreds of servants on the front lawn kneeled one after the other, before Sri to worship The Intended Queen.

By the time Sri reached the reflecting pools, it was hard for her to remain completely focused on her own space when everyone around her was dropping into a genuflect. Her pace slowed considerably to look at the worshippers on the left and right of the pools. *"Why today?"* she thought to herself. For her people—for her sanity—Sri nodded her head at the servants gracefully, once to the right and once to the left, in a gesture of appreciation for their humility.

"They have never seen me alone outside the temple grounds before…" Sri said to herself. *"I have never been alone—always with Ajan. They have always stared. I just never saw it. I was hypnotized."* Sri's steps continued to slow down as she grew more and more aware of what was around her. *"There must be more."*

The forest path began only a short distance from the reflecting pools. Sri's pace returned to normal and she wandered through the banyan and mango trees. How many times had she gone on this walk with Ajan—and not really seen what was around her. Sri suddenly felt ashamed at her ignorance. Gripping her braid protectively at her shoulder, Sri continued onward until she came across the figure of a small, old man. He almost blended into the forest with his green cotton pajama suit and funny brown bald head covered with a miserably woven straw hat. He was crouched over, plucking at some weeds.

The servant stopped from his work, and looked up at Sri. His eyes were not good and he squinted to be able to get a better look at who he was before him. No one should be outside at this time. The sun was directly above at mid-day.

In a voice that was both aged and kind, the man spoke a greeting to Sri in a language that the servants spoke but she could not understand completely. It was a hybrid of Kasimian, Goane and *ruda*, the language of the slave class. "*Namas namas...*" the man said. He smiled up at Sri and cheerfully repeated, "*Namas namas!*"

Sri could not help but smile. This old, little man seemed so kind and seemed to want to speak to her. He didn't stare or gaze—he was just simple. She looked at the servant man, and kneeled down beside him. "*Namas namas,*" Sri attempted to repeat. "*Namas namas...*"

The servant laughed at Sri. She had not perfected the specific accenting of the words. He repeated, and exaggerated the parts with special intonations. "*Nahhh-maaas nahhh-maaas...*" He shook his head and muttered something very quickly that was no doubt about a silly girl speaking silly things.

Sri laughed too. She nodded her head to follow the corrected pronunciation after the man. "*Nahhh-maaas nahhh-maaas.*" She laughed again and let go of her braid.

"*Goot, ver-y ver-y goot!*" said the old man, waggling his head back and forth. He was delighted to play the role of teacher and continued on. "*Nehm ees Brahma* after god," he said resolutely.

It took a while for Sri to understand what the servant was saying until she repeated what he had said out loud. *"Nehm ees?
Nehm ees?* Oh! Name is *Brahma* after god. After the god *Brahma!*
Oh! Hello Brahma, I am Sri." Sri smiled gently at the old man and
took a seat on the patch of grass where Brahma worked.

"Sri, *thees* yes I know!" Brahma laughed heartily, slapping his
hand down on his thigh. This was the most entertainment he'd
had in years. *"More learn of* Brahma!" he insisted. He pointed to
her and said in his broken Kasimian, *"Queen, you speak."* He
then relaxed into his slang and pointed to himself. *"Rani, I speak.
Ra-nee."* He pointed back at Sri. "Try you *pluus?"* he asked.

Sri's bright smile dropped immediately when Brahma said his
word for Queen. Not wanting to hurt his feelings, she quickly
replaced her smile and repeated on cue. *"Rani."* The pronunciation was perfect—as if she had chanted the name as mantra. Her
eyes looked sadly at the pile of cut weeds. *"Rani."* She pointed to
herself weakly and whispered, *"Rani."*

The old man was very perceptive. He could see there was something wrong. He waggled his head again, his eyes looking at Sri
with concern. *"So sorry…"* he muttered. He pointed back at her
and said in the best proper Kasimian accent he could, "Queen."
He thought he had offended the Intended by using his language to
address her role instead of Kasimian.

Sri gently shook her head. "No Brahma, you haven't done anything to upset me." Sri leaned in and kissed the old man on the
cheek. "Thank you, Brahma-uncle." She said. "I have to go now…"

Brahma waggled his head in delight again. The apology was
enough for him. He shrugged, figuring the intended had some
special worries of her own that he could not understand. *"Viseet
Brahma man-y man-y time!"*

Sri nodded and then stood up to continue her walk through the
forest. She knew where she needed to go now—the sanctuary—

and as quickly as her feet could carry her. But, she did not walk
with the usual speed that moved her through the forest. She had
weights attached to her hands and feet that made her body collapse in on itself. A sick feeling revolved around her stomach and
she was light headed. A cold sweat broke out just above her upper
lip and for a while she lost sight. Sri had to pause underneath a
canopy of leaves to catch her breath.

Sri curled her knees to her chest, and hid her head from view.
She repeated to herself, over and over, "*Rani, me Rani, me Rani,
me Rani, Rani, Rani, Ra-nee...*" Sri let her tears begin to fall to
mix with the cold sweat on her upper lip. "*Rani...*" She could not
let go of this word.

After a few minutes, Sri used the trunk of a nearby tree to raise
herself to standing position. She centered herself as best she could
with a deep set of breaths, and then walked carefully the rest of
the way to the sanctuary. She had never traveled to this place
before, only with Ajan.

Sri placed her sandals outside the sanctuary opening, and crept
inside the space. The sanctuary was not grand like the temple. It
was more humble than the servants' cottages on the outskirts of
Ajan's property. It was made of different rocks, woven together
from a dozen men's scavenging the forest. The roof was not symmetrical, made of thick layers of straw and assembled by unskilled
men. Inside, however, was another part of Kasimi. The floor was
an aged black marble, having sheltered many scholars for thousands of moons. The elder priests would come to paint the
prophecy into the wall in ancient Kasimian. The sky god was the
third miracle, and with him would come the telling of the fourth
and final tale.

Sri walked into the sanctuary lit by one torch on each wall.
Like Ajan's study, there were no windows. In the center of the
room was an elevated table that was big enough to sacrifice a

man, and even had a red stain on it that no one could identify. *Blood?* The table was meant to raise the worshipper off the ground so that he may read the prophecies by simply shifting his sitting position in meditation.

She was supposed to cover her hair when in the sanctuary. Women were not allowed here. But, since she was the Intended, she would have to learn the religious texts as a man would, and must enter. The elder priests agreed that if she covered her hair, the gods would forgive a feminine presence in their sanctuary. Sri respected this rule—her reverence for the gods was definite. But there were no cloths to be found to hide her hair.

Unlike most Kasimian women, Sri had never been told that her body was shameful. No one was in the sanctuary, and no one was sure to come. She must cover her hair—and she only had her silk purple wrap for material. She could rip it; but that would cause question in the temple. Sri removed her dress over her head, her hands pulling opposite sleeves until it tumbled to the ground. With some skill, Sri converted the wrap into a veil. Her hair was covered—the gods would forgive her presence.

Sri walked to the wall that held the tale of the Intended's King. It was strange to her, that the story focused so much on her arrival, rather than on the arrival of the King. Her delicate hands traced her collarbones in an unconscious pointing to herself while she read the words about her great grandparents. Her fingers reached in limbo between her body and the wall to touch the names of her grandparents, Osra and Putana. Putana was legendary for her beauty—how Sri would have loved to know her. Her hands reached onto the wall on the discussion of her birth parents. Varuna II and the grand niece of Varuna produced Sri. She read this part of the prophecy carefully:

Varuna's favored had a grand niece through the bloodline of her brother, who was of proper breeding to attend to Varuna II.

She had been raised to be a noble concubine just as her great aunt, and felt blessed to be given to the direct descendant of the sea god.

Sri had not been born to a proper consort, since Varuna II wished not to marry formally. Since her birth mother was not a wife, her name was not part of the scripture and not part of the miracle at all, except in the bed of Varuna II. Sri traced her fingers tenderly over the one sentence that addressed her birth mother, and then traced the wall to the ground as she collapsed to the floor. She curled her bare form into a fetal position, and wept quietly to herself. Her salted tears left marks where her cheek touched the floor.

It was not Ajan that found Sri.

Brahma had heard sounds of weeping in the sanctuary when his weeding brought him to the dirt path outside. His bare feet tracked mud inside as his small body was involved in a physical search for the sad man inside. Brahma shouted, "*No oh!*" on seeing the bare body of Sri shriveled in the corner.

"What?" Sri asked, shaking herself from her tears. She propped herself up on one elbow and squinted through her water strained eyes to see Brahma. Sri's lack of modesty didn't even occur to her, having never been directly told that the female body must always be covered. She leaned up against the wall using her knees as a shield against her breasts. "Brahma…" she said, in relief that this kind man had found her.

Brahma was not at all taken aback by Sri's bare form. In the villages, clothes for children were a luxury that not everyone could afford. Whatever scraps of silk or cotton could be found would have to do. The body would have to show. It didn't occur to him that Sri was immodest. He just saw a very sad, little girl much like the ones he left behind in the village when he was sold to the temple.

"Sri, crying not goot," said the kind old man. He walked over to Sri and sat down next to the girl with purple covered hair. *"With you, sadness?"* Brahma looked with concern at the little girl.

For some reason, Sri felt very comforted by this old man. She nodded her head a few times and said in a soft tone, "I can't help but cry, Brahma. I don't even know where I come from." Realizing that she might have not spoken clearly, Sri repeated her statement in simpler words. "I am sad. Who am I?"

Brahma laughed with concerned eyes, and pointed up at the wall where the prophecy was written. *"There!"* He looked sadly at Sri, his laugh somehow making his pain more apparent, and said, *"Brahma ees know where from. Brahma ees from temple now."*

Sri knew of Brahma's unfortunate fate. The slave classes of each house were subject to the whims of their owners. Brahma was most likely from a poor, land owning family that was forced to sell him. The temple was a merciful place to send the slave. Maybe Brahma had a wife or a child. It didn't matter—*"Brahma ees from temple now."*

Sri looked tenderly at the little old man. She brought her lips together into a thin line, not knowing what to say. She just placed her arms around him, and leaned her head on his shoulder. The two people sat together feeling a common loss, finding comfort in each other. Sri had never been taught to shun servants or the slave class. Their purpose was just as carved out in society by the gods as hers was, albeit to serve. It has never been said that she must not speak to one. And Brahma was so kind.

"Rani Sri back temple." Brahma waggled his head at Sri.

"I will, Brahma." Sri replied. She removed her head from the comforting place at his shoulder and began to mentally prepare herself to return to the temple.

"*Goot, ver-y ver-y goot!*" said the old man, waggling his head back and forth in a gesture that was becoming very amusing to Sri. Brahma stood up with some help from the young girl, and walked out of the temple yelling behind him, "*Viseet Brahma man-y man-y time!*"

Sri smiled, the heavy part of the sadness now lifted. She stood up and walked to the temple entrance, undoing her head covering slowly, and slipping it over her body at the same time. At the front of the sanctuary, she grabbed her sandals in her hands having decided to go barefoot.

Brahma had continued his weeding and stopped to offer a goodbye with a deep smile on his well wrinkled face. "*Viseet Brahma man-y man-y time!*"

Sri waved as she walked past Brahma, and smiled brightly at a man who had so instantly become dear to her. "I will, Brahma," Sri responded truthfully.

The return path through the forest was not so bad. She could actually smell the mangoes that grew beyond the banyan ones. She felt empty instead of weighted. Brahma had been sent to her out of nowhere as a friend and advisor, someone who attended to the paths where she walked. She would visit him, many many times again.

~

The temple was on full alert that Sri was missing. As she walked up the path through the reflecting pools, the servants raised their voices at the spotting. Some bowed—others pointed—others did both. They seemed relieved that she was back and everything could return to normal.

Sri distanced herself from the chaos by not looking directly at the people. As the servants bowed, she gestured broadly with her hands for people to rise deciding that she could not handle any-more ceremony for today. She blazed past the hordes of concerned people and walked with meticulous posture up the temple steps, not stopping to kneel before the divine symbols. The guards looked relieved as she entered the temple.

Knowing that Ajan's red clad form would be standing and wait-ing for her in the direct center of the worship room, Sri walked with her dirty bare feet past the pillared entrance and into the heart of the chamber. "Ajan." she stated, without looking to see if the priest was there or not.

Ajan responded back harshly, "Sri." He walked towards her to meet his ward halfway. "Where did you go, child?" Ajan crossed his arms and looked down at his beautiful ward. Even though he tried to sound angry, Sri could see the worry and nervousness in his body language.

"I went for a walk, Ajan." Sri responded calmly, looking Ajan straight in his light blue eyes. "And I have something to tell you."

"First, Sri, I have something to tell you…" Ajan muttered quickly. He grabbed Sri by the hand, and dragged her into his study. His grip was firm and demanding.

Sri did not resist—she was going to ask to speak to him in pri-vate anyway. Sri skipped a step from being dragged hand first, but then quickened her pace to the study.

Ajan threw Sri in the room, and then closed the door. He stared at the dark wood doors, banging his head against them with a thump, before turning around to face Sri. He drew his sword from its sheath and pointed it at Sri, "Do you know what I do with this sword, Sri?"

Sri's eyes fluttered nervously at the site. "Yes…you fight with it," she whispered while moving her eyes away from the weapon.

Ajan glared at Sri, his anger showing itself fully in private. He was not aware of the emotions that soared through his own body.

He waved the sword in the air, in the same way he would wave his army into battle. His voice was a chilling whisper, more effective than the loudest scream in scaring an enemy. "You will not worry me like that again, Sri. You will not disobey me again. You may be my Queen. But, I am your protector, your warrior, your guardian. I am your life, Sri. Do not destroy yourself by disobeying me."

Sri opened her mouth to respond with her eyes pressed to the ground. But Ajan placed a finger in the view of her gaze to signal her silence.

He circled behind her still holding his sword in his hand. Squeezing her shoulder firmly, he made a hushing sound pushing air through his front teeth. He whispered in her ear, "I am not done." Ajan completed the circle so that he was right in front of Sri, with only one inch between her and the fully extended sword. "Do you know what I do with this sword, Sri? I protect you with it. I protect this temple with the sword. Do you have any idea how many people would like to see you dead? Do you even fathom what will happen to Kasimi if you are not safe?" Ajan's rage was building inside, until his voice could not control itself. He screamed for an answer, "Do you?"

Sri detested the way Ajan would use his sword when he felt emotional. He used it as a shield more than anything—to ward off his own fear and terror—to appear strong when he was trembling inside. Her eyes fluttered when an answer was demanded of her. She looked up slowly, and pushed the sword away to Ajan's side. "I will respond when you put that weapon away, Ajan."

Ajan tightened his grip around the sword, and biting his tongue, resheathed it.

It was Sri's turn to speak, but she did not raise her voice above the chilling calm whisper she had learned from Ajan as a tactic for control. "And who is responsible for me not knowing, Ajan? I walked for the first time on the temple grounds by myself today.

I had never seen what was around me. You sheltered me from it all, Ajan."

Today, everything would come undone.

Sri walked in a circle around Ajan, needing movement to free her words. "People want me dead? No, I didn't know that, my mentor. How could I? You were always keeping my eyes on something other than what was around me, my mentor. You were teaching me how to handle my role, but never told me what that role was, Ajan! Look at yourself if you are angry." Sri could not believe her tone, or how her relationship with Ajan had changed from yesterday to now.

He was furious. This honesty slapped him in the face with his own teaching. He unleashed his voice freely, while gripping the sheathed sword at his hip with a clenched fist. "I protected you, Sri! You need to be something beyond this world. You are not human Sri—you are of the divine. I needed to make you more pure than this world. It is what your King will need, what Kasimi will need."

Sri stood her ground, unwilling to back away from Ajan's challenging words. "What were you protecting me from, Ajan? Who I am and what do I represent? From these people who would somehow make me less pure? I am their Queen, Ajan—as you so grandly announced this morning. I am supposed to protect them." Sri blinked, feeling too young at fifteen to be engaged in this debate.

It was an impasse. Ajan looked up at the imperfection in the ceiling and then back at Sri. Reverting back to his chilling whisper, he asked, "What is it that you wanted to say to me, Sri? Did you come here to tell me what a bad guardian I was? Because I refuse to stand here and have my ward curse me."

"What I wanted to say to you Ajan has no meaning now that you have spoken. For fifteen years, Ajan, I was a child. And today you threw me into my role without any help. This protection that you've showed me all my life. I could have used some of it while you pushed me away from my childhood." Sri was pleading for Ajan to understand her.

The mentor loosened his grip on the sword's handle. He clasped his hands together, and rested them under his nose. He bowed to Sri, humbly. "What do you want me to do?"

Sri pleaded to her mentor again. "I need you, Ajan. You and Jabie are all that I have. I will not walk away from my path, but I need you to be honest about the direction I'm going in. Give me some guidance, Ajan—don't just lead me around by the hand, screening my eyes from everything. I won't know what to do when I'm Queen, otherwise. Please, Ajan." Sri held her delicate hand out to her Grand Priest. "Can you do this for me?"

Ajan nodded a few times, aware at how old Sri seemed all of a sudden. "I just did not think that I was worthy of guiding my Queen." Ajan took his ward's hand and brought it to his lips to kiss. He closed his eyes and exhaled—he was at peace when his Queen loved him again. "I will guide you, and listen to you, Sri."

"Then I will tell you what I needed to tell you. And, I am not asking." Sri squeezed her mentor's hand to reassure him. "I want to go to the place where I was born. You must take me there before I can even begin to find what you've asked me to find. I have no idea who I am, Ajan." Sri placed her arms around Ajan's waist and brought herself to embrace him.

"Your birth parents are dead, Sri. They were killed in the rebellion years ago. You know that. Why do you want to go to a place that holds nothing for you?" Ajan held his ward against him tightly, protectively.

Sri buried her head in Ajan's red silks and murmured exhaustedly, "I want to see that there is nothing there instead of you just telling me."

Exhausted himself, Ajan's tall form sank into the much needed affection from Sri. "All right, Sri. We will go when the full moon ends." The Grand Priest sighed and looked up at the ceiling above, longingly, and then back at his ward. He kissed the top of her head and rocked his child and Queen in his arms.

3

Ajan kept his promise to Sri. At the end of the full moon, he made arrangements with guards, hand maids and the elders for the coming of the Intended to *Videha*, where the girl had been born in the Northern Kingdom, a little over fifteen years ago. He was diligent in his tasks, making sure that the entire journey would be planned to the last detail. Sri began to prepare herself for her return home, to see the nothingness that awaited her.

It was a tricky journey that required Ajan to dip back into his warrior's bag. He did not want to draw attention to his caravan. The temple was separated from the rest of Kasimi by the mountains. *Govandhara* was not part of any kingdom, designated as the property of the divine. If they took direct roads, the caravan would need to go through the Southern Kingdom which might be dangerous since Sri was technically born in the lands of the North. While Sudha could help to keep rebels away from Sri, it was still a risk. If they took the unmarked paths through the rocks of the mountains, they would be deposited directly into the Northern Kingdom and near Sri's village. It was highly unlikely that they would be seen. Ajan decided it was better to risk the treachery of land over the viciousness of the southern fighters. The gods would be watching them, and would make their travels safe.

Ajan required that the other three priests would go on the journey to *Videha*. He claimed that it was necessary for Sri—that was
true in part. Ajan did not want to leave Vishal alone in the temple;
things were too tense. Ajan could watch the men if they all came
along, and the temple would be peaceful with the elders looking
after the property. Jabala would come. Both Sri and Ajan needed
her. Another dozen royal guards and servants would accompany
the caravan, for safety. There would be two covered carriages,
marked with the symbol of the temple. Sri, Ajan, and Jabala
would be in the first carriage, while Sudha, Vishal, Devyn and a
literate and loyal servant would be in the second carriage. The
guards and other servants would travel alongside the carriages on
black horses. White horses were rare, and therefore, conspicuous.

After just a seven days, the temple was ready to let Sri go. It
would be the first time she had left the temple grounds. The morning of the journey, Jabala and Sri did not speak. Jabala took extra
care grooming her sister-child and placing her hair in a more
ornamented sari. She was more tender when she brought the
brush through Sri's hair, each stroke an expression of love. Sri
stared back at Jabala, her black eyes wide with terror and joy.

Ajan did not visit Jabala's chamber during the planning of Sri's
journey, which is the longest he had stayed away in ten years. He
spent much time alone, or making arrangements or taking silent
walks with his Queen. He could see that she needed to go to
Videha, even though there was nothing for her there.

The journey through the unmarked paths of the mountains was
uneventful. They would travel in the earliest parts of morning,
and then again in the temperate parts of the afternoon. Though
the air of the mountains was cooler than on land, a Kasimian
spring day was still unpleasant when the sun was directly overhead. Ajan had made journeys back to the North Kingdom for
meetings with the royal families, and the path felt comfortable for

him to navigate. Sri, who had never seen such beauty, watched every part of the journey with wide eyes, either in the arms of Ajan or Jabala. The gods kept the weather stable for the journey, each sun as predictable as the next, leading the caravan with welcome arms into *Videha*.

And then, the carriages went without ceremony into the heart of the Northern Kingdom arriving at the palace of the Lord Janaka in *Mithila*, the center of the territory. There was an assembly of neatly dressed servants and grand looking noblemen waiting for the Grand Priest as the carriages made their way up the long path to the palace grounds.

Lord Janaka was old, but in good health, and known for being both an impatient and fair man. He was Ajan's uncle, and proud to be connected to Kasimi's spiritual world. He had little interest in politics since he was one of the richest men in the North. He had no use for games of power when he could buy it at any time. He showed all the symptoms of privilege, flaunting jewelry on every acceptable place on his body. Rings and necklaces of thick yellow gold added extra weight to his already girthy form. He wore a long tunic of rich cobalt silk, the color of the North, and a fitted pair of white silk pants. A sword rested at his side that he did not know how to use; but, the rubied handle was more than enough reason to add it to the ensemble.

There was a resemblance between Ajan and Janaka, especially in the powerful way they carried themselves. The Lord was a handsome man, who had pleasantly accepted age. His cerulean blue eyes deepened by the moral trials of Kasimi were even more shocking against his white hair.

The Lord walked towards the carriages, leaving his entourage behind, and waited for his visitors to depart.

Ajan exited first, wearing a cobalt blue pajama suit, and went into the waiting open arms of his uncle. "Lord uncle!" he exclaimed, happy to be united with a kinsman.

Janaka lifted Ajan off the ground in the embrace, happy to see his nephew, the Grand Priest. Everyone in town knew who Ajan was, and specifically, how Ajan was related to *him*. "Ajan!" the older man exclaimed. "You look poor, Ajan. Can you not find some better gold?" he joked, fingering Ajan's thin gold necklace.

Ajan shook his head, smiling at Janaka's famous disposition. "And you look fatter than when I last saw you, Janaka-uncle. Well done, old man." Ajan laughed heartily, and gripped his uncle's shoulders. He kissed Janaka's cheeks and then looked into the elder's eyes. "I have brought some people you should meet."

Janaka furrowed his brows. "How many people?" The fat old man placed his hands behind his back in a disciplined manner. "Get on with it, you know how I hate meeting new people."

Ajan nodded, smiling at how some things never change. The three priests had assembled alongside their carriage, and were not concerned about how ridiculous they looked while picking private holes to straighten out their clothes. None of the priests wore cobalt blue. This was the North Kingdom—it was not home for them. Ajan shot a stern look at the men, and gestured for them to join him.

In a deep voice, Ajan proceeded with the proper introductions. "Lord Janaka of the Northern Kingdom, I would like you to meet Priest Sudha of the South, Priest Vishal of The Isles and Priest Devyn of Goane." He motioned broadly to present all three at once.

Sudha was polite enough and nodded his head to Janaka. "My lord." He then stepped back towards the first carriage. He had had enough for today and just wanted some food and wine.

Devyn was straightforward. He bowed at the waist, knowing his place as a Goanian before a nobleman of the North. "Lord Janaka, I am happy to be at your home…" he said quietly. To this, Janaka raised a brow. Devyn could not hide his halfbreed blood-line. It was not clear whether Janaka was dissatisfied by the Goane Priest's presence.

Vishal didn't do anything. He just blinked, and crossed his arms in judgment at Janaka. It didn't matter. Janaka had dealt with Vishal's family before, and had met this priest in the past, before he held the title.

Janaka looked back at Ajan and gave him a knowing nod. Formalities—he understood. "And where is the person who I wish to meet?" He pointed at the first carriage, knowing that she must be in there.

Ajan walked up to the covered carriage and put his hand inside to motion that it was time. Jabala came out first, and dipped into a curtsey before Janaka. She looked like a noblewoman herself, wearing a cobalt blue salwar-kameez and a sapphire pendant betwixt her brows. Her dark brown hair was pulled tightly back into a bun, offsetting her features. "My dear lord…" Jabala whispered, before claiming her place by the carriage.

Janaka's eyes swept over Jabala's form a few times. "Lovely…" he whispered to himself, following Jabala's body with his blue eyes. "Lovely…"

And then, Sri walked out of the carriage. Jabala had spent nearly three hours fussing over the girl. Her raven hair fell in rampant curls around her shoulders and face—unfettered. She wore a formal gold and cobalt sari, folded in the way of the north. Sri had managed to bargain with Jabala for a few select pieces of jewelry rather than a tasteless sprawling of gold. The stone of Varuna, emerald, had been applied as a bhindi between her brows. A choker of inlaid sapphires and yellow gold fit around her slight neck, and one white diamond ring was placed on her thumb. The clothes were wasted, however, against the maiden's beauty. Sri's large, black eyes were mesmerizing in their natural state of awe and curiosity. Her impossible mastery of innocence and power held the attention of the onlooker.

Janaka knew exactly who Sri was when she made her entrance. He, and the entire entourage, the priests—everyone—dropped to one knee. "My Queen..." Janaka whispered with his hand on his heart, entranced by the young girl.

Indeed, there was a physical feeling of awe from the crowd as the beheld their Queen for the first time. Jabala had warned Sri that this would happen, so the girl was prepared. Her wide eyes carried her gaze across the bowing people. In a refined voice, Sri commanded. "Please rise, my good people." She then walked to Lord Janaka and helped him up with her hand. "I thank you for your kindness, in guiding me through my personal journey to my birth place."

Sri had practiced this moment in her mind on her way out of the carriage.

Janaka stared at the Queen, impressed at the elegance he saw in the youth. "Yes, your Highness..." is all he could manage to say.

Ajan chimed in, to move the meeting forward. He stood up from his kneel, and gestured to people to carry on and continue. "Lord uncle, we would like to make this trip as brief as possible. There is much to do back at the temple, making our time very scarce here. Can you get us to *Videha* tomorrow, and provide us with an escort in your name?"

Janaka slapped Ajan on the back. "Done, Ajan-child. Simple. I would be happy to have my escort take you back to the temple as well..." Janaka was a clever man—he knew that going to the Grand Priest's temple was a very rare honor, that had never been granted.

"You know that is not possible, Janaka-uncle. But, anything you do to help us here will be looked upon with favor by the gods. We appreciate your help." Ajan put a hand on his uncle's shoulder and on Sri's arm. He smiled softly between the two people.

"I thought I should try, Ajan. Anyway..." Janaka clapped his hands together to get the attention of the crowd. He raised his arms in the air over his round body and bounced up to make a spectacle. "Attention, Attention!" he yelled. "Tonight, to honor our guests, I will be having a feast starting at the rise of the moon. It will continue until the moon sets, and we bid our guests a farewell. There will be wine, dancing and food!"

There was a wave of cheer over the assembly. Sudha looked especially relieved. Who wouldn't be pleased at the prospect of a wealthy man having a feast to honor important people? The women began to gossip about their adornments for the festivities. The men began to cheer loudly at the thought of politics and wine. The servants marveled at the thought of taking part in something so festive.

Sri looked at the ground, uncertain if she wanted to have to play her role for the evening. This was supposed to be her time, and she was scared for the next morning. She looked up at Janaka, and inclined her head to him placing a proper smile on her stained lips. "Thank you."

Ajan could see that Sri was less than pleased, though it wasn't apparent to the rest of the crowd. So could Jabala. He put the hand on the small of Sri's back and led her back to her nurse for comforting, away from the crowds. He would take care of politics and face making until this evening—it was the least he could do. "Perfect, Janaka-uncle. Now, let us go talk of your merchant adventures until then, shall we?"

The two men walked arm and arm towards the palace, while Sri and Jabala were shown to their guest quarters by the women servants. Ajan looked back at his ward, waiting to catch her gaze—Sri was already staring at him. They smiled quietly to one another, and made a silent agreement to seek one another out at the feast later that evening.

~

Janaka bought the most beautiful slaves that the territories had to offer. A tiny, dark haired beauty served the two men spice wine inside the lord's smoking parlor. She kept the glasses filled, and slipped in and out of the shadows on cue. She was always ashamed of her dissatisfactory state, not letting her eyes look up at Ajan or Janaka, unless asked to.

Ajan stretched his legs, and slumped back into his overstuffed chair to take an extended puff of his cinnamon wrapped smoking roll. "Janaka, where did you get these? They are delicious…"

Janaka's eyes were momentarily distracted as he watched his slave pour him wine—looking at the curves he had purchased as they all seemed to effortlessly bring bounty into his cup. He sat at attention on his chair, with his elbows helping him further forward. He took the liberty of bringing a fat, jeweled finger to the girl's chin to thank her for a job well done. "Thank you, sweetness…" he whispered with his eyes half closed before releasing her along with the smoke from his inhale. He slumped back into his chair, and took his time at the smoking roll before engaging his nephew in conversation. "In Goane, Ajan. In Goane, the land of beauty and spice. Did you know they have women merchants there?"

Ajan rolled his eyes and asked the obvious question, "What was her name?"

Janaka's mischievous smile curled around his smoke. He exhaled, parting his full into a skilled O for effect. "I don't even know her name, Ajan. But I did know her, many many times…and

I do hope to know her again. A woman who turns smoking into a recreation of her body deserves my knowledge...oh Ajan, you must get to Goane. There are things there you have never tasted before."

Ajan was not virtuous. He had his fair share of women, from all different classes and backgrounds, and all were beautiful. The Grand Priest shook his head in the negative, "I don't have time for these things, right now, Janaka-uncle."

Janaka's eyebrows went for his forehead, and he removed the cigarette from its loyal place between his fingers to put on the clay pot. This was a change he did not like in his nephew. "Hmm, I don't recall the gods ever asking a man to give up women. Is this a personal choice or?"

Ajan furrowed his brow, and sat up on his chair, slightly annoyed at his uncle's questions. He took a quick puff of the cinnamon smoke and then retorted, "No, uncle. With my responsibilities, I don't have the time for those kinds of complications. I just don't have time."

"Ah..." Janaka nodded his head, still incredulous to Ajan's words. He leaned forward on his chair, and held his blue eyes against his nephew's. "Let me see if I can interpret what my nephew is really saying...he is in love and doesn't have time for other women. Am I right?"

Ajan exhaled his smoke into an O and closed his eyes to enjoy the stain of cinnamon on the inside of his upper lip. He narrowed his eyes at his uncle's mocking. "Old man, I will never be in love. It is not on my path, at least for now..." The nephew hoped that this would stop the questions. Janaka always had a way of pressing Ajan for truths that he would not admit to himself.

Janaka watched Ajan with no expression, studying the subtle tension in his nephew. If he didn't have a woman, why would the subject cause such nervousness in him? Janaka gripped his spice wine, taking a generous swig at the cup and then lifted it to Ajan in a half toast. The subject would be done with for now. "She is beautiful, Ajan. You've done a wonderful job with her…"

Sri, of course. Ajan also grabbed his spice wine, and lifted it respectfully to the toast. He relaxed to the sweet taste of the liquid mixing with the cinnamon fumes—how long it had been since Ajan had indulged in these exotic tastes. "I just guide what is already divine. She is…" Ajan paused, contemplating the wine in his cup, "…the hope for Kasimi."

"*Acha?*" Janaka asked, his eyes widening in confusion and curiosity. "The temple has made you vague, Ajan. Good for a politician, bad for a merchant. I don't understand…your words. What of this Queen?"

Ajan placed his wine down, pushing it away for the moment. He sat on the edge of his chair, and watched Janaka to see if the man was trustworthy. Janaka was a fair man, who would not double cross blood, even for the highest bidder. Pursing his lips together, and extinguishing his smoking roll, Ajan grew serious in front of his uncle. "Sri is going to be the one to find the sky god. I have read the scriptures, and prayed, and meditated—it is she who will find Him. Of this, I am certain…so yes, she is…" Ajan reclaimed his wine, "…the hope for Kasimi."

"*Acha.*" Janaka stated, closing his eyes in understanding. "It's the most brilliant thing I've seen you devise yet, Ajan." Janaka beckoned his servant girl over to refill the men's glasses. He did not seem shocked or disapproving of this extraordinary historical event.

Ajan was taken aback by his uncle's lack of a response. "Brilliant?" This could not possibly be a compliment. "What do you mean, Janaka-uncle?"

The serving girl came and quickly refilled Janaka's spice wine, but did not escape without being touched. Ajan did not want more wine or he would fall asleep from already onsetting exhaustion. Janaka placed a new smoking roll between his fingers, and tugged at the servant girl's waist for her to light it. She did, trembling with the candle in her hand, and then pattered quickly back to the shadows.

"It's logical. Shift the responsibility to the child—and what's even better—a girl, and away from the priests. If she succeeds, you will be hailed as a hero. If she fails, well then..." Janaka inhaled the cinnamon and released it through his nose. "...well she was just a girl and you were blindly following the gods which is still worthy. You will either be a hero or a disappointed worshipper. Either way, you will not lose face. Brilliant, Ajan. I couldn't have come up with something more sound, myself."

Ajan blinked in disbelief at his uncle. "No, that's *not* it. You don't understand, Janaka-uncle." Ajan leaned forward over the table to argue his position. "I actually believe that Sri is the only one who can find our King. I am not trying to find a way to..." Ajan had trouble finding his next words. "...way to maintain my position or power. I am trying to serve..." Ajan paused, feeling strange about his argument, but continued, "Trying to serve the gods as purely as I can."

"*Achaaaa.*" Janaka said, nodding to himself. He continued to puff on his smoking roll, putting this topic to bed as well.

Ajan had said something that clarified a question in the old man's mind. Janaka did not believe his reasoning—he was not convinced of things so easily. Ajan's words must have given him another insight, another answer. He quickly changed the topic. "How will we get to *Videha*?"

"It is not a far journey, especially if you bring my horses. My guards will take you through the forests rather than the roads for privacy, and you should be there by mid-day if you leave at dawn. You won't have any problems, and I will make sure everything is taken care of." Janaka smiled over his cup of wine, his eyes bright with support for Ajan.

"Thank you, Janaka-uncle." Ajan bowed his head and then refocused his cerulean gaze on his elderly relative. His lips challenged him for a smile, but Ajan remained in control of his expression. Ajan then asked the question Janaka had been waiting to respond to. "Will you come with us, Janaka?"

Janaka didn't control his smile, which burst over his cup of wine but was quickly hidden by a sip. "Will that delicious woman that I saw in your caravan be going?"

"*Acha.*" Ajan grinned, mocking his uncle.

"Then I will honor you with my great presence." The old man laughed happily and brought his glass with surprising energy and focus to the ceiling, like a sword. "To our journey!"

Ajan raised his glass up, in a more refined fashion, and then curled his lips over the side to down the last of his liquid. "To our journey," Ajan agreed.

~

Sri and Jabala were comfortably in the ladies guest chambers, relaxing for the afternoon before they would have to make an appearance at the feast. They were not alone, however. The servant women could not take their eyes off these two mysterious creatures, especially Sri. This was the experience of a lifetime, of one thousand moons, and they were not going to leave their posts for one moment. They might miss something.

Jabala, with the overly attentive help of four servants, helped Sri out of her sari and into a soft resting gown. The servants giggled in voices that were too shrill to be claimed by women, thinking that high pitched sounds would amuse Sri and her maid. Jabala was very protective of her sister, making sure that these servants didn't get too close to her. When Sri was finished, Jabala stepped out of her salwar-kameez and into a pink sarong.

Jabala was shocked as the same women who had helped Sri ran to her side to attend to her. She had no issue with shewing them away in their language, "*Nehi, nehi...*"

Sri had seated herself in one of the four offered chairs, beside the window that overlooked the palace grounds. Her cold hands sought warmth, one under her leg and the other in her hair as she traced the raven locks from end to end. Jabala saw one of the eager hand maids arm herself with a brush and head over to Sri, happy at this open opportunity to serve the Queen. Jabala skillfully intercepted the servant, and claimed the brush with a quick *thank-you*, and sat behind her lady to brush her hair.

"How are you, child?" Jabala said, stroking through the Intended's hair. The servants would not be able to understand most of their conversation if they spoke in proper Kasimian.

Sri sighed, enjoying the familiar touch of Jabala in this very strange place. She looked outside at the palace grounds, and focused on a particular set of mango trees in the distance. "How am I, Jabie?" Sri asked, knowing that Jabie would know better than she did.

Jabala pulled up a chair to continue brushing in comfort. She looked around to see if the servant women had found something else to occupy their time. "You are both frightened and relieved. Frightened because you are going to a place you have never been and relieved because soon you will have been there."

Sri tilted her head back, to enjoy the diligent brush strokes. Jabie was right, as always. "How are you, Jabie?"

Jabala inhaled the perfumed scent of her child's hair, and then kissed Sri in the middle of her head. "I'm fine, Sri." She was always fine.

Sri's eyes went back to their gazing at that spot of mango trees outside. "Jabie, what will I find tomorrow?"

Jabala brought her eyes back to the spiral curls she loved tending to so much. "You can't ask me that question, Sri."

The servant girls had finished with their gossiping, and returned to attend to Sri and her maid en masse. By now, they had brought in the sweets and fruits for the ladies afternoon refreshment. Jabala pointed for the girls to bring Sri's favorites: *cha* and *chumchum*. Jabala would just have *cha*. Five servants argued over who would carry the silver tray. Jabala eyed the girls in warning, and focused Sri on the food.

Jabala took her tea, and stood up to share Sri's view outside the window. "Child, you should eat and then get some rest. You will be the center of attention tonight, and you will have to be everything the people want. The best thing you can do now is to sleep."

Sri appreciated this honesty. She brought her eyes up to her maid and pleaded, "Hold me, Jabie?" Sri asked, tugging at her maid's sarong.

"I suppose." Jabala answered quietly with a smile, placing her cup down on the tray. She took Sri by the hand, and led her to the bed. Jabala lowered herself to the cushions, arranging the pillows around her to support the figures of both women. She then held her hands out for Sri to join her in a maternal embrace. Sri was Jabie's little girl and found her comfortable place in the nurse's arms. It was a picture of innocence. Two loving women, dressed in soft colors, holding onto one another on the single bed of white blankets.

The *cha* had gone cold, and the servant women were too distracted to bother with cleaning. They were not sure how to react to seeing their Queen so vulnerable, in the arms of her maid. It was so strange to them, the relationship that existed between Jabala and Sri. It was not proper, not supposed to be that way. Jabala should be standing by Sri's bed as she rested, not holding her like a mother.

Jabala and Sri were unaware of the curious stares, too caught up in their own embrace. Jabala pressed her lips to Sri's head, and stroked her little one's hair whispering terms of affection from time to time. Sri was curled up next to her maid, her arms submissively around her Jabie's waist. They would stay this way until it was time to get ready for the feast.

~

The feast was outdoors so the people could enjoy the palace grounds without the confines of walls. Over one hundred servants proudly tended to the gardens. Janaka rewarded his servants handsomely, even the slaves, and none wanted to lose his place at the palace. The Lord's gardens were known for their exotic beauty—plants and flowers from his journeys to lands far off Kasimi had been carried to his palace. Papaya and mango trees lined the grounds, to protect the borders and send a natural perfume through the night air.

A visual blend of color and fire created the feast. There were a dozen randomly scattered bonfires roaring, with servants cooking all kinds of meats and spiced vegetables in an endless procession of food. Another hoard of servants passed out wine, to make sure that there was wasteful consumption throughout the night. As usual, Janaka's party would leave people fed for weeks. Musicians wove their sounds in between the bursts of delighted voices, strolling from group to group to engage them in song. The tabla drum, when played next to the warm fires, was the seductive chanting of the gods.

Janaka wore the fur of a white tiger to his feast. Only a man so devoted to his own wealth would wear fur in the Kasimian spring. He wore all white trimmed in cobalt blue, knowing that this would offset his jewels, which were proudly displayed. The Lord wanted to be the center of attention, next to the Queen, of course. Already happy from an afternoon of drinking, Janaka moved from person to person to welcome them to his home.

Everyone had dressed for his or her part, and everyone from the North by blood or land wore cobalt. Men wore the emblems of their title (if they had one) and carried ceremonial swords on their right hips. Moustaches were slicked into neat lines, and beards trimmed to fine angles. Position was very important, and appearance was one way to decree or deny power and affiliation. The women were styled just as the men, wearing silks in creative combinations of cobalt and gold, and as much jewelry as their frames and purses would allow. Hair styles that would take the care of a hand maid or two, were woven in dark hair, more a sign of class than fashion. They were all waiting for Sri.

The priests from the three other houses were speaking privately during the feast, not concerned with making polite small-talk with the other guests. Sudha and Devyn were dressed politely enough, in neutral Kasimian reds, a color without affiliation. Vishal wore a decisive and haughty yellow, to distinguish himself as a member of The Isles. They wove aimlessly through the trees, and Sudha ensured that several stops were made at various bonfires.

Vishal walked with his eyes scanning the crowd, and his arms comfortably behind his back. He stood in between Sudha and Devyn, staking claim as the tallest member of the trio. Without his eyes looking to the other two, he asked, "And why again are we wasting time here?"

Sudha accepted a refill on his wine from a pleasant looking woman servant and grabbed another kebab from an attendant by the nearest fire. He had to quicken his stumpy legged pace to get back into line with the other two priests. "I am having a wonderful time, Vishal. No time wasted here."

Devyn laughed under his breath at Sudha's comment. He took an idle sip from the wine he had been nursing all night but did not say anything.

Vishal sneered at Sudha and shook his head disgustedly at the man's avarice. "Sri wants to see where she was born, how nice." Vishal shook his head again, obviously annoyed and not wanting to participate further in the feast. He feigned a loud yawn, his wide open mouth a rude gesture of boredom.

The men continued to walk, examining the scenery and refreshment. A few moments after Vishal's tantrum, Devyn said dismissively—as an afterthought to Vishal's comment—"Too bad Sri wasn't born in The Isles, eh?" A throw away comment, no one paid any attention to the quip.

One of the most seductive and majestic events for the evening was the display of Janaka's tigers that he kept with trainers, for amusement. It was rumored in *Mithila* that the Lord had lost three trainers over the past ten moons; still, many men went to Janaka for the position since the pay was more than an average merchant would make in one year. No man could fill the position—Janaka selected an exotic, yellow haired woman who was from a land worlds to the north of Kasimi. Her journey to *Mithila*, her existence in Kasimi, was something of a mystery to the people. The tigers, however, seemed to know her and respond to her like sickly entranced boys.

Her lustrous yellow hair, worn long and free, made an announcement for her spectacle most unnecessary. Men stared at the site of this strange and beautiful bird. Pale skin, so rare and treasured to the Kasimians, was obvious. Not being Kasimian, she was excused from all the laws that applied to their lives with pleasure—she wore a tight fitting demi blouse of cobalt blue, blatantly showing off the lines of her bosom and muscular arms. The skin of some animal had been died to cobalt, and pronounced softly rounding curves through comfortably snug breeches. She gave no name, so the people called her *Radha*.

Radha led her line of beautiful golden tigers out to the central bonfire, without restraint. The crowd did not back away in fear, seeing that the beasts had been captivated by her spell. They crept on the grass, moving so slowly to torture the onlookers who would want to see the tigers in their athletic runs.

Radha did not make the loud yelling command sounds that most trainers would, or use whips to herd her tigers in positions. When they reached their point, she purred at them much the way a lover would indicate desire to her mate. She ran her hands through their fur passionately, taking time to appreciate all of them—but somehow making them all feel individually loved. The affection of the tigers for this woman rose as she touched them, and they turned on their bellies, squiggling their spines in the grass submissively. *Radha* continued to purr at her tigers, who so willingly followed her.

She whispered something to the animals, and the tigers began to perform a dance for their mistress. *Radha* stood back, looking at her tigers with an enigmatic expression, guarding her children as they soared. Their sinuous, lithe bodies twisted in the air, as they jumped over the fire in a choreographed sequence of lines. There was no growling, no sound—the animals were being led in this dance by *Radha's* beauty. The trainer waved her hands, and the tigers lined up again side by side.

Radha laid down in front of them, arching her back as if to accept the embrace of a lover. The crowd was uncomfortable with this, and some of the men reached for their swords in case the golden tigers grew angry.

In the midst of the crowd, Sri watched the golden haired beauty lead her tigers with such love and affection, while remaining so untouchable to the Kasimians who watched with wonder. *Radha* had captured Sri. *She is able to transcend everything I know and place herself above it.* Watching the white woman, Sri brought her hands to trace her own body the way *Radha* had touched the tigers. She understood—the animals, like herself, had been swept away by this beauty who had communed with their desire.

The tigers roared passionately with *Radha* sacrificed before them. But the beasts were not growling out of hunger for her, they were moaning in jealousy at all the people who tried to take away their attention from their mistress. *Radha* purred from her place beneath them, and the glorious animals stretched their front legs to her, in the gesture of a bow.

Radha rose and smiled alluringly at her tigers, and beckoned them to follow her back to their keep. In a quiet and slow walk, torturing the onlookers again, the golden trainer took her tigers to rest. There was not a trace of worry on her face, not a bead of sweat, from the tigers or the fire. The audience had experienced the anxiety for her.

After *Radha* had exited completely from the view of the crowd, Janaka clapped loudly, and then held his hands up in the air to gain the attention of the crowd. He paced to the center of the garden, where the largest bonfire raged, and called for silence. He moved his body in a circle with his raised hands, quieting the crowd from their whispering on *Radha*.

"My guests!" Janaka proclaimed joyfully. "It is my honor to welcome the people of The Temple on *Govandhara* to my home." The Lord paused to receive the loud cheers and clapping. He signaled silence, and continued with more serious words. He looked out into the crowd and folded his hands neatly behind his back.

"It was five years ago that our Kingdom was ravaged by rebels who sought to destroy what we had all worked to build, and to kill the Northern lands. We lost many cherished members of this Kingdom, including our own Varuna II, a member of the divine...I lost many a friend in that dark time. We have worked to rebuild our Kingdom, to restore it to its former glory, and that, my friends, is what we celebrate tonight! We have been reborn. We have returned. Join me, my friends, in this celebration of life!"

Janaka spoke with both pride and sadness, fighting back tears through flared nostrils. The crowd did not applaud, having joined the Lord in remembering the dark time of civil war. Janaka continued on.

"Tonight, my friends, we have some very special guests. Their presence has given me hope, and has mended by broken heart." Janaka gripped his chest, closing his fingers into a fist. He bowed his head, and then returned his voice and gaze to the crowd for the last part of his address. He was sweating, exhausted from the flames of the fire and his heavy emotion. "Please join me in blessing Sri, The Intended Queen..." Janaka stepped a few paces forward and held out his hand to the girl who had been mingling casually with the guests.

Sri took Janaka's sweaty hand in her own tiny one, and walked with her eyes locked on the old man. From her spot on the grass, the nobles and servants began to drop into a kneel and bow their heads. There was a full silence interrupted only by a crackling fire as Sri made her way through a maze of people to the center of the feast.

Sri straightened out her sari and then motioned with a raising of her hand. "Please rise, my good people." She swallowed against the constraint of her choker, and looked out at the pool of brown faces with her own awe in return for theirs. She would speak—her heart was full.

"I have returned home." Sri began. Her focus claimed that specific set of mango trees from her earlier meditation, and she continued in a sweet voice. "Or should I say, I am discovering my home for I have never had the honor of knowing the good families of the North. I can feel your loss, my good people, for my father was Varuna II, killed by the savages of civil war." There was no desire for tears, as there had been previously in Sri's eyes, just determination to deliver a message. "I am wrong to say that the North is my home for I am not only your Queen. I belong to all of Kasimi's people, and sacrifice my existence for you. This celebration tonight is not only about the rebirth of the North, it is about the hope for Kasimians as an entire people. That is the purpose of my life. I came here to find my reason, and now...I have."

Ajan's eyes guarded over Sri for her entire speech. He could not believe the strength and purity that his ward portrayed to the people. She had enlightened and moved him. Tears dared to flash over his blue eyes, and he claimed Jabala's hand in his, while pride overwhelmed him. The crowd, some weeping and some cheering, dropped again to one knee and began to chant in worship to Sri. Janaka began, "Behold Sri, Our Intended Queen!" He pounded his fist to the sky, each thrust ripe with feeling from his heart, "*Sri, ya! Sri, ya! Sri, ya!*" The crowd joined in the ceremonial worship of their god's wife. Fists and jewels, swords and hands thrown up to the moon, "*Sri, ya! Sri, ya! Sri, ya!*"

The chanting and cheering continued on for a long time. Sri quietly left the people to the ceremony and went straight to Ajan's side. He drew her to him with an open hand meant just for his ward. The two people slipped unnoticed, away from the feast. They found sanctuary underneath a leafy papaya tree, and sat down at the trunk to speak quietly for a while.

Ajan's hands pressed Sri's curls to either side of her face as he placed a lingering kiss on her forehead. "Sri, darling..." he murmured. "You did so well tonight, and you look so beautiful."

Sri pressed her hands to her mentor's. "Did I, Ajan?" She needed approval still from her mentor. She closed her eyes, and held her breath, awaiting an answer from him.

He kissed her forehead once, and then again. He pulled his cherished ward against him, possessively. How could she be so humble when she was so magnificent? "Sri, darling...you were...you are a Queen and a goddess. You were wonderful."

Sri breathed. Her black eyes remain closed inside of Ajan's powerful arms. "Tomorrow," she sighed. Ajan might have responded back with reassuring words, but she did not hear them. Sri just enjoyed being a little girl again, in her mentor's embrace. In the background, the haunting chant, *"Sri, ya! Sri, ya! Sri, ya!"* deafened the girl's ears. She buried her head in Ajan's silks, until the sound went away and her exhaustion released her from night.

4

It was still dark when Sri awoke to the sound of Jabala's hoarse morning whispering. "Sri sweetness, it is time."

The last thing Sri remembered was being held by her mentor, and drifting off. Ajan must have put her to bed after the feast.

There would be no protesting this morning. "Yes, Jabie..." Sri said quietly.

Like the morning when Sri had left the temple, Jabala and the Intended did not speak. Sri stared at Jabala as she helped her to get ready. *Videha* was more traditional, so Sri had to wear more coverings around her face and hair. Sri wore a plain, red salwar-kameez, and a cobalt wrap around her hair and neck. Jabala was dressed in the same way, wearing heavier coverings since she was older.

The two women made their way down the narrow staircase to the front hall, where everyone would be gathered for the journey. They were the last two, and most anticipated, members of the caravan to assemble. Sri took Jabie's hand, and watched as the men went about their talks on arrangements. Janaka was preparing his guards to work alongside Ajan's, and deciding who would have which horse. The carriages would weigh them down too much for a journey that would only be one day.

Janaka and Ajan were a powerful duet, with decisive and efficient arm gestures to who needed to be where with what weapon and when. They had a clear vision of the way things were supposed to go for this day, and communicated it with precision. The informal arrangement was that Janaka would be in charge for the day, making the decisions regarding the journey and Ajan would relinquish his usual controls. This made the most sense.

Without a grand announcement, everyone made his way to his assigned horse in the front of the palace. In a seemingly meaningless arrangement, Vishal was placed in the group with three guards. Janaka would ride with Jabala, and Sri would ride with Ajan—they would be together in the center of the group.

And, it was time. Everything was in place and arranged. The servants gathered outside the palace to bid their master and his guests farewell. Sri looked at the women servants who stared back at her, and smiled. She wanted to remember every part of this day.

"*Acha!*" Janaka yelled with his sword in the air. On his signal, a masculine choir of voices yelled, "*Acha!*" and the horses rode forth into the rising sun, for *Videha*.

Again, everything went smoothly as the group made its way to *Videha*. They made it to the village by mid-day, in time to escape the heat. Ajan frowned at the clouds that appeared to be coming in from the east, and hoped it was not a sign from the gods. Janaka laughed, knowing that it didn't rain during the Kasimian springs. "*Clouds travel, just as we do...*" Janaka mused.

Sri's arms found a tight grip around Ajan's waist for most of the journey, and her head found a place on his red tunic. It was as much a sign of affection as an apology. She felt like she was shunning the man who had raised her, her only real family, for the people who created her. Now, Ajan would have it no other way. He held his head like a warrior and brought his Queen to battle her demons. It was as it should be.

On reaching the main road in *Videha*, Ajan felt a surge or memory and emotion in his heart that he had not expected. This was the place he had come fifteen years ago to claim his ward. *"Everything has changed..."* Ajan thought to himself as his blue eyes swallowed the sights of a glorious land that was still recovering from war. *"Where are the people?"* He had remembered lots of smiling children when he first came and the sounds of day: women gossiping, sparrows singing, girls laughing, goats complaining, horses drinking. He had remembered the stands of merchants and artists selling their bounty, with bright eyes. There was nothing. There were people, but none that wished to make eye contact. There were no children to be found. *Videha is dead.* Ajan caressed Sri's hand.

Sri did not know what to expect. The town looked empty to her, but she had never known it to be anything else. She leaned up to Ajan's ear and asked, "Is this what you remember?" Her eyes were wide with curiosity for the war-ravaged town. The stone houses showed signs of destruction or fire, but no one was there to rebuild them.

Ajan leaned in to where Sri whispered and kissed the top of her covered head, pausing to inhale the scent of rose that Jabala had sprinkled on his ward. "No, Sri. This is not the same place where you were born. You were born in a glorious *Videha*, my darling."

Ajan led the group off the main road in the direction of Varuna II's house, near the coast. Even Varuna could not protect his grandchild from the savages that wished to control Kasimi. After Sri was taken, he and his mistress decided to live a quiet life in their home by the ocean isolated from most of the town's people. Varuna II was still an influential member of the noble houses and could sway the people in his direction, if he chose to. His death was a symbol to the people of *Videha*, and to the people of Kasimi. The rebels would not even spare the divine.

The group stopped at the base of the winding rode to Varuna
II's manor. Ajan had agreed that Sri could explore the house without the entourage while the guards stood at attention at the base
of the road. He promised not to follow her, and Jabala would
watch the Grand Priest to ensure this. Sri had made it very clear
that she would go alone to the house.

The world did not move or cry out as Sri made her way down
the stallion, and walked the few paces to her family's home. She
looked back in slow motion, bringing her black eyes with her neck
in a graceful turn, and picked a moment to freeze in her mind.

Janaka's black horses stood, swooshing flies away with their
tails, and eating treats that the guards had brought for them. A sea
of cobalt blue washed over the people with the color of blood
mingling on various limbs. The people were participating in the
usual rituals of waiting by chatting or sitting under nearby trees in
hope of rest.

Ajan looked back at Sri, his cerulean gaze that she knew and
loved so much, such a burden in her journey towards the house.
And, Jabala, her cherished mother—*Have I ever called her that?*—
stood calmly by Ajan's side. She mouthed something that they
could not see, a promise. It made her so sad and nervous that the
taste of nausea tempted her dry mouth with drink. *Goodbye.*

And Sri's black eyes focused on the promise of a house off into
the distance. She didn't remember how she walked there, but it
seemed like a thousand moon had passed when she reached the
doorway. She was a ghost looking back on where she had begun
and ended her life.

The stone house was ravaged and abandoned. It was not
large—but grand even in destruction. Her father had chosen modesty, having the position and status to claim a palace in *Videha*. Sri
kneeled in front of the doorway, running her hands over the broken wood desperately. "*Nehi...*" she whispered.

Sri crawled through the door and went inside the one level house. There was no color around her—the light was too dim. The shadows were broken by touches of sun to guide the intended on her journey. The house had been raped, there was no warmth left. Sri's eyes widened thinking about Varuna II's last night in Kasimi—how this home had been destroyed. It smelled like death. Animals had sought comfort and shelter inside the house, without regard for whose territory it was. Sri's desperation was suddenly replaced by confusing twitches of anger that threatened to over-take her tears with vomit. *"Brahma!"* Sri screeched, reaching for a nearby wall. "Oh *Brahma!*"

Brahma led her to the fateful room where she had been born. A bed, big enough for two lovers, called out for Sri. She obeyed, picking herself up, and walking to the destined place. Her hands, shaking, moved slowly to stroke the red blanket in the middle. She spread the molded quilt out, while water dripped restlessly from her chin. She could feel the pangs of childbirth through her arms, which made her scream out in pain—for her mother and for her father—for the loss. "Oh *Brahma!*" Exhausted, she received the bed to her body writhing restlessly in a tearful fit. "Oh *Brahma!* Why, why, why?" Sri tensed her body, while arch-ing up her back to the Omnipotent King for sacrifice. "Take me! Take me, *Brahma!*"

Sri grabbed her hair from underneath her head covering and pressed her fingers against her skull—attacking her parents' mur-derers in her mind. She beat her head against the floor, hoping to shed her blood in place of her father. Sri screamed out, as her mother had, to drown out the pain.

The sound of a young girl screaming awakened someone's attention and footsteps could be heard approaching the bedcham-ber. Sri continued to scream loudly, the rough sound of weight against a wooden floor not able to bring her back to sanity. The shadow of a young male figure loomed at the entrance, and glared at the trespasser on his property. A low male voice asked with contempt, "Why are you in my house, girl?"

Sri, with her eyes more red than black, looked up at the boy in fear. He had a sword on his left hip, and a saber at the other one. Would she die in the same place that her parents had? "I...please forgive me..." she swallowed, quickly bringing her hands to wipe the water from her shiny skin. "I...did..." She looked at the boy again and slowed her tongue. "not kn..." Her lips froze. She was moved to silence. Something, again, was strange.

Sri was suddenly struck by an overwhelming sensation of love—in its purest, most undemanding form—and her soul changed. She felt bonded to this strange boy before her. She wanted to give him everything, be everything for him. Her hand crept to her face, her temperature had risen. "*Who is he?*" she asked herself, suddenly wishing the demoness would have an answer. His face was so familiar—she had seen him before in the night. His colors had been drawn on her. She could hear the sounds of her body on the inside—the rhythm of her mind, the sound of breath inside her nose all in time to the beating of her heart. These sounds orchestrated the beat of thunder outside; the storm clouds must have paused over *Videha*.

The boy halted at the foot of the bed, and his contempt for the trespasser was replaced by sudden curiosity. The tall, lanky youth dressed in servant's clothes gazed upon the familiar girl. His black eyes, with a ring of red on the pupils, locked on to Sri's. "*You have my eyes jahan. Do you share my soul, too?*" The boy reached his hand out for Sri with a combination of fear and need. "*Who is she?*"

The rain had made Ajan worry, and he had walked up to the house against Sri's wishes to retrieve her before the storm became ferocious. They would have to spend the night in *Videha*, in camp near the house. By the time he got to Varuna II's house, his clothes were slick against his body. With careful footsteps, he made his way into the dimly lit house. For a moment, their silence was broken by the sound of two voices: Sri and a boy. *Sri...danger?* With skill, he crept into the house towards the sound, only to hear conversation rather than harm. The rumbling of thunder masked the weight of his body, and warned Ajan not to intrude on the coming miracle. The Grand Priest remained with his wet body pressed against a wall in the shadows, listening to the two voices in the dark.

Sri reached her hand out for the boy's and grasped it tightly. It was the uniting of flesh that had been separated for too long, forever. She knew. Suddenly, she knew. It was so obvious and real—*Videha* had given her the answer. *"Brahma..."* she murmured affectionately, in thanks to the Omnipotent One who was overhead.

"Brahma..." the boy chanted in return. He moved to take Sri's other hand in his, and bring it to his lips. "Who are you?" the boy asked, moving closer to look in Sri's eyes which held him still.

"I am..." Sri paused, feeling that her name was too insignificant to speak in this moment. She leaned forward on the bed to better see that ring of red in the boy's eyes that looked so achingly familiar. "the person who you are supposed to meet." Sri was moved to say things as if she had practiced them all her life. *"I am...made from something that is intended for you."* Sri's eyes burned furiously, and she was taken over by the heart of her ancestors while the thunder beat on the drum.

And you are, he is,

He is their father, he is their son,
He their elder brother and their youngest:
The One God, entering the mind,
Is the first-born; he is in the womb.

From the full the full he raises up;
With the full is the full besprinkled.
Would that today we knew from whence
That full is sprinkled round out.

The boy brought both Sri's hands to his heart, and pressed them so they could feel his soul. He returned the speech as captivated by the gods as the girl he now loved so much.

And you are, she is,

She, the entrant, was born in right olden times;
She, the primeval, all things encompassed:
The great goddess, lighting up the dawn,
Looks out from each single thing that blinks the eye.

The two children sat on the fateful bed and became One, while the clouds cried tears of joy outside Varuna II's house. The third miracle had happed—the divine had been united. The rolling waves of the ocean that swept Varuna's II's home hailed the God and his Queen. The gods rejoiced in the coming of their kin to Kasimi.

Ajan dropped to his knees in a silent, breathless fall. "*It is the third miracle, Brahma.*" His heart both ached and rejoiced in witnessing the greatness before him. He could see the union and feel the gods' celebration in the sky and sea. How he wanted to chant! But the miracle must happen, so he kept silent as the children united.

Sri and the boy laid down side by side on the bed and held on to each other's hands as they exchanged promises. Sri asked, "Who are you, My King?"

The boy could not imagine life without this woman now. He closed his eyes and sighed, "My Queen..." The boy led the hand of his Queen to his lips, and closed his eyes in peace. "I am...*Marici*."

PART II

5

Ajan had been listening to the miracle on bended-knee, praying in his heart to *Brahma*, in thanks. His King had come and united with his ward. The thunder stopped long enough so he could hear the announcement of the King to his Queen.

"I am...Marici." Marici said.
"I am...Marici." Sri heard.
"I am...Marici." Ajan repeated.

No. "I am...Marici." *Not possible.* "I am...Marici." *How is he still alive? He is not the King.* Ajan stood, frozen by his own doubt until the thunder stunned him back into the moment. "I am...Marici." *This is not the third miracle.* Ajan needed to leave behind the sight of the bedroom before he was smothered by the sense of confusion that laid claim to his body. Ajan used the sound of thunder to guide him outside of Varuna II's house. He could barely stand. The heavy rain that beat against his skin was a welcome stimulus to wake him from what had just happened. "I am...Marici." *He was left behind.*

In a state of half consciousness, Ajan returned to the group without Sri. Only a few people stood waiting for him. The others had taken shelter under a canopy of pepul trees, south of the house. Ajan was weak and faint. He did not walk properly—it was the stagger of a man who was about to fall to his death.

Jabala waited in the rain, holding a wooden cover over her head. She was worried since Ajan had been gone so long, and Sri had not returned on her own from the rain. When Ajan stumbled back toward Jabala without Sri, Jabala ran to retrieve the warrior and take him to safety. She tossed the wood covering in favor of speed.

In the rain, Jabala's clothes began to melt around her. "Ajan?" Jabala asked, smoothing the priest's hair back from the water. She searched his blue eyes for an answer. "Ajan? Can you hear me? Where is Sri?"

Ajan stopped to let Jabala nurse him. He could not fully hear what she was saying, until the word Sri was uttered from the worried woman's lips. He gasped, and uttered hoarsely, "Shhhhr-i?"

Jabala cupped Ajan's face and stood calm though her own body was weakening with fear. Something had happened. She knew. "Ajan, where is Sri? Is something wrong?" Jabala shook him as hard as she could. "AJAN!"

He still would not respond, his eyes focusing off in the distance. Jabala closed her eyes in regret and brought her hand up to slap the wet skin of Ajan's face. He needed to be returned to her at all costs.

Ajan was snapped back to reality by the sting of Jabala's hand. "Sri?" he asked Jabala. It took him a few moments staring into Jabala's light brown eyes to regain balance. "Oh Jabala, please...I...saw..." Ajan could not find the words. There was so much that had just happened. "Jabie, please. Please." Ajan collapsed against the woman. "Please?"

"Oh Ajan...here..." Jabala brought the man to her bosom and comforted him as the rain poured around them. Whatever had happened to Sri did not have to do with danger. It was something else. "Come with me…" Jabala led the Grand Priest to a cluster of trees where the rain would not disturb them as much. It did not matter though—both people were drenched and could not feel the water anymore.

"Ajan?" Jabala pleaded.

The Grand Priest grabbed Jabala's forearms gently. "Sri met Marici inside the house." There was obviously more to the story, but Ajan wanted to ensure that he had spoken each word correctly.

Jabala stared intently back at Ajan, with a slight smile. "Sri's brother is alive?" The woman leaned in and kissed Ajan's cheek, thinking that this was good news. "We never told her she had a brother. Does she know now? Is she angry?" Jabala's eyes darkened, suddenly realizing the sense of betrayal her sister must feel at the kept secret. "Oh, I…I see."

Ajan shook his head and moved his hands up to grasp Jabala's shoulders. "No, no, she does not know who he is yet. Not that way. But, she has claimed him, Jabala. They…"

Jabala blinked, not getting the message clearly. Her pupils moved back and forth quickly, wanting the answer.

"They recited the miracle to one another, Jabala. Sri has found the King." Ajan hesitated with his next words, and dropped his voice to a whisper. "Sri thinks that Marici is the King."

Jabala did not react with the same negativity as Ajan. She let the thought run through her mind for a while, and then returned with her judgment. "This is complicated, Ajan, but not impossible."

Ajan looked back at Jabala in total frustration. His voice rose in volume—*Jabala did not understand.* "Jabie, Sri cannot marry her brother. Does that make any sense? She is the Intended Queen, and claims Marici to the King? It's not possible!"

Jabala examined Ajan for a moment, trying to realize the real problem underneath the complicated turn of events. A gentle smile came on her lips—"The only problem with Marici is that Sri can't marry him, in your opinion."

Ajan's face tensed as Jabala began to argue with him. He gripped on to her shoulders more tightly, hoping that he could make her see the gravity of the situation. "Explain yourself, woman!" Ajan said, tersely.

Jabala did not wince from the pressure that was applied to her shoulders. She looked back, without contempt, at the confused priest. "Everything else makes perfect sense, doesn't it, Ajan? He was born on the same day as she and is already connected to the gods...and to Sri. The only problem is that they are sister and brother, and not husband and wife. Sri is his intended Queen and partner. No where does it say that she has to be a lover too."

Ajan looked briefly away from Jabala and back to Varuna II's house. "Jabie..." It made sense to him. "But what will Sri be? She was bred to be a..."

Jabala removed Ajan's hands from her shoulders and placed them at her hips. "Do not turn away from something that is so obvious, Ajan. You are enforcing a rule that need not apply." She leaned her hands up to Ajan's wet hair, and ran her fingers through the mass of black waves. Her eyes found a spot on his forehead where she imagined the center of his confusion rested, and kissed it. "Go, bring them."

Ajan nodded obediently at his friend. She was right. Again, Jabala had managed to find that one thought that would convince him of his own foolishness. Even though it did not appear to make sense, he was enforcing rules on the situation that need not apply. *Jabie is right.* He did not want to doubt, or to falsify the third miracle. The gods were an enigma, and once again they had brought Kasimi their kin in a confusing riddle. It made sense—it had to. Looking at Jabala, Ajan stroked the dear woman's face tenderly before he returned his gaze to the house of Varuna II. It would do no good to turn away from Sri's choice, now. He must go to them, and find out more.

~

Marici and Sri had risen from the bed, and were walking out of their father's house to receive the rain. Sri must bring the King to the Kasimian people—and first to the priests of the temple. She was sure. She did not need to question Marici. The boy just stared intently at this strange woman who he had suddenly loved—not aware and not knowing of the story unfolding around him—but uncaring. He must be with her.

Ajan walked towards the twins with long, uncertain strides. He held *Brahma* in his heart, and Jabala's words in his mind, and went to claim the King and Queen. He was still confused. *I want to know what's going on, Brahma!* He stopped a few paces from the children, and waited for them to find him.

Sri's black eyes, with a ring of red on the edges, looked back at Ajan's with an intensity he had never seen before. She was certain. There was no doubt in her eyes. There was blind faith. Her hand gripped Marici's and the two stood before the Grand Priest, united. Sri uttered certain words. "My mentor, my guardian, my master, my Grand Priest..." she chanted, still touched by the gods. Sri kneeled down before the two men. "Behold the King." She looked up at Marici, entranced—hypnotized—by the boy.

Marici's immediate reaction was to move to Sri and help the girl to her feet. Ajan brought his hand out to pause Marici from doing so, signaling him to wait.

Ajan dropped to one knee alongside his beautiful ward and looked up at the boy. "The King..." he whispered. He then motioned for the two children to follow him to a private place where Jabala would be waiting. There would be so much to tell and understand—and they did not have a lot of time.

~

Ajan returned to the canopy where Jabala stood, waiting. Without taking time to look at Marici, Jabala took Sri quickly away so that Ajan could speak with the boy in private. Sri, protested, but then surrendered to her nurse's wishes after a few whispered words. The women walked further in the line of trees, escaping from view.

Marici looked as Sri was led off and then turned to Ajan with a worried expression, "Why did you take her away?"

Ajan looked at the boy. He was definitely his ward's twin. The two were exact complements: a male and female set. He had the same beauty and fiery inner strength as his sister. One gesture with his eye or hand, and his point was effectively made. Marici did not show promise of developing into a physically intimidating man. He was lanky, and stood about Sri's height. What he lacked in physical presence was made up for in his eyes. The same black pupils, ringed with a thicker line of red than Sri's, impressed meaning and understanding in their gaze. Even in old, ragged brown clothes, Marici looked noble and of a different place than Kasimi.

What should be his first words to Marici? Ajan did not answer the boy's question immediately. In a soft voice, he welcomed the child who he had seen being born. He had come out of their mother first. "Hello, Marici. Do you know who I am?"

Marici took a few paces back, wary of the strange man before him. The boy placed his hands on the two familiar weapons at his hips and spoke timidly to Ajan. "How...how did you know my name?" He blinked rapidly.

Ajan took the sword off hips hip and dropped it on the ground, and placed his hands up in a gesture of peace. "I mean you no harm, Marici. I am Ajan, of the North Kingdom and Grand Priest of Kasimi. I watched you being born, child." After declaring his identity, Ajan took a few steps toward the boy.

Marici did not let go of the weapons on his hips. Ajan had only dropped his long sword—not abandoned it. "I recognize your face. My father spoke of you from time to time." Marici's thoughts were nowhere close to logical at this point. He jerked his head back in the direction he remembered Sri leaving in and asked again, "Why did you take her away?"

Ajan continued to walk forward calmly, taking his own time to communicate with the boy. "You weren't killed by the rebels, Marici? What happened?"

Marici felt for his weapons with more vigor, withdrawing the saber slightly. "Did you come to finish the job? Do you know who I am?" Marici's eyes burned with both fear and anger as he calculated how much of a threat Ajan just might be.

"I am not going to hurt you, child." Ajan whispered in a low baritone voice. He continued to inch towards the King with his hands raised in the sign of peace. He kicked his sword out of the way, so that Marici was in control of the situation—though, the boy was hardly in any state to be. Still in soothing and hypnotic tones, Ajan continued. "You are the son of Varuna II, direct descendent of the sea god. Yes, child, I know who you are. But do you know who you are...now?"

Marici arched a brow, and dropped his jaw to answer. His eyes worked up over the canopy of leaves. He jerked his head again to where Sri had been taken away by that strange woman. In a louder voice, supported by rumbling thunder, he demanded, "Why did you take her away!"

Ajan clasped his hands under his nose and bowed at the waist, pleading to Marici to understand, and begging *Brahma* to give him wisdom. "She is safe, child and you will see her again soon." Ajan finally reached the boy's place, and put his slender fingers around the boy's wrists to hold him still. It was not a move of aggression, but one of compassion and mercy. "She makes you who you are, child. Do you know who she is?"

Marici did not shove Ajan away and instead let himself be drawn in by the Grand Priest. He stared back at the man, wanting to answers now, more receptive to inquiry. "My lord, I have no idea who she is, but I do know that she makes me what I am." He was determined, unwavering in this statement. "Whoever she is, I must be with her."

Ajan closed his eyes and positioned himself to let Marici fall into his arms if need be. Marici knew he had a sister, but did not know the woman with whom he had bonded on the birthing bed was she. If Ajan released Sri's identity, Marici would begin to see what this meant. "She is Sri, the Intended."

Marici's mocha face went yellow, and his eyes searched the forest for an escape. His gaze found no center except in Ajan's eyes, which held truth. Marici swallowed—his hands wanted to find his weapons for use on his own person—but Ajan held them down. Painful sounding response gasps vocalized themselves from his abdomen when Marici failed to find words. "Sri? My...baby *jahan* sister? The Intended?"

The real truth was even more complicated.

Ajan just nodded, and let Marici find the questions and conclusions on his own. He would have answers—but Marici needed to find the words.

Marici tried to pull away from Ajan and run into the storm that loomed around them. The thunder grew more ferocious and threatened the land with punishment. Ajan stood as a rock, holding the boy in place. He could not run from the truth. "She called me the *King*?"

Ajan nodded again, and let Marici work through his own thoughts. Ajan could not tell him, only respond to him.

"Impossible…" Marici responded. "I was born before Sri, I am older…"

Ajan dipped his head so that his cerulean gaze met Marici's eyes. "Yes, you are older. You were born first. And, I watched you being born, Marici…"

Marici knit his brows together in confusion. He ached. He had lived alone since his parents had died—it had taken him so long to find peace once he was left alone. In this moment, everything would change for him. "It's not true? You watched me born…I am…"

Ajan answered for the boy, realizing it would be merciful to do so. He whispered in the boy's ear, "You are her twin. And you have bonded on the bed where your mother gave you to Kasimi. You are…the King."

Marici's first response had nothing to do with him or how this would effect him. His eyes bulged and he asked, "Does she know who I am?"

"She knows who you are, my King. She does not know you are her twin." Ajan dropped his hands from the King and bowed slightly in deference to the boy. "We will go to her now."

Marici just nodded. He could not find the words.

~

Jabala moved Sri away, running with her through the trees, to a spot out of view of the men. Sri was too confused to question—and assumed that Ajan and Marici would follow behind. They arrived at another hole in the forest, where the leaves of papaya trees would shelter them from the storm.

When Sri did not see Marici or Ajan, she looked to Jabala and asked softly, "Where are they?"

Jabala looked at her little girl, and pressed down the water from her clothes taking time to let the silk mold itself into the curves that were becoming so obvious in the rain. "They will come along shortly, child. I need to tell you something so that you will understand what is going to happen when we leave your father's house." Jabala walked up to Sri, and placed the girl in her arms and found a place to whisper in the girl's ear.

Sri whispered, still in a magical trance, "I know him, Jabie. He is the King and I...love him. It is what I have been told to find all my life..."

Jabala would not give Sri time to question her words. She would be honest and direct, and then let the consequences and complications take their course. Jabala stroked the place where Sri's hair would be underneath her head covering. "My love, that is Marici. You were not told everything about your past, but we have known the truth all along, child."

Sri pressed her body into Jabala's, and tugged on her skirts to make this moment pass quickly.

Jabala looked off into the rain, and whispered the message to Sri, as gently as she could. She told her the truth. She told her about her twin. She told her how the boy had been deceived as well. She told her that not everything would make sense now, and how it would get more complicated that evening. She told her to be strong, and that she would never be alone. Sri could either run or stay, it was her choice.

Sri collapsed in Jabala's arms, and Jabala sank to the muddy ground with her Queen. The rain would not hurt them for long.

Ajan would come with Marici, and they would figure out what to do.

~

After the rain had subsided, Ajan, Jabala, The King and The Queen walked towards the group in the camp that had been arranged, south of Varuna II's house. Janaka spotted them off in the distance, and jumped up and down to attract their attention.

"*Acha!*" Janaka yelled, relieved to see that the group was safe. "Here, here, here!"

The group walked slowly, not wanting to rush the next moments in any way. Ajan and Jabala stood behind Marici, who held the collapsed body of his Queen and sister in his arms. They approached the camp with determined eyes. They had a message.

Janaka's weighted body ran up towards the quartet and he stopped short when he realized there was a new member to the troupe. He paused, and observed the expressions on Jabala's and Ajan's faces—and wondered why Ajan would let a stranger carry Sri—unless of course the Grand Priest was too exhausted to do it himself. Marici was dressed in servant's clothes, and Janaka addressed him as such. "Ajan, how much does the boy require for his services here?"

Ajan stared at his uncle. But, Jabala was the one to respond. "A lifetime, *Janaka-uncle.*" She smiled quietly at the Lord, and directed the group past Janaka to the center of the camp.

The sight of Sri collapsed and broken in Marici's arms drew the attention of the camp from inside the covered tents that had been set up. All at once, the servants, guards and priests hurried forward into the rain to see if the Queen was all right. There was not one person that did not look worried, not one person who did not go to Sri's side—even Vishal. There was a sea of questions around the quartet, *"What happened? Is she all right? Sri? Did she fall? Did the rain hurt her?"*—all spoken in chorus. Ajan let the group grow tired of its own questions before announcing the miracle that was before them.

Janaka herded around the four people creating space for some kind of announcement. The group quieted—*Is she dead?*—and moved in a circle around the people in the beating water. *It never rains in Videha in the spring.*

Ajan started the speech he had prepared for the glorious triumph of the third miracle. The powerful figure of the warrior stood still, with humility before the good people that had come with him on this journey. He would begin with ceremony, and end with the truth.

It is the Person in the sun whom I revere as Brahma...

Marici looked at Ajan with his sister stirring in his arms, and grew wary of the priest's tale. He brought the girl to him protectively. *Brahma is One.*

It is the Person in the moon whom I revere as Brahma...

The thunder boomed overhead loudly as a warning to the people to remember that *Brahma* is omnipotent.

It is the Person in air whom I revere as Brahma...

The water began to beat down harder on the people.

It is the Person in fire whom I revere as Brahma...

The other priests knew what was coming—these sacred words which Ajan had preached in debates and meetings—were meant for the Grand Priest to introduce the miracle. The words were highly controversial—for they would declare the third miracle to all of Kasimi. The priests began to look for each other in the circled crowd, for one another's responses to this proclamation.

It is the Person in the self whom I revere as Brahma...

Ajan stopped his prayer, and drew his sword into the air to declare the King. The water had turned cold and hard, beating down on the people in the rhythm for the next words. Sri had stirred to half consciousness, and Marici used his body to shelter his Queen from the anger of the sky.

"Our Queen has found the King, my people! I witnessed the exchange, the third miracle. Kasimi will delight in its god and goddess, and the are One. Hail, people, this boy who holds his Queen. Hail, my people, the son of Varuna II. Hail, my people, King Marici and Queen Sri!"

As the announcement was made, the servants and guards cheered loudly in the rain. First jumping up and down for joy and raising their voices to the rain despite the cold water that beat them. They then went into a kneel, waving their fists up in the air to yell, *"Marici, ya! Marici, ya! Marici, ya!"* There was no confusion, or question. The people of Kasimi had been expecting and praying for a King. When The King was announced by the Grand Priest, they cheered and prayed as they had been planning to for years. This was their day of glory as much as it was Marici's.

Three distinctly confused faces could be picked out of the crowd—the three priests—who knew who Marici was. They quickly pushed through the people around them to approach Ajan for an explanation. Seeing the questioning faces, Ajan directed his court to the inside of the main tent, leaving the worshippers to hug and kiss, and rejoice in the King.

The tent was as plain as Marici's clothes. A few wooden poles worked alongside sticks from any given tree to hold up some animal skins for shelter. The ground was bare and wet, since the camp arrived after the rain commenced. The water and wind introduced the scent of whatever dead animal had been sacrificed to keep the people dry. It was a bare place, much like the temple's meeting chamber—a place for frank and brutally honest words.

Once inside the tent, it was clear that Vishal would be the one to voice discontent. Sudha looked hopelessly lost for words and Devyn sat in the background, waiting to be informed of Sri's decision. Jabala cradled Marici who was holding Sri, keeping them mothered from politics as best she could. Marici however looked with wide eyes at the priests, watching each of their movements with intensity. He wanted to be aware of everything in what he was coming to understand as his kingdom.

Ajan began to speak without letting the others ask meaningless questions. His voice was calm, a whisper against the haunting chant of worship outside. "When I went to find Sri, she was inside her parents' room with Marici. They had no idea who the other was, and they recited the bonding poems to one another. I dropped to my knees—I could feel the bonding had been complete. I felt the presence of One. And then, this boy Our King, said his name, and I doubted as much as you do. I have told them—they know that they are brother and sister, now. Twins."

Ajan shifted in his position, and looked back at Jabala who was comforting the children with a maternal embrace. He was about to either lose his court for a King, or unite them. "It seems wrong, I know. But let them speak to you, and they will convince you. They are One. Our problem is that Sri is supposed to be the Intended Queen. Perhaps, my lords, the answer is that simple. The only one that could serve and entertain Our King would be the one created from the same seed. She will be his guide and comfort, his Queen. It does not say she must be in his bed."

Vishal's fury was growing inside him and he growled a response to Ajan. "I want Marici to speak. Make the boy convince me." He glared at the boy in Jabala's arms and then back at Ajan. "Make him speak."

Marici sneered at Vishal from his place in Jabala's arms. The fifteen year old boy was strong, despite his lanky frame. He had seen his parents murdered before his eyes with no mercy and he was not about to let this man do anything to hurt the woman he held in his arms. Marici walked forward with Sri, holding his sister protectively. "You do not make me speak, sir. Because I speak by my own free will. I am the son of Varuna II, and you will honor that fact even if you do not believe what has happened today."

Marici walked right up to Vishal and dared the man with each word he would bring forth. He created ancient scripture with his tongue.

The Lord of Creatures stirs within the womb:
Unseen he comes to birth in many forms and places:
With a half he brought the whole world forth:
With his other half, oh, what is the mark of that?

Like a woman bearing water in her pitcher
He bears the water up:
All see him with the eye; not all know him with the mind.

Vishal loomed over Marici and looked down on him. His eyes narrowed to slits, and his lips twisted into an evil grin. "You are a fool, Marici." He looked up over Marici's head to Ajan and shook his head twice. "Your King is a fool!"

Marici continued on, fighting Vishal back with words. He matched Vishal's smile with a carefully crafted one of his own and looked upon his beautiful sister with love. He knew this display of beauty—of Varuna's children—would hurt Vishal more than insults. His father had taught him well.

Whoso revered the eternal God who reigns on high
Becomes of use, an eater of much food.

Eternal, do they call him, and yet even now
Is he ever again renewed.
Day and night are each from the other born
Each in its different form.

Vishal's anger could no longer be restrained. He walked forward, pushing Marici and Sri toward Ajan with each stride.
Marici grinned at Vishal, holding his Queen to him with pride and
continued on:

In the house of mortal man there is a maiden
Fair, unengaging and immortal
He for whom she was made lies flat;
He who made her has grown old.

Thou art woman, thou art man,
Thou art the lad and the maiden too,
Thou art the old man tottering on his staff:
Once born thou comest to be, thy face turned every way!

He is their father, he is their son,
He their elder brother and their youngest:
The One God, entering the mind,
Is the first-born; he is in the womb.

From the full the full he raises up;
With the full is the full besprinkled.
Would that today we knew from whence
That full is sprinkled round out.

She, the entrant, was born in right olden times;
She, the primeval, all things encompassed:
The great goddess, lighting up the dawn,
Looks out from each single thing that blinks the eye.

Marici stood proud and strong in the middle of the bare tent. He was worthy as the son of Varuna II, and his confidence made him a solid rock to strike upon Vishal. There was nothing that the Priest from The Isles could say or do to harm him or the woman he loved. His black eyes, with a ring of red around the edges, glared back at the challenging priest and dared him—dared him to respond with anything but utter and complete loyalty. He was the great grandchild of a God and stood now, rightfully as King.

Ajan felt that Marici could only be The One. This strange, young boy who fought with such eloquent thoughts and speech, had moved him and enlightened him the way Sri had. Devyn and Sudha were already kneeling to the ground, chanting prayers to *Brahma* in thanks. Marici had made them aware that He was The King. There was something so powerful in his youthful presence, and more meaningful with Sri in his arms. He would be received in Kasimi.

Vishal pushed Marici towards Ajan, but not before grabbing Sri from the boy's arms in the moment Marici lost balance. Anger soared in his blood and he could not control it anymore. He would make his mind known without regard to the diplomacy that had been betrayed in his mind. Vishal's face spread into a mask of hate. His nostrils flared across his cheeks and his eyes lit with rage. He yelled loudly and viciously at the assembly and towards the sound of prayer outside the caravan. "*Nehi*! I will not have it!" Vishal screamed at the half conscious girl in his arms, "You whore! You bitch! You slut! You harlot queen!" He threw the girl towards Marici and Ajan with the rage that had made it to his arms. "Die!" he screamed in a violent shrill, as the girl moved through the air. He stood, breathless in his spot, and pointed an accusatory finger at the Grand Priest with one strong motion of his arm. "You, Ajan. You cunning, deceitful man. You, who use the position of religion to promote your own goals. You will pay. Why did you bring us here? *Acha*, Ajan? Why? I will tell you why!"

Sri had been half-caught by Marici and taken over to the corner with Jabala. This fight was between Ajan and Vishal—he could sense that. He would not impose his presence where it was not needed. He would only be in the way.

Ajan stood strong in his position, with a readied hand at his sword in case Vishal tried anything more. Ajan would not physically protest the abuse of his ward—it would be unwise with Vishal in this state. How he wished Vishal would pull his sword—it would be a valid reason to kill him. "It is the coming of the third miracle, Vishal..." whispered Ajan.

Vishal put his face up to Ajan's and spit on him from a pleghm-based point in his throat. In a low rumbling tone to match the thunder outside, he declared himself. "You orchestrated this. You brought us here because you wanted a Northern boy to be King. Now, all the power is for you. Everything is North! You clever, clever bastard." Vishal put his hands up, his rage turning to his mind in thought rather than physical gestures. "I am leaving here, and with my departure go The Isles. We will have nothing to do with your new child King. We will have nothing to do with Kasimi. When I leave, I take my land with me." Vishal backed out of the tent, his feet beginning to pick up pace to run.

Ajan let Vishal go. He did not protest or hesitate. It would only be a matter of time before Vishal's Isles seceded from Kasimi. Sudha stood up and thought about trying to calm the man down, but Devyn brought a hand to the man's shoulder. The Goanian whispered to him, "Not now. Let him go."

Vishal ran into the thundering storm, and grabbed the nearest horse to take into his possession. He kicked the stallion and yelled his commands, and was gone in a moment of weakness. It would not be the last time they would hear from him or his people.

Marici left Sri to the care of Jabala, and walked in between Ajan and the two other priests. He was both angry and calm, and his eyes glared at Vishal's exit from *Videha*. He watched and watched as his presence grew further and further from view. Marici decided that Vishal would be an enemy, regardless of apology. He would be punished and The King would show no mercy. He then looked out the people who chanted, *"Marici, ya! Marici, ya! Marici, ya!"* and smiled thinly. *I know exactly what I am.*

"Sri and I will be One. I will be your King and she will be my Queen. I don't know how we will do this, since she and I are from Varuna II on the same day. But, it must be." Marici stood tall in his servant's clothes, and put His Priests to rest on the issue of the validity of the third miracle. He was the son of Varuna II and brother to the Intended, worthy King of Kasimi.

6

Ajan decreed that the group would stay near *Videha* in *Mithila* at Janaka's palace, until they decided what to do regarding the difficult situation of Marici and Sri. He did not want to leave the site of the third miracle, but could not stay at the pillaged and destroyed house of Varuna II any longer. It was best to leave the place behind before it tormented them more. Despite the hard rain, Ajan demanded that the group ride back to the palace at once. With the united presence of King and Queen, Ajan was certain that the gods would protect his group in the storm. The people could hardly notice the rain as they chanted their prayers and thanks to *Brahma* above for bringing the King to Kasimi.

As Vishal declared war on Kasimi, the clouds overhead grew black and dark with danger, and the sound of thunder ceased. There was something even more disruptive about the piercing silence, that allowed every gallop of the enemy priest's horse to be heard through the forest. The sound of rush and panic went undisturbed by the gods, perhaps as a warning to Vishal. There would be no hiding from his own actions. They would be as plain and evident as his anger.

Soon, word of the King would spread throughout the lands along with his other identity as the son of Varuna II and twin of

Sri. The priests, now three instead of four, would need to decide what this meant to have a companion message to the people to temper expectations and rampant rumors. Ajan would invite the counsel of his uncle, a most honest and outspoken man, because he needed to hear as many opinions as possible before deciding the fate of Kasimi.

Ajan rode alone on his horse back to *Mithila*. He had given Sri to Marici, and the two held on to one another in the rain. After fifteen years of separation, the twins had found one another. They were identical images in the form of boy and girl—the two children of Varuna II. Why had the gods chosen to make it this way? What would become of Sri now that her role was undefined? Ajan's heart sank as he watched his collapsed ward being protected by another. *She will need me now more than ever.*

The storm was only over *Videha,* and as soon as the group went past the main roads, the sky brought sunshine and blue. It was a welcome relief, and plenty of bright smiles were exchanged. The sun was hailed as another part of the miracle—the gods brought tears of joy over the house of Varuna II—and welcomed the King with bright light into the rest of the Kingdom.

Marici sat tall on the black horse that had been lent to him by Janaka. Unlike his sister, he was immediately comforted by the constant chanting of his name and by the predetermined role of his destiny. He had grown from boy to man the night he watched the rebels kill his mother and father. He had been so weak, to sit and scream out as swords slashed flesh before him. He would never forget the cry of his mother as a powerful, dark man sliced her throat while cursing her womanhood. The bloody saber was then turned on him, but the assassin chose to let him live a life with these nightmare images rather than give him a merciful death.

Marici kept that memory in his mind's eye, as a reminder of the deed. When he found that man who had killed his parents, he would punish him. It would be merciful, in his mind. Make him do penance in this life, so that he would be spared in the next. And now, with his beautiful sister in his arms, Marici made a promise to her. He would never let anything hurt her—he would not have two women in his life killed due to what he believed was his own cowardice. He would look after Sri, and protect her. He now knew why he had been spared. It was not to live with images of death, but to be the son of Varuna II—and to love Sri.

The tired caravan returned to Janaka's palace late than night, and lazily began to unpack the horses and get settled back in their manor. Janaka spoke quietly with servants to prepare more appropriate long-term quarters for his guests. There was no telling how long they would be in *Mithila*, and the priests would need more clothes and other items. The old lord was pleased that the coming of the third miracle and all the spiritual glory that accompanied it would be in his palace.

Ajan bid everyone a goodnight. He watched his trusted group break for the evening. Sudha and Devyn, to whom he felt closer, were led towards the guest house next to Janaka's palace. A train of young, eager maids trailed behind Jabala and Sri as they were escorted back to their original rooms. More quiet man servants would show Ajan and Marici to their quarters, which would be opposite Janaka's apartment, in the main part of the palace. Guards would be posted everywhere.

Janaka put an arm around Ajan and asked, "Are you coming?" He was concerned about his nephew after all that happened today.

Ajan shook his head and replied. "I think I am going to take a walk along your garden."

Janaka would protest, but realized that it was futile. Ajan would probably need time alone tonight. The old lord nodded and bid his goodnight.

Ajan stared at the train of women going up to the ladies' quarters and hoped—prayed—that Jabala would see his message.

~

An hour had passed since Sri was asleep in her bed. Things had quieted down in the ladies chambers, as all the hand maids retired one by one. As much as they wanted to stare at the Queen, they needed to rest or else they would miss out on the next day in her service. Jabala waited patiently by Sri's bed until she heard the girl's breathing come to a steady rhythm in sleep, and her nervous tossing and turning had stopped.

Jabala walked to the mirror, and took a few moments to fix her appearance. She was in her night dress—a soft, white gown of silk that worked to hide her curves on the outside and free them from within. Her dark brown hair was pulled into a braid, by one of the hand maids, to be kept out of the way for the night. That would not do. Jabala spent a few moments unfastening her hair so that it fell long and loose, against her dress. She grabbed a blanket from beside Sri's bed—a grey one—and put it over her to ward off the night air. She would be gone for a while, but not long enough for anyone to notice, hopefully.

The unusual, but discrete sight of a gentle woman making her way down the candlelit spiraling staircase was ignored by the guards who stood on duty that night. Jabala moved with an easy grace and goal in her eyes which was not questioned. She was not noble, nor was she important—she was a servant. If she wanted to roam, she would do so, without protection or inquiry.

Jabala floated out of the palace, and went to that certain patch of trees where Ajan had been standing just over an hour ago. When she had eliminated herself from public view, Jabala searched the area but did not see any figure of a man. She went further into the gardens, looking for the person who had called for her in the darkness. But, there was no one. Her breath was visible in the Kasimian night air, and was growing quicker while she searched from tree to tree.

"Lover?" she called out, in a whisper. "Where are you, old friend?"

Jabala had wandered quite a distance from the main palace gardens. She was beginning to shiver, and pulled the grey blanket around her body for more warmth. Just a few more paces, and then she would return to her room to sleep. She would have enjoyed seeing Ajan in private tonight.

A male figure crept in the darkness toward the sight of a feminine body. Jabala's ears picked up the sound and she whispered, "Ajan?" to see if this was her priest. No answer. "Ajan?" she called out again. The man continued forward towards her, without responding. Jabala asked, in a more alert tone, "Who goes there?" No answer.

The male figure, still cloaked in darkness, pressed Jabala's body against the tree where she stood. Before she could scream out in pain, the man put a strong hand over her mouth to stop the sound. With the other hand still in place, he put his free hand inside Jabala's white night dress to feel the gentle curve of her stomach and swell of her bosom. He pressed his lips to her neck, and bit slowly along the edges that decided her shoulders.

Jabala bit the man's hand playfully, and brought her own hands to feel the dark male form around her. She traced along the familiar body that had been away from her for so long. She had intended to counsel Ajan tonight—but gave in to her own carnal needs. "Oh, darling..." Jabala moaned, and begin to claw hungrily at the priest's clothes.

Ajan pressed with urgency against Jabala's body, digging her into the tree. His kisses grew demanding along her neck, and his hands began to resent the white gown that kept her skin from his lips. His arm tensed as if he were going to tear the silk, but Jabala stopped him just in time. "No, Ajan...they will know."

Ajan began rocking his hips into Jabala's body and commanded in her ear. "Take it off."

Without effort, the blanket dropped to a space between the woman's skin and the tree. Jabala struggled to pull the gown over her body with Ajan's own form unrelenting in its position against her. The subtle twitch of her hips and arms to wriggle the dress of made the priest even hungrier as his hands moved to help the silk off and to the ground. With more flesh exposed, Ajan's desire unleashed further.

The Grand Priest's hands and lips were everywhere at once. His tongue traced the woman's sweet skin to the space between her bosom. His hands went to cup both breasts, and squeeze suggestively around the nipples. His hips began to work a rhythm against Jabala. It would not be long before she would be tempted to join him.

Jabala closed her eyes and enjoyed the overwhelming pleasure of being taken in the dark, in a strange and beautiful place. She had missed Ajan's touch and his hunger—his pleading—was matched with her own. To complement his rushed, hurried pace, Jabala relaxed her hands on Ajan's back and stroked him tenderly. She slowed her breathing to a lulling calm, and let her kisses become slow and affectionate. "Take me, Ajan..." she whispered.

Ajan kissed Jabala deeply, and probingly as she gave him permission to enter her. He pressed himself into her, and closed his eyes in relief as he slipped further inside his dear, old friend. His eyes clenched shut, and his mouth opened into a low groan. "Oh, Jabie..." he murmured.

Jabie whimpered as Ajan entered her. She had missed him—his touch—the closeness. Her legs wrapped around the priest, and she began to partake in a desperate rhythm with the man while the blanket comforted her back against the tree. Jabala's strong thighs embraced Ajan as he took her, reminding him that she was there. "Aj...ahn." Jabala leaned her head on the man's shoulder and let her body be ruled.

Ajan was sweating from how vigorously he was working on Jabala's form. He was somewhere else—he was not making love to Jabala, but taking her—and satisfying something he felt inside. Or was lacking inside. His thrusts quickly became too powerful to sustain, and he reached his point of pleasure while letting out an emotional cry. "Oh, Jabala. Jabala." he whispered, while his body recovered from the shock.

Jabala rested between Ajan and the tree, and held her dear friend to her. She realized that he had used her. He had no intention of making love to her, but he needed to take her. Jabala knew this before she came to the garden, and was happy to comfort her friend. "Shhh, lover..." Jabala whispered to Ajan. "Let me hold you, Ajan."

Ajan began to sob, and gripped Jabala to him. "Oh Jabie," he managed, in between cries. He pressed the woman against the tree, and held her there while he let water escape from his eyes into Jabala's hair. "I'm lost..." he said. "I'm lost..."

Jabala stroked Ajan's hair, and whispered into his ear. She spoke sweet words, and kissed his neck and lips from time to time. It was all she could do for him now.

7

At dawn, the men would journey to the river just south of
Janaka's palace to discuss the future of Kasimi. Meeting in the
palace was risky—Janaka's servants were far too educated and
might be able to pick up on the intimate details of the unfolding
drama. Janaka decided to disguise the meeting as a fishing trip
and only bring one or two illiterate servants, and a mute guard for
protection. He would also bring his tabla players—to seduce the
fish from the water. That's what he said.

The day was perfect for fishing, and Janaka looked forward
to the retreat near the water. That's what he kept saying over
and over again, as the horses were being packed with covered
items resembling glass bottles. He had the men dress casually, in
cotton white pajama pants and tunics with no jewelry. "The
fish might take that as a sign of disrespect..." Janaka would say.
The old lord also insisted that the men take the white horses to
the river to match their clothing. When a few of his guests
snickered at this choice, Janaka would retort with, "I have a
reputation to maintain!"

At the sun's first appearance, the men rode their white horses
through the garden and onward into the open land and newly lit
sky. They rode slowly, and not together—each taking his own

space for the easy ride to the river. Why bother with conversation when they would spend a whole day together? The men would indulge in the comfort of their own thoughts for a few hours.

Ajan lingered purposefully behind Marici during the ride, to observe the new King. How much he reminded Ajan of Sri. The gods had created such a divine image in the boy. Servants had spent time grooming him this morning, and he looked like a true nobleman. His black hair had grown long during the years alone, and the mass of curls was tied back into a tail. His appearance was more robust that Sri's—more definition to his features and a sense of hardship in his expressive eyes. A richer tone of brown coated Marici's skin as he made no effort to hide from the sun. Why bother? His beauty was not in his face, but in his being.

"How are you, Ajan?" Marici asked, picking words from nowhere. Ajan's horse was quite a few paces behind and Marici did not look to see who was following him. The boy somehow knew that the Grand Priest would watch him.

Ajan kicked his horse to catch up with Marici. "How did you know I was behind you?"

Marici laughed for a few moments, leaning his head and hair back in a grand gesture. He turned his neck to look at the Grand Priest and put the situation back on Ajan. "If you were me, who would you suspect of shadowing you?" He cocked his head to one side and grinned with youthful pride. "I guessed. More importantly, I was right."

Ajan smiled faintly and molded his horse's rhythm to match Marici's stride. He looked out onto the open green field for a few seconds, and then snapped his attention back to the boy. The inquiry, although serious, was put to Marici in a light tone. "It's simple to ask, Marici—but what is going on in your mind about what's happened here?" Ajan returned his gaze to the comfort of the open plain.

Marici leaned his head up and exhaled the Kasimian air with delight. He welcomed the inquiry, and seemed to have an answer prepared for it. He shook his head, and closed his eyes to receive a gentle spring breeze that played along his hair and skin. "I was waiting for something to happen, Ajan." Marici opened his eyes and took another deep breath to appreciate the air that he now ruled. "I knew my whole life that I'd be the true great grandchild of Varuna..." Marici's eyes dimmed as he looked over at Ajan. "If I'd known she were my twin, I would have come for her before she came for me..."

Ajan's eyebrows arched upward in surprise at the boy's confidence. Marici was certainly aware of who he was, and accepting of his position. It would make his training easier. One part of Marici's answer confused Ajan, however. "Why did you not seek Sri after your parents died?"

Marici let a newly jeweled hand smooth his raven hair in place, similar to the way Sri would. "What would be the point, eh Ajan? I'd lose her to the King, eventually." The boy's ears honed in on the tabla player's beat who was only a few paces ahead. His head began to move in rhythm to the drum, adding conviction to his next words. "I did not /know/ what it meant to be the son to Varuna II until I saw Sri in our mother's bed. She makes me what I am, Ajan. I won't lose her..."

Ajan intentionally blocked out the sound of the tabla, and watched Marici's movements without music clouding his thoughts. *I won't lose her, either. I am glad you love her because anything less would be most unacceptable to me. I say that especially to the man who is to be her King.*

Marici lost his casual smile and swept his black eyes to Ajan's sword. He then traced the length of the weapon up to Ajan's eyes before letting a grin return to his lips. "Then we should think of something today, eh?" Marici caved in on himself, and then burst out his torso. "*Acha*!" he yelled to his horse. Galloping forth with power and strength, Marici found his place next to the tabla player.

Ajan could not make up his mind about Marici. On one hand, he was pleased with the boy's confidence in his identity and worthiness. On the other hand, he was frightened that such pride at young age would lead to foolishness.

As a young warrior, Ajan had been much the same way. He was worshipped by his people—*his people*—as he began to call them—because of his success and his family name. He let the hero worship get the best of his spirit, and felt more powerful because of it. In truth, he was just an individual—without the support of his neighbors, he was nothing. What Ajan hoped that was Marici, after being alone in the world for so long, would realize the difference between confidence and foolish pride. It was a distinction that Ajan wished he had made before massacring entire peoples— a distinction that would have let him sleep without nightmares.

One thing that would save Marici from himself was his seemingly genuine love for Sri. A Queen so pure and yet so strong, was the most precious gift the gods had given the King. She had been raised in a way that allowed her to be the Queen that Kasimi would want, without attaching predestined glory derived from the name of Varuna. It would be a proper match—Marici's pride to Sri's innocence—and they would rule Kasimi in peace.

Marici had a jovial spirit. He was playing with the young boy tabla player, making his horse dance around in no particular way. The King would suggest new beats and rhythms through precise motions of his hands and neck—sometimes invading the boy's drum with his own jeweled fingers.

Ajan used the rest of the journey to pray to *Brahma* up above for wisdom, and for the future of Marici and Sri. He trailed behind, letting his horse's pace grow slower and slower. He was getting older, and felt the effects of middle-age, especially today.

The river arrived after a few moments, and Janaka began to set the tabla players in place for fishing. The covered bottles then surfaced from the many horses' sacks—and were actually large bottles of wine instead of water. Janaka's fishing trips were relaxation festivals of herbal smoking rolls and drinking. It was a way to give his male friends a day away from their disapproving wives, female servants and mothers. Why the river? Just beyond this spot was a house known for its loose women. They were discrete and magnificent—and at least the old lord would have somewhere to go and something to do in case the meeting got boring.

The wine and smoking rolls were lavishly arranged, along with some wool blankets for napping and sitting. Everything was a blinding shade of white from the men's clothes, to the clay cups to the wool blankets. Janaka enjoyed the irony of it all.

Ajan laughed at his uncle's show. "You never change, Janaka-uncle! All those years, I thought you and papa were actually fishing. And all you were doing was drinking?"

Janaka lit up a smoking roll and his fleshy body shuddered as the herbs swirled around his nose. Ajan didn't know everything yet about what his old man did. He grinned, letting the special blend of weeds cloud his face in a exhale. "Mmm, hmm Ajan. All we did was drink." Janaka rolled his eyes while the smoke pleasantly invaded him. "Drink...*acha*..."

Devyn looked at the luxurious spread of drink, weed and tabla. He took a glass of wine and asked half-jokingly, "The drums make it sound like a mating call."

Janaka's full lips grinned around the smoking roll. He nodded his thick neck both to the rhythm of the tabla and in Devyn's direction. "*Acha*!" he responded both in approval of the smoking and to Devyn's comment.

Sudha finally arrived. He was out of breath and sweating so much that his white clothes had become translucent. The short, round priest plopped off his horse and pointed both hands behind him. "There..." he put his hands on his knees and breathed heavily for a few moments before returning to his tale. "Over there!...were...masses of...screaming...women...chasing me!...didn't see...why...*acha*...chasing me..." Sudha was still huffing and puffing and kept pointing as if there were something really scary right behind him. "Women chasing me!"

All the men laughed heartily—Janaka loudest of all. The servants and tabla players waggled their hands in delight. Janaka walked up to Sudha and put an arm over the priest's equally fleshy shoulders. "Tell Madam Shopa and her girls hello from Janaka-uncle next time. They're all good friends of mine..." he then added as an afterthought, "They must be fond of you! I can't get them to chase me without lots of gold falling behind!"

Sudha grinned weakly and went to get a cup of wine. He giggled nervously—a high, squeaky sort of laugh.

Ajan waited until Marici had retrieved some refreshment before opening the discussion. The boy did not touch the wine or smoking rolls, a sign of either discipline or undeveloped tastes. Since the boy did not bother to examine the other items, and dismissed them so intently, it was most likely discipline. He chose some mango pressed juice instead. Ajan was watching him—he knew—and so he gave the Grand Priest a nod of confirmation.

Ajan sat in the middle of the troupe without refreshment. Janaka paused him with two waving hands and wide eyes of caution. He beckoned his servants to him and whispered in their ears while slipping a generous portion of gold into their hands. They'd be gone a good, long while with that amount of wealth on hand. Ajan began again, and had to stifle a laugh and regain composure.

"I really don't have anything planned my lords...we have a strange and enigmatic situation on hand. And a solution to find. Does anyone have any thoughts?" Ajan lowered his knees to sit meditation style in an unconscious gesture.

Sudha, as usual, was the first one to speak the obvious at this meeting. His squat legs were in a *V* in front of him, and his hands supported the weight of his growing belly. "So, we are baffled because sister and brother cannot marry? And Sri is an intended wife?"

Both Ajan and Marici shook their heads at Sudha's lack of grace. They wouldn't even dignify the priest with a response. Janaka did the honor—he laughed out loud, his back buckling forward in a physical gesture of amusement. The laugh gave in to a cough, over the smoking roll, which quieted the old lord.

Marici raised his hand up symbolically, volunteering his words. He had not intended to speak so soon—but with the thought of Sudha speaking more, he had to end this. "Ajan, I have something. In fact, I know what I want."

Ajan widened his eyes and spread his hands out in front of him. "Please, Marici. By all means..." The Grand Priest sat back on his hands, relieved that at least one of them had an idea.

Marici drained his mango pressed juice and then turned the cup upside down on the grass. He brought his eyes up and began to dictate his wishes in a tone that implied fact, and did not ask for commentary. "I want Sri to belong to me, symbolically—in every way. No one else will be able to protect her the way I can. She found me, and declared who I am. I want to make her my Queen. She's the only one worthy enough as the child of Varuna II, and my twin. It's so clear."

Janaka added the crude element to the meeting. The strong fumes of his herbal roll penetrated the air, and the old lord showed the signs of deep relaxation. "Are you going to bed your own sister, boy? Be serious. I've known people who have done that to keep money in a family. It's downright foul!"

Marici snickered and shook his head at Janaka. He examined the large diamond on his right-hand middle finger, and responded without bringing his eyes up. "I don't plan on bedding my sister, old man. In fact, I believe her too pure to be in the bed of any man, ever. But we'll get to that, eh?"

Sudha chimed in his need for clarification. "So what will Sri be to you? I'm not following here..." This was probably one of the few times that Ajan appreciated the Southern Priest's inquiry. They were all confused.

Marici stroked the diamond on his finger, polishing it so it would reflect the light better. He cocked his head to one side and mused, "Hmm..." He waved his hand up and continued. "All right, I'll define Sri to you. She will be every relationship that a woman can be to a King. She is my mother, because she named me and created me King. She is my sister and twin—both from Varuna II. She will also be my wife and Queen. It will be a symbol to my people—she and I, united in every way..."

Janaka spoke right up, "But she will not be the mother of your children?"

Marici glared at Janaka's outburst. "No. Wrong...she won't give birth to my children. Sri will be chaste and pure. But, she will help me raise my heir."

"So you will take concubines?" Ajan asked, quickly before Janaka could call out again.

Marici's eyes widened with impatience at the manner in which he was being questioned. "I must provide Kasimi with an heir, eh?

Yes, I'll keep a warm bed. I'm already impure, my lords. It is no use trying to make me something I'm not."

Janaka seemed satisfied. "As long as you don't bed your sister, your plan's as good as any, my King. Besides, think of how delicious it will be to pick mistresses..."

Marici laughed politely at Janaka's joke and then looked at Ajan for his answer, or judgment. It was clear that Marici did not want or intend to receive permission from Ajan. The Grand Priest knew this was a test of his loyalty, since he had a good twenty years of experience on the boy. He murmured in an noncommittal tone, "I will start preparing you both for the ceremony..." and left his opinions for a more appropriate time.

A voice that did not usually speak up, did. The cultured accent of Devyn came calmly from his place, set off from the group, near the water. "Do you think it is fair to talk about Sri when she's not here?" This was more than a question. It was the signal of discontent over the entire subject. The red haired priest raised his eyebrows and awaited a response from the group.

Marici answered as diplomatically as a rash teenager could. "I appreciate your concern for my sister. But...she has little to do with this. A King defines his Queen." The boy kept his black eyes locked on Devyn.

Devyn shook his head, unsatisfied with the response. "*Nehi*, no. I'm not being precise..." When Devyn did speak, it was meaningful. He never wasted time or words that he had not thought about carefully. He was never aggressive or rude, but direct. He never raised his voice, no matter how insulting the adversary became. "Sri was born into her role, and with circumstances changed, we are molding her existence to fit certain rules. It seems like we are making her suffer the consequences of something we do not entirely understand."

Ajan turned around, shifting his torso abruptly, to better see Devyn. Where had these words come from? A priest with few opinions and neutral standing had managed to say in one verse exactly what Ajan had felt in his heart. Ajan would have to speak to Devyn later, to thank him for his courage.

Marici looked at the Goanian with contempt. The boy already held Devyn as a lesser individual because of his bloodline. His position was due to the grace of Varuna's friend. His eyes narrowed to slits and then released into their full ovals. "It is the burden of her birth." Marici raised one eyebrow to his forehead to silently inquire on Devyn's satisfaction with the response.

He was not satisfied. Devyn finished a slow, lingering sip of wine, and let his tongue lick the remnants of red brine that stuck on the skin of his lips. He started again. "Why deny Sri the joy of love, Marici? If this is really a symbolic marriage, why must she keep a cold bed?"

"Cold bed! She will be warmed by my undying love for her as a King, brother, father and husband. Are you going to insult Sri— saying that for the only way for her to be happy is to accept some man between her legs? Eh?" Marici was about to lose his temper. His voice was simultaneously rising in volume and pitch, and his limbs were poised to spring up from the sitting position.

"No, my King. I'm not saying anything about Sri." Devyn drew his hand from his heart and appealed to the boy on a more personal level. He softened his tone, and dropped his head in deference to the boy. "I have five sisters, Mari—"

"I am painfully aware how many offspring your mother birthed, Devyn..." Marici interjected with a biting tone.

Devyn exhaled and began again. "I have five sisters, Marici. I would not deny them any happiness, if they wished it."

Marici was fully barking at Devyn by this time. If he had been able to speak directly after Devyn, he would have acted with the rashness of youth. Ajan—because he agreed with Devyn—stopped the fight.

"I think our main concern is Sri, for all of us. Marici you have given your wish and Devyn has just stated concerns. Let's remember that we are all focused on Sri—Sri—is our main purpose. Our Queen." Ajan leaned forward on his stomach to grab some more wine. He had a pounding headache and hoped that an excess of wine would help. How he hoped it would.

Marici went for the wine as well. He really had nothing left to say, and hoped that Devyn would be quiet. His decision was final. Who was this half Kasimian to question the King?

Devyn eyed Ajan and picked up on his cues. The Goanian was genuinely sad for Sri. He respected Ajan, which is why he backed down. But, he did not like the way Marici had rationalized his own desires in the name of his love of Sri. Some may overlook the fact that Devyn had been named Goane's spiritual advisor at the young age of eighteen, and had been the only one of the four (besides Ajan) who had watched Sri grow. He did not have a lot to do with her upbringing—but he was bound to the girl through time. Sri was also as old as one of his sisters. That alone made Devyn look upon her with tenderness.

Janaka broke the gross silence that was ruining his high. In a slurred tongue, he asked, "Anyone wanna come with me to fetch the servants?" His impish grin suggested that he had other things in mind besides fetching wayward servants. Janaka turned to Sudha and inquired in a squeaky tone, "Come with me, please? They'll let me in for free if you come…"

Sudha might have accepted the invitation if Ajan and the King were not present. Instead, he chuckled under his breath and shook his head violently in the negative—as if to convince himself that he really didn't want to go.

Janaka shrugged and decided that persuading his guests to indulge in the very essence of manhood inside womanhood was not possible while Ajan was playing the part of celibate priest. The short, squat man in white stood up and waddled down the river towards—most likely—the house of loose women. He yelled back over his shoulder, "Knowing me—I won't be too long!"

The group welcomed the chance to laugh at the old lord. They used it as a way to forgive each other for the tension that existed during the meeting. In Janaka, they were all together again—bonded through a masculine round of mockery.

Words at this point would be dangerous. There was a comfortable silence among them that did not need to be broken. The white clad men chose to appreciate the beauty of Kasimi's winding river instead. The water was cobalt blue with the sun directly overhead, which was the historical source of the Northern Kingdom's color. The river was both calming through its lulling whisper and dangerous in exploration. Rumored to flow from the North to the South of Kasimi, the river had trapped many an explorer who attempted to discover that truth.

When it seemed that Janaka would take a longer time than expected, the men split up to do their own exploring. Sudha was fast asleep with a cup of wine on top of his belly. A long day of drinking and thinking for the Southerner would do that. Marici was content to do some reading with his bare feet dangling in the river.

Devyn began walking south, appreciating the calming sound of water running its course. He walked with no set pace, and his hands folded gently behind him. His hair was getting more towards blond with the sun hitting it at certain angles. Ajan took the chance to catch up with the Goanian while keeping a protective eye on Marici.

Ajan cleared his throat as his position approached Devyn's place by the water. He subconsciously mimicked the Goanian's posture and stance—loose strides, hands folded behind his back.

Devyn smiled and nodded—not saying anything—but welcoming Ajan to come along if he wanted to. He didn't stop, or slow down. Just continued to stare at the cobalt water and the curious distance it held.

Ajan kept pace with Devyn for a while, with silence between them. Devyn did not know that the Grand Priest had approved of what he had done. That alone made the walk awkward. After a moment, Ajan whispered, "Thank you…"

Devyn kept walking forward with his eyes on the water. "For?"

Ajan didn't know how to respond. He shrugged and brought his arms in front of him to gesture. "I'm not sure, Devyn. But, thank you. Someone had to say something."

Devyn lifted his head and turned in Ajan's direction. His feet remained firmly planted in his place by the water. "Why didn't you, Ajan? Your words carry more weight that mine…"

Ajan picked at his own spot with his feet, tracing a semi-circle in front of him. He made eye contact this time. "I didn't think it was the right place for objections. Opposing my King…what good with that do? His choice is law."

Devyn shook his head from left to right in wide swings of disbelief. He chose to bring his eyes back to the water. "I didn't think you to be so cunning, Ajan. Of course—what I said had no real effect except to be said and heard. Do you only say things when they get you what you want, Ajan?"

Ajan walked up to Devyn's place but still allowed him a comfortable personal space. There was a certain pleading in his voice. "No, Devyn…That's not it at all. But why bother saying something when it will only prevent you from acting in the end?"

Devyn sat down, and dangled his feet in the water. He was so calm and so clear in his thoughts. Ajan envied this kind of natural control. He didn't need to be liked or respected. He had his own code and held himself to a higher standard. Devyn ran a bare hand through his greying red hair and looked from his space by the river at Ajan. "I don't live that way, Ajan. I can't. If there is something that I think and feel to be unfair or wrong, I say so."

Ajan squatted on his knees by Devyn. He wanted the Goanian to see where he was coming from. "Aren't actions more important in the end, Devyn? Why weaken that position?"

Devyn stretched his legs and feet to their most extreme points and took in the fresh Kasimian air through a deep inhale. "You said we can't act anyway—against our King. He's the law? Our only option is then to speak. Even if nothing comes of it. Someone needed to speak up for Sri..."

Devyn had the last word.

Ajan was shocked by the honesty of the statement. *Someone did need to speak up for Sri.* He used the strength of his legs to grow to standing position again. He rubbed his wrists into his eyes, and began walking carelessly back towards the camp. *Why didn't I speak up for her?*

He fussed with his tunic as he walked back to camp. His clothes just didn't seem straight enough, or precise enough. *Why didn't I speak up for her?* He paused and stared at his distorted reflection in the quickly moving water. The unfocused stare conjured up the image of Sri's birth night in his mind's eye. Marici had come out so quickly, bringing much blood and pain to the mother. But Sri—so sweet—had come out gently, as if concerned for her mother's body. And then, Sri was put into his arms and his life had started. *Why did I not speak for her?*

The Grand Priest was rallied from his self indulgent dreaming by the sound of his uncle's loud, commanding voice. "Let's go!

Acha! I'm hungry!" Ajan warily dragged his body towards camp. *Why did I not...*

"*Acha*, Ajan?" Janaka asked, putting a hand on his nephew's back with concern. Janaka had spotted the lost looking man only a few paces from the horses, and went to retrieve the boy. "*Acha?*"

Ajan just smiled at his uncle and put away the thoughts of Sri for now. "Let's go, Janaka-uncle. I'm hungry, too..."

Janaka laughed with his whole body, and his back moved to and fro with amusement. "You didn't even give yourself a chance to be hungry, Ajan!" The old man bobbled his head, with bright eyes. He encouraged his nephew with a push and an affectionate slap on the bottom.

Ajan forced a breathy laugh through his weighted thoughts. "To *Mithila*, uncle..."

8

Marici requested to have dinner alone with Sri that evening. He left instructions with the hand maids to have Sri waiting at the rise of the moon, in formal Northern Kasimian dress. No detail was to be spared in her appearance. If Sri asked questions, the hand maids were to tell her that her King simply wished to dine with her and appreciate the more perfect child of Varuna II.

This was very exciting news for the hand maids who hurried up to Sri's chambers with quick feet and high giggles. They all began speaking in broken Kasimian or *ruda*, much to the confusion of the Queen who just sat at her place by the window with her mouth agape and eyes squinting in confusion. One of the sturdier maids managed to raise her voice above all the others and screech out a "Dinner alone with King!" which gave Sri an idea as to what the attention was for.

Jabala stood from her seat to enjoy the immediate power of being a full head taller than the gang of Janaka's pretty hand maids. To quiet down the increasing volume and pitch of the women, Jabala directed a stern and unwavering glare at the group and placed her hands on her hips in the posture an angry mother would take with her daughters. That worked wonders on quieting down the immature servants. Jabala then, in one efficient gesture, pointed the women towards the door and commanded them to leave. The defeated servants protested slightly with whines and brief complaints under their breath, but Jabala was determined to keep Sri in peace.

Sri laughed at Jabala's exaggeratedly commanding presence. "Maybe you should be Queen, Jabie." She rolled her eyes and shifted her position so that her feet were flat on the ground. "So, what am I being summoned for? I kind of understood dinner with Marici, but I didn't get the rest."

Jabala sat beside Sri, and put a protective arm around the Queen. Her eyes looked to the door to make sure the gossipy hand maids were out of sight and mind. "Yes, too many messengers...Marici wants to dine alone with you tonight. You're to be in the formal dress of the Northern Kingdom." The message delivered, Jabala stroked Sri's hair with tenderness. "Now, what do you want to wear?"

Sri smirked at Jabala, and voiced her bitterness at not being able to go on the fishing trip this morning. "Marici didn't say whether I had to dress in man's or woman's attire, did he? If not, I'd like to wear a cobalt pajama suit with jeweled toes. Hmm?"

Poor Jabala would have to deal with her attitude this evening. Sri was just ready to pick a fight.

Jabala would have none of it. She knew the gravity of Marici's request and would not stand for Sri to be anything but completely cooperative. Jabala flashed a grim look at Sri, and held her lips in a thin line. "Hmm, Sri? I think you will wear a silk, cobalt salwar-kameez, with appropriate jewelry. I haven't thought about your hair yet...I'll get to that as we dress you..."

Sri might challenge Jabala on another day. But there was no humor in her nurse, and her bratting would get her nowhere but into trouble. In a conciliatory fashion, Sri murmured lightly,

"Why not the sari? It is more elegant and fitting for the evening, no?" Sri smiled quickly, to show she was done with her tricks.

Jabala nodded once. "You're right. The cobalt sari will be more appropriate. Would you like the plain pattern or the one with gold birds woven into the silk?" She gestured to herself with a hand. "I think the more ornate one is best for this evening, Sri. Yes?"

Sri nodded and shrugged her shoulders. She didn't care what she wore. Her appearance was the farthest thing from her mind. "Prepare me in whatever gown and style you need to prepare me in, Jabie. I don't want to think about it…" Sri stood up and walked over to the heavy dark wooded trunk that held her silks and jewelry.

Jabala smiled to herself. Rarely did she get this kind of permission to create Sri into the beautiful woman that she had grown into. This would be an extreme pleasure. "We'll start with your dress, and then on to your jewelry. Then, I will know how to paint your face and arrange your hair, my Queen…" The dinner was very important—Jabala knew.

~

Marici paced about the long cherrywood table in Janaka's dining room. The moon had risen an hour ago, and the Queen was not ready yet. The table was long enough to seat ten on either side, but only two places were set: one at the master's position, and the one to its right, both overlooking the roaring flames in the black marble fireplace. Sri would sit at the head of the table. Marici had already decided.

With long strides, Marici was able to climb the length of the table in five paces and pivot and turn around again in another five. *She will learn to be on time.* His hands turned to fists on reaching the ends of the table, and Marici used its length to release his hands before balling them back up again. Occasionally, he would fuss at his cobalt tunic or pick at his loose hair in frustration. He growled under his breath. His mother had never been late for his father.

The room was quite simple, and had been decorated by Janaka's first wife. The fine, cherrywood table was functional and long without ornate carvings or inlaid marble. Twenty-two simple, matching chairs fit perfectly into the table with tiny red cushions in the seats. The only thing that distinguished the master's chair from the others was a set of arm rests—it did not sit higher or grander than the others. A few, small tables rested around the room to place food and dishes. Candles in silver holders and a black marble fireplace would light the room, the only wealth.

Janaka's wife Uma was a very humble woman born to a common family. She did not want to surround herself with unnecessary comfort. The room would be filled with the laughter of her friends feasting on meals she would prepare with her own hands, and that is what would define its character. Janaka took his bride when he was forty, and she was eighteen. She died just six months later, taking a child who was almost to full term with her, to her tomb. Janaka did not entertain himself in this room, ever again. And, he commanded that it would never be changed.

Marici had paused in front of the fire when Sri arrived. She stopped by the doorway, allowing her fingers to trace the frame behind her before completely entering the room. Sri then lowered herself into a formal bow, which she had practiced especially for the constraint of her sari. "My King..." she murmured, and awaited permission from Marici to rise.

Marici walked slowly to Sri, each step draining the frustration he had felt on her tardiness, and hovered over his sister. Gently, he said, "You never have to lower yourself to me again, Sri. We're the same." He offered a hand to Sri to help her rise. "It breaks my heart when you bow to me, sister." Marici looked with tender eyes on his sister. "Please?"

Sri accepted the hand in hers, and rose to regard Marici. "If it is your will, Marici," Sri said. There was still a formal feel between the two. Familiarity would take time, and their roles and relation were the only bond they had right now. In time, Sri would drop the polite speech and formal tone, and come to regard her King as family. "...brother..." she added.

Marici looked over his sister's form. She was a child of Varuna II, both glorious and beautiful. Her appearance was much like the room: simple. She did not need finer silks nor heavy jewels. She wore the plain cobalt sari, after all, with no gold or silver threads. It was just a lush line of blue silk that swept in the traditional folds of the Northern Kingdom across her developing body. A tighter than normal blouse of white raw silk was fitted on Sri's arms and breasts—Jabala knew she was ready to start displaying proof of her femininity.

There were no sapphires or emeralds in the Kingdom fit enough for this Queen tonight. A set of combs, decorated with perfect white diamonds, drew back Sri's thick hair on either side of her face before letting it drop in heavy waves over her body.

Marici leaned in and kissed his sister on her cheek. "You look stunning, sister..."

Did she look stunning? She would not know. She had intentionally not looked in the mirror from the time Jabala had wrapped her body until the last bit of coloring had been placed on her lips. She didn't want to know what she looked like. It would only distract her from the insecurities and doubts that helped her create her own thoughts.

Marici walked with Sri's hand held in his towards the dining table. On reaching the side chair, Sri was about to take a seat but her brother directed her to the master's place.

"No, sister. You're the head tonight…" He then pulled out the chair for the Queen, and waited for her to place herself.

Odd. Sri moved hesitantly to the directed spot at the head of the table. Silently, gracefully, she let Marici pull in her chair and perform etiquette as a gentleman would.

While Marici seated Sri, a servant had quietly entered from the shadows and placed the meal on the table, and poured the wine. He had been instructed beforehand to do this, and then to leave. He would then be dismissed for the evening. The wafting smell of hot lamb with cinnamon and pepper spices, alongside lemon and onions quickly crowded dominated the air. Spiced lamb was Sri's favorite meat combination. Her sense of hunger became aroused as she eyed the plentiful amount of food on the table.

Marici raised his glass of rose wine to the sky, "To our union, eh Sri?" He nodded in her direction, for her to agree or contribute.

Odd. Sri raised her glass in a more feminine, half toast, and repeated, "To our union, brother." She timed the wine's placement at her lips with her brother's so both would drink at the same time.

Marici took a strong drink of his wine and then made a face. He had not realized how potent the drink would be and had gulped too much at once. The cup was placed back in front of his filled plate only to find Sri staring at him. She was obviously waiting until he started eating before daring to take a bite of her own food. And so, Marici took a piece of nan and began tasting the sauce surrounding the lamb with a healthy appetite. Sri was still staring at him, and showing no signs of changing the position of her eyes. Marici put his nan down and placed his hands flat on the table. "What is it, Sri?"

Sri now decided to pick up a piece of her bread and begin tooling around the edges of the plate to pick up specific parts of the sauce that she knew would flavor it nicely. "Hmm…" she said, thinking on Marici's question. She took a tiny bite of her prepared nan and nibbled it slowly. "Hmm, well...brother..." Sri placed her food down, and also placed her hands flat on the table in a similar gesture. "Why did you ask to dine alone with me?"

Marici raised an eyebrow, and a slow grin took over his lips. He thought that a woman would be swept away by the idea of a special reason to be decorated and to dine alone with an important man. He thought Sri would enjoy the chance to be beautiful for her King. But, that was indeed not the reason he asked her to dine alone with him tonight. She was clever—he'd have to remember that. "You don't want to dine alone with your brother and King?"

Sri could tell by the tone of his voice that if she pressed him further she would get the real reason. She also raised a brow, in identical fashion to Marici, and retorted. "Of course I want to dine with you, brother. But, that isn't the reason you brought me here, is it?" She smiled, to soften the directness of her words.

Marici shook his head. She was very clever. He clasped his hands as a temple over his steaming food that was now beginning to settle into a milder temperature. "No, Sri. It's not, I..." Marici shifted slightly in his chair. "I came to discuss the details of our marriage with you."

Sri raised and lowered her eyebrows quickly, "Ah..." Satisfied that the necessary conversation would now take place, the girl began a comfortable rhythm of chewing. She was determined to enjoy this dinner.

Marici cleared his throat. Sri had clearly taken over the power in the conversation. "Ah, yes. Hmm..." How would he go about this? His concentration was shifted, unbalanced. He had a plan, and Sri had seen right through him. "Well, I think we should have a symbolic marriage."

Sri cleared her throat while chewing through her bread. She expected more of an explanation. She did offer a question to guide Marici towards the information she wanted. "How will it work?"

Marici watched his sister eating, and wished he had been harder in keeping the topic of this evening to himself until the time presented itself. "For the people of Kasimi, we must be brother and sister, twins…King and Queen…and husband and wife. We'll wed as a symbol of our unity, before the gods." Marici exhaled, and hoped Sri would understand.

The statement—husband and wife—changed Sri's mood, suddenly. The taste of the lamb on her lips and mouth turned from pleasing to painful, and the pepper burned on her tongue. Her usually healthy appetite had waned. She dismissed her food by pushing the plate aside, and then brought her eyes to look at her brother. "What will you expect of your wife, Marici?" she asked, in a slightly choked tone.

Marici grinned to himself, realizing that he had reclaimed the power in the conversation. His posture grew in his chair, and his tone calmed to sooth his hesitant sister. "Sri, it won't be what you think. I won't take you to my bed…we won't produce children together…but you will be my wife and I your husband, and we will share the commitment of a husband and wife. We'll share our lives, sister."

Sri breathed out, relieved of this one point. But, she tensed on the other details. If they would not bed one another, how would heirs be produced? Sri settled her hands in her lap, and closed her body off from Marici. Her feet came together, as did her knees, and she suddenly looked like a girl much younger than her years. "How…how will children come, Marici?"

Marici swallowed and sucked down his own throat. They had come to the hardest part of the conversation. He reached next to his sister and brought her hand in his, to reassure her that this—

this part—wasn't so bad. It was just something she would have to do. "I will take concubines for my bed, to produce heirs." He hadn't said everything yet.

That would make sense, yes. Sri searched her brother's eyes for the rest of the answer. Her bed had not been described yet. There was something more or else he would have said "We" will take lovers to "our" beds. Her face began to flush, and several scenarios ran through her mind. She knew what the answer was behind all the possibilities. But, women did not have other lovers so..."Will I keep a cold bed? Will I be a mother?"

Marici leaned to take Sri's other hand in his, and shift her in her chair so that she was looking at him completely. His heart did ache. He could sense that his sister wanted motherhood by her question. It pleaded for a "No." to flow from Marici's lips. The water that came to Sri's eyes when that answer did not come was wiped away by two tender kisses from her brother's lips to her eyes. "You will be chaste, yes, sister. But...but...the only people who will raise the heirs that come will be you and me. You will be their mother and they will be raised to call you their mother and Queen."

Sri's tears fell openly. For a woman to be told that she will never experience the tenderness of a man's touch or the birth of her own little one breaks her heart—harder, when it is not her choice. Why had she been intended if she would never be able to do what she was intended for? Wasn't that her purpose—to entertain the sky god? Didn't that really mean to breed with him? She knew that consorts were just tools for proper breeding, no matter how nicely one dressed them, or what titles they held. The gift was—the love they would hold for their little ones.

Marici led his sister by the hand to the fireplace that was just before them. He loved her so much—he would make this pain go away by his commitment to her happiness. He kissed both her hands, and kneeled before her. "Oh Sri..." he whispered. Marici brought his head in to her stomach, and pleaded for his sister to embrace him. "Oh Sri..." he gripped his arms around her slender waist and took comfort there. "Please...I...will make you so happy. I...will see to your every wish...please, Sri...be my Queen? Please, Sri...for Kasimi..."

Sri's tears grew to sobs that commenced from her abdomen and went to her eyes. She would have buckled over if it were not for Marici's grip around her body. She embraced him and fell over his form in front of the hot flames in the fireplace.

"Sri...we do this for our people...we must. But..." Marici loosened his grip on Sri's waist to hold her up. He needed to look in her eyes for this last part. "I won't do this unless you give me permission. So, my sister..." Marici took his sister's small hand in his and kissed each individual knuckle tenderly. "My beautiful sister...you created me. I can call you mother. We were born from the same seed. I can call you sister. The gods gave us our role. You are the Queen..." Marici took out a generous emerald ring inlaid in platinum—the stone of the gods. "...will you be my wife?" He brought Sri's hand to his forehead, and lowered himself further before her.

Sri continued to let water escape from her eyes, but the sobs subdued. *He has asked my permission.* The tears continued as she watched her brother express his love for her. There was no turning back. And though she had been given a choice, she had a certain destiny she knew she must fulfill. And, if the priests had decided that this must be the way of it, she could not betray her people. "I will be your wife, Marici. Yes, my King."

The emerald ring was slipped on her ring finger, and it was done.

~

Sri decided to take a walk that evening, along the lighted path
in Janaka's main gardens. That set of mango trees that she had
been staring at from her window helped to center her, so Sri
decided to go there for a while to understand what had happened
this evening. Maybe even find a way to make peace with the decision that she was asked to make. Or was she it the decision she
was told to make?

Sri held her gold sandals in her hands, and wanted to feel the
water that would settle along the grass in the cool of night. She
slid her feet through the lush, wet carpet of green that led her to
her mango grove, enjoying the private rebellion of being so common in a Queen's clothes. Most likely guards or servant girls
would be watching her, but—it would give them something to
gossip about before bed. Her sari itched around her. The blouse
was too tight, and the folds too precise. When she got to the
mango trees, she would rewrap the silk to her liking.

Someone was already at the cluster of trees when Sri arrived. The
distinctive smell of liquor lingered in the humid air, characterizing
the person as lonely, or pensive—even melancholy. Sri approached
the trees with curiosity, already tugging at her sari, and was surprised to come upon the seated figure of the red-haired Goanian.
"Devyn?" she asked, her tone rising from low to high in question.

Devyn finished the brief sip of his moderately filled glass of
Goanian rum, and smiled up at the Intended. "It is I...am I interrupting you, Sri?" He had been here for some time, and intended
to stay for a long while. Devyn had brought the entire bottle with
him. He needed space from the day's events.

Sri actually liked Devyn. He had been a very solid presence in
her life without giving her obvious affection or disapproval.
Devyn was always quiet—and simply there. His bond to her was
in this consistent sense of companionship. They would speak—he
was honest but silent—and he would listen. Devyn never made her

feel like anything more than a growing woman. She—liked that. She could use that kind of company right now. "Not at all, Devyn. Mind if I...have a drink?"

Sri—drinking—with a Goanian? Devyn certainly had no problem with it. On other days, he might discourage a young person from drinking something so strong, so late in the evening. But, Devyn knew what Sri had just been through, and from the presence of the emerald on her ring finger, he knew that she could use the comfort of a bottle. It was the best thing she could do for herself tonight, most likely. Besides, she wanted it.

Devyn didn't answer. He just moved over beside his place at the tree, and offered the bottle up to Sri.

Before taking a seat, Sri gripped the bottle in her ringed hand and squeezed so that the platinum would dig painfully into her flesh. She clenched her jaw, and shook the bottle to communicate her needs to it. The opening was then at her lips, and her back arched her body to ease the flow of liquid inside her throat. The burning sensation of the alcohol was welcomed. She wanted to feel the pain—the sting and the burn. Sri removed the bottle from her lips, and handed it back to Devyn with a mischievous grin, thinking she had proved something. Now, she was ready to take her seat by the tree.

Devyn accepted the bottle, and watched Sri use what would be the last of her perfect balance for the evening, in taking a seat beside him. "You will regret that in a few hours, Sri...but it will feel nice soon enough. You all right?" Devyn knew the answer. But, this would give her the chance to tell him what had happened.

Sri's stomach couldn't handle all the liquor that was reaching it, and a small exhale of sound came forth from her mouth. "Oh, excuse me, Devyn..." she laughed in new found giddiness, while covering her lips with her ringed hand. Feeling the right to be a more bold this evening, Sri started with an answer to the question straight away. "No, I'm not all right. Whose idea was it, Devyn? Ajan's?"

Devyn could pretend that he had no idea what she was talking about. That would further complicate Sri's confusion and pain. He was straightforward, honest—even if it did not please the ones deemed as important. Before he did tell her the truth, however, he would make sure she wanted to know. "Does it matter, Sri? Why do you want to know?"

"Because it is my life, Devyn. And I want to know who is responsible for it now. It is my right." Sri's voice was getting louder, and her mood was affected by her drink. She grabbed the bottle and went for another turn at it. It was giving her the confidence she so desperately needed.

Devyn grabbed the bottle from Sri's hand, and held it tightly in his to deny Sri access to it. "Don't, Sri...don't drink out of need." He managed to secure a loosening of Sri's hand on the bottle and then put it on his left, out of her sight. "It's not my place to tell you who decided this, Sri. I can't explain it to you. But..." He turned to the girl and put a hand on her shoulder in a reassuring sign. "I'm sorry I couldn't do more for you."

Sri looked at Devyn with worried eyes. *Do more for me?* She enjoyed his affection. It was so undemanding, comforting. She placed her ringed hand over Devyn's, and continued to question the Goanian without raising her voice. The liquor had exhausted her. "Who do I go to about this, Devyn? I want to understand..."

Devyn would be honest with her. It would hurt, sting—maybe scar her. But as she said, she had the right to know. The Goanian turned his gaze out towards the trees and spoke to the thick night air. "You go to Marici, and you ask him why." He then returned his eyes to Sri and continued, "But there's nothing that he'll tell you that you will not figure out in time...he can only deny you the chance to really, really understand, Sri."

Marici? My brother? Sri just closed her eyes and let water streak down her cheeks again. She felt so betrayed. She should have expected nothing less. Sri just brought her knees up to her forehead and let her tears come as they pleased. If it had been Ajan, she might have been able to speak to him and persuade him to help her. After what had happened—and the dinner before the fire—it was done.

Devyn didn't try to stop Sri from crying. That was not his place either. He didn't offer a comforting arm, or whispers of how things would be all right. It would be a lie. There was no hiding from this place, from this life that Sri had started. There was no comforting available for reality. And so, the red haired man sat next to Sri as she wept, as a silent reminder that he was there.

9

The months that passed were comfortably busy and structured. The wedding would happen on the sixteenth birthday of the twins of Varuna II, and much needed to be done to prepare Marici for his role. For the time being, the crisis of The Isles was put aside for thought for after the coronation. Vishal had not been heard from since he stormed away on one of Janaka's horses, many moons ago. Ajan had too many other things to organize, than to prepare for battle with Vishal's house.

It was too risky to go back to the temple right now. If Vishal were to strike, it would be first against Ajan at the temple and then on to the Northern Kingdom. So, the Grand Priest decided to stay in Janaka's palace to complete the arrangements and for the preparation of Marici to his ascension. The temple near *Govandhara* was deserted, and all its inhabitants (elders, guards, servants and slaves) would come to the Northern Kingdom. There was room enough in *Mithila*.

Sri had been trained to be a Queen, separate from the rest of Kasimi. She knew her role her entire life, but not the world in which she would practice. Marici had been thrown into the world that he would lead, without understanding his purpose. With two very different approaches to the creation of leaders, and two people of the same seed, Kasimi would have an ideal pair: the lightning and the thunder of the sky god.

Marici, as predicted, was easy to train. He had confidence in his title, and accepted his training with equal dignity. He had already been taught by his father how to concentrate and reach inner peace through exhaustive meditation and focus. His education was refined and broad, due to his affiliation in the Northern Kingdom. His understanding of Kasimi, the culture, the history and the politics, was well developed because of his ancestors. Marici was very self aware—perhaps too self aware.

Marici took to his lessons with a feverish pride and energy. He was determined to memorize every bit of scripture, every bit of Kasimian law and make it his own. With the aid of Ajan and understanding of his Queen, Marici was able to become a master of the ancient texts and scriptures. He would grow impatient and angry when Ajan would tell him he needed to rest or that he needed to stop for the evening. His temper would flare to almost uncontrollable heights. Only Sri, and Sri alone, could calm him.

It was written that Marici would be able to harness the power of the sky in him. He would be the mortal translator of the strength it held, and be able to tunnel his desires by thought and prayer with his ancestors. There would be no way to teach Marici how to use this gift. He would have to experience it on his own. The change, as the elders called it, would come in time. It was written that way.

Marici did begin to start this process of change, and to experience a kind of transformation during his months in preparation. At first, the signs were almost unnoticeable—the King's preference for as little sleep as possible as to watch the colors of the sky change or his impatience with the way the clouds would move too slowly.

His temper was short, and sporadic. His body would seem to grow in might from its thin stature, and the red rings around his black eyes would rotate during these bursts of rage.

And then, one night in the Kasimian autumn, Marici changed for good...

Sri woke up in the middle of the night in a cold sweat, her entire nightgown slicked against her body like a second skin. Her hair was drenched from the perspiration, as well, and was smooth against her face and forehead. The water around her body made her shiver—but it was such a warm temperature in the room fed by the constantly roaring fireplace. Sri's body felt out of control. Even her mind felt drawn, or called, to somewhere. And a voice in her head wanted to claim her from her sleep.

The voice called to her in a whisper that a mother uses to sooth a sick child. Sri could even feel the comforting touch of a mother's ice-cold fingers against her sticky, wet skin. "*Sri, I am you. Come to me.*"

Sri moved her hands out to feel where the ice-cold hand was moving on her cheeks, and smiled slightly in her distant state. "*I will come to you. Lead me...*"

The voice breathed against the inside of Sri's head—the scent of her favorite cinnamon and vanilla lingered in her mind and found its way to her senses, tempting her. Sri's mouth began to water, wetting it as her body had been drenched. "*Go Sri, to your brother's room as you are.*"

Sri tried to protest. Marici was sleeping, and it was not an appropriate time to visit him. She began to speak the words to the voice in her mind. But, this voice was of something that already knew her thoughts and her words before she spoke them. Suddenly, her body felt a warm breeze blow over its skin. It was a reassurance that she must visit her brother.

Though Sri was shivering slightly, she did not take a blanket with her to her brother's room in the main part of the palace. She went as she stood: a Queen, drenched from the night effects of fever, to where she was told to go. For some reason, the guards did not call out to her or try to stop her. Or maybe they did, and Sri just could not hear them.

It was as if she was not really there. Sri did look straight at one of the black clad guards who stood at the end of the staircase, holding a sword at attention in his hand. Her black eyes searched to make contact with his if for no other reason than to prove her action inappropriate to herself. She stared and stared, standing in front of his hulking form for a long moment. To further her presence in his space, Sri's delicate hands went to trace the edge of his sword's blade. He did not see her—his eyes were very aware of his surroundings—and he looked straight through her.

Sri continued across the palace hallway towards the main wing, welcoming the feel of cold marble under the hot skin of her feet. Each step, gaining that new pleasure of a chill, was relished. Her toes grasped at the floor, and Sri felt sadness in the pit of her stomach, that the cold would abandon her and leave her in the flames. There were some steps where she wanted to trace through with a circle, to make the moment longer. But, she had been summoned and must go.

The stairs ascending to Marici's room could not be felt on Sri's feet. The sensation of cold had moved to her hands as she crawled up the winding, black marble path to reach the King's bed chamber. The wet of her nightgown made the material thinner, and allowed her knees to enjoy the pleasure of cold.

That voice began again in Sri's mind. The tone was a hissing whisper of wind that created a gentle and cool breeze around her body on the ground. *"Rise, Queen, and greet your King."*

Sri obeyed and rose to her full height before walking in to the bedroom of the King. The feel of her soft palms on the wooden handles of the doors burned to her hands. There were hidden flames inside the wood, and blistered the skin of her fingers.

Marici stood in his white night shirt, waiting for his sister. The billowing silk material was simple on him, and went down to his knees to provide the King with an acceptable garment for the night. His eyes were closed, and his arms were folded across his body. Though he did not look upon her as she entered, his voice whispered the identity of the visitor. "My Queen, you have come."

"Yes, Marici, I have come." Sri stood at the door, frozen until the command could break her from her moment. Somehow, near Marici, the feeling of control was completely gone. She was answering, understanding—in the presence of something greater. Sri was not sure what would happen in this room.

His voice was deeper, and rounder, the unity of many ancestral voices tuned to one in chorus. "Walk forward to me, Sri. The doors will close behind you." Marici did not open his eyes yet. One hand motioned for his sister to come to his side, with a gentle roll of his fingers towards him.

Before Sri obeyed physically, and had made the mental decision to walk towards Marici, the doors closed with resolute movement behind her. She walked forward, her feet gliding against the marble floor, towards her brother. "How are you, brother?" Sri asked lazily, as her unblinking eyes focused on Marici's closed ones.

Marici did open his eyes when Sri requested looked upon him. The heavy lids opened to exhibit a change. The red rings around Marici's eyes had taken over his pupils so that only two dots of black remained within his usually onyx pools. There was fire in his body that heated the room. The flames were hidden, buried— unwilling to come out to view. Marici's arms opened to welcome Sri into an embrace. It was not an open gesture of affection, but a command. He needed her near his heart and mind, in this ceremony.

Sri went to the imposing embrace of her brother's arms, feeling the welcoming warmth of fire. The pleasure of sun drying away water on skin began, drawing the Intended closer and closer into the ceremony. But when Marici's arms did draw in to bring Sri to him, the Queen yelled out in pain from the hot flames burning on her skin. There was no sound that could be heard from her mouth by others—it only echoed in her head and in Marici's heart.

"Oh, sister…shhh…and be still. The pain is but a sacrifice that will pass. And your wounds will heal, my Queen…" Marici leaned in and whispered in her ear, adding a cool breeze to the fire that would burn his intended wife and Queen. A kiss with lips that were heated with fire went to Sri's forehead.

The burn was ferocious against her skin. Sri yelled out in the carnal call of pain, and tried to break away from the embrace against the possessive control of her brother's fiery limbs. "Marici, let me go! Please!" The screams of uncontrollable terror worked to emphasize each movement of her arms against his in trying to free herself from the burning.

Marici looked upon his sister with his red eyes in a state of demand. His recent growth had granted him a few inches over his sister's height, and he could look down upon her and be the more powerful of the two. "You will not escape, Sri. You must be a part of this, my sister…it will all be over soon." With these words, Marici scooped his sister up with surprising strength in his arms, and walked towards the window that overlooked the property. The windows threw themselves open at the mercy of the King, and accepted a warm blast of air into the outside.

Marici held Sri outside the window as if to throw her to the ground. His grip on her body was too tight, however, to offer any remote chance for her to fall—even in the discomfort of the fire racing through Sri's body. He explained in his breath of ice, "It is to offer ourselves to our ancestors, Sri…"

Sri just closed her eyes, and focused on the separation of the physical and mental realms—to try to distinguish her physical discomfort from the reality that this was an act of the gods. This distinction allowed her to keep her squirms to simple responses to the pain rather than decisive movements to rid herself from her brother's embrace.

Marici then held his sister out to the open grounds of Janaka's palace and lifted his voice to the sky above. His red eyes were wide with focus, and were no longer communicating only with the Kasimian mortal realm. He had channeled, communicated—gone beyond the level that had restrained him for so long. He proclaimed his power to the land:

Others again with wisdom's sacrifice
Make sacrifice to Me and worship Me
As One and yet as Manifold,
With face turned every way, in many a guise!

I am the rite, the sacrifice,
The offering for the dead, the healing herb;
I am the sacred formula, the sacred butter am I,
I am the fire, and I the oblation!

I am the father of this world,
Mother, creator, grandsire, that need be known;
Vessel of purity. Ohm!
And the four Kingdoms am I too!

The Way, Sustainer, Lord and witness,
Home and refuge, friend—
Origin and dissolution and the stable state between—
A treasure-house, the seed that passes not away.

Marici's voice had lowered to a piercing boom that could call the thunder with its breath. His grip on his sister was strong, and desperate. He needed her near him to make this proclamation, and to gain his strength. If he had not summoned her tonight, he would not be able to pronounce his moment to the Kingdom of Kasimi. And he coronated himself that night, as Sky God:

It is I! Who pour our heat, hold back
The rain and send it forth!
Death am I and deathlessness
What is not and that which is!

The ancestors granted him His Right, and a flash of lightning came down to where Sri was held out the window. The flame did not burn her or even pierce her skin for Marici would not have it. He would protect her and love her, and no harm would come to her while she was His Queen. Marici looked down on his Sri, and a twisted grin began to tug at his mouth. He was The Omnipotent, The King and The All. And, in his arms was the only woman who possessed the ability to be his partner. He did need her.

Just as the proclamation was coming to a close, Marici released his channel to the ancestors and spoke his own words out on *Mithila*:

I am the Night, both darkness and power!
I am the Dreams, both the pure and the sinful.
I am Glory, both rejoice and fear me!
I have come, with my Queen, I have come.
Behold the progeny of Varuna II, and be saved!

Marici's red eyes flared with yellow and cast a light over his Queen and lit the many lightning strikes that soon followed. He looked to the sky, and his show of lights began. And with a dark smile, Marici harnessed the power he was given from the gods to display his might. Sri was brought back inside from the window, and held to his heart so she could be the purity of soul that he was not.

The night sky began to be overwhelmed with jagged bolts of light that descended en masse across *Mithila*, and could be seen from *Govandhara* and on into the Southern Kingdom. The striking silvery glow of the gold bolts burned away the clouds that had begun to swirl over Janaka's garden into a cone. Marici's eyes just watched, and commanded the storm of His Reign with a slight smile and his Queen in his arms.

The clouds began to shift from the black of night and bring forth a silver reflection—jewels in the sky. Around the movement of the funnel, emerald in its color of the gods, was pushed through the thick texture of the rain clouds. *"Be saved..."* whispered Marici, while cradling Sri to him. His lips pressed against her hair and he closed his eyes to again murmur, *"Be saved..."* On command, the rain came with the gentle thunder that would announce the storm. Marici had the power of the sky in him, and his Queen in his arms.

IO

Two weeks before the moon would celebrate the sixteenth year of Marici and Sri, Ajan's band would begin the journey to the sacred wedding site, in the lush gardens of *Vrndavana*. The tropical garden was on the ocean, at the point where the Northern and Southern Kingdoms came together as one. To the west, was Goane and to the Southeast were The Isles. *Vrndavana* looked upon all the members of the Kasimi, it is lair of flowers and waterfalls, and cradled the Kingdom as one.

They arrived to what *Vrndavana* had to offer in its flawless blue skies, and gently sweeping sun filled days. It was the place where the gods had been united with their consorts since the beginning with *Brahma*, a place where fruit grew with bounty and flowers bloomed moon upon moon. A garden created by the Omnipotent *Brahma* for the purpose of love, *Vrndavana's* wind would whisper that message gently in its warm breath off the ocean.

Each day begged for its visitors to play outdoors. Each flower bloomed with fierce color and fragrance. The birds sang their prayers to the gods. And, Varuna looked on his kin with delight in his turquoise depths. One could not leave *Vrndavana* without knowing what true beauty was.

Everything would be as it had for generations. Marici would take his bride by the ancient waterfall that led its way into the ocean. The vows would be taken at the rise of the moon, on the night of their sixteenth year. The union would be in the most beautiful place that Kasimi had to offer, and nothing but joy would be felt throughout the Kingdoms as the King and Queen became bound for eternity.

Ajan's caravan arrived one day before the ceremony would begin, as planned. It was a large group of people that followed the King and Queen to the marriage garden—hundreds of servants to attend to the smallest details, guard upon guard to risk his life for the nobles, and the guests that would witness the consummation of the third miracle. The palace that would shelter the nobles, stood on the ocean, and was built of the purest white that Kasimi had to offer. It could house the entire following without effort, and all could get lost in its endless display of luxury and delicacy in its confines.

Slowly, after the arrival of the Grand Priest, more nobles and their servants would follow for this glorious event. Even though one needed to be of certain blood to witness the day, all of Kasimi would feel the epic event. Word of the wedding had spread throughout Kasimi, and on the rising of the moon on the sixteenth year of the twins, the entire Kingdom would look up into the sky in praise of their savior.

~

Marici was in the beginning part of his dressing rituals, to be completed by his entourage and servants. For the men, this was a treasured part of the noble ceremony. Every guest who held a title of affiliation to the Northern House would be welcomed into the groom's quarters at midday for feasting and drinking, and even women if they so chose. Marici would sit in his chair and let the servants, whose lives were meant to attend to him, wrap him in silks and fineries. He knew the true beauty of the day, however, would be in his Queen.

There were twenty men and fifty guards to be present for the dressing event. Somehow, all were needed to ensure that the King would be ready to be a groom, at the rise of the moon. The other nobles were standing or lounging on the various pillows and divans spread around Marici's quarters, drinking expensive wine and eating whatever the bare midriffed women would bring by. Marici had no interest in those things, but enjoyed the banter that these nobles provided for him while he was being groomed.

A faceless servant with strong, exact fingers was attending to Marici's raven hair, strand by strand. He would keep it long for the wedding, but would allow it to be smoothed back. Not a strand could be out of place, not a part of the painting could be wrong. This servant's hands moved masterfully along the black threads, for a task that would take painstaking effort.

Ajan looked over at Marici with a thin smile. He enjoyed watching the King surrender to vanity for this occasion. The people would want to watch a man of beauty take the hand of a worthy woman, and be swept away by ceremony in all its grace. Bringing a cup of finely spiced wine to his nose, Ajan inhaled its scent slightly and spoke. "Your Queen will still outshine you, Marici…no matter how much you groom."

Marici laughed, careful not to shake his head in the process. He knew this. He enjoyed the fact that Sri had turned into a beautiful woman over the past few moons. He didn't want to outshine something that should be so filled with the light of His Sky.

Janaka replied the retort to Ajan, all while eyeing which food looked best according to midriff. "With that jewelry, Ajan…you could come close to looking like the Queen!"

A round and hearty laughter accompanied Janaka's taking of a kebab from the same light-eyed serving girl that had been walking past him throughout the afternoon.

Ajan rolled his eyes towards Janaka and gave him a flat smile that said, *"This is old."* His uncle had been nagging him about jewelry and garments since they left *Mithila* to come to the sacred site. His lips then took refuge in the comfortable and relaxing aroma of the wine. Janaka was better at these sorts of large social gatherings, and Ajan was happy to be fodder for his performance.

Janaka nodded his head to some rhythm he wished were there and then looked around for it. "Where's the tabla? What?...This is a party, and there's no drum? Oh, it's more fun in *Mithila*!"

The relaxed group of noblemen rounded out the King's quarters with rounds of chuckles provided by Janaka. He had provided a good show, and a nice background for the boy's grooming ritual. The old man, sweating slightly from his own outbursts, threw his fourthly filled glass of wine up in Marici's direction to draw the nobles from the merry laughter into a hearty cheer. *"Long live King Marici, ya!"*

The men were easily focused into this display of worship. With wine in hand and cheer in heart, the toasts came from all levels— from their lounging positions to their standing poses against the wall—*"Long live King Marici, ya!"*

Almost on cue, Marici's hair was finished and had been put neatly into a tail of black silk that fell with weight on his back. Each strand was pulled back across his head without flaw, and shined slightly with a hint of rose oil. He stood to accept the praises and cheers, and nodded a thanks to Janaka for his merriment. Marici was steady and calm about the day, and quieted down the hail with a rise and lowering of arched fingertips.

He walked to the center of the room, and folded his hands neatly behind his back to address the noblemen—and dismiss them for now. "Thank you for your company, my lords and elders. But now, before I take my Queen, I request a few moments to center myself for the event...to meditate...to pray to *Brahma*..." He bowed forward and fluttered his eyelashes a few times. "Even I need the peace of the One..."

The invocation of *Brahma*'s name is all it took to clear the noblemen from the chamber. Yes, they understood that the King would need his privacy. Even the guards took posts such that Marici's immediate space was fully cleared of human presence. They strategically positioned themselves outside the windows and doors, with their thick arms readied at their swords if the King called for help. But, with the power of the storm in Him, Marici could unleash wrath a thousand times the power of a sword. He watched silently as his court exited his chamber, with a quiet smile. This event had made him feel older.

Finally, when everyone had been removed from the room, Marici stood alone. His black eyes, with a circle of red, looked upon the fine silks for which he would later exchange his simple white resting gown. The gold jewelry and ancient long sword were ceremoniously placed on a circular wooden table, attended to by thin white candles that emitted a vanilla fume—a gift from Sri.

Marici wondered what his sister was doing now. All the women were gathered in her room for a similar ceremony of merry making. Her appearance would be much more elaborate and would require specific attention. Already, there had been two ceremonies for the painting of her hands and feet in mendhi and gold, in the intricate swirls and designs that made fingers so hypnotic. He could only imagine how insignificant *Vrndavana*'s beauty would be compared to His Queen's. *Sri.*

And then, the pure thoughts of Sri were clouded over with a dark presence of some other energy. Marici opened his eyes from his daydreaming and stood still to concentrate on this strange feeling that invaded his peaceful meditation. It took him a few moments to realize that he was not alone. He began to turn on his heels towards the source of human warmth that he could feel a few paces behind him. The motion was accompanied by the necessary question in a low tone, "Who goes there?"

A voice hissed from the shadows, his black clad form a darker silhouette against the ebony of the corner. He had most likely been there for some time, because Marici had watched all the nobles exit one by one. He was most likely a specialist for him to be able to stay unnoticed. "King Marici, son of Varuna II?" he asked in a tone that was barely distinguishable as male.

Marici's eyes went to the corner of the room, from where the sound was produced. He then closed his lids tightly over the pupils—something was so familiar about the presence of this stranger. Marici was not certain what it was—or how it could be so—but he was certain he had met this man before. Inclining his head at angle, up towards the ceiling, Marici answered back, "Aye, this is your King. And who...who are you, eh?" Marici's hands tensed into fists. This stranger was not bringing fear into his soul—but anger—and the purest form of hatred was raw in his blood.

The voice continued. "I am the end my king, of your third miracle...your savior." The body of the figure began to emerge from the shadows towards Marici's place in the chamber. In a stronger tone, with a more definitive and distinctive tenor quality, the voice stated with conviction. "I am the bringer of justice from my people..."

Marici's eyes clamped shut, and his mind took him back to the place. His covered eyes began to move back and forth inside their lids to hurriedly examine the details of the memory in his mind's eye. *It was there.* There was rain and thunder outside, which skewed his perception of the room. It was dark—everything was black and grey that night—and there was lightning to highlight the blood. That, Marici remembered—the way the blood lit up against the flash of a silver sword when the lightning pierced the waves outside.

He remembered the triumphant scream of his mother as she refused to denounce her house—the song of a woman who upheld her convictions, even as a brutal instrument pierced her flesh. And when the man took what belonged only to Varuna II, his mother screamed out her defiance in minor tones of the purest pain. She would not denounce her kingdom even with her husband dead, and her child in danger. And with each refusal, the man was fiercer and angrier with his savage work on her tender body—ripping with his manhood what he could not with his sword—and then bringing the two blades into a fierce rhythm of murder. The man said to his mother as she gasped her last bit of air, "*I am the bringer of justice from my people…*"

And then, that black clad man turned his sword on the child in the corner. The blood of the newly dead mother was thick on the edge, and a few drops tumbled mercilessly down onto the boy's tear stained face to emphasize his mother's end. But this murderer would not grant the child a peaceful death—but wished him misery in a world without family and protection.

Marici's eyes opened with full red anger in them. He could smell the blood of his mother on this man, and there would be payment. The King unclenched his fists and brought his arms up like wings to build his might before the murderer. The thunder had begun in his mind, a contorted rumbling of anger and pain. The movements were slow and calculated against this uncontrollable rage building inside of him, driven by a memory. Reaching for his ceremonial sword with a simple flick of his wrist, the King began to generate his red eyed gaze at the villain while remaining deceptively calm. "You. Welcome back to my life."

The black clad man showed himself from the shadows and moved forward with the steady grace of a trained assassin. He was covered in the dress of his trade, the haunting black silks that made him one with the shadows. Only the amber of his hard eyes showed through his mask. Marici had memorized that shade—and had grown angry when the sunset would dare bring forth the color of a murderer. The assassin looked on his victim with the intention that it be his last civil glare before the blood would come.

He still uses the long, silver sword. Marici's eyes, now fully red, glared back at the assassin. His ceremonial sword, though smaller than the weapon of the killer's, would be more powerful. He did not need his guards, or his watch. This was his revenge, and he was the son of Varuna II. He was even more powerful than his father, and he held all of the sky's might in his soul. The rage began to transform in Marici's hand, and the instrument was his channel. The calm changed—transformed—and the thunder that had rumbled in his body began to turn and control Marici. He was Vengeance.

Marici inclined his head and watched the assassin with his red eyes, invoking heat and burn in his own manners. The ceremonial sword was lifted, and then ripped and tortured...once...twice...into the middle sections of flesh that had invaded his mother. The King did not scream or yell—it was done in the piercing tones of silence with the calculation of a leader. He closed his eyes, and made the assassin's screams go muffled against the ears of the guards, through a quick settling of his rage's thunder around the room.

The assassin's knees buckled and his hands went to the blood stained section of his groin. He opened his mouth to let out his sounds of terror, but his voice had vanished. He dropped to the ground, powerless, and his sword was easily taken by Marici. The assassin was at the mercy of His King. He would open his mouth to beg. He was only a hired servant.

"And so, Murderer, you are at my will. My mercy. I am your King. Say it!" Marici stared down at the helpless servant, his anger now subsiding to command. "Say it, now!"

The servant, now powerless without his sword, looked up help-lessly at Marici. He removed his black mask as a sign of humility, and bowed his already lowered body as best he could. In a voice that grasped for air, the assassin whispered, "You are...my...King." He then returned his hands to the focus of his pain, to try and hold it from the constant state of imminent throbs.

Marici watched his victim and his mother's crucifier with a sick delight and satisfaction. He then demanded, "Who sent you?" while pacing around the bleeding man.

The servant closed his eyes and prepared for his death. He would not betray his master to simply exist in this realm. A silent shaking of his head, and the villain thought his fate was sealed. He prepared himself for one final wound.

Marici laughed, and put his bare foot on the assassin's tumbled body. How amusing! To let this man receive the merciful blessing of an honorable death! To die because he would not renounce his master, with a single cut to the body. No—it would not be this way. The King brought his sword down in the man's groin one more time, and then spat out his words as the stranger glowered in pain. "Your death? No, no...you will tell me who sent you, or you will remain in my presence for as long as you can hold on to this realm...and I will make it a long time..." Marici pressed down harder with his foot, and continued. "You will tell me your master, or I will create ways of inflicting pain on you and will find out your family name and create generations of punishment for them. You will tell me your master, or you will be cursed for-ever by me and my ancestors, and will receive no mercy."

Marici's lips curled into a thin, cruel smile as he finished with, "If you tell me, I will be kind."

The servant buckled in more pain as his manhood was mutilated further. The blood had flowed out onto the smooth floor, and showed no easy signs of stopping. In the whirlpool of mental intensity of His King and the sensation of pain, the assassin coughed the name of his master quietly. "The Isles."

Marici swallowed, and let his foot return to the floor from its hold on the servant's body. *Vishal.* There would be payment, and death. Families would suffer. *But not now.* He had an answer. *The answer.* Marici closed his eyes and focused—for somehow this had brought him peace. His anger could now be directed—his might could be channeled. But, the murderer before him was only the messenger of blood—a servant—and not fit for a simple death. Though he had destroyed everything for Marici—he was obeying a master. It would be the master who would pay, and pay severely. *The Isles will learn my might.*

The King watched the servant bleed for a few moments, while he stared out the window with his soiled ceremonial sword in hand. He was calm and peaceful after this deed, and the arrival of his decision. When his verdict came, it was in the voice of a withdrawn man giving a decision to an insistent peasant. "You will serve me." He decreed, while the man bled on the cold floor. "You killed people of my blood...and you shall pay...but not with death. You were just a servant of your house." Marici then turned to the man and loomed over his helpless body. "You will watch over my Queen's guards from afar. I will know where you are, but they will not...if anything should happen to her...anything at all...as little as a scratch...and you will wish my wrath were as forgiving as it was today." Marici's red eyes fixed on the criminal, as he knelt beside the man to place a burning hand on his skull. He dropped his head to whisper in the assassin's ear, "Do you not know? I am the sky and its might is mine...you will serve me...I will know your every move...I will have people watching your every move. Your life will be in fear and that will give you your penance for the next realm." Marici then rose to his full volume over his new servant. "That is My Mercy."

Marici waited until his new man faded into blackness before calling forth a trusted guard to see to the man's health for the evening, and days to follow. No questions were asked though the guard peered curiously at his King. Marici waved away the inquiries with a shaking of his head and a flicker of his red eyes. As for the trail of blood on the floor, it was only the beginning of what was to come. Why bother with a few drops, when the storm would pour it down later. It was unimportant for now. He must see to becoming a husband.

~

The moon held its glorious position over Kasimi in one whole circle that glowed with a thin layer of green around the edges in the night sky, *Vrndarvana's* jewel. The sky was covered with a lush blue blanket as the sun lingered its dying rays with the moon's light. It would soon be a black sky, but for now it was content to sit in that vague in-between of evening and night.

Ajan had arranged everything for this wedding. Though the festivities were joyous, there was still a feeling of divinity in this love garden of the gods. There was nothing more beautiful or inspiring as the uniting of a god and his consort.

All of Kasimi's major nobles and their wives, scholars, priests and elders had journeyed to watch this event and to bow to the King and Queen. Varuna's ocean welcomed the boats that journeyed through the water, and the earth below kissed the feet of the traveling horses to bring the good people to their god. There was a sense of great peace at this event, whispered in each warm wind that blew over the merry crowd as they mingled and chatted with one another.

The wedding would take place on the stone patio before the ancient waterfall in the central gardens of *Vrndarvana*. The waterfall cascaded over the entrance of an old stone cave, that was rumored to have been the opening to ancient temple ruins in the Age of No Moon, when the Kasimians were separated from their gods. The garden was filled with green of every shade and texture in amounts that craved the attention of scooping hands. Tall trees sprouted protectively around the waterfall, with their branches growing inward and curving over the ground. Each gentle breeze would release a few wayward leaves of flower petals in gently-slow motion. As the land led up to the stone patio, green grass united with wildflowers of yellow and red in haphazard fashion making sweet perfumes. And though it was not attended to by servants, the gods had created an eternal space of beauty that needed only its eye.

The smooth stone that claimed the edge of the lawn and circled the waterfall—the place of marriage—was smooth and black. The patient coating of water that trickled off of the cascade's ends had persuaded the rock to age gracefully and had promised to never abandon it, and to always warm it even when it faded into the night's black.

The Kasimian guests waited for the event with wine-filled hands along the lawn. Some of the more agile youth, opted to sit in the welcoming spaces that the strong branches in the tree provided. The hum of pleased voices, happily waiting what would be a beautiful event, echoed in and out of the space as the evening slipped further and further away into night. It would start when the moon went straight overhead and reflected in the ocean.

Servants soon began with the preliminary details. A group of four men came with firelit torches to place at the four ends of the stone patio for light. The men, dressed in pajama suits of sturdy brown, moved with exquisite grace—even the preparation tasks needed to be performed in a dance-like manner. As soon as that fire had been lit, the tallest servant took his guiding torch and walked down the aisle that had been cleared for the procession. Tall white candles, with a vanilla fragrance, marked the boundary—and were lit one by one with a quick shift of the servant's feet. The servant bowed to each candle, as a symbol of his devotion to his King and Queen.

With the fire in place, the rest of the stage could be prepared. A small servant girl with fiery red hair, came out on the platform and placed three crimson pillows in the center. She had been taught how to place her feet for this event, curling her toes forward before putting her heel on the black stone. Another tiny servant girl, most likely her sister, took the pillows off of the pile and leaned to gingerly place them one by one in a semi-circle. They bowed in to the center of the circle, and then turned to kneel to the ancient waterfall, before exiting the stage.

And now with the details completed, the musicians began to take their anonymous places for the ceremony. They were wearing neutral beige, but were colored by an array of yellow and red flowers in front of their line. The rich and alluring sound of four drums coming together in different flavors and timbres began, with a pleasant duet of sitars blending tones. The music directed the energy of the people in attendance for this wedding—to passion, desire and love—in the subtle nuances and rhythms of the music.

The Grand Priest, dressed in the traditional white dhoti made his way down the candlelit path towards the stone patio with long, purposeful strides. Even in a costume that was meant to be humble, Ajan looked fine and grand. His bronzed skin was somehow more warrior-like, than priestlike—more noble than spiritual—against the soft folds of his robes. He wore no jewelry, and his feet were slipped into simple sandals for this event. He was coming as the supreme spiritual leader to be a bare and humble union maker this night. With his chin held high, Ajan ascended up to the wet stone block and stood in the center to await his King and Queen. Though, he was losing a part of his himself tonight.

Like a burst from the sky, dozens of multicolored parakeets carrying flowers in brilliant blues, reds and yellows flew down the candlelit path. Their wings spread with pride as they glided silently towards the waterfall, and the Grand Priest. The flowers were released over various points on the aisle, adding more color to the festivity. The creatures found resting places alongside the waterfall, on cue—uniting air with water.

The guests had quieted their whispering, and now knew that the King would soon be making his grand entrance. His coming had been heightened, and all the details were in place. The tabla began to quicken in pace, and the sitar began to play more rhythmically and feverishly in response to the demand. And then, the King did come.

On a white horse, trimmed in gold and emeralds, and groomed to perfection, the King did come. Marici rode slowly down the candlelit aisle, alive with moonlight. His black eyes, with the thin layer of red, focused upon the Grand Priest and the waterfall behind him, and only seeing the Queen who would come soon enough.

He had grown into a man over the past few moons, and it showed on this wedding day. The lanky body of a boy had turned into a fuller form, and filled out his white clothes. The churidar on his torso was tailored to fall squarely around his shoulders and arms, and fall simply to his hips. And the kurta pants dusted on the young King's lightly muscled legs that squeezed around the white horse's sides. Finally, a jacket of gold thread fit around the churidar. Subtle shades of yellow and white gold were woven into the symbols of his ancestors that were only visible on careful inspection. But, Marici could feel them close by. Every ornament was a subtle reminder of his lineage from the gold medallion on his heart to the emerald clasp in his long tail of black hair. The sword at his hip, newly cleaned of a man's blood, was his ready symbol.

Marici's horse moved slowly past the vanilla-scented candles, and closer to the sound of falling water. The fast rhythm of the drums could not force the King to rush during the moment he knew his people would watch with awe. At the edge of the stone patio, the white horse lowered its front legs slightly—as if in a bow to the leader—and Marici dismounted with grace. He locked his eyes on the cerulean gaze of the priest, and waited.

From the position of the musicians came the voice of an older woman singing in the subtle notes of an ancient Kasimian song, with no words. The other musicians went silent to mark the solo voice in the humid night air. The richness seeped through its density—the blending of minor half tones that worked effortlessly into a tale of beauty became the music that would soften the hearts of the most vicious. And then, the Queen did come.

Emerging from the opening of the temple ruin to place herself before the ancient waterfall, the Queen did come. There were tears from the people, as they beheld the purest form of beauty in their goddess. It was not that she had transcended the standards of feminine beauty—she had defined them this night.

The Queen wore a blending of dark and light reds that emphasized mortality in the stain of blood while enjoying the vividness of such a spectacular visual shade. The sari was a deceptive crimson of many undertones, as the brilliant light of the moon and candles called out the gold threads underneath. The silk was wrapped and folded in subtle angles to completely cover the full curves of the Queen, while making her sensual figure obvious to the Kasimian eye. Tiny diamonds of white and pink were woven into the silk of Sri's sari to make it glisten against her mocha skin in the moonlight—indeed, she shone more. And unlike most Kasimian women, Sri's face was not covered with a traditional veil. Instead, the sari had been gently folded over her knotted blue-black hair and fastened in the center of her head.

As Sri walked forward to the two men in her life, the designs of paint and jewelry were more noticeable on the Queen. An emerald bhindi had been marked betwixt her brows, a symbol of her divine lineage. Layers of yellow-gold fell over Sri's neck, crafted by Kasimi's finest artists in the most complex designs. The jewelry continued onto Sri's hands—webs of white and yellow gold that encased her fingers over the stained vines of mendhi. Her bare feet followed the pattern of her hands, dressed in a web of thin spun gold that swirled in mysterious designs around her toes, and towards her ankles.

Sri had fulfilled every promise to grow into a lovely woman. There was beauty in the coupling of distinction and delicacy in her aristocratic features. Her eyes had become definitively almond-shaped, and the red rings around her black pupils had mellowed into a burgundy. For this event, faint shades of coloring had been added to her youthful skin. A dusting of gold was placed over her cheeks and nose to contrast the silver glow of the moon. Lips that would never smile quite as brightly again, were dressed in the crushed powder of rubies.

Marici looked at his sister with tears in his eyes. His Queen was something so pure, so perfect, that would always be his better half. Of the two that were born sixteen years ago, she was clearly the better. He would spend his life defending her honor, and ruling his kingdom in his mother's memory. As His Queen approached the circle, Marici could do nothing but kneel before the woman that would be his life's purpose.

The soloist completed the welcoming of the bride to the marriage circle. The tabla began a steady sensual rhythm, to accompany the ceremony. The guests, who had not breathed since the Queen entered from the waterfall, relaxed to the comforting pattern of the drums. The Grand Priest, who was overcome with pain at the site of beauty, found his center in the music.

Sri claimed a garland of red flowers from a faceless servant who came readily to the her. She placed it over her kneeling brother's head and murmured her wishes. "I willingly take you as my husband."

Marici rose from his position before Sri, and took a garland to place over her head, while placing a chaste kiss on her forehead. "And I willingly take you as my wife."

Ajan began to chant "*Ohm…*" over the King and Queen, with his hands placed in open acceptance of the power of *Brahma*. He then stepped back to present the two willing partners who would begin this path towards immortal union. The tall warrior spoke his blessing in a whispered tone. "As guardian of the King and Queen, and Grand Priest of Kasimi, I bless this union of the sky god and his consort. May no man deny what the gods would have as right. *Ohm…*"

The three people took their seats on the pillows around the circle. Ajan and Marici held Sri with their eyes to ensure she could find a seat gracefully under the heavy folds of her bejeweled sari and plentiful gold. Ajan closed his eyes and said a hymn to *Brahma*, and then created a fire in the center of the three people using two rocks. It was the invocation of Divine Light, and the channel where all the ancestral gods could give their blessing.

Ajan threw *Darbha* grass around the fire while chanting the invocation of the twin's ancestors.

We meditate on the lovely light of the sky god,
May it stimulate our thoughts!

"*Ohm...*" was recited by the trio while they bowed towards the growing flames. Ajan continued to chant this meditation prayer a few times, to bring blessings to the union. Each time, he would throw the sacrificial *Darbha* grass into the fire with care. Finally, when the flames were burning with intensity, the Grand Priest invoked the Divine Light further.

To the god of fire!
You, o fire, are King Varuna, give wealth to him who serves you.
You are the bestower of property, as god!
O king, you control riches, you are a protector of the house of
him who has revered you!
Ohm.

"*Ohm...*" was sung by Marici alone. He then threw grain into the fire, to bless the fertility for the union. Usually, the woman would bear such a gift, and ask for children from the gods. Sri did not need this. Marici bowed his head towards the flames, his eyes flickering slightly. "*Ohm.*"

Sri looked between the two men who had defined her. She knew the chants to the gods by heart, and had practiced her part for this very moment since she was a girl. *It is what I was intended for.* But somehow Sri did not expect to feel that this ceremony would be a sacrifice of her life. She did not expect to feel a loss of children that would never be born. She did not expect the site of her husband to bring tears to her eyes. "*Ohm.*"

And, Ajan began the final invocation to *Brahma* for the ultimate blessing. His voice was just a whisper, gently bringing the presence of the god into the Divine Light.

To the overlord!
You who with furious energy cause sustenance to burst forth for the one that presses and cooks, verily you are reliable. May we, o overlord, be ever dear to you. Having heroic sons, may we address this place of union!
Ohm.

To the One!
Let us today invoke you!
Master of All, inspirer of mind,
To help us at the time of union.
Let him take pleasure in all our invocations,
Bring us blessing, working good to help us in this union!

"*Ohm.*" Marici looked into the flames of the fire and felt the blood of his ancestors flow through him. In this moment, Kasimi was centered around him and he was the center of His Kingdom. The gods had blessed him, and brought forth their desires with hot fire that intensified against his rich brown skin. And his Queen was by his side. "*Ohm.*"

And when the invocation was complete, Ajan began to chant his prayers in classical Kasimian for the union to be bound for all eternity. He begged the ancestors of Marici and Sri for a good and peaceful life—for the reign of King and Queen to be filled with truth. The Grand Priest opened his hands on his knees, and closed his eyes to submit his guidance to the gods. Each word was uttered with precision, as he had memorized these chants on the day Sri was born. It was not with a light heart that he could perform this task. He, like his Queen had showed him, would separate his physical duties with the pain of his breaking heart.

Ajan settled into a rhythm of recitation alongside the steady sound of the sitar that accompanied the slight vocal intonations of his prayers. Bowing his head in on himself, he became the spiritual channel to praise all the ancestors that had intended this union.

Marici could do nothing but stare at the beauty before him, glowing from the glorious yellows of fire. He dare not blink, to ruin the image of Sri. Each prayer that Ajan chanted slipped further and further into the background of his mind as the sight of this woman grew more intense in his eyes. She was everything to him. It was obvious the gods knew this too.

After Ajan completed the long prayers of necessary blessings, the King and Queen rose from their place by the fire to make their personal vows to one another. Ajan slipped back towards the waterfall, to allow the twins to unite without his intervention. He did not turn his back on the couple, and moved with backward steps into the water's cool mist. This part of the union was the promise. Only the man and woman could utter these words to one another, and they had been written by each for the other.

Marici moved across the circle to face his Queen directly. Somehow, the pure white of his costume did not change in color even against the gold blaze of the fire. He spoke simply across the flames, and presented the terms of his bond as a man. He bowed over the fire, and lowered his head before Sri. He stared into his sister's hypnotic black eyes for a moment, before beginning. He exhaled, his breath carrying the fire in beauty's direction, and confessed his sins. "I lower myself before you, Sri, as a man…"

Marici stopped. He had prepared his promises in meditation, and thought he had found the words for the bond. But looking into the face of his young Queen, Marici knew no words that could dignify the surrendering of his heart to this woman. His love for her was pure, and above any that a man could have for a common woman. Marici bowed further, to ask forgiveness for his inadequacy. His voice, now deep in texture, spoke with solid tones. "I give you my protection, honesty and devotion, and the confession that I am less of a King without you. For your purity, and your presence, I will fulfill your every need and your every wish. You will not want for anything. I am lesser than you. Less pure and less worthy. Accept me as your husband and make me better."

Marici straightened his posture without lifting his intent gaze on Sri's eyes—such hypnotic eyes. He awaited the response. Her promise. If only she would say she would try to understand his promise. That would be all he needed.

The Queen looked over the fire with resignation. Her eyes, with a deep red ring around the black, shined brightly with the layer of water that threatened to fall against her pools. Sri could only gaze upon her King with a blend of understanding and surrender. For, he had betrayed her in his words, even now. Because he would not be able to provide her with every wish, and that was done of his own will. She would never look on her brother with the same blind love. Instead, she would practice compassion and unconditional understanding for the man who would be her husband.

Sri bowed her head over the fire, and the diamonds in her crimson folds of silk became warm with the flames. The red of her sari shifted slightly in color with the nearness of fire, settling into a deep blood tone that was alive in the light. She was sacrificing herself, of her own free will, for her people. And yet, her words were still filled with love. Closing her eyes to the heat of the fire, the Queen recited a simple answer:

In the beginning was the Self alone. He was afraid as a man who is all alone may be. Since nothing existed other than this one, what is it that made him afraid? It was the longing for another that did not exist that made him afraid. He longed for a second.

And so, the Self split in two: and from this arose husband and
wife. Accept me as your wife, and become One.

Sri gazed upon her brother with compassion. She would be his
guide, his companion—his family. The King needed her, and the
Queen would understand. She would forgive him forever, and love
him without condition. She would see his flaws, but choose to
love him anyway.

Marici held his hand for Sri to take across the fire, with an open
palm. The flames roared upward on the abrupt movement but
tamed when the King looked down upon them. His eyes, black
with a ring of bright red around the pupils, searched his sister's for
the promise. Sri moved her hand inside Marici's, interlacing her
fingers with his in the tying of the symbolic knot. The delicate
chains of gold that encased each of her refined fingers began to
feel the energy of the fire, and bring the skin of the twins together
to one. The two would circle the fire together, one across from the
other, seven times to represent the seven truths of marriage: life,
character, wealth, joy, health, peace and truth.

One circle...and then two...three...four...

On the fifth circle, Marici slowed down the pace, and tightened
his fingers around the gold in Sri's hand to combine the warmth in
his soul with the energy of the fire. He would soon be a husband
made. *Be saved.*

Five...

On the sixth circle, Sri let her eyes divert to the flames and she
felt her body slowly become a part of the sacrificial fire. She imagined all the details held in the heavy gold on her neck melting like
liquid and pouring off of her skin into the circle—like the waterfall to the smooth rock beneath her feet.

Six...

Ajan invoked the prayer of peace from the gods as the King
and Queen neared the completion of the bond, "*Ohm. Shanti,*

Shanti, Shanti!" The tabla drums began to play faster and the people of Kasimi began to chant with the Grand Priest *"Ohm. Shanti, Shanti, Shanti!"* with more energy as they approached the seventh circle. The union of the King and Queen was almost complete, and the rumbling of drums and prayer in the crowd were filled with anticipation.

The last step of the seventh circle was done. Marici looked at his wife with burning red eyes, and led her by the hand around the fire to his side. He brought his free hand to her emerald bhindi and cast it with the color of his eyes to signify their bond as husband and wife.

And then the union was made a promise, and a sacrifice. The Queen, both beautiful and pure, stood in her finely decorated state before the good people who came to witness the consummation of the third miracle. She had been united with Marici, and married to them. Even as she stood in the finest silks of red, and the luxurious jewels of her position, she was merely a servant. Though she was beautiful and could command the hearts and desire of her people through her very image, she was only their Queen.

Marici stared at the vision of purity—of beauty—that was now bound to him in every way possible. In his mind and heart, he loved her more than any man could love a woman. For he was her god and King, brother and husband, and she was worthy. They had walked the seven rings of marriage together, but that was only a weak symbol of the true bond they shared. Sri was his savior.

"Ohm. Shanti, Shanti, Shanti!"

PART III

I I

After the events of the wedding had calmed in *Vrndavana*, the King would lead his people back through the mountains to the palace built in *Govandhara*. The last King to inhabit this sacred palace was Varuna, and it had been left unoccupied until the third miracle. Just one day's journey south of the Grand Priest's temple, the palace was built in perfect harmony with Kasimi's spiritual center. And yet, Sri had never been allowed to see her future home in all her time at the temple.

Marici took six moons before finding himself at his palace. Against the wishes of Ajan and the elders, Marici went to visit several cities in the Northern and Southern Kingdoms, to meet with leaders and to replace others. Several titles were rearranged during his trip, and the subject of The Isles did come across many a discussion. Those of influence who pledged their gold and property in the name of King Marici would be granted status, and favor in his court. The young King was able to make many a lord see Kasimi his way.

A group of servants were sent ahead with some guards to see to making the palace acceptable for the King's arrival. Sri, who did not want to participate in this political tour, asked her King if she might go with them to oversee details and to get some rest from what had been an exhausting ceremony for her. Marici needed Sri by his side, and got down on one knee to beg her for her presence. After one hour of kissing Sri's hands and crying into her bosom, the Queen decided to stay.

And finally, Marici's caravan approached his palace on the end of the sixth moon. Two servants had gone ahead on faster horses to inform the castle's attendants that the King and Queen would soon come. As the line of horses, both black and white, made a single trail on the ocean's white sand towards the palace, Marici looked towards the castle with the moon reflected in his eyes. With Sri asleep behind him, and her head tucked on his shoulder, he could whisper promises to her that she might not hear. He would confess his sins to his wife. He rested his lips on the crown of Sri's head and whispered:

A man should love his wife, be pure, support his servants, devote himself to the performance of ceremonies in honor of the Ancestors. He should not neglect the five sacrifices which are to be performed with the mantra namah!

Not injuring living beings, truth, not stealing, purity, control of sense and action, giving, restraint, compassion, forbearance are the means of accomplishing the moral duty of all men.

"Oh Sri, help me to be a married man. Help me, my Queen. Help me control my rage, guide me...be my wife."

Sri did not hear these words whispered by her brother, and remained with her head silently placed on his strong shoulder. Marici looked upon the beautiful face of his sister, and sighed—content that she was there. He would have plenty of times in the future to confess to her, and beg her for forgiveness. Finally, the line of horses arrived past the glowing ocean water to the Palace of *Govandhara*, which would be home to the King and Queen.

Marici gently nudged his sister awake with a gentle kissing on her ear.

Somehow, the generations of emptiness that marked the palace, after the death of Varuna, had vanished. It was as if the King were returning home after a short sojourn. It was not the size of the palace that made it fit for a god, but the worship yielded to every bit of marble. To mark the full moon, the palace had been lit with candles in every crevice, and along the many fountains leading towards the estate—like the Grand Priest's temple.

It had been built with perfect marble. The palace was decidedly square along the exterior, and was framed by a marble white fence that paused at the opening side to open to the white sand and ocean. The fence was not a barrier, for it could not prevent an average man from jumping nor did it frame the sprawling gardens. It was a simple reminder that the King's true power was not in his fist, but in his blood.

And then the palace began inside the simple walls. There were three clear layers to the expansive home of flawless white marble, each drawn out by a distinctive character in the windows. The first layer of windows was very symmetrical and utilitarian: one after the other in equal spacing, separated by green marble pillars carved within the wall. The rooms on the first level had specific purposes—from the throne room to the conservatory, and did not require a creative light flow to set a mood that was already predetermined.

Upon the second level, where rooms became more personal and crafted, the windows began to fall in double sets to allow more light inside. In the middle window of the main opening, a balcony came forth from the parlor of the King and Queen—with rails in the shape of outwardly curving rose vines—to present the royal couple for large hails on Varuna's beach.

The third layer of the palace held the personal chambers of the King and Queen, and thus, had few windows. Some curved in semi-circles at the top, while others remained symmetrical and square. Balconies appeared without pattern, as did the inlaid green columns.

But, it was the massive dome of gold that truly made the palace the home of a King. Extending from the four corners of the home towards the sun, the gold cupola began its gently rounding motion until it reached a clear single point after stretching the height of many men. The purest yellow gold of Kasimi had been brought to *Govandhara* to press into each inch. The slaves had worked the hot flames below, melting the gold into its liquid form before handing it off to the artists, who applied the King's honey gingerly with brushes of fine horse-hair. The dome took one hundred moons to complete, and was crowned with an emerald at the top—the one last touch to make this palace above the mortal realm.

"We are home, Sri…" Marici whispered into his sister's ear. "Behold something that does not come close to your beauty…" Marici let his lips kiss the soft bit of flesh at the lobe of Sri's ear. "Wake up and see…"

Sri stirred slightly in her contented sleeping position on Marici's shoulders. As the warm words were muttered in hear ear, the Queen's lids lifted open to behold a vision of magnificence—a palace of Divine Light. "Oh!" she sighed. She gently lifted her chin to look up at the moon and candlelit palace. "Oh Marici, it's—beautiful."

Marici let a hand stray from his reigns to hold Sri's fingers affectionately. "Let us ride forth, my Queen…" He waited to feel Sri's grip around his torso tighten, before coaxing his stallion into a gallop towards his palace's walls. Symbolically, Marici had his white horse run in the ocean's gentle tide while the others in his following rode along the white sand.

The servants of the palace had dressed in festive colors to make it a happy occasion for the King and Queen to enter their home. Hundreds of servants lined the courtyard, and cleared an entrance aisle from the ocean to the palace. The brightest and most exquisite shades of red and blue were displayed before the silvery night ocean, to welcome the King as he would ride forth.

And finally, the stallions and mares rode triumphantly on the beach and into the welcoming line of the palace's servants. Voices and hands were raised to the sky in prayer and cheer that the King and his Queen had arrived peacefully to *Govandhara*. There were no drums in the night. The air was dense with the rhythmic clapping and cheering of many joyful male and female bodies in the sand of Varuna's beach. Colors came alive, as people shifted in their positions to twirl one another in heart felt dance, and to embrace in the coming of their leader. *"Marici, Sri, ya ya! Marici, Sri, ya ya!"*

Marici rode past the worshiping servants with his ceremonial sword high in the air, and his Queen near his heart. The fierce gallop of his white stallion was an angry pace—the King wanted to claim the palace in the night. His eyes, focusing more in red than black, gazed obsessively at the entrance until finally his white beast delivered him to his home. The King petted the animal once, and resheathed his sword. He awaited Sri's grip to loosen around him before dismounting the horse with a quick motion of his strong arms, and agile legs.

Marici looked out onto the line of servants cheering for him and His Queen, and placed his hands on his hips. *It is as it should be.* He let his lips provide a smile for His People, and brought a fist to the air once in a sign of his might. *It is as it must be.* Marici raised his open hands to the sky and turned around so that all of his servants could see his glory. *It is as I want it.*

Marici stopped his gaze on the crowd, and looked up at his Queen. Even in a simple salwar-kameez of purple silk, she was glorious and more beautiful than any jewel of Kasimi. His arms went to reach for his Queen's waist, and Sri effortlessly accepted the aid of her husband to dismount the white stallion. Marici closed his eyes as he felt Sri's touch, and pulled her up into his arms to carry her. Only now could he enter the palace.

~

The Queen's rooms were across from the King's rooms, and separated by a long hallway of black marble. Marici would not enter the bedroom of Sri, so there was no need to place the apartments side by side. Instead, they would be near to one another but with the necessary privacy for brother and sister.

Jabala remained with Sri, in a special room just off of the Queen's bedroom, to be in constant attendance to her lady. Sri had given special instructions to the servants who would prepare her chambers to make sure that Jabala's room was elegant—to befit a loyal friend who had served her with kindness. The Queen was now in a position to express her love for Jabala, to show her what her quiet companionship had meant all these years.

The only difference between Jabala's chamber and Sri's bedroom was size. It was as if the nurse's room was an extension of Sri's own, decorated in the same grand styles. Where windows did not offer the yellow paintings of the sun or the moonlit candles of the sky, rich tapestries of the many gods and their consorts covered the walls and floor. The tapestries were miniature fairytales in themselves, expressing generations of history in one masterpiece. The hand could not help but reach out to touch the seductive history of

Kasimi, with Sri a part of the tale. Inviting, tempting, dreamy pillows were placed in the many crevices of both rooms in the subtle colors of the tapestries. Even the bed was an extension of these rich weavings, rich with silks and blankets in the colors of the weavings—to unite everything in this royal composition.

The stunning focal point of Sri's chamber was the entrance to the balcony, marked with large glass doors. On either side of the windows were solid, yellow-gold statues of voluptuous women in the feminine symbols of wealth and fertility. The goddesses were crafted by the same artists who had composed the palace's dome, and were meant to guard the fertility of the Queen. A layer of the finest, white lace when moved by a gentle breeze, would beckon the Queen out on to her balcony to overlook the royal gardens. Roses of yellow had been woven in and out of the vine-shaped steel, to bring the fragrance of such beautiful flowers to their Queen.

In Sri's room, there was no purposeful furniture since the Queen had a dressing room with her blackwood vanity, and bureau. But in Jabala's room stood a vanity table that was specifically crafted for her. It was carved of white marble, with a smooth surface across the top to place many jewels and bottles of perfume. The holding drawers on either side had been designed with affection, with inlaid designs of grapes and mangoes. Any crevice created by these cravings had been painted with yellow gold. And on top of the vanity, Sri had placed many items of jewelry—some new and some of her own. A stool of the softest purple velvet welcomed Jabala to adorn herself.

At dawn, the nurse threw open the doors and made hasty steps to Sri's bed. The weight of her body could be heard against the lined floor, since each step was directed with the quick pounce of Jabala's body. She threw a few of the pillows to the ground that had hidden the Queen's body from ready touch. "Sri! My

Queen!" Jabala shook the Queen, wanting to wake her and hold her. Jabala managed to coax the woman from her fetal position to look up at her nurse. Jabala took the opening and dove into the girl's arms. "Oh thank you!"

Sri would never enjoy mornings. The hug felt more like an attack on her peace of mind, and the gratitude sounded more like the chirpings of a loud raven before dawn. Sri submitted her arms around Jabala's waist and murmured some sounds—nothing that amounted to language.

Jabala continued on through her tear restrained voice. "Sri, Sri, Sri! Why did you do this for me? Why...oh it is so lovely! I have never seen such beautiful things...the jewelry...oh Sri, you really shouldn't have...you know I don't need such things to stay with you—you don't need to do this." Jabala's mass of brown hair fanned out over Sri as she gripped tighter.

Sri became more fully aware of the situation as Jabala's affection grew stronger around her body. She placed her hands tighter around her trusted friend, and stroked Jabala's hair tenderly. Her voice, still tired from sleep, whispered back, "It has nothing to do with you staying, Jabie...you've been my...you've been there for me forever...and this is just something small I could do. You deserve so much more." Sri brought her torso out of its blanket-swaddled state and embraced Jabala.

Jabala continued to hold Sri for a moment before bringing herself back to her normal state. She pulled herself out of the embrace and put her hands along either side of Sri's warm face. "Well, my Queen..." she mused, "...it is time to prepare you for your first court today...there are many nobles waiting to see you and the King..."

Sri closed her eyes and let a sleepy smile grace her unstained lips. What use was there in protesting? Even as Queen, she was subject to the desires of her King and her court. Her hands began to tug around the blankets, and her body felt the disturbance of the cold morning air. "I suppose, Jabie...I suppose." Sri leaned up on her elbows and let out a loud yawn. Her eyes found the sunlight outside, and the blooming yellow roses around her balcony. "Let's wear the yellow sari this morning, Jabie...no jewels, just the silk..."

Jabala disappeared into the Queen's dressing chamber, and began to find the silks and wraps that her lady had ordered. She called out, playfully, "Eat your bread, Sri and drink your tea. We won't have a weak girl."

Sitting at the edge of her bed, Sri stretched her arms overhead. She inhaled and exhaled, brining fresh air in her circulation. Instead of playing along, Sri just agreed, "No, we won't."

The Queen walked out onto her balcony where tea and bread did await her attention and began to enjoy her morning meal as Jabala made the proper arrangements for her dress. "Jabie...come eat with me? Talk to me?" she called out. Sri poured two cups of tea, and prepared two plates of bread and honey in anticipation of her nurse's acceptance.

Jabala rushed out from the dressing room with a look of shock in her eyes. She peered outside on the balcony, and asked hesitantly, "Sri...you want to be seen eating a morning meal with your nurse?" She paused, and then added the explanation in case the Queen had not realized all the ramifications of such an act. "...now you are in your palace and to eat with me is socially...people may talk?" Jabala smiled apologetically, though she had done nothing wrong.

Sri finished putting honey on her bread, and took a large bite. In between chews, she pointed at the chair next to her and said, "If you don't join me, I'll eat all the bread before you can get any."

Jabala smirked at Sri's stubbornness. She joined her ward, and took a refreshing sip of cha while enjoying the rising sun over the royal gardens. The two women had simple conversation this morning, enjoying each other's company. *It is as it should be.*

"What do you think court will be like, Jabala?" Sri asked, while picking a few crumbs off of her resting gown.

Jabala scraped some of the excess honey off of her bread onto her plate. "Well, Sri...I don't think it will be all that different from the way Ajan held his meetings in the temple. The nobles will come—they will seek your ear—and will want a decision. It is a duty." Jabala took a small bite of her bread and washed it down with some cha.

Sri nodded into her cup of tea, and diverted her gaze to the immaculate blue sky. "And what do you think my role will be at court, Jabie?"

Jabala put her cup down, and turned in her chair to focus on her ward. She realized—Sri was worried about her place in this palace. What exactly would Sri do? Would she be a traditional type of Queen, who simply stood in her jewels and carried babes? Not this reign. Jabala could barely find an answer to give Sri. "I...I don't know, Sri...I think you will define your own role."

"How will I do that, Jabie?" Sri asked, handling her cup of tea idly.

Jabala chuckled and took a few dainty bites of her bread. "I think...if you are defining your role, that my definition would be useless?"

Sri turned her gaze back to Jabala and motioned to herself with an idle hand. "I am asking for your help, Jabie. In defining my role." She narrowed her eyes at Jabala.

Jabala sat back in her chair and brought her tea to her lips for a long sip. "Well, Sri," she said, while inhaling the herbal fumes, "I think what the court sees in the Queen will not be who you are. If you want to be a meaningful Queen, it will be done silently."

Sri thought about this for a moment. Her first impression at court today would be the most important. The nobles would make judgments—on her appropriateness. Word would spread about how the Intended had turned out. Would she be a pleasing Queen for her court? Or, would she object to her life's circumstances by disobeying tradition. She needed to decide what she wanted to do. And, now.

"There is a lot I can do, Jabie." Sri stroked her hands through her raven hair, and combed it back into neat waves. She was growing aware of her femininity, and learning to enjoy it. "But for the masses, I will just be Marici's Queen…" A slow smile came to Sri's lips, as her mind began working its mischief.

Jabala drank down her tea and stood from the table. Her smile shared her Queen's mischief, and her eyes had a mature twinkle in them. "Shall we see to your morning dress?"

Sri stood with an overly precise sense of etiquette from her position by the balcony. Feigning the voice of an old noble lady, Sri played, "Yes, we shall see to it. Please, lay my things out and I will be with you in but a few moments." Her mischievous smile grew wider, and Sri plucked a rose from one of the balcony's garlands.

Jabala dipped into a perfect curtsey. "Yes, Your Highness."

~

Most of Kasimi's influential nobles had journeyed to the palace in *Govandhara* for the first court of King Marici and Queen Sri. The early hours of the morning kept the servants busy in tending to the arriving people, placing horses in stables and showing honored guests to their quarters. Marici had ordered that music, fruit and wine would accompany the arrival of his court. He wanted to create a feeling of welcome at *Govandhara*.

The underlying shadow of this court was The Isles. No ambassadors from Vishal's kingdom had come for this event, and several letters of formal secession had been sent to Marici. The nobles who were invited to keep court with the King were those who had pledged their loyalty and gold in this pursuit. The others—had been banished quietly to The Isles. This would be the topic of discussion over the next few days.

The King had already made up his mind about The Isles. While he would allow an open hearing for discussion and debate, Marici did not intend to break down from his position. No one knew about the assassination attempt on his life. No one needed to know. The only thing his nobles needed to understand was what they would do after his decision was rendered and made law.

The nobles had gathered in the central room of the palace, underneath the magnificence of the gold dome. The splendor of marble—both flawless white and rich green. The room screamed out for conspiracy. Little alcoves meandered in and out of the main meeting space, where secret words could be exchanged before presenting a final message to the King.

Unfortunately, the intricate work of the floor could not be seen over the sea of nobles standing on foot, or lounging on pillows and divans before the throne. A mosaic of tiles in the image of Varuna and Sona had been painstakingly made upon the deaths of the King and Queen. Birds that flew to the top of the gold dome would be able to see their sea power and his consort staring back.

Candles of vanilla—the Queen's favorite—had been lit around the domed room, to bring out the warm glow of gold against fire. Musicians and servants continued to entertain the masses until King Marici and Queen Sri finally made their entrance to hold court.

When the King and Queen entered, the tabla played to beat their rhythm into the hall. The nobles dropped to one knee and bowed their heads to the ground in humility of their King. As Marici and Sri walked into the chamber, arm in arm, some did divert their eyes upward to gain a quick view of the leaders that they had only seen in paintings and never in the flesh. Until now.

"You may continue, my good people..." Marici said as he reached his dais in the front of the room. The King was clad in a black silk pajama suit, with a large emerald medallion at his heart. His black hair was worn loose and free about his shoulders, despite his servant's desire to cut it into neat angles. Meticulously placed on his head, however, was a thin circlet of gold with one emerald in the center to signify him as the supreme ruler and god of Kasimi.

Sri was dressed in a fashion to complement Marici—a simple yellow sari folded neatly around her still developing curves. To match her twin, she wore her black hair unfettered, down her back and shoulders with petals of yellow rose dispersed between the rampant curls. Instead of a crown, Sri wore an emerald stone betwixt her brows drawn back into her raven hair with fragile gold chains.

Two opulent pillows of cobalt sat upon drapings of multicolored silks on the dais. Marici helped his smiling wife to her place, before settling beside her. The court shuffled to regain their previous positions before kneeling to the King and Queen.

Marici accepted a glass of mango presse from a servant, while Sri politely declined with a gracious nodding of her head. He raised his glass to His People and took a refreshing sip of the pulpy liquid while murmuring, "To Kasimi!" before the assembly.

The mixed voices in the crowd—mostly male but some distinctly female—responded back in kind. "*Ohm...*" while bowing their heads.

Marici rested a hand affectionately on the small of Sri's back to allow her more comfort on her pillow. She sat with the dignity of a Queen, and the subservience of a wife. Her eyes focused on Marici, seemingly entranced with every word that he uttered. The King nodded to his advisors: Ajan, Sudha and Devyn, who sat just to the left of the dais, before opening his court.

Marici raised his hand in the air to bring eloquence to his mind, and then gazed out upon his loyal servants. "Kasimi. Our home. It is not One anymore, my good people."

Marici brought his hand down to rest by his side and continued. "For the past six moons, we have received word from The Isles that they wish to secede from Kasimi. They have established their own kingdom, separate from us. It was a dark day when the Vishal, the Priest from The Isles—assaulted my caravan—and rode off with his wishes of terror on Kasimi. And now his father has named himself King with Vishal as Prince Regent...of The Isles...Our Isles...My Isles!"

Marici paused, and looked to his sister for grounding. His free hand had balled into a fist and his jaw had tensed to add a rough edge to the proclamation of "My Isles." If he would be able to continue, he would need his sister's support and purity. He slipped his hand from her back to hold her slender fingers, and continued with her strength as part of his own.

"My lords, I need you to speak your minds this day, to tell me what is on your hearts and lips. We will act, and we will bring The Isles back to Kasimi. The question is—how? I refuse to acknowledge the secession. It is the ultimate act of sin against *Brahma*. For, *Brahma* teaches us that we are all One. We are One kingdom, with many parts...but one together in those parts. To deny this...to deny the One...is treason. I cannot, as King of Kasimi, and direct descendant of the gods, acknowledge such a thing!"

Marici pulled his hand from Sri's grasp and motioned towards the assembled nobles. "Please, my ears are yours."

There was silence across the assembly. No one wanted to speak after the King. No one wanted to lose favor with him. He was a divinity, and to raise one's voice either in harmony or discord, may curse the soul for the next life. At least, that is what most Kasimians thought. Most of the nobles just nodded their heads in understanding and agreement.

An older woman from the Northern Kingdom, Lady Bali, stood from her place on the divan near the Queen. She was held as an equal, and revered among the Kasimians, as a wise and virtuous woman. Her husband had been killed by the rebels during civil unrest, and she had ruled the lands in his name since then. It was said that even before his death, she was the brilliant mind behind the wealth in her lands. And so she stood with confidence, in her heavy cobalt blue sari, and turned to face the King.

Her face was never beautiful, but elegant in the way her refined and sharp features rested so well on her light brown skin. Fine lines formed by years of true joy and pain echoed around her light blue eyes and the corners of her dark red lips. Bali held an ageless wisdom in her expression, seen in the slightest of movements.

"Your Majesties..." Bali began, while dipping her head decidedly before both Marici and Sri. "I wish for nothing more than Kasimi to be one again. But it seems that we should go about this effort with peaceful means. It is my understanding that we have not even tried to speak with the Prince Regent. And thus, should we even continue further without having accomplished this?"

Marici's mouth dropped slightly in disbelief. A woman, regardless of her age or position, should not speak this boldly. But, she was Lady Bali, and so he allowed her a few moments of the court's time. When she was done, Marici answered in an overly polite tone.

"Lady Bali of the North, you have served the Kingdom well, and there is much wisdom to your words. But, there are many things that you do not understand. The Prince Regent, as he calls himself—Vishal as I call him—is beyond diplomatic negotiations. I do not see any other option besides action, do you?"

Lady Bali took a few steps forward to more clearly address the King. Her gaze was momentarily distracted by Ajan's presence and she nodded respectfully in his direction. She knew Ajan from her time spent at Janaka's palace over the years—and had seen the Grand Priest as a baby and a warrior. "Your Highness, I sense the energy of a youth in your crown. I do honor you, my King. But I must warn you, that youth can often bring a kingdom to a most unnecessary peril. Please, I beg of you Your Highness—if act you must, do it with peace in mind."

Marici gritted his teeth and pressed down on his lower lip. "Woman, be silent!" Marici said in a definitive tone. He did not yell, but he was resolute in his command. "Peace...Lady Bali...is not on the mind of our Vishal. I will not beg The Isles to return to what is and always will be, a part of Kasimi. They will submit or they will die."

The nobles went silent. Not everyone wanted a war. The people from the Southern Kingdom shifted slightly in their spots—a sea of swaying green tunics and saris among the blues and reds of the court. The notion of war had finally been uttered. It was no secret that the South had close ties to The Isles due to many marriages between the families. Bloodshed was not a favorable solution.

Sri could see the tension in her husband's face, and the subtle pain evident in the eyes of the women who thought of losing their sons and husbands. She moved one of her jeweled hands to Marici's and squeezed through his gripped fist to release as much of the anger as she could. She leaned in to his ear, a veil of black hair shading her face as she spoke private words to him.

"Marici, be calm. Whatever your desires are for The Isles, you must remember that everyone is here for you—to honor you and to find a solution with you. What…" She paused and placed chaste kiss on her brother's cheek, masked by her curtain of raven hair. "What you should do now is let Lady Bali continue with her plan, and then see if perhaps it is feasible. Do not strike down a lady that holds tremendous weight with your court. If you want The Isles, you must look for their support. *Acha*, Marici?"

Marici listened to his sister's words—truly listened—and was visibly calmed by her wisdom. He nodded a few times, and then affectionately straightened the emerald on his Queen's head. "*Acha*, Sri…" he muttered to his Queen before looking out at his court once more.

With a gracious gesture of his hand, and a clear change of his tone, Marici pointed to Lady Bali. "My fear, Lady Bali, is that if we choose to pursue peace—The Isles will view us as weak. Dissenters in the future may believe that we are weak, and fol-low." Marici raised his chin slightly and rolled his hand in the elderwoman's direction. "Speak what solution you may offer."

Still, Marici had no real intention of listening to the woman.

Lady Bali straightened out the cobalt of her sari, and continued forward to the dais of the King and Queen. Despite her age, the woman moved with the grace of her younger years—an elegance that caught Sri's eye. The woman kneeled at the marble steps of the platform and spoke her mind with a booming voice, unbroken by the pride of a youthful King.

"The Isles are our blood, my King. And as *Brahma* has taught us that we are One. To take violent action against The Isles is to attack part of the One, part of us. And so, I implore you to invite the leaders of the secession movement to come forth and answer for their sins in a peaceful setting. That is my heart and mind on this matter, my King."

Marici directed his eyes on the older woman. Despite his Queen's words of calm, rage was beginning to build in him again.

He did not tighten his body, and show any obvious tension to the masses. However, his black eyes began to cloud with red once more as the rings around the edges closed further and further in on his eyes.

In a low, rumbling tone—that held a chilling calm—Marici asked, "And what if I had evidence that the rebels who killed your husband, Lady Bali, were from The Isles? What if I had evidence, Lady Bali, that the civil unrest that raped the Northern Kingdom was caused by The Isles?"

Such an accusation, without hesitation from the King, startled the court. The noblemen blinked in disbelief towards the dais. Some who had been standing found walls to lean against, or pillows to share. The women began to nervously toy jewelry at their collarbones, and cling to their husbands for reassurance. People searched for the eyes of their friends to find reactions—impressions—of such news.

Lady Bali, however, did not break her confident position before her King. The accusation did make her blink. The thought of her dead husband did not bring water over her crystal blue pools. She was not the type of woman who cried in public. Her mood only mellowed further against the rage of a youthful King. "And if they did? I would not fault The Isles with the blood of my Northern kinsmen, but the family who was behind it. There is no question that they should be punished with the Might of your crown for their crimes. But action—as you speak it today—is against an entire Kingdom, your Majesty. Innocent people will pay for the actions of one family."

The King's eyes, now fully red, looked upon the graceful noblewoman with resigned contempt. Marici held his Queen's hand in his, and dismissed the woman from the dais. "The ruling family of any Kingdom takes responsibility for their crimes and understands that when they act, they do it in the name of their land.

Consequences…are for the people, not just the man." Marici waved his hand at the kneeling woman, excusing her counsel.

Lady Bali dipped her head once, and then rose. She paused to look at the Queen and offer the woman a small smile—maternal and sympathetic. The elderly noble pivoted, and walked back to her original position among many important men wearing cobalt blue.

Would anyone else speak after Marici had made his mind clear? It seemed now that the only people—men—who should offer counsel are those well versed in war. It would also be a Northerner since the South would be hesitant to offer advice that may mar their kin across the sea. And so, Ajan's mentor in battle, Lord Ashok of the North spoke next.

Raising his cane in the air, Ashok announced himself to Marici with an arrogant and assured tone. Ashok, like Ajan, was a powerfully built man. He was a head taller than most Kasimian men, and large everywhere in his body. He was not heavy set—just massive—from years of treacherous journeys and hard battles. He wore a cobalt blue tunic, and white pajama pants that fit tightly around his largely muscled legs, to make him an imposing and proper noble figure of the Northern Kingdom. Everything about him was typical of the North from his cerulean blue eyes to his chiseled features set in mocha marble. Everything, except his massive body.

The warrior had lost the better use of his left leg during the civil uprising, and used a plain wooden cane to aid his steps. This humble pole seemed farcical alongside the long sword and dagger that Ashok still wore at his hip. But, it was his most powerful tool now. Ashok held his age well against the youthful King. His stark white hair was worn loose and long about his shoulders, like Marici's. He too had a touch of rebellious youth in his soul, and that may work well with this new King.

"Your Majesty!" Ashok proclaimed, while shaking his cane in the air to attract attention. "If Your Highness wishes to take action, then action he will take. And if I may, Your Excellency, I have several ideas that will help you in your quest!"

Ajan smirked to himself. Ashok would never change. He would always seek the leader and ingratiate himself in his favor, and be successful for it. Ashok had taught Ajan everything—from how to lift a sword with grace to how to win a battle. Ashok had also taught Ajan ruthlessness, and to act without passion on the battle-field. The Grand Priest listened to the older warrior with a mixture of curiosity and concern.

Marici's red eyes looked with great interest upon Ashok, and the boy wholeheartedly granted, "Continue, please, continue!"

Sri looked straight at Ajan. Her mentor would be able to see the disquiet in her black eyes. She did not like the way the way Marici was handling this. She was confused—The Isles and the Northern unrest—what did they have in common? Inside, she was growing frustrated at her own ignorance and lack of authority in the court. Ajan did meet her gaze, but only nodded in her direction in respect. He could not be seen staring at the Queen.

Ashok reached the dais, but did not kneel due to his injury. Instead he bowed deeply at the waist, with his eyes straying quite obviously to the lovely face of his Queen, before returning full attention to the King. "Your Majesty," he said in a softer tone, "I have ships and men who have been training in the mountains of the Northern Kingdom that are ready to fight. They are versed in swords and strategy. They are good strong men, who wear the blood of their families on their backs." Ashok turned to face the court, his voice filled with the anger of his rising army. "All these men had mothers and fathers murdered by the rebels. The Isles as our King says. And they will show no mercy in returning these wayward people to their proper ruler!"

Marici honed in on the key words on Ashok's speech. *Northern Kingdom. Blood of their families. No mercy!* Marici grinned at Ashok and nodded approvingly at him. "Lord Ashok, you have served your King well with this knowledge. You shall stay with me at the palace, and we shall discuss a potential attack. I place the responsibility of gathering men and swords in your capable hands, my old warrior."

The King motioned to Ajan with an open palm. "Perhaps you and Ajan may work together on this? It will be a reunion of the most fierce and victorious heroes our Kingdom has known." Marici smiled from Ashok to Ajan, his red eyes beaming at how his plan would now unfold.

Ajan did not smile. His blue eyes clouded over with the nightmares of war once again, and the demoness that would forever haunt him. He had not touched a sword in the name of war in over sixteen years, and in that time he had changed. He had raised the Intended, and had become a spiritual figure to his people. To ask the Grand Priest to reclaim a post as a warrior would destroy him. Though his distress would not be apparent to the strangers of the court, his ward would be able to see the nightmares behind his blue eyes. Sri noted his gaze and nodded once in recognition, for she could not be seen looking at another man for too long.

"I am glad to know that the beginning of my warrior troupe is in progress, with such a competent set of men to lead me in strategy." Marici's voice was filled with newfound confidence. Ashok and Ajan, as a team, could lead him into victory in any battle. "And this brings us to the question of when we shall begin?"

And with this, Marici had made his impression on the Court. He was an unwavering, confident King who was comfortable with his power. He would be feared. If there were dissension or discontent from his people, it would not be tolerated. He angered quickly— but it was not the rage of a weak man—evident and obvious, and easily tamed. It was the passion of a calculating leader. The madness went in extreme waves, with comfortable states in between. And this King held the power of the sky in his soul.

The court resigned themselves to this impression. If he wanted war, it would be so. Some nobles stared in awe at the strong leader, amazed at the strength they saw before them. There were mutterings of *Ohm* underneath the breaths of many people, in thanks to *Brahma* for providing the people with this King. They had been blessed. Others stared in fear at the King. His word was law. Blood would shed from their flesh at His Will.

The question of when. This caused more uneasiness in the court. The blending of blues and greens in the court, moved to distinct clusters of the colors. For, Kings could talk about their might, and try to enforce it in court with words. But Marici wanted to know when. This King would act, and even the blood of his own people would not stop him.

"When?" Marici asked his court with red eyes and raised brows. "When?"

Silence. The court did not know how to answer this. An awkward silence vibrating the tension, fear and angst of the nobles.

"When!" Marici commanded. His red eyes glared out on the masses of royals who had assembled. His youthful rage was beginning to rise once again.

Sri leaned in and gave Marici a kiss on the cheek. She too had made an impression at court today. A gentle Queen with yellow rose petals in her hair. There was not a trace of challenge in her eyes, though her heart ached to speak her mind. She was simply the jewel by Marici's side—the calm of a woman matched against the rage of youth. She had power in her spirit, though no one could see it yet.

A faceless noble called out from his position amongst the court. "As soon as possible, King Marici!" Though his face was not visible—it was clear that the young man's voice was coming from the group of cobalts. A Northerner. "As soon as possible!"

Matching the Northerner, was a young man who spoke from the back corner of the room in a section heavily flooded with green silks. "Why so rushed? Let The Isles respond to the judgment of the King!"

Disagreement over the calls of time began in private murmurs and raised voices of objection. Men with louder and stronger voices could be heard alongside the higher intonations of protesting noblewomen. It was a clear divide. The North wanted blood now. The idea that The Isles were responsible for their civil unrest inspired anger. The South wanted patience.

Marici stopped the growing chaos of his court by raising his hands in the air and calling forth a well supported, "Silence good people!" His eyes flicked across the crowd in warning.

Immediately the nobles quieted. Marici commanded that much presence, already with his court. He brought his hands down to his knees, and looked at his Queen for grounding before addressing his nobles once more. "It is obvious that we will all need to think about this in greater detail. Perhaps Lord Ashok and The Grand Priest will be able to recess and discuss this issue, eh? But, I will make myself clear—I want this done soon."

Marici cleared his throat, a rattling of mucus against strong vocal chords, and changed the topic. "Until now, I will recess to speak to my Queen regarding this incident. Until we gather in court again, please, my people, be my guests and wander the palace to make joy."

The King motioned to his advisors to follow him. Marici stood, and then turned to help his Queen rise beside him. He took a moment to appreciate her quiet and loyal presence at his side, playing with a few of the rose petals in her hair. The King and

Queen went arm in arm off the dais, and towards the parlour for more private conversation.

~

"Brother, I think you were too quick to dismiss the counsel of Lady Bali...she has seen many wars in this land...survived the civil uprising in the Northern Kingdom...and prospered all that time. She is wise. I real..."

"Silence, Sri..." Marici commanded gently.

He was lounging on an emerald green divan in the parlour. It was one of the only pieces of furniture in the room. Marici did not like the clutter of tapestries and seats that had clouded his space and had ordered the cleaning of the room. All that remained were a few chairs and pillows scattered randomly about the white marble floor. The walls were bare save one grand portrait in oiled paints of Varuna and his consort. The last worthy King. Marici intended to have he and Sri sit for a mural for this room once a suitable artist could be found. The King had not found ornaments grand enough for this parlour—and preferred it bare than decorated in mediocrity.

"Silence, Sri..." Marici commanded gently. "You do not understand war the way I do. You grew up sheltered...you grew up removed from politics. I appreciate your counsel, Wife...but on this, you must realize you are blind."

Sri moved a chair to be seated directly in front of Marici, blocking his view of the fire with her body. She sat quickly, and immediately felt the heat of the flames pressing against her yellow sari and raven hair, alongside the beams of sunlight that came in through the balcony windows. She did not understand the need for fire during the afternoon, but it had been commanded by Marici.

"Marici. I know I am not versed in the way of politics. But, I am versed in the ways of peace. More so than you. It was my life's teaching, Marici. And. I sense that The Isles do what they do not out of direct defiance to Kasimi, but some greater misunderstanding." Sri motioned broadly with her arms to reinforce her next point. "Lady Bali can help us discover the truth. She has tremendous re…"

Marici cut Sri's words off with a direct and harsh. "No." He also motioned broadly with his arms before resting his hands warningly on Sri's knees. "My decision is final, Sri. Do not make me angry."

Sri closed her eyes and sighed under her breath. He was the King, and she could not argue with him and change his mind. His words and decisions would be final. It was not her way to become angry and use loud sounds to reinforce her beliefs. She would resort to other methods to do what she knew was for the good of Kasimi. Opening her black pools to look at Marici, Sri asked, "What do you intend to do now?"

"Ajan and Ashok are the two most powerful and brilliant warrior minds we have. I am certain the two will devise a plan quickly so that we may fix this once and for all…" Marici moved one hand from Sri's knee to hold hers, as an apologetic gesture for his scolding.

Sri simply nodded, not offering her opinion on the matter. She knew that Ajan would not want to reclaim his role as a warrior, or be any part of the fighting of war. The details, she did not know. But he had mentioned a nightmare, a long time ago. His devotion and energy was meant now for the gods and—for her. "I meant, when do you think you will go there, Marici?"

"I will speak with my two advisors tonight. If the plan is sound, I will send my men there at dawn. It must be that quick…it must be immediate. I will not tolerate disobedience in my people." Marici withdrew his touch on Sri's person and then stood from the divan to pace on the pristine white floor. "I may go with the men..." Marici said casually. "To make sure everything is perfect."

Sri stood immediately on hearing these words. She went and placed a firm hand on her twin's shoulder. "This, I will protest, Marici. You cannot go to The Isles, in the name of war. You may be hurt—killed. The people need you alive. Marici. No."

The King rested his hand on Sri's softer one, and leaned his cheek on her wrist. Though his gesture was tender, his voice remained strong and resolute in this wish. "Only I can see that this is done right. I will not die. I am a god and a King."

Sri shirked her brother's affection from her fingers and circled around him while claiming both her hands in a clasped plea under her chin. "Being a god does not preclude you from death while you are in mortal form, Marici. Mortal flesh is weak....insignificant. Your power, while in this realm, is ruled by the limitations of man."

Marici's red ringed eyes began to be claimed by red on Sri's challenge. How quickly the boy could change from affection to anger, even with his sister. How he could seemingly use his pure love for Sri in the most sinful ways. In a gentle voice, Marici retorted. "No, Sri. You must understand. I am the powerful one. I am a god. My flesh is subject to my demands—as are you. I will go to The Isles to oversee my men, and you will be the sovereign in my place."

"Send me, Marici. You trust me, I know you do. If you must, send me to The Isles!" Sri unclasped her hands and reached to draw her brothers red eyes to gaze upon her. "You are mortal, Marici. If you must see the battle, let me be your eyes...stay safe in *Govandhara*."

Marici's eyes widened at his sister's selfless loyalty. His red eyes began to cool to a clear brown, the anger dissipating through his form as affection for Sri overwhelmed him. "You...you would do that?" Marici brought Sri to him in a tight embrace. "Would you really risk yourself like that—for me?"

"Of course, brother." Sri embraced Marici and rested the emerald of her forehead into his shoulder.

"I cannot let you do that...but...I will think about whether I should go or not. Will that be all right...for me to think about it?" Marici tightened his arms around Sri's back.

"Of course, brother." Sri responded again.

The crowd of nobles in the front of the palace on Varuna's beach began to chant for the vision of their King and Queen. The twins were supposed to hail the court from the balcony moments ago, and were late. The voices had grown from a rustling stir of impatient cries to a unified plea for Marici and Sri. And so, the embracing twins went hand in hand onto the terrace to greet their people. No one would know of the division Sri felt at this moment in time.

~

As directed, Ajan and Ashok met to discuss their ideas for the attack of The Isles. As directed. The two men walked side by side, barefoot on the sand of Varuna's beach. Their discussion would be private if it looked like the two were enjoying a reunion rather than a strategic discussion. Idle laughter and smiles were exchanged— some by force and some brought on by the interlacing of memories—as the two men became master and apprentice once more.

Ajan did not want to return to this role. He has been a warrior, a good warrior. He had led his people to victory many times. When he announced his retirement to the North, and his intention to serve the gods by religion rather than war, it was met with contention. Some people saw him as a coward, by leaving the life that best suited his talents. Some members of his family threatened to disown him, and distance him from their circles. Some people saw him as a martyr, giving up glory for something more humble. It was only modest for a while. Until he rose to power as the Grand Priest. His new life suited him. He did not want to turn back.

Ashok relished this moment. Slightly taller than Ajan, he fit the role of mentor with pride. Looking down at his younger apprentice, he smiled and laughed easily. Ashok had been bred from warriors. Every man in his family had been a brilliant fighter, and had served the Northern Kingdom in battle. His ancestors had been selected to be explorers with Varuna, and warriors with Osra. Ashok's ability was well revered throughout Kasimi. When he found Ajan as a boy, he felt kinship with the young one. Here was a promising warrior, cut of the same cloth as he. Ajan was strong, powerful, graceful and most importantly, cunning. Ashok taught Ajan everything he could. He had no sons to mentor.

Ashok walked less heavily on his cane while strolling next to Ajan. His aging eyes held a youthful twinkle and his voice more of a gentle air than an authoritative one. "I knew we'd be together again, Ajan. Two warriors united for the Kingdom. Things are not the same without you in battle!"

Ajan nodded quietly, while staying a few paces on the sand towards the water. It was that part in the late afternoon that one had to enjoy before it disappeared into evening. And the ocean seemed to know this too, practicing high waves and roars just one more time for the nearly setting sun. Ajan had always found peace by Varuna, and searched him now for an answer. "It is good to see you again, master." Ajan spoke with precision. He purposefully did not comment on the other parts of Ashok's statements.

"The Queen is a beauty. I am shocked you could create something so gentle given what I remember of you, Ajan." Ashok laughed sloppily, his voice raising up and down while he made heavy footprints in the sand. To bring the insult to a close, the lord pushed his cane in the Grand Priest's bottom. "Such a beauty!" he added.

"I did nothing but teach. She's beautiful by birth and blood." Ajan answered dryly. His responses were distant, and he refused to become involved in this back and forth bantering and joking. In rhythm to his mental distance, Ajan wandered further in the water and the white of his breeches dampened against his skin.

Ashok sighed slowly under his breath. He navigated his own path by the water, but only so that his toes got wet from the stained sand. He could not go in the water with his wooden cane. After a silence, Ashok changed the subject to something away from battle. "So, how does this work? Sri is the twin and wife?" The warrior walked slowly, dragging his toes through the cool surface.

Ajan turned his head to look at the man's expression once. It was enough to catch the slight sorrow in his old master's eyes. It was not Ashok that distanced him, it was the prospect of war. In a more engaging tone, Ajan began to explain the situation of Sri and Marici in the most simple words possible. "It is a symbolic marriage. Marici wanted Sri to be His Queen. She was raised to be— and of divine blood. But, they are only companions, not...lovers."

Ashok raised his refined white eyebrows up over confused eyes. "I never understood royals. So be it. If the King wants to marry his sister, who am I to say otherwise." The warrior walked closer to Ajan, his feet and white pajama pants grazing the edge of the water. Filling awkward pauses, he repeated, "She is beautiful."

"Indeed." Ajan responded tersely. He continued to walk forward, his pace becoming too fast for Ashok to comfortably handle.

"*Acha...*" Ashok said, again trying to fill in the space of conversation held by an unwelcoming partner.

Ajan verbalized some of his own tension in a direct question to Ashok. "So what made you speak up today in court, Old Man?" The priest's steps began to slow, and angle in towards the sand.

"Loyalty. A need to serve my King...boredom..." Ashok answered simply. He began to use his cane more readily now with each step, digging it well into the sand with each full stride.

Ajan stopped, and turned around in the ocean to look at Ashok, swooshing the blue water in a semi-circle. He was about to say something. He was about to state Ashok's real reason for wanting to pursue this campaign—to lead it and win it. But he did not. It was good that he was not facing the lord, or his words would have spilled too easily. The time of movement had saved him from ruining a relationship that had carried him through his youth. Instead, Ajan smiled softly and said, "I'm glad to see you again, Ashok."

Ashok stopped, feeling the building and waning of energy in Ajan. He could read the cerulean gaze of Ajan as he could read his own. The slightest gesture in his apprentice, even if in passing, would be noticed. But, Ashok would not comment. Whatever it was in Ajan that seemed strange, had passed. It was not his place to question him. He nodded, humbly accepting the words of affection. "I'll be here awhile now, Ajan. We can make it like old times, *acha*?"

"Absolutely, Ashok. Absolutely." Ajan reclaimed his strolling pace, and walked closer to Ashok. And then the topic that was inevitable. "So...The Isles..."

Ashok nodded deeply again. His voice became rough—authoritarian—calculating. "The Isles." His wooden walking stick was forced more powerfully into the sand while his feet pounded the ground. "The Isles. I don't need to think much about it. I know what I want done..."

Ajan sang the part of the skeptical warrior. "It is not what you want done. It's to find a way to achieve victory in the style of the King. He wants something quick and efficient. Not one of your...shows..."

"Nonsense! He wants blood just as any Northerner does. His family was killed by those bastards, didn't you hear him? He wants a show all right. I have the men, the swords...The King has horses and gold. It is simple. We bring in the power of *Govandhara* bought with its men and gold. We kill everything in our way. We win. That is what the King wants." Ashok kicked up the sand with his toes, his strides becoming march like.

"Blood for blood's sake?" Ajan shook his head. "I will have no part of that, Ashok. I am Kasimi's Grand Priest. I cannot condone massacres anymore."

Quickly, Ashok retorted. "You used to do them. You used to kill, and take pleasure in victory. Don't tell me you don't crave blood anymore, Ajan. You are a Northerner too."

Ajan would not continue this conversation. He rose above this scene to realize that Ashok simply wanted things to be the way they had been. Before Ashok had grown old and lost the ability to wield a sword with both legs running. Calmly, Ajan spoke his piece. "I will help you with a rational plan that will bring Marici to victory. But, we will use minimal men and horses. This isn't about blood. This is about defeating Vishal. We are not out to destroy a part of Kasimi."

"Then we disagree." Ashok said, shrugging his strong shoulders. "But that does not mean we cannot present two plans to the King. Mine and your more...spiritually conservative one."

"My plan is to bring Vishal and his family down, quietly. Your plan is to create blood in The Isles." Ajan conceded. "We can present both to His Majesty, and see which he desires. That would be acceptable I think."

"Good." Ashok approved, leaving the topic of battle behind. Things were not fine. Ashok would have liked for Ajan to scheme with him on the grand show. He could have used his brilliant apprentice's insight in designing this battle. The lord relaxed his pace, releasing his anger into the lapping ocean. He would just walk beside his old friend for now.

The two men walked side by side in silence for a little while longer. Ajan had to step back onto the sand as the water temperature got colder with the sun's strength diminishing in late afternoon. They let the gentle laughter of the nobles at court be their background noise, while trying to enjoy an awkward reunion. Occasionally, Ashok would slip in an idle comment to fill time and space. "You really did a good job with her, Ajan. She is beautiful."

~

Lady Bali had changed into a looser set of silks for an afternoon ride along the water. Her equestrian ability, and her unusual skill with a sword, were the centerpiece for many rumors and stories. In any other woman, this kind of display would be frowned upon. But in Lady Bali—it was hailed as the mystery of the goddesses that a woman could carry herself with the power of a man and the grace of Sona herself.

Lady Bali looked like a true noblewoman on her black mare. Her silver hair, proudly streaked with raven, flowed in straight folds down to her waist. Her salwar-kameez of silver and white silk was brilliant against the dark hair of her horse. In her clear blue eyes touched with grey, a quiet storm was growing...

"*Acha!*" Lady Bali proclaimed as she leaned forward on her mare, coaxing it into an athletic run. She was fit despite her age and gender, and was outracing her gentleman companion.

"*Acha!*" her companion bellowed breathlessly on his more grand white stallion. Of course, he was dressed more elaborately than the Lady in fine white silks and tremendously heavy jewels. He wore a cap of white tiger fur over his head, to emphasize his status. But, the finest tailoring and gold could not hide his mediocre equestrian skills. "*Acha!* Wait up!"

"You old man!" Bali laughed, as her hair flowed behind her and her mare carried her with a winner's pace down Varuna's beach. "You've never beat me, and you never will!" Bali laughed loudly, spreading her mirth to the nobles who cheered her on in the race that had begun.

"I surrender to your beauty, Lady Bali! I could never win with a woman so fair..." the companion belted as his horse struggled under his weight. The prints of the stallion were much deeper in the sand than those of Bali's mare. "Have mercy!"

"*Acha!*" Bali screamed in strong, alto tones. The lady leaned forward, her thighs poised around her mare and as she led the horse for the few final paces on the sand. She looked victorious with her hair whipping behind in her own created wind, and her long sword at her hip. The Lady brought her weapon forward above the black mare's head and signaled her victory. Random clapping and cheering resulted from her gesture, hailing Bali as the Lady of War.

The companion trotted his horse near Bali's place, building a path by the tide. "You still have it, Bali. You're still so beautiful when you ride." whispered the man, when his stallion latched on to the noblewoman's mare. The man let his horse press up against the black mare and discretely put a hand from his side on the woman's resheathed sword. He whispered again, "You always did know how to ride..."

Bali closed her eyes and sighed at the sweet words of her male companion. "I always won our races. But you could always ride better than me...Jankie dear..." Bali took the hand that rubbed on her sword and lifted it for just a moment to her breast. "Isn't that what you meant to reach for?" Then, she slapped the man's hand and returned it to his side. "Shame on you!" she laughed, playfully.

Janaka and Bali rode their horses side by side, taking on a slowed pace to enjoy the last bit of the afternoon. The two people were old friends. No matter how much time had passed, the two could pick up conversation easily, as if the friendship had just frozen until they could meet again. Janaka had not seen Bali in more moons than he could count. Her husband was still alive when she last visited him in *Mithila*. That he remembered. And now he was dead.

Noticing Ajan and Ashok in the distance, Bali commented while keeping her blue eyes on the pair, "The last time I saw Ajan, he was leaving a warrior's life...from the looks of it...he has returned to those ways, *Acha* Janaka? What does The Uncle think of this?"

Janaka gave a small wave to Ajan off in the distance, and then turned on his stallion to answer his Lady. "Hmm. I hadn't thought that it was something that needed commentary. Why do you ask, Bali?"

"It seems that Ajan is a priest not a warrior. And Ashok—I know Ashok well, as do you. He is a warrior through and through. I am uncertain about Ajan working with him again." Bali rolled her eyes and craned her neck to look up at the sky. "I am uncertain about this escapade! He is a young and most inexperienced leader, Janaka."

"Shhh! Bali." Janaka looked quickly around him to ensure that ears were not close by. "Shhh! What you've just said is treason. I know what you are thinking, and what you have said. But don't speak directly in the open, Bali. You know better." Janaka softened his scolding with, "*Acha*?"

"*Acha.*" Bali agreed. She turned her head to the left and right to see if ears were falling upon her words as well. "I hope the youth will think on his decision, and let not his anger rule his actions. It will inevitably be his d...will not be good for him. I will pray to Varuna for Him." Bali threw her silver hair forward, creating a mask for her lips. "It will lead to his d..."

Janaka straightened up on his horse, and with quick motion, cut Lady Bali's words off with a lingering kiss. He brought a finely jeweled hand to stroke her still smooth skin, and whispered softly to her. "You will forgive me for the kiss later, Bali..." He then darted his eyes towards the sand to a young, Southern nobleman who was casually walking close to where their horses met in the water. "Don't speak words of treason with Southerners at bay, Bali. I don't want to lose another beauty to unfair circumstances." Janaka smiled sadly at the woman, and finished tracing her skin.

Bali's eyes went wide when her lips were claimed so abruptly. But as soon as she felt Janaka's touch once more, her eyelids fluttered down to concentrate on the touch. It had been so long. "I...I understand." She trembled slightly as the man moved his hand down her face. "But I will not deny my feelings on this matter. And, I will not stand idly by as innocents go dead. I will act in my own way." Bali eyed her companion intently. After a long while, she raised one eyebrow, asking Janaka without words.

He knew what she wanted from him. "You have no idea what you ask, Bali." Janaka shook his head, and nudged his stallion onward. "Come let's ride further in the water." The black horse trotted along the ocean's depths, and further out of the reach of the court's ears.

Bali's mare picked up pace alongside the light stallion. Her own silver hair began to ripple in rhythm with the ocean waves, and her blue eyes grew fiery with her new mission. "Janaka...join me...you know what I speak of...we have done it before." Her smile grew brilliant, drawing alive the warm lines around her eyes.

Janaka nudged his horse to quicken its pace in the ocean water. He was beginning to sweat underneath his tiger's fur cap, despite the cool breeze blowing off the water. "Bali, you know I'd do anything for you—we have been such good partners before. But it is different now, my sweet lady. I'm an old man, and left politics years ago. And my family is well connected to our King...I just can't go back to this."

Bali kicked her bare heels into her black horse to catch up with Janaka. A soft hand petted her mare's mane affectionately, to thank her for riding in the ocean waters with her. "Think about it, Jankie...I need you. And, I have never needed a man. But...I need you...I have always needed you." Bali turned her face away from Janaka, so he could not see the pleading that was in her eyes.

Janaka could understand Bali's words without listening to them. Her alto voice always went deeper when she truly wanted something—needed something. Few things affected Janaka, or mattered to him these days. But she had always mattered. "My dear old friend...Lady Bali..." Janaka paused his horse in the water, and shook his head back and forth.

Bali's mare stopped on cue, following the stallion's movements even. She leaned her hand over to Janaka's horse and pat it softly. "Yes?"

Janaka sighed loudly and stared out at the sun that was preparing to escape into the ocean for the evening. He looked back at Bali with an expression of annoyance, tenderness and surrender. "Then need me." His lips turned downward into a pronounced frown. "I need you." Janaka was not happy about this confession. He felt weak—and had worked to never have to be weak ever again.

Raising his hand up towards the sky, Janaka yelled loudly. *"Acha!"* and dug his heavy heels into his stallion's belly. The horse took off at heroic speed further down the ocean path.

Bali smiled weakly and opened her lips to say something in return. But as usual, Janaka rode off before the woman could confess. Her own heart. They were two old friends. She supposed, they did not need to say the things that time had built around their relationship. *If things had been different, maybe we would have...*

"Acha!" Bali exclaimed, as she kicked her horse forward to compete with Janaka's stallion. Her mare could easily overcome that beast of a horse, since she was the better equestrian. "You old man! I will get you!" The point was Bali had already won.

~

Varuna's ocean went calm during the sunset. The waves that had entertained the court all afternoon as the nobles made love and merry went flat, in honor of the sky above. Varuna had his time as King, and had served Kasimi well. But now he had passed from the mortal realm to the ocean, and deferred to the sky power who now ruled on land. The King and Queen looked out on their ancestor from their rose crafted balcony.

The lords that had engaged in sports and drinking during the afternoon parted ways to look for their ladies. There was something about the Kasimian setting of the sun that made lifemates seek one another to walk on the sand. Even those whose marriages had been arranged found a moment of pure intimacy, hand in hand on Varuna's beach. After just a few moments, the sand was claimed by couples who exchanged whispers of romance and stolen kisses. The water reflected the last of the sun's sparkles just for one more moment...one more kiss.

Those who did not have mates found comfort in dear, old friends. A setting sun just could not be viewed alone. There was always something that one could find in the smile of a trusted and old companion that makes the sky that more beautiful. In solitude, the Kasimian sun was nothing more than a reminder of the heat.

~

The King was displeased. The Queen was upset. The Grand Priest was confused. The warrior was shamed. It had not worked out as everyone had planned.

"Is this the absolute best that the two most reputable warriors to have walked on my ancestor's lands can come up with?" screamed The King on his place at the divan. Marici seemed to be more eloquent when anger pulsed through him. His eyes would always be his visual weakness. The rings of red began to overtake his pupils and his muscles tensed to make him the picture of an angry King.

Sri, who was perched on the edge of the divan near her twin, found reason to stand and pace. Away from Marici for now.

"This is wrong! Unacceptable! I wanted details! The Isles must suffer for their insolence. For disobeying their King!" Marici also stood, and blankly went to Sri's position. "And all my two advisors can come up with is an intention to send masses for blood or the other option…to simply kill Vishal? Unacceptable. Where is the strategy? The timeline? The art of war!" Marici's red eyes flared at Ashok and an accusing finger was thrust in his direction. "Answer me!"

The old warrior leaned heavily on his cane and brought his head down to look at the marble floor. It was difficult for a man who had proudly served his kingdom to be shamed by a young boy. But the boy was his liege and that weighed heavily on Ashok's heart. "It will not be difficult to draw up a detailed plan for you, Your Highness. We only had a few hours and…"

"Silence!" Marici almost growled under his breath while listening to Ashok make excuses. "I am tired of hearing about weaknesses. You had a few hours to work together to come to me with a sketch of battle. You come to me divided even though you know my wishes?" Marici grabbed Sri's hand to give him some comfort in his growing anger. His eyes intensified to a liquid crimson and his gaze darted all over his parlour.

Sri gently extracted her hand from Marici's grip. She did not approve of his anger—of his plan for The Isles. She could not speak against him in public. They must be unified in all ways—in the Kasimian eye.

Ajan would not stay silent. Though he respected and worshipped his King, he could not let his duty to the gods remain unheard. Bowing before Marici, Ajan spoke in soft, reverent tones. "Your Excellency…Marici…I am not a warrior anymore. I do not think like one—I'll never think like one again. I am your Grand Priest. Don't anger at Ashok. It was I who refused to collaborate on a plan."

Marici clamped his eyes shut and hurled his accusing finger at Ajan. But then, Sri placed a comforting hand on the King's shoulder. This affectionate gesture centered him for a moment, allowing the Queen to speak her counsel in his ear. His eyes remained red, but became more mellow in shade.

Sri whispered her words of reason into the King's ear. "Ajan raised me, Marici. How could a warrior bring up a gentle girl? Let him go and speak with Ashok alone. Ajan is a priest." Sri squeezed her brother's shoulder again.

Marici gritted his teeth and then murmured through a clenched jaw. "Both of you go. And tell no one what was done in my parlour tonight." The King cast his gaze on the fire, and the flames obeyed the King's call by growing in heat and intensity.

Sri darted a warning look to Ajan and Ashok and raised her arched brows once. *Leave without protest.* She commanded without words in her intent look. Her eyes, black with a ring of red around the pupils, returned to their protective glance on Marici.

Ashok bowed over his cane. Ajan dipped his head in a low nod. Master and apprentice left the King's parlour without words. Ajan paused by the chamber door to give Sri a small smile. He had raised her well—he could see that now. *May Brahma be with you, Sri. Ohm.*

The King watched the servants exit, and the red of his eyes began to relax to a browner shade. He returned, with Sri in hand, to the divan by the fire. His anger was still present, but Sri had given him the strength to suppress it for now. He laid back lazily, and pulled Sri to him to embrace. Anger was still there, but love was the more powerful emotion.

"They have disappointed me, Sri. Ashok and Ajan." Marici closed his eyes, and began to tangle Sri's hair with his hands. His grip was tight and caused her discomfort as she murmured a sigh of pain. Marici stopped and kissed the place where he had been rough. "You are right about Ajan...but I expect more from Ashok."

Sri moved up from Marici's embrace and turned to face her brother on the divan. The fire, always burning, began to roar more steadily and cast a nice glow against Sri's brown skin. She spoke resolutely, and firmly. But gently, and with love in her voice. "Marici..." she said, centered. "I think you are acting too rashly. They were charged with this task just today and your expectations are too high. They came with two ideas. Ajan was a warrior, but is a priest. He gave you an idea to work towards that would make peace with religion...in his eyes." Sri shifted on the divan, and brought her yellow silks around her. "And Ashok gave you what you wanted. Just no specifics. Why are you angry? What is the real reason?"

"I want blood." Marici said under his breath. His eyes narrowed to fine lines, and red began to leak through his pupils. "I want to avenge our mother's death."

Sri went silent, and jilted her head towards the fire. *Mother's death*. Sri returned to her brother's arms and rested her head against his shoulder. This way, she could at least pretend he was not angry—not having to see the rage in his eyes. "What was our mother like, Marici?"

She never did know her. Marici was shocked by his sister's question. Bound by blood and yet she knew nothing of the family that bred her. It was difficult to vent his rage with the softness of Sri around him, and the melancholy that she seemed to possess. "She was very beautiful, Sri. She was gentle…kind…tender. She loved our father very much." Marici paused, and gazed at Sri for a moment. *Such similar beauty*.

Sri's eyes locked on one flame in particular that seemed to match the yellow hue of her own silks. She breathed—and brought herself to the flames. Feeling like she was part of the fire. Feeling the heat beat against her skin, she was suddenly younger and on the temple's beach. The thoughts could come so easily. "If she was gentle, Marici…would Mother want her death avenged?"

Marici answered flatly, while looking at the fire. "She is not King."

Even the invocation of their mother's name could not bring Marici from his bloodlusting thoughts. Sri turned to her brother and gave him one last piece of reason. Her voice held strength and passion, for she too was a child of the gods. But she held forgiveness and peace in her tone. "If it is blood you want, it is

blood you will get. You are King." The Queen brought her fire
warmed hand up to Marici's red eyes and traced them in circles
with her slender fingers. "Just see what you do with more than
anger, Marici." That would be all the counsel Sri could afford her
brother on this night.

Marici took his sisters wrists in his hands and brought them to
his lips. "Sister..." he murmured. He inhaled the scent of coconut
on her fingertips bringing him further into her spell. "I see my
anger with all my senses and I know it is Virtuous Anger." He
drew her hands over his face, forcing her fingers to drag the
length of his jawline. "It is clear to me now that I must avenge
Varuna II's downfall alone. Alone." Marici brought Sri's hands to
his lips and spoke through the small gaps in her little fingers.
"Come with me, now..."

Sri trembled as her brother touched her. She could feel his
rage in her hands and it burned in her fingertips. "Marici,
don't...please...don't..." Tears began on her face, but they
could not cool her hands which were in the King's possession.
She whimpered as the skin of her hands caught fire. "Please let
me go..." The hatred—the anger of her brother was inside her
now. She could feel his pain. "Oh Marici...I had no idea..."

Marici leaned in and kissed away some of the tears that had
fallen on Sri's feverish face. "My Queen..." he said, darkly...almost
growling under his breath. "Don't ask me to deny what I am..." His
lips reached for her eyelids and coaxed them closed. "The pain you
feel is because you deny what you are. Come with me, now..."

Sri's tears grew into sobs. "No!" She shook her head to release
Marici's lips from her skin. "No!" She cried out to the flames of
the fire. "You will not take me to this place inside you, Marici!
Don't do this to me!" Sri's own heart began to break in its place in
her rib cage. "I know who I am...it is not this."

Marici swept Sri off the divan. He grinned down at the woman and said in a darker voice that matched the sharp crackling of flames. "You do not know who you are because I will decide that. I asked you to come with me. Now, I will take you with me."

12

Marici ignored everyone as he carried his Queen in his arms down the spiraling staircase towards the main entrance of the palace. His feet barely touched the ever-twisting marbled steps. The King moved with a quick, determined pace—his eyes shined with red as he swept past the guards. The look in his eyes was enough of a command for the warriors to stay at their posts, and to leave Marici alone in his pursuit.

Sri shivered in her brother's arms, and bit down on her trembling lip. Her skin was inflamed by the anger of her brother; but her heart felt the solitude of his mind. He had isolated himself in his fury, and only she could reach him. But he would not let her. Sri buried her face in Marici's black silks. Her tears disappeared into the folds of his suit, and the warmth of his body.

The King reached the entrance of the palace and the doors were held open by the guards posted on either side. The door was made completely of yellow gold and etched with the story of the third miracle. The young boy stopped for a moment and looked at the drawing—his eyes narrowing more. *How inadequate. They will be replaced.* Marici continued forward onto the sand.

His strides became more demanding. The length of his legs kicked up the tiny grains beneath his toes. He marched forward towards the roaring waves. He needed the power of his great grandfather tonight, to mix his own blood with the water. The rage inside him found its way to the water, and the tide grew longer on the beach—to meet the King's feet. "You are Varuna's child, Sri...like me."

Sri's muscles tensed as her body began to cave in on itself in Marici's arms. It was not physical pain that she felt, though the heat on her skin was the temperature of fire. She would not become him. She would not permit Marici to bring her to the place where his rage was held. If she surrendered this night, she would never feel pain again. She would be invincible, like her brother. She could not—for herself, for Kasimi. She resisted, and growled loudly against her place in Marici's silks. "I am not like you!"

Marici's feet made contact with the water and he closed his eyes to inhale the smell of salt mingling with cool night air. His sister's protest did not phase him. "Let your pain go and be with me, Sri..." The red eyes of the King looked up at the waning moon above and whispered his reign to the holy creature. "I am the King of all Kasimi. I determine your fate, sister."

Sri twitched in Marici's arms, trying to break free of his grip. "Don't do this, Marici...I love you...I forgive you...always..." Her teeth bit against the King's shoulder and she murmured. "Don't make me be what I cannot."

Marici let his arm holding Sri's legs free, so she could stand in the water. He pressed his fingers into the small of her back to create a pressured embrace that would not be easily escaped. Molten red eyes burned on the pure woman. *Only she rivals the moon. But she rules it with my heart.* His lips traced a path along Sri's cheeks to consume the water that glistened on her skin. "And I need you, my Queen. I cannot exist without you." Marici pulled Sri tighter against his body. "Make me better, Sri..." he whispered.

Sri relaxed the tension in her jaw, and breathed a sigh of relief at her brother's words. Her head rested against him, and she welcomed the tenderness. "Come with me...Marici..." Sri implored. She did not know where to take him—away from where he had isolated himself. "You are lost...let me guide you before you go there again..."

Marici continued to guide his lips over Sri's cheeks with increasing intensity. Occasionally, his lips would stop to suction against the delicate skin of his Queen's face. "Dance with me, Sri..." the King murmured. "Guide me in your embrace..." Locking onto his sister's eyes, Marici took both her hands in his, and led them to rest on his shoulders. He kissed her right hand, and then her left while closing his eyes to enjoy her touch. Replacing his hands on his sister's hips he then commanded. "Dance with me."

"I..." Sri said, tilting her head to the right in confusion. *What does he want?*

The water began to swirl and twist around their feet. The sound of the waves was as persuasive as the low tones in Marici's voice. Sri then realized that she must surrender her body to her King on this night. She did not have to release her mind or betray her heart. But her body could do what it must, in the arms of her brother. She clasped her hands over Marici's neck and then arched her back towards the ocean to obey her brother's request.

Marici examined his sister's body with interest. The gentle line of her collarbones and how they came together near her neck. The silk skin of brown laced with a thin layer of ocean mist. Rampantly curling black hair alive with the moon. *A child of Varuna II.* Marici let his fingers play along Sri's hips, as the two began to move in circles deeper in the water, towards the waves.

Sri looked up at the moon through her black eyes. If only it were another night...another place...it could be in her mind. But her body was not hers at the moment. I will dance with you,

Marici. I surrender to Your Wish. Her feet were not moving of her own will. She let them drag in the water, guided by the circles that Marici marked.

Marici pulled Sri's body tight against his, so he could feel the sharpness of her hip bones against his. He pulled her across the waves. Their bodies went deeper into the ocean while they twisted in circles together. Marici's red eyes burned down on Sri, and the he began to draw the dance into a sweeping circle in the waves. "I see so much of our mother in you, Sri," Marici said as his waist bobbed in the salt water. "I avenge her death to save us."

The dance began to take on a sweeping rhythm, as the two children circled in the dark salt water. The King began to draw the waves around him, and the speed of his twirling forced the water to follow the couple. The ocean began to roar with pain—the King's pain—and the waves crashed onto the sand with devastation. The blood of the North was in the salt, and it found the wounds of the earth to sting. Each exhale of the furious Marici blew against the ocean, feeding it rage and energy. But it would not heat beyond its cooling tones and touch for there was still a calm element in its grasp. *Sri.* Varuna would cling to that for comfort.

Sri was not aware of her surroundings anymore. She had separated her thoughts from the sensations that overwhelmed her body. The intensity of her brother's red eyed gaze disturbed her. His anger was manifesting itself in too many ways, and it was beginning to seep into her being. When she was pulled close against the King's body, Sri felt her own blood grow cold inside her veins. It was a foreign feeling to the girl's body, but somehow she knew it was wrong. The Queen closed her eyes and went elsewhere in her mind, isolating herself from the anger that swept around her.

And the sky was harnessed next. The water roared with pain, and was ready to meet the power of the sky. Marici craned his neck against the cradled fingers of his sister and spoke his piece to the night:

This whole moving world, whatever is,
Stirs in the breath of life, deriving from it:
The great fear, the upraised thunderbolt;
Whoso shall know it, becomes immortal.

For fear of Me the fire burns bright,
For fear, the sun gives forth its heat,
For fear, the gods of storm and wind,
And Death fly!

The King was moving violently through the water, thrashing his Queen's body through the water while the ocean splashed up towards the sky. He brought his lips to the delicate skin where Sri's collarbones came together and kissed there feverishly before tracing a line with his tongue along her neck. "I need you...tonight, Sri..." he chanted continuously between the moments when his lips went unoccupied. "Do not shun me, do not deny what you are." Marici gripped at Sri's skin with his teeth and tasted the salt mixed with her perfume. "What you have become...my Queen..." he growled.

Marici pivoted their path in the water, needing to feel more of the ocean's waves around him. He pulled his Queen to him so that both were immersed in the water and carried further before Varuna. They floated—Sri atop the King—deep within the sea. The twins surfaced as the waves ceased for a moment to roar, and the King dragged Sri with him to a calmer part of the blackened water.

The two gripped on to one another in a dark union. Sri's black hair was a heavy cloth of curls that lazily spilled over Marici's and her own shoulders, closing off the embrace. The only thing that could draw the boundary of Sri's body was the clinging yellow of her sari silks, that clasped desperately onto her body. Marici's black silks and hair controlled Sri further, refusing to let her rid herself of the ocean. The King pulled Sri against him again, as the two were brought under the water by Varuna's strong arm.

And underneath the water, Marici pressed his body to Sri's and showed the girl his need. The Queen opened her mouth to scream, but the flush of salt water gagged the sound. The two plunged further until they were consumed by a chilling depth of the ocean—where the sky could not even reach—and then Marici dragged his Queen to the surface to unite the purity of Varuna with his own grace.

When the twins reached the sky's territory, Marici let out a low, fierce growl of anger and pain. His eyes—a glowing, violent red—looked up at the night sky with the untainted moon. He would bring his rage into the sky so The Isles would feel his pain. He would not be alone in his darkness—it would be felt throughout Vishal's land. "BLOOD IN THE ISLES!" Marici screamed with force. "BLOOD IN THE ISLES!" he repeated over and over again.

Sri could not return to her body. She had traveled to a memory of long ago, when she had first seen Varuna's beach from the temple grounds, with her own eyes. She had played in the waves, and remembered the way her grandfather had played so gently with her. The sun had felt so pleasing on wet skin. So different from the whipping sensation on her body now, as Varuna grew angry with her brother. Sri preferred the moment when she laughed with her great-grandfather and went there—to hide—from the anger. *I will not go with you, Marici.*

Marici threw Sri's body over his shoulder when her muscles refused to follow his lead. She must touch me. He raised both his arms to the sky as he was gently nudged up and down by the water. "Obey me, my gods!" Marici screamed again. Pounding his fists to the moon, he chanted:

In the beginning was darkness swathed in darkness;
All this was but unmanifested water.
Whatever was, that One, coming into being,
Hidden by the Void,
Was generated by the power of heat!

Marici closed his eyes, and brought his rage to a resting point. He could feel Varuna's strength in him and it tunneled through his body in the water until it reached his glowing eyes. He waved his hand across the dark sky and brought the sea's rage to it. *Obey me.* Marici could feel his own power, and the wisdom of his gods. *Obey me.*

The moon dimmed slightly, making everything still. *Obey me.* The water calmed its fury, and lapped gently against the twins. *Obey me.* Marici tilted his head back to look upon the sky and brought open palms above him. *Obey me.* He could control his rage, and turn it into power. He would be heard in the sky, and The Isles would pay this night.

He was obeyed. A single streak of heated light flashed across the sky and landed in the water before Marici and His Queen. And then there was silence for a good, long moment. But, the King was not done. He began to walk in the water, towards the shore with his hands raised to the sky. With each step, a strike of light slashed down into the water taunting the waves to obey. The King had summoned the sun to strike at night, and so it obeyed alongside Varuna. The waves began again, rolling slowly over one another. As the light flashes grew progressively stronger and faster, the water began to reach upward to put out the flames.

Marici marched in an ellipse around the shallow depths of the ocean. He approved of the sun's work with the water, and began to lead the light in the circle with him. The water followed—obediently—for Marici was King now. The light and water began to swirl with passion, following the King with extreme force. *Obey me.*

Marici paused in the center of the fiery whirlpool and began to feel the rage flee his body. He gently lowered Sri's to him, and held her against his heart. He kissed the emerald bindhi that still sat obediently on her forehead. *You are mine.* The water soared higher in the night air as the King's touched his Queen, to shield the twins.

Sri's eyes fluttered open as the waves united with these foreign objects of light in the night sky. She said breathlessly, "How beautiful…" as the light made patterns against the water. Still coming to consciousness, and returning from her thoughts, Sri was not aware of what the King had done. Her own eyes, black with a slight ring of red around the edges, looked back at the King and she murmured, "What did you do?" *The sky will be raped.* Realizing the horror of the light, as the waves rumbled mercilessly towards the fire in the sky. "What did you do!"

Marici spoke harshly at his sister. "I am bringing justice to The Isles, sister! Do not speak to me in such a way!" He shook the girl's body violently as he heard the disapproval in her voice. "I will determine who you are! And only me! Do you not see my might, sister?"

Sri screamed up at the sky. She was trapped both by the arms of her brother and the watery wall of her King. The arms of Varuna were lifting the water towards the moon's canvas, using the sun to pull it up. Sri looked in horror at the twisting water as it reached to the sky around her and Marici. "No!"

Marici roared up at the sky, while rocking his sister in his arms. "BLOOD IN THE ISLES!" His hands worked gently against His Queen while his eyes burned against the moon. The water completed its journey and united with the sky in one cylindrical line. The King continued to chant his rage to the power around him.

Finally, the sky repeated Marici's rage and a soft rumbling of thunder came across the dark blue painting. He had channeled His Will, His Might, His Power and His Gods in the ocean and the sky, and The Isles would see blood. The ocean's waves had been led by his energy to meet the sky, and the light flashed around the whirling bridge to celebrate the union of water, fire and air. The serene night was given the movement of the sea, and the two would seek revenge as One.

"Do you see, Sri?" Marici whispered in His Queen's ear as the water met the sky. "I am King and god of all Kasimi." He began to kiss along the girl's neck, admiring how pure she was. Though he was powerful, she was still better than him. "Come with me, Sri," he whispered, as his lips traveled across her salty cheek.

Sri looked up at the magic in the night sky, surrendering once again to her brother's commands. She would not go with him. She would not isolate her heart in rage and anger. Sri's eyes began to let water drip for them, as she prayed for The Isles with her heart. "*Ohm. Shanti, Shanti, Shanti.*" she murmured with her lips.

The prayer was sent with Varuna's power, for the mercy of a Queen is the saving grace of a land. The sky consumed the water that the gods brought forth, and became more powerful by the command of the King. There would be terror, and blood soon. Marici had released his anger and pain to a receiving sky. Vengeance was done. For now. He looked up at the water twisting images in the sky, with the sun's fire and thunder to accompany the glory. Soon, it would be done.

Sri, who would be a part of Marici forever, sent her calm and mercy into the center of the sea's storm. Forever, there would be kindness in even the harshest power because a Queen had refused to make her heart cold. This was perhaps the most tragic part of the night. In forgiving her brother's madness, Sri had lost a piece of her already broken heart.

Marici's lips hovered at the edge of Sri's lips. His hands worked soothingly down her back to hold her in place. The twins were again one—Marici placed a chaste kiss on his sister's lips to claim what was truly his.

13

The sun came up on the next day, and Marici was a gentle King again. He called for a celebration of victory, a party that would last indefinitely and without pause. The King sent messengers to fetch artists, musicians and entertainers that word could reach, to join the merry making on the beach in *Govandhara*. He wanted color—the vivid colors of the bright afternoon sky and the setting sun—and murals painted on the palace walls. He wanted to hear non-stop music and the rhythm of a demanding drum. He wanted to be happy, and to show his loyal subjects how much he loved them.

People queried the sanity of the boy. What victory? But, the court would not argue celebration and revelry. This is the type of madness that Kasimi could tolerate. Their King, who was so angry just the day before, was now full of life. He smiled brightly and joked with the nobles, and he loved his Queen. The nobles felt encouraged that Kasimi would reach greatness once more, with a leader who would love them.

It did not take long for the palace to be transformed from a home of the King, to a palace of fantasy and delight. The King raised his hands to the gold domed roof and winked at its sweetness, and servants followed behind throwing flowers from the garden. The happiness of the King was contagious, and the court strolled through the marble floors of the palace with candles and roses to place around chairs and crevices. The guests worked together, smiling from room to room, leaving color and the scent of mango presse. The tabla player danced around Marici and Sri, inducing the royal twins to create merry. They were beautiful together.

The King danced around the palace walls, with the court behind him. The ladies and lords would prance atop the walls and leave the flowers behind to mark their territory of joy when the caravan moved forward. The train moved like a Kasiminan snake, twisting around the white marble of the fence.

The servants listened to the laughter and danced from their spots near the windows of the palace. The young hand maids even removed their sari silks to display the marks of their femininity. Such beauty was its own distraction. Inspired, the servants found flowers and greens to mingle outside the many different windows which added to the many colors of marble on the outside. A few of the older men made drums of the balcony walls, adding a rougher sound to the rich texture of the tabla.

The palace on *Govandhara* would be one of pleasure, decreed the King. Luscious roses and vivid flowers were so plentiful along the palace's boundaries, and along the windows of the structure. To serenade the perfumed air, musicians would be at constant play on balconies and in the gardens so that the King could whisper his love to the people in music. And they could hear his desire and his strength in the constant knock of the tabla.

When the sun would tire of day and leave the party on *Govandhara*, Marici decreed that fires would be made alongside Varuna's sand to keep the light alive at night. Even during full moon. The dark sky must be so lonely without the warmth of its sun, so the King would provide the night with comfort. The fires would burn until sunrise, when the ocean's morning tide would sweep them to rest.

And there would be wine, and feasting at all times. The nobles would not want for anything as servants walked with filled trays of meats and fruits through the gardens and sand. The King ordered Goane to produce more wine, and the word was sent through Devyn. He commanded the sun to release its heat over the dry region, so that rain could fall from time to time and the sweet crops would be plentiful. His command was obeyed, and the sky knew his might.

When the artists and entertainers arrived, Marici selected the most reputable to bring Kasimian art into His Age. He wanted them to paint murals of Him and His Queen, and to draw the glory of His Palace in this golden age, where he reigned supreme in the land. There had been nothing new in the way visions were recorded and nothing new with the written hand except in religious texts. This would change! The King's glory would be known in art, and Marici would restore beauty to the Kasimian lands.

The palace on *Govandhara* would know no pain nor need. It would be a glorious place of fantasy and delight. The name would echo through the lands beyond Kasimi, and would draw people to the promise of happiness. The King wanted to spread his love in pleasure, and devote his palace to the court. In art and merry, the King would truly be known forever.

Marici dedicated the feast on *Govandhara* to the Queen. Without Sri, there was no happiness or music.

~

On the late afternoon of the tenth day of festivities, Sri walked alone on the beach. Her King had gone hunting with his men and she was allowed a few moments to herself. Guards kept a close eye on her from their posts—she could feel their dark eyes from every angle but learned to ignore their focus. And one strange man—who nobody identified except Marici—always seemed to be watching her from his place by the palace walls. He seemed harmless, and the King was certain that he was just an old lord who admired beauty as much as him.

With no men to please, Sri wore a white salwar-kameez of rough silk that caught the breeze of the ocean. She wore no shoes or jewelry, and her raven hair went free around her. The only symbol of her status was the emerald bindhi that marked her as Queen. She was certain people whispered of her modesty in dress—it was a virtue.

It seemed that only women were strolling along the beach for this afternoon, due to Marici's trip. The sunset would not be as lovely without the whisper of a masculine voice against a waiting ear. For Sri, the solitude would make her appreciate the way her own eyes could interpret color.

Growing from a small dot on the horizon along the ocean came the image of a red-haired man who appeared to be riding towards her. Sri squinted to make out the image, as it moved forward in the water. "Devyn?" Sri called out loudly. She had not seen the Goanian since arriving at the palace, and missed his company. She waved her hand at the priest to attract his attention. "Devyn! What are you doing here?"

Devyn slowed his horse a few paces from Sri, and trotted towards her side by the sand. He smiled down at the girl with his equally black eyes and said smoothly, "I did not feel like killing beasts, Sri." Devyn dismounted his horse, splashing his feet in the cool water. He turned and bowed at the waist towards the Queen. "Your Highness," he chuckled, and then straightened his posture. "What are you doing alone on the beach? Where's Jabie to walk with you?"

"I couldn't find Jabala or Ajan, actually." Sri shrugged. "Besides, I have been very demanding with my nurse these days. She could use an afternoon away from me." Sri beamed, at the sight of her unconditional friend. How she relished his company! "Oh, Devyn! It is so good to see you! I've noticed you in court, but I am not allowed to seek people out without them…" Sri motioned with her eyes towards the fierce looking guards who were staring at her.

"Ah," mouthed Devyn with amusement. He cocked his head towards his horse and asked, "Want to go for a ride?"

"Where will we go?" Sri asked in a sigh. "I could really use some conversation, Devyn. Things are not…right…" She went to pet the creature. "Do you know anywhere less crowded?"

Devyn shook his head. "They don't let you out much, do they, Sri? Come here." Devyn held his hands out to raise Sri up on his mare. "You haven't been to the sanctuary in the gardens, yet? It's restricted to the priests—and the King and Queen of course. We'll go there." He gestured with his open hands again. "Shall we?"

Sri's eyes widened in surprise. "I had no idea." Her waist found itself in Devyn's hands, and she was quickly hoisted onto the mare. "Let's go!" she commanded, her eyes surveying the gardens in the distance for sight of this magical sanctuary.

"Yes, my Queen," mused Devyn as he mounted the horse. "Put your arms around my waist, Sri," he said in a gentle tone. The priest's heels dug into the horse, and the two went forward from the water to the back gardens of the palace with haste.

There it was. The sanctuary was actually just out of the view from her balcony window, hidden by a small patch of banyan trees. Like the one near the Grand Priest's temple, it looked like a modest home. It was made of smooth grey stones, collected from Varuna's depths and placed together to form a single roomed house. Atop the stones was a woven straw roof that looked black due to the constant shading of the trees above. The sanctuary looked like the palace's one little secret, that should be kept in the shadows.

Devyn dismounted his horse and tied its reigns to a nearby tree where she could graze. He gestured toward the sanctuary and said in a slow voice, "Not even the guards can watch you here, Sri." He brought his hands up to support Sri's waist as she stepped down from the horse. "Here, let me help you down."

Something happened inside Sri when two masculine hands were placed around the side of her waist. A cold sweat came across her upper lip. Her mind flashed to the touch of her brother from the ocean and went black to welcome two warm hands on the white silk of her salwar. She gasped quietly when his fingers curled around her sides, and then centered herself.

Sri walked towards the sanctuary entrance and then turned to look back at Devyn. "Should I cover my hair?" she asked.

Devyn peered inside the doorway to find the sanctuary— empty. He looked back at Sri and shrugged. "I'm not covering my hair, so?"

"But I am a woman and the elders said that I should cover my hair in the sanctuary, so…" Sri bit down on her lips. Again, she did not appear to have any cloth with which to hide her hair.

"And you are Queen, which is a higher rank than elder. If…if you are going by the rules."

Sri nodded a few times at the Goanian. "I see…" She smirked and puffed brazenly at him, and then entered the sanctuary with her raven hair uncovered.

Devyn entered the sanctuary behind Sri, grinning at her daring entry. His eyes looked upon the familiar space. It was all his. Ajan had his own apartment in the palace, and did most of his think-ing in the study. Sudha and Devyn had their own rooms, but the space was claustrophobic. Sudha took comfort in the gardens with various female nobles. This sanctuary was the place where

Devyn went to be alone in the merry of the court, which had proved too grand for him.

It was a simple space, and Devyn preferred it this way. The Goanian had almost finished inscribing the scripture of the third miracle on the wall. He had spent many nights with the chisel, making sure each word was perfect. There were a few stools in the dark room, and candles of vanilla that burned constantly. A few bits of straw had fallen from the roof to the ground. The sanctuary was still fragile.

Devyn pulled two stools close together in the position that conversation would warrant. He pointed to one, inviting Sri to sit, and placed himself on the other. "So what's on your mind, Sri?" Devyn asked, while retrieving a nearby glass and a bottle of Kasimian rum.

Sri did not take her seat right away, and paced around the sanctuary reading random bits of scripture. "Why are you wearing cobalt, Devyn? You're not a Northerner?" Her eyes continued to scan the scripture, without looking at the Goanian.

"I like the color." Devyn downed his shot of rum and held the bottle out to Sri. "Care for a drink?"

Sri waved her hand and answered, "No thank you." She continued to pace, her eyes wandering across the second miracle. "As to what's on my mind," Sri sighed and placed a bare hand against the cold stone wall. "I...am very worried about Marici. I...he's...I..." Sri walked over to the stool, and sat down intently. "Did you see what happened in the ocean ten days ago?"

Devyn pushed the bottle towards Sri. This time, he would encourage drink. She would need it. "Of course I saw the storm...but it was late and we were all asleep. But out my window, the sea did look spectacular."

Sri grabbed the bottle and let it dangle in her hands. "It wasn't a storm, Devyn...it was Marici. He and I were moving through the waves and then I...my mind...I wasn't there all of sudden, but my body was." Sri dropped her voice to a low whisper. "He made the storm."

Sri was unable to put the events of that night into words. She struggled with the thoughts, and tried to think of the translation. There was none. "Marici can harness the sky. And what he did was wrong, Devyn...I can't explain it. But there was anger, and rage—and it consumed Marici. He made the sea angry and the sky went mad. It was wrong, Devyn—I could feel blood in the water."

Devyn squinted in confusion and tilted the bottle in Sri's hands to fill his glass. His pale fingers gently brushed along the Queen's as the rum poured. Her hands were cold, and they sent a shiver through Devyn's arms. "It was a storm, Sri. Whether or not Marici used his powers with anger—it's over. He left it behind in the sea. Look at him now!"

Sri took a long drink of the rum and then locked her black eyes on Devyn's pools. "It was the blood of The Isles, Devyn. There will be pain there."

Devyn's eyebrows arched over his eyes. "Ah," he murmured. He did not understand Sri, but he knew that she felt something very real. Running a free hand through his red hair, Devyn admitted his confusion. "I don't understand the King, Sri. He has powers that we do not. I don't know how he wields them. I don't know the extent to which he can control the sky, as the edict commands. What I care about here and now—is you. How does this affect you?"

Sri had not thought about this. How did it affect her? Sri's eyes strayed to the wall beside her, and her hand traced the cold rock. "It affects me because I don't want pain in Kasimi. That is not what the gods intended for the people. No matter what Vishal has done, those innocent people don't deserve the bloodshed that is coming."

Devyn downed another glass of rum, and then gestured at Sri with his empty glass. "If you don't agree with him, what will you do to right that, Sri?" He looked calmly back at the Queen, offering no sympathy.

Sri answered quickly, almost defensively. "I try to guide the King with my words, and to calm him."

Devyn retorted. "You can do more."

Sri snapped, "No I can't. I would be defying the man I'm sworn to guide, and love. I must be loyal." Her eyes went back to the wall, and traced the words of her history that she knew so well.

Devyn sighed heavily and pulled the bottle from Sri's hands to place against the wall, alongside his glass. He took the girl's hands in his, and spoke gently to her. "Sri, you were intended for a reason. You can continue to live in the shadows, behind your King, counseling him in his ear. Or, you can take action." He leaned forward and cocked his head to one side to catch Sri's glance away from the scripture writing. "I know you have sacrificed yourself in this marriage. And I will openly say that I do not agree with the life that has been dictated for you. Now you have a choice, Sri. You can be Marici's Queen or Kasimi's Queen—you do have power."

Devyn had spoken the dilemma in her broken heart. "I know my choice, Devyn." She could not deny the choice she would have to make. Her hands were not tracing the words that described her birth. Her eyes soaked in the tale that was written of her blood:

Varuna's favored had a grand niece through the bloodline of her brother, who was of proper breeding to attend to Varuna II. Rani had been raised to be a noble concubine just as her great aunt, and felt blessed to be given to the direct descendant of the sea energy.

Rani. The name was there. Sri's eyes glowed and she jerked her head to gaze at Devyn with her outer hand still in his. "The name...it was not there in the temple's sanctuary." Her eyes went back to stare at that one word. *Rani.* "You are carving this? Devyn?"

Devyn nodded softly. "Your mother has a name, Sri. She deserves to be part of your birth, and not buried from history."

Sri's fingers trembled as they traced that name repeatedly. *Rani.* "Oh Devyn..." Sri sighed. She leaned to bring her lips to her mother's name and kissed the carving softly in honor of the woman. She gained her mother's strength in this motion. "Devyn..." She turned back to the Goanian and placed her hand back into his. "I will not live in the shadows. I will continue to love and guide my King. But, I will be Kasimi's Queen."

Devyn looked intently into Sri's eyes and a smile flashed on his lips. "I knew you would."

The two people continued to holds hands, while looking honestly into one another's black eyes. After a moment, Sri spoke again. "I will need help with this, Devyn."

Devyn continued gaze into Sri's dark eyes. He was proud of the woman she had become. And, she was so very beautiful. He shook his head to break the trance and murmured, "There is someone you need to meet."

"Who?" Sri asked, with both surprise and curiosity. *People to meet.* Sri did not know that Devyn had such contacts into the Kasimian court.

"Lady Bali." Devyn replied. "She can help you, and she wants to meet you." Devyn rubbed his thumbs over Sri's hands to reassure her. "She is very powerful in the Kingdom, Sri."

Sri nodded. Lady Bali had impressed her at court, and if anyone could help her on the subject of The Isles, it would be this noblewoman. She was well aware of her accomplishments, and her reputation in the North. "I want to meet with her as soon as possible."

Devyn's lips calmed into a subtle smile. "I will arrange every-thing." His eyes narrowed, and his voice became soft and sharp. "Don't tell anyone of our talk, not even Jabala. The men will be drinking tonight to celebrate their hunt. Look for me there." The Goanian's eyes searched the Queen's for her answer. It was one thing for Sri to vow her heart. It was another thing for a Queen to agree to treason.

~

The men of Marici's court had dressed in their recreational whites to spend a merry afternoon in a hunt. The King had ordered the party to follow behind the royal caravan. He wanted a tabla at constant play—to hear the heat of the drum against the sun on his face. No women. Not even his Queen was allowed on this adventure. He remembered how Janaka had prepared trips for the men in *Mithila*. Marici would do the same.

The lords left their women behind at the palace in a farewell scene where the ladies could kiss their heroes goodbye. Wives, daughters and mistresses admired how ceremonial their lords looked with long swords and sabers attached at the hip. It gave the lords a chance to be gallant, and to feel the pride of the hunt. Mounting their stallions decorated with emeralds to symbolize the presence of Marici, they braved into the forests of *Govandhara* while blowing kisses to the women would later receive them in bed.

Men could be men on this trip. As soon as they were certain that the women were not watching them, their behavior became more relaxed. They laughed more easily, on easier talk. Flasks were revealed from underneath tunics, and shared among friends. This was their time to enjoy, and Marici had created the celebration.

Servants were given access to horses so they could ride along the train of the lords' stallions and refill flasks with wine and rum, and to ensure that every man had his heart's desire. Music accompanied the journey into the forest, as they traveled nowhere in particular. They enjoyed the freedom of the afternoon, and would pause for a kill if one was readily available. This trip was not about hunting.

Marici requested that Ashok ride alongside him, so they could talk of politics and other things. This morning, the King had a single white rose delivered to the old Lord as a symbol of his gratitude. Ashok was again in Marici's good graces, and wore a smile as his white stallion trotted alongside the King's noble black horse. The two appeared to be friends, and the child listened with great interest at the words of the old and revered warrior.

"The campaign for The Isles is over?" Ashok asked, with his bushy brows raised over his cerulean gaze. The man was only slightly disappointed. While he wanted revenge and The Isles to feel the North's sword, he did not want to experience Marici's temper during the throws of battle. Perhaps the boy had come to the conclusion that anger was no way to run a battle.

Marici nodded once. "I have no further business with The Isles, and have reclaimed them into my Kingdom. They will soon see my way, I am sure." He flashed a smile of his white teeth, and glanced with his black eyes in the direction of Ashok's long sword. "Sometimes we don't need to wield our swords to demand blood. Eh?"

Ashok squinted. "Eh...*acha*..." he mumbled, though he did not understand Marici's. It did not matter. If the war were called off, it would not be spoken of again. While Ashok wanted revenge, he wanted a happy King most of all.

"I would like you to stay on, Ashok. Be an advisor on my council, and be at my side in times of strife?" Marici made his request for this most esteemed position without looking at Ashok. He

knew the old lord would be embarrassed by the offer, and would
need to hide his blush.

Ashok gasped. The sound was hidden by the horse's steep trot.
He managed to murmur a heavy, "Of course, Master Marici,"
after a few moments.

Marici smiled thinly. "Good. I knew you'd be pleased." He did
not look back at his new advisor. It was not something that
deserved a moment of ceremony. "And now, I feel a kill coming
on!" Marici kicked his horse, and drew the train of nobles faster
into the forest.

Even the forests were tended to by servants. Mango trees were
the predominant members of the grove, spreading fruits and green
leaves artfully along the grassy paths. It provided many animals
with food while creating a colorful vision for lovers who would
stroll on its secretive paths. This made the King proud.

"Stop..." Marici whispered, while bringing his horse to a halt.
One by one, the line of nobles paused while the King's eyes sur-
veyed what appeared to be a blank horizon.

Marici cocked his head in Ashok's direction. "I hear it and I'm
going to kill it." The King dismounted his horse, and reached for
the saber at his hip. His eyes looked at the trio of pepul trees in
front of him, and at the shadows of the leaves against the ground.

Ashok, along with a few guards followed protectively behind
the child. "Your Excellency, there is nothing there." Ashok whispered. The old man reached for his long sword, and the suit of
young guards followed the gesture.

Marici waved his hand behind to silence the old lord, and continued with his saber held protectively in his left hand. He crept
silently, pressing his bare feet into the carpet of grass. He moved
with minimal effort and refined steps. He readied his saber, and
his eyes began to grow red as they focused on the one tree.

The nobles began to crowd in a semi-circle watching the King move with determination toward what they deemed as nothing. Ashok warned the men to be quiet with a flash of his hard eyes. The King sensed something—who were they to question the dance of a god.

Marici reached the foot of the tree and pivoted in his tracks to glare at the tabla player who had ceased his rhythm on the drum. The King's red eyes coaxed the faceless servant back into the music, and Marici's lips started a smile again. He turned back to stare at the bark of the tree. The palm of his right hand went to press against the tree, and the King closed his eyes.

His breathing steadied to a violent system of inhales and exhales as Marici pressed his palm against the tree. He was reaching into his mind, and into the energy of the forest, to feel something. The hollow sound of the tabla played against his hot breath and the two became one instrument.

The King raised his left hand, readying the saber and struck at an angle behind the tree. A high pitched whimper was heard, in a call for mercy from something inhuman. This made Marici's eyes flare red, and he brought his saber up once more and stabbed again. This time, the beast's call was a low growl of relentless pain. And so, the King granted the beast mercy with one last strike to the heart. The beast sighed peacefully as *Brahma* claimed its soul, and the King smiled with his sword in hand in the name of the One.

Ashok cued the guards to retrieve the beast that Marici had sacrificed to his anger. The lord's eyes were wide with curiosity. No one had seen nor heard the animal, but somehow the King could still see it was there. He stepped to the side of the boy and whispered, "How did you know?"

Marici eyed his bloody knife with interest, noting the clean lines of red against the sharp blade. He paused to consider Ashok's question. He answered while stroking the blood.

Who slew the dragon and made the seven steams to flow, who drove out the cows by disclosing the demon of darkness, who created the fire between two stones, winner of booty in battle is he.

Ashok did not understand the King, and stepped a few paces back in awe of the boy. There was a force at play that he did not understand. He went to look upon the animal that had been slain by Marici.

The King walked idly around his guards and lords as they dragged the hulking, white bull out from its place behind the trio of pepul trees. A trail of blood from its sliced neck mixed with the fresh green grass, making it hot with death. Marici looked at the animal with a combination of pity and pride. He raised his bloody saber over his head and continued.

In whose control are horses, cattle, villages and all chariots; who created the sun, the dawn and who guides the waters!

The lords dragged the beast to the center of view and loomed over the magical animal who had given his life for the glory of a boy. They looked at how the creature must have suffered as it received three thrusting blows to its flesh. Finally, the chest was cut and it was granted mercy. The lords began to chant prayers of worship to the King who had done this deed with his own hand.

Marici motioned to the tabla player to continue a pattern on his drum. He reached for his long sword and motioned to the people to kneel as they chanted. Most fell to the grass, in awe of the realization of the King's power. The heat of the drums drew a trail of blood from the bull, as it continued to steak across this cove in the forest.

Who slays with his bolt, before they know it, all those that have committed great sin; who does not forgive the insolent his insolence, who slays The Isles!

The men began to chant "*Ohm* Marici!" after the King's declaration of his hunt. His message was mysterious, but they were hypnotized by the actions of this boy.

The mighty bull of seven reigns, who let loose the seven streams to flow, who club in arm, kicked down as he was scaling heaven!

"*Ohm* Marci!" the lords shouted.

Marici kneeled before the bleeding bull in his white silks and stroked his hand across the dead beast's back. His lips went to kiss the animal's face as he whispered to the people.

You who with furious energy cause sustenance to burst forth the one that presses and cooks, verily you are reliable! May we, O Brahma, be ever dear to you! Having heroic sons, may we address this place of sacrifice!

"*Ohm...*" the men said against the lilting timbre of the tabla.

Marici stood up, and motioned to his men to tie the bull to bring back to the palace. He spoke in simple, light tones, but his message was grave. "Glorious! I hunted today in my own forest. A beast that had hidden from view. But I could sense it, and I killed it. Let that be the lesson to The Isles. The blood of this bull is shed for them."

The King's eyes became black again. The lords looked up at the boy with fear and wonder at the words of someone who had just killed. Some men, who usually favored green attire, clutched their swords as the King spoke of The Isles. Those who favored cobalt looked with amazement at the brilliant child-King who had brought a bull down with three strikes.

Soon, the nobles returned to their horses to continue forward in the forest for more sport. The chatter was not as bright, and voices were kept at a minimum. The pace of the horses was slow, and dulled.

"Wine! Music!" Marici yelled, with a winning smile on his full lips. "Forward we go!"

The dead bull was given its own horse, by decree of the King. The blood of the animal streaked down the white of the stallion's hair, making it dirty with death. Marici was grateful to the beast that had given him strength, and wanted his journey to the palace to be of peace.

~

Jabala moved her hips slowly against the throbbing of the Kasimian sun as it streamed inside the rock alcove. Her hair, which was darker in hue and wet from salt water, was spilled against the sharp rocks, causing a sensation of pain as love overcame her body. So many things pressed against her skin and begged for attention that the woman found herself lost in the afternoon.

They had traveled quietly on separate horses to a place on Varuna's beach that was in between the temple and the palace. Ajan had found a secretive rock alcove, in a palisade overlooking the ocean water, where no one would find two lovers. It was foreboding. The place was dark, and the ocean water lapped inside the rock when the waves were heavy. The sighs of passion were quiet against the sounds of the water.

Ajan's bare body moved slowly against his lover's form. The water taunted his hips, making them cold against the warmth of a woman's body. He withdrew his lips from Jabala's and let his eyes gaze out at the ocean. He whispered tenderly to his faithful servant...another promise...and her tears of salt rejoined the ocean water.

They had spoken already about the burdens of Ajan's mind and heart. He had confessed his reservations of the King's youth and decisions to Jabala while they held each other inside the hidden cave. And Jabala had held him quietly because she had no advice to offer him that he had not heard before.

He had said that he did not want to be a warrior again. He had confessed the vision of the red headed demon girl who had told him how he must serve the gods. He feared bloodshed, because Ajan knew *Brahma* would be displeased with cruel wars.

As he kissed Jabala's lips and stroked her silk hair, he had murmured his confession of loyalty. "I serve Marici and Sri faithfully, and will do anything to help them in the name of Kasimi. But I will not create blood again...I will not return to my night-mares...my glory is no longer in war. I will kill myself before I become a Protector again."

Jabala had looked longingly in Ajan's eyes, saddened by the thought of her friend's fears. It had been a long time since they could be intimate. It was harder now, since Jabala was at the palace. She had longed for his friendship, and knew she would be said without it. She wanted to scream to him that he would never have to make that choice. But with Marici as King, things were uncertain. Jabala did know that there would be much pain in this reign. She would not lie to Ajan. She kissed his lips and whispered, "Part of my heart will die if you go...but my soul will be restored by your strength and conviction."

If the two people were in love, it would be natural to confess "I love you..." before the passion overcame their bodies. Ajan almost made that promise, but Jabala put one finger to his lips and stopped him from sinning.

She kissed him once, her tongue tracing over the outside of his lovely mouth. She whispered in his ear, "How dear you are to me..."

He kissed her passionately, moving his lips and tongue suggestively with hers. He did not love her. But how he needed her. It
began to take over his blood, as his hands moved from her wet
hair down to her back to feel the strength in the servant's body.
"How..." he leaned his lips against the woman's bosom and
sucked on her nipples. "...dear..." he continued and then licked
his way across to the other side. "...you are to me, Jabie."

His lips moved further down the body of his lover, and clothes
were carefully removed in the process. Soon, two naked bodies on
the bare wet rock of the cave began a slow, long afternoon of lovemaking. Ajan's lips found refuge in the sweetness of Jabala's femininity, as he showed her the joy he wished he could always give
her. She shivered underneath him.

And when Jabala was about to scream Ajan's name, she begged
him to come closer to her and touch her on the inside. Before the
words could make it to her lips, he was moving in and out of her
with passion. Her hands moved to guide his flesh to hers, making
him work harder against her. She could not feel enough of him.
Her body rang once, twice, and still demanded more.

Ajan throbbed inside Jabala, and his movements became more
urgent as his hands went to lift Jabala's hips off the cold rock.
He focused his rhythm inward, creating short, deep strokes
inside his friend to bring her to a climax. He could not give
enough to her. Or apologize more for his distance. He closed the
gap with each movement.

Finally, the Grand Priest's lips found Jabala's in that one
moment that a man and a woman share during lovemaking. Each
moaned the other's name, and the passion seemed to last longer
than usual this time. And when they had made love once, their
bodies began to work towards more joy again.

~

The men returned from the hunt shortly after the sacrifice of the bull. The lords found the forest heavy and filled with blood rather than a place for a merry hunt. The King was tired, too and wished to find His Queen for a walk on the sand as the sun went to rest. The caravan turned around, and went back to the palace on *Govandhara*. The trip took longer on the way home. The lords and their horses could only move at the pace of their thoughts.

Marici placed the dead bull at the head of the train, and rode his horse behind the animal. He chanted to *Brahma* on the way to his Queen, and prayed for the honor of the bull's soul. His eyes remained black, and his lips did not smile. The Lords followed in the chant, paying homage to their King and god.

When water was in sight once again, the train of stallions and nobles grew happy. Their eyes softened as Varuna's gentle ocean filled their senses, and the caravan moved more quickly towards the palace. Their women were walking quietly on the sand, and engaging in a dance. The lilting sound of a flute and the roar of Varuna's voice guided the ladies through the beauty of the afternoon.

The lords were hypnotized by the grace of women on the sand, and brought their horses to the edge of the beach to observe the spectacle. They had no idea what awaited them—but as soon as their eyes approached the gathering of women—they had no choice but to stare. It was poetry against the setting sun. Words that had yet to be written.

The noblewomen in their light, flowing silks and loose hair watched the dance before them while they squatted and lounged on the sand. Some of the younger women played the flute and Goanian drum, to make the music for the dance. Only two partook in this classical Kasimian dance that was usually performed by sisters or dear friends in praise of *Brahma*'s beauty. The elders did not look on, for it was crafted to explore the curves of the woman's body and to evoke passion.

The dance was in its final stages, and the Queen was perform-
ing each step with beauty. Her black eyes were dimmed in that
subtle way before a man would claim her lips, and her hips moved
rhythmically to the drum. Her feet stomped in place, making
tracks in the sand. Fingers were styled in the exact positions, to
symbolize the language of the prayer. Sri had danced this dance
many times as a girl, usually with Jabala.

Lady Bali, who had known this dance through her life, performed alongside the Queen with closed eyes. Her arms wove
intricate designs over the space that Sri's hips circled and her neck
jilted stiffly on the offbeat. Her smile was warm, and genuine.
Even at this age, the blue eyed noblewoman enjoyed the feeling of
music around her. Her eyes opened to look upon Sri, as the two
continued to step in time.

Marici gazed upon the women with discomfort. He did not like
Sri engaging in merry with Bali. He could feel something wrong
about the companionship that had developed between the two,
and thought it the fault of the brazen elder noble. But, he watched
with a grin on his lips because Sri looked so beautiful as her body
twisted and turned. Sri's black eyes caught his from time to time,
and he blew a kiss to his sister.

Sri joined hands with Bali, and the two women stepped together
in mirrored motions. They bent their knees to join together and
moved their heads in opposite isolations. Eyes blinked with precision in time to the flute, and the women began an intricate set of
twirls together with both feet in constant contact with the sand.

Bali's older hands gripped Sri's gently in hers. Warm, more
experienced fingers guiding the younger, naive ones in a bond. The
circles were completed one after the other. Sri and Bali comple-
mented one another. What Bali lacked in agility, Sri made up for.
What Sri had yet to develop in intricacy, Bali nurtured. They were
lovely together.

Janaka watched Bali with a certain longing in his eyes. He scanned the crowd for his nephew, and could not find the youth for comfort. He was forced to focus on the Lady who he had known for so long. He was committed to helping her now, but he didn't want to watch as his heart fall once more for beauty that would not diminish. "Bali..." he whispered to himself, while his old body was hidden among the women.

"Sri..." Marici whispered idly while watching his sister spin on the sand. The two women had now begun walking forward to the sound of the Goanian drum, bringing their arms down with flat palms to heighten the ending of the dance. Marici locked his eyes on her, hoping that her gaze would fall his way so he could blow one more kiss to her.

The Queen's eyes were dimmed, and she looked not to her brother in these last moments of the dance. Her gaze fell upon Janaka, and she saw his admiration for Bali. She smiled in her eyes which glowed at the thought of such appropriate love.

Her black pools moved towards the ocean, in the rhythm of the Goanian drum and the girl felt the weight of a new gaze upon her body. She blinked. She shivered.

Something very warm went through her blood and spread to her toes that squirmed in the sand, and to her open palms that gestured to the sky for *Brahma*. Her breath felt light, and her head spinned with the feeling of those eyes on her body. Sri closed her eyes, and felt a need to make her hips move more smoothly and to raise her bosom with a deep breath. Her back arched slightly when she turned this last time in the final movement of the dance. The Goanian drum tapped lightly, and Sri's blood grew thick with desire.

Bali spinned in the sand next to Sri, and the two women completed the dance. They waited a moment for the music to end before opening their eyes to curtsey in gratitude. The applause that had started on the final twirl swelled, and the men cheered for the elder noblewoman and the Queen.

Marici stepped off his horse, and walked towards the two women with slow strides. His eyes were locked on Sri's, and she smiled sweetly in return. Such beauty should go rewarded. The King fell at Sri's and Bali's feet as he raised his palms up to *Brahma*. "The jewels of *Govandhara*, you both are!"

The people cheered and laughed joyously at the proclamation of the King as he kneeled before his Queen. The older lords yelled "Bali!" to signify their adoration of the woman. Some yelled "Sri *ya!*" to celebrate her delicate nature. Marici lowered his hands and simply stared at Sri. Such beauty should go rewarded.

Sri and Bali bowed before Marici, both giggling under their breath like fresh maidens. They joined their hands and presented the clasped fingers to the King for him to receive. Bali looked over at Sri and gave her a specific yet playful nod.

Marici chuckled and bowed low over the hands. He yelled again. "We will drink tonight to the Jewels of *Govandhara!*"

The old lords laughed and smiled, the afternoon of blood long forgotten now. And their women went to join them on their stallions, to enjoy the sunset before the party at Marici's palace turned to the night festival. There was laughter and music, and the King's ears were soothed.

Marici turned to His Queen, and took her free hand to his lips. He leaned in to whisper softly to Sri. "Child of Varuna, you have never looked lovlier...dance only with me?" The King drew Sri away from Bali, and turned her around his arms as they danced in the ocean's tide.

14

It had been the land of gentle breezes, and plenty. The people would walk carelessly through the plentiful grass and feel the bounty of *Brahma* underneath their feet. The people had been blessed with an easy life, and found time to create art and make love. All the children smiled as they played during long afternoons. There was little work to be done.

Food dripped from every garden, and no one went hungry. Bananas, mangoes, papayas—blessed by the gods to their people—fell into the hands of waiting women who would sing praises to the gods. And fish willingly sacrificed themselves from Varuna's surrounding arm, to the men who cast nets along the borders. There was no need to hunt, but weapons were crafted to kill men.

The people were peaceful, and spent many hours in the sun making music and happiness. There was no need to suffer, or to feel jealousy of the ruling family when life had been blessed by the gods already. It was not uncommon to see a husband and wife making love on the sand of Varuna's arm during an afternoon, when most men in Kasimi might be working. Time stood still in The Isles, and the golden sun spread over the land like a crown.

Vishal's father Parnath ruled this land, and had been in power for nearly seven hundred moons. When Osra claimed the tiny

islands to the south of The Isles, the house was given the right to
reign over the new lands. Most of Kasimi thought this to be an
increase of The Isles's power. But, it had ruined the kingdom's
chance of gaining an influential seat in Kasimi since half of their
population was not of pure blood. Though intermarriage was permitted, Vishal's house had remained pure. However, The Isles
were never regarded with as much respect again. That was the
only source of anger here.

The inhabitants of the land did not care for Kasimi's politics.
They were happy to take part in the glory of a land so perfect, and
to thank *Brahma* each day for their lives. Bloodshed and hatred
were things that happened only in the palace.

Within less than one moon, the smiles of children had been
wiped away. People did not make love along Varuna's gentle arm.
The Isles were dark, and the sun had forsaken the good people for
the length of almost one full moon which did not shine at night.
Varuna had angered around them, forcing people to make their
own salt water within their eyes.

The gentle whispering of the wind on the palms of trees grew
violent and strong, forcing up forests and homes and tossing them
into the ocean. The water came from a black sky, an endless night,
and poured with force upon the land. Soon, the ground could not
hold the water, and rivers grew in the villages. Animals and the
weaker elders and children were swept away into Varuna's ocean
while mothers screamed to *Brahma* for help. He answered the
mother's prayers, and washed the women away to the ocean to be
reunited with their children.

Thunder bellowed with the rain and announced its might. It
held the voice of divinity in it, and it promised to be a companion
to its victims. To not leave until it was done. To visit until it had
seen destruction and revenge. To never let there be silence while it

performed its deed. When men cried to the sky in pain, the rain and thunder only came harder.

The wind joined in the act and tore the ground up to the sky in sporadic bolts. The twisted cylinders of air carried animals, gardens and families and sacrificed them to the sky's power. With the presence of each one, the sky grew angrier—and more pleased that it had showed its might. It released more water to the land, as more lives were sacrificed.

Vishal stood in the middle of this nightmare, in the remains of his father's palace. He had been such an angry man, so filled with hate for those that had forsaken his people. Just as Parnath and Parnath's father. The Isles had seceded from Kasimi with pride. It was time for them to form an independent nation.

When *Govandhara* did not respond to the formal letter of secession, Parnath had grown wary. He had expected that King Marici would send a letter demanding that Vishal return to the court for an audience. There should have been a confrontation, and a direct statement of disapproval from the King's court. Silence worried the old ruler. It meant that the King was thinking about punishment.

Parnath had been swept away to the ocean when the flood waters crept inside his ancient stone palace. It reached for the elder as he slept, and enveloped his thick white hair before bringing him fully into its embrace. Before the aging noble could scream for help, he was gone in the depths of Varuna's ocean—too weak and old to fight against the current.

All that was left of the ruling family was Vishal and his two younger brothers, who were barely of age to rule. There were no women in the palace—the elder mother of the sons had died after the birth of the youngest. She was in no condition at her late stage in life, to carry another child to full term. But, she blessed the family with another boy and was received to heaven in *Brahma's* arms.

Vishal collapsed in the middle of the ruined palace and screamed to the sky. "Marici! You have won! Do not kill my people!" He raised his fists in the air and let out a loud sigh of pain that echoed in harmony with the thunder. He brought his hands to pound violently against his chest as he yelled at the water that lapped against his kneeling body and threatened to swallow him whole.

Finally, Vishal took his wet hands and placed them over his face. He sobbed for a long time, while the rain kept beating around him. He cried because his father had died, and left him alone to be responsible for The Isles. And though he was head-strong, he loved his people as his father did. To see the corpses of newborns floating with water-eaten flesh through the roads, and to hear the screams of women and men night after night as they suffered, made Vishal weep. He felt the weight of one thousand deaths on his shoulders—Vishal, the ruling noble of The Isles.

He wandered aimlessly towards the ocean, the water from the flood tugging against his torso. His eyes could not tune out the misery that surrounded him, and the haunting silence of death that drifted out to the sea. A little boy, no more than two and dressed in yellows, lay decayed underneath the water where Vishal walked. The priest and ruler paused and bowed his head in grief, while his own tears continued to come.

Vishal knew that Marici held the power of the sky in him now. He did not doubt that Sri had indeed found the magician that would rule Kasimi, and The Isles were being punished for his own insolence. Vishal had only meant to restore The Isles to their glory—he had not wanted the blood of his people painted in Varuna's face.

Vishal arrived at where he thought the ocean lied. The boundary became more vague as the rain poured day by day, and the trees wilted against the light rods from the sky. He dropped to his knees, so that only his face emerged from the water. He raised his palms to *Brahma*, and prayed for the lives for his people.

We understand Him as a river of five streams
From five sources?—crooked, cruel—
Its waves the five vital breaths
Its primal fount fivefold perception;
Its five whirlpools swirl wildly
With fivefold misery:
Fifty tributaries it has, five branches.

Vishal's eyes widened during his prayer, as he felt a breeze of clean air across his face. It was a dry breath from the sky, and the ruler looked up to see if his eyes had deceived him. They had not, and the sky had stopped raining on the spot where he kneeled. The breeze was *Brahma's* breath, and it carried calm around the sky. *Brahma* continued to breathe on Vishal.

The powerful figure of Vishal rose from his knees to look off into the ocean's waves, that still held energy in them. His eyes widened at the miracle that was coming to him. Above the trembling water was the hint of a blue sky, and the rays of the sun that had been trapped by a think layer of black clouds. *Brahma* had answered his prayer, and a layer of calm would sweep through the storm that fell on The Isles. The ferocious sky was being pushed away by this calm set of clouds. It could only be through a divine force, for this miracle.

A new hope sprung in the heart of Vishal. Was the storm finally gone? Had Marici let up the rain? Would he be able to start rebuilding The Isles? Vishal rubbed his eyes with fisted hands, and looked up to the sky once more. *Brahma*'s dry breath was still upon him, and the blue of the sky still approached him. A new fear came into his heart—what if this was only a break in the storm? A trick. A way to get the people out towards the ocean, to find rafts to get to safer land in the South. And then the waves, and wind would start up again to swallow an entire people.

Vishal looked blankly out onto the horizon, and exhaled in resignation. He was powerless against the might of the sky to help his people. After loving The Isles in his heart and mind for his life, Vishal would have to let nature sweep across the land and claim the lives of innocents. He gazed out onto the tired ocean, and was met again with another divine signal.

Walking on the horizon's border was a dot. Something that was larger than a sea creature. Vishal walked closer on the sand to see better. His heart pounded in his chest, and his already clammy hands began to sweat nervously. Marici's fleet. The King must be sending vessels to destroy his people while they were already vulnerable. The calm was Marici's magic over the sky guiding the warriors as they came to destroy what was left of The Isles.

It was a whole fleet of ships that grew closer on the horizon, and were approaching the north shores of The Isles. They grew bigger in appearance, as more blue sky peeked through a thin layer of white clouds. The light of *Brahma* against the dark of Marici's storm. Soon, the King's forces would be here and The Isles would be no more.

Vishal crumbled to the ground and began to weep once more. He would suffer the fate of his people, and welcomed death. He had done nothing wrong in this life, except forsake a King and insult a Queen who had been raised with grace. But, he had loved his people. So, Vishal wept on the sand for all the children that had died for his mistake and cursed Marici for slaying his father.

15

Sri wove in and out of the palace's central room, trying to make her presence as unnoticed as possible. She wore red, just as all the other women had that evening. And like some of the more traditional Kasimian noblewomen, Sri covered her face and hair to make her appearance less obvious. Her eyes, black with a red ring around the pupils, distinguished her as Marici's sister. She kept them downcast to the ground, so the more discerning nobles would not recognize her as Queen.

She was looking for the red-haired Goanian among the drinking men and women who celebrated the hunt. Sri had seen the bull in the middle of the room, placed upon a white blanket so the warm blood of the beast could let freely. Candles—her favorite vanilla—were placed around the creature to bless its soul as it made peace with *Brahma*. This sight had disgusted Sri—the senseless sacrifice of an animal so that the Marici could show off.

The people were lazily socializing underneath the gold dome, while indulging in glass after glass of red wine. Even the King had had his fair share of alcohol, and was too busy to watch Sri cover her face, and leave the pillow where she sat beside him. Marici had worn red as well, the color of his sacrifice's blood. Sri watched her brother through the night, until she saw him lose control of his smiles and bring his words together lazily. She kissed his cheek and muttered something about finding a friend, and then disappeared into the sea of red that filled the throne room.

She quickly covered her hair and face, and walked along the green and white marble tiles in search of Devyn. Flirtatious whispers and drunken laughter invaded Sri's ears, and she grew more anxious to find the Goanian. Then, a strong hand squeezed Sri's shoulder and Sri felt a shiver go through her body. She turned to look up at the red haired man, who sipped his wine as he signaled her. He cocked his head towards a secretive alcove in the back of the central room, where Sri could escape unnoticed to the gardens of the palace. His fingers made a three across his cup of wine, and Devyn went quietly to the alcove to escape towards the gardens. Sri looked up at the gold domed ceiling, and took three long breaths. Now, it was time to drift beyond her subjects in the direction of Devyn.

Sri walked casually past the revelry, and slipped into the dark alcove, and the door that went to the narrow corridor—she walked quickly, so that guards would not have a chance to observe her while she moved nervously towards the secret entrance. Then, she was outside. The cold night air of Kasimi whipped warningly around her face. It was Marici's wind, and it lingered around her suspiciously. But, the Queen moved further. She knew where to go—the sanctuary.

The Queen ran through the lush gardens, inhaling the sweet scent of bursting flowers. In her empty stomach, the smell was digested like too much sugar and made her feel ill. She ran aggressively, faster, in the direction of the sanctuary. The trees blurred past her, and the girl thought she was going to vomit. But Devyn found her just a few paces before the sacred shrine, and took her damp hand in his. Sri found stability with him, and could then enter the sanctuary

Inside, the room was dark save two red candles that burned underneath crystal blue eyes. Lady Bali stood in the modest and secretive structure, and bowed deeply to the Queen who would help the people of The Isles. Words must be scarce, and the red-clad elder paid homage with her lowered form instead of her voice. Sri nodded graciously, and took a seat on one of the two stools against the wall. Devyn found a place standing in the shadows, while the two women conducted their meeting.

The flames flickered against Bali's aging face. Sri took note of the heavy expression in the woman's beautiful eyes, brought out against the fire. The elder lady began in hushed tones, directing her words to the point of the issue.

"My Queen, I am honored that you have followed your heart. Be assured that *Brahma* will look down on you with mercy and pride that you protect the innocents—your people. We do not have much time, my Queen." Bali looked over to the shadows where Devyn stood, and then at Sri. A small smile of reassurance and comfort came to the girl.

Sri nodded efficiently. "I am hesitant, Bali. I am afraid, and I am defying my brother and King. But I will help you—I do this because it is right." Sri stared at the elder woman for comfort, not knowing where else to turn. Though there were people who believed in this cause, Sri was alone.

"I have no plan, Sri. All I know is—something bad will happen in The Isles, and we must do something. Organize an underground movement against this hatred. Organize the people. I am sure the Southern Kingdom is unhappy about this." Bali whispered into the darkness.

Sri shook her head, and interrupted Bali's statement. "No…no, Bali. You are wrong. Something…very bad is going to happen in

The Isles. This is not about organizing support. We must send it. We must send it now." Sri sat at the edge of her stool, and leaned in towards the elder noblewoman. She was speaking with force, and feeling all kinds of emotions running through her blood.

Bali brought her hands up, and spread them before Sri. "What, what do we do? The King has not openly discussed a plan for aggression against The Isles. How do we plan something when we do not know what will be done?"

Sri closed her eyes and brought a finger up to where the sky would be. She sat, frozen in that position for a moment, and then said in a voice lower than she would normally use, "It will fall from the sky, Bali." She brought her black pools to look at the noble. "I was part of it, Bali...and don't ask me to explain...and I tried to be calm, and I tried to make Marici stop. And yet I do not remember."

Bali's eyes widened. In her age, her very experienced and advanced age, Bali had seen the work of the divine. The confused words of the child-Queen were a sign of a power that only a descendant of Varuna could hold. She squinted, and prodded Sri to explain further. "Go on, child."

"We danced in the ocean, Bali. We swam in the waves. Marici screamed to *Brahma* above, and made our great grandfather angry. Do you remember that storm just nights ago?" Sri dropped her tone. "Do you?"

Bali nodded once. "Yes?" She was beginning to understand.

"The water grew violent, and I could feel anger and rage around me. I don't remember what happened after that—but it was no storm, Bali. It was Marici...and before I fell asleep in the water, I heard him call for blood in The Isles." Sri's eyes looked down, her story now complete.

"I see." Bali searched Sri for more details, clarification. The elder was confused. "The storm was Marici's anger. I understand. But...how does this involve the people of The Isles?"

Sri smiled faintly, and grabbed the elder noblewoman's hand to place against her heart. "Do not ask me how I know things, Bali. Marici made me a part of that storm, and I can feel the thunder in my mind. I can't sleep, and I have no peace. The storm is part of the ocean, and it is moving. I can feel it inside me. I am not the sky god, but I am linked to him. I can feel Marici. I know that the people there will feel the storm. They have to get off the islands."

Bali squeezed the Queen's hand and kissed her knuckles. "All right, Queen Sri." She sighed. It was a risk to trust the raw emotions of a child with the energy of a rebellion. "All right." What choice did Bali have but to believe Sri? Something in her own old soul wanted to trust this sweet youth. "All right."

Bali released Sri's hand. "And so..." The impasse.

Sri stood from her stool and walked towards the wall where her mother's name was carved. She traced that beautiful name, and let her fingers linger on the cold stone. "I...have a plan."

Bali laughed nervously under her breath, and turned on her stool to look at Sri. "By all means, Sri."

"We need to get the people off the islands. Quickly." Sri walked idly in the sanctuary. She asked a rhetorical question. "How do we do that?"

Bali did not answer. She didn't have an answer. She sat patiently, blue eyes wide with wonder. She motioned with a flick of her head for Devyn to come closer so that he may participate in this strategic discussion.

"The ports in the Southern Kingdom. We need to get ships to sail from there to The Isles—as many as we can get. They will have to risk Varuna's strength. But, I know the ocean will carry them. And they must gather the people from The Isles, as many as they can gather, and take them to safer land." Sri sighed, and turned to Devyn who stood only moments from her. She looked apologetically at him, "These people cannot go to the Southern Kingdom, Devyn. There is too much danger, and too many people who are adamantly loyal to my brother. This is where my plan is weak. I do not know where to take these people when it is done."

Devyn thought for a moment, and tapped his lips with a finger. "I have asked you to make a sacrifice, Sri. So I will make one too." Devyn sat in the empty stool and looked between Bali and the Queen. "My people would never condone violence against innocents. It is not our way in Goane. I will send word to my family to expect refugees in the port. Goane..." Devyn turned to face Sri. "Goane is at your disposal, Sri. Send the people there. It is not a far journey from The Isles."

Sri looked quietly at Devyn with a grin on her lips. "I know." She had read the priest. If he had not volunteered his land, she would have doubted the purity of his convictions.

Devyn winked at Sri. "I see."

"Sri, I think your plan is brilliant. And, it could work. But..." The elder noblewoman put her head in her hands and sighed. "I think you believe me to be more powerful than I am. I assume that I would be the one to organize the ports in the Southern Kingdom. While I have a few contacts, and have gold, I do not have the power necessary for this great a task. I would need the support of many, many merchants who would be completely loyal to me...who would not betray me...for this to work. I am afraid I am just not that influential. There are few who are." Bali looked up at Sri, upset at her own inadequacy. The plan could work, but even she was limited in Kasimi.

"I am." A familiar, but new voice, came from the dark corner of the sanctuary. The man walked closer to the source of light. "I am one who is that powerful."

The body of Lord Janaka made itself visible. The elder lord, clad in red silks and holding a glass of red wine, had been in the corner of the sanctuary for the entire meeting. He looked at Bali, Devyn and Sri with amusement.

Bali looked at Janaka with frustration. She stood and walked to his side, and gripped his forearm forcefully. "Janaka. You said you would not make yourself known. You put yourself in danger."

Janaka placed his hand over Bali's and spoke with resolution. "You asked me to help you, and I am." He nodded to Sri, and to Devyn once more. "I trust you two will not let my name leave this room?"

Devyn bowed his head to Janaka. "Of course not, my lord." He was still shocked to see the rich nobleman and merchant inside the sanctuary. He had not expected one of such status and seeming apathy to be a part of this.

Sri's went to sit in Bali's stool, surprised by the sight of Lord Janaka. She was wary, at first, when he emerged from the shadows. But if Bali trusted Janaka, he must be pure of heart. She nodded quietly in his direction. "You are safe, my lord."

Janaka smiled. "Thank you, my Queen." He kissed Bali on the cheek and continued. "I can organize the fleet of ships to go to The Isles and take the people to Goane. It's simple. I have the contacts. Consider it done."

Sri walked to Janaka, and embraced him while he stood next to Bali. "Thank you," she murmured, with her head pressed between the lord's and lady's shoulders. "Thank you...you have no idea..."

Bali placed a maternal hand on Sri's back and comforted the girl, and looked over at Janaka. "Thank you, Sri. You have sacrificed a great deal to come here tonight, and we are grateful."

Sri smiled, and backed away from the elder nobles to sit near Devyn. She took a deep breath, and looked among the people. "I will leave the sanctuary, and go to my room as if nothing has happened tonight. Should you need me, send word quietly through Devyn." She flashed her black eyes at the Goanian and smiled. "Devyn has a way of finding me when no one is looking."

There was silence in the sanctuary now. The meeting was done, and the candle was blown out so that only the dark of night remained. The door opened, and Bali exited with Janaka, arm in arm. Though it could not be seen, Sri smiled at the couple that appeared to find much comfort in one another. There must be a past between them.

Sri waited a few moments, and then stood to make her exit. She whispered in the darkness, "We will speak soon." She began to walk towards the door but the Devyn had moved silently before her. His breath was warm and near, and he put his hands around Sri's waist. There was another shiver that went through her body, and she leaned in just a bit to feel him. Her hands trembled as they moved around Devyn's back. There was a moment of hesitation, and the night air was suddenly thick and warm. His lips were near as he whispered, "Go, Sri. The party will end soon and Marici will seek you."

In the dark, Sri's heart pounded in its cage. Her hands tightened into fists, and moved through the air back to her side. She swallowed against her jeweled throat, and ran out of the sanctuary.

16

Sri ran as fast as she could back to the palace, making the colors of the garden a blur against her black eyes. Soon her feet were making pace with the stairs that would lead to her suite. Her red silks could barely keep up with her moving form, until she finally reached the Queen's chambers and closed the door behind her. She did not want to think about what the guards or attendants must think of her for being in such a state. Sri just paused by the doorway, and let her eyes search the room.

Her black pools were captivated by the gold statues of the fertility goddesses at either side of the glass doors of her balcony. Sri wandered towards the women, and stared at the carvings. She examined how the curves of their bodies seemed so smooth and beautiful—so perfect. The gentle twist of the hip, the subtle tilt of their necks made Sri feel hot underneath her silks. The Queen brought her hands to her body, and began to feel her own curves beneath the sari. Her delicate hands, strong and limber, massaged the beginnings of her full bosom.

Sri moved the sari aside to fall at her hips so that only her skin-tight blouse rested on her torso. Her hands worked around her elliptical mounds and squeezed...and released...squeezed...and released. Until the large brown nipples in the center were so erect that it hurt. Sri ripped open her blouse, sending a few of the pearl buttons to the floor, and let her fingers squeeze over the flesh that felt so tender. The Queen sighed lightly, and removed her hands from her body to feel the gold statues.

Sri pulled apart the sari and unraveled the folds, letting them slip to the ground in a massive whirl at her feet. Her hands felt her own waist, tracing the smooth mocha skin with her fingers, and then feeling the lilt of her soft hips underneath. Sri closed her eyes, and indulged in her body for a while longer. Her hands went to feel the uplift of her bottom, and how the cheeks pinched together so artfully.

Finally, Sri's hands found her womanhood and began to explore what was inside her. The rubbing made her feel so in touch with what she had felt before, when the eyes of a man were on her body. She massaged her sex, gently at first. The touch got thicker and more aggressive, and Sri's breathing grew heavier with pleasure. Finally, out of nowhere, her body shivered in vibrations and collapsed to the floor with an overwhelming feeling of peace. Her eyes looked at the tapestries that surrounded her, and the stories seemed to make much more sense.

~

Jabala walked to sit near Sri, and to stroke her long black hair as it spilled on the cold marble floor. She did not attempt to wake or move the sleeping girl, and simply watched her. The lightly dozing Sri stirred as Jabala's cold hands made contact with her forehead, and her eyes drifted open. Sri did not appear embarrassed in the accepting arms of her nurse.

"Jabie?" Sri asked.

"Yes, Sri. It's me, little one." Jabie brought Sri's head to her lap, and worked her fingers in the girl's hair. "You looked so peaceful, I did not want to wake you."

Sri smiled slowly, and stretched her body from the makeshift blanket of clothes. She wrapped her toes in the bottom of her sari silks, and then looked up at Jabala. Her eyes searched her nurse's for a moment. "How did you know, Jabie, what it felt like to be a woman?"

Jabie laughed lightly, and settled the red silks around Sri to hide her body from view. "It depends on what you mean, child."

"I mean…to feel pleasure as a woman would." Sri blinked once, and waited for the older woman to explain to her.

Jabala nodded to Sri, and paused the caresses of the girl's hair. "I lost my virginity at an early age, Sri. Younger than you are now. I came upon my womanhood earlier than I expected. My body had not given me the signals that yours seems to be giving you."

Sri hesitated but then admitted, "I felt a man's eyes on me, Jabie. I didn't know that it would feel so…sensual?"

"Sensual, yes. The look, the scent…the touch of a man can do that." Jabala leaned in and kissed Sri's forehead. "Does the way your brother look at your make you shiver, sweetness? Indeed, it is not wrong to feel that way, child."

"No, Jabala, it is not Marici." Sri paused, and wavered upon her next words. How she wanted to confess her feelings for another man. She had promised—vowed—not to feel this way. No, she would not betray that feeling that was festering deep within her heart.

Sri bit slowly on her lip, and murmured as an afterthought. "I…have defined myself today, Jabala…as a Queen." Just an afterthought. Said lightly without much weight or eye contact. If Jabala took the subject further, it would be fine. If she ignored it, even better. A passing confession.

Jabala would never prod Sri to go further in conversation to satisfy her own curiosity. She would encourage direction only to help Sri clear her mind. Jabala started to stroke the girl's hair once more, only adding a quick "Oh?" in polite inquiry.

Sri unsettled herself in the red blanket of silk and sat up to look at Jabala. Her bare breasts were covered only with long tresses of black curls. Her eyes held a certain passive intensity as she spoke. "Jabala, I am no longer innocent. I am not pure as everyone thinks me to be. I have done something tonight that is irreversible. I have sinned, but I did it by my own will and my own choice. And I am not ashamed."

Jabie raised her hands to Sri's head and pressed them against the Queen's ears. "Shhh," she motioned to the Queen with the puckering of her lips. She brought the girl to her heart, and whispered slowly so only she could hear. "There are times when we must do on our own, without fear. Whatever you have done, my child, does not make you impure. You have been your own lover. What has been denied to you, you provided for yourself."

Jabie coaxed the girl into her lap once more. "Nothing to be ashamed of. Women must do what is necessary, without a King or without a man."

Sri eyed Jabala for a moment. So wise, Jabala was. She fumbled with her lips, wanting to speak—add something to this. But there was nothing she could say, that would be meaningful. Sri gathered the red silks around her and stood up near the golden statues in silence.

Jabala remained on the floor for a moment longer, and craned her neck to look up. "Just remember, Sri. That you can trust me. I understand there are some things you do that I can't know. But everything that you tell me, stays between us. My loyalty is to you." Then, Jabala stood and walked over to the Queen's bed to unfold the blankets and prepare it for Sri.

It would be better if Jabala did not know what she had done, just now. Sri smiled and blinked. "Yes, Jabie...I know." The girl walked to her bed and retrieved the white resting gown that had been tucked neatly away under one of the pillows, and placed it over her body. "And thank you."

Jabie nodded quietly, and did not speak more on this topic. Her hands traced along the edges of the many pillows and blankets and made sure that the bedding was in place. "Here you go, child. Time for bed."

Sri began to slip into the comforting bed, and feel the pillows around her when she heard a demanding knock at her door. It was not a request—the sound was a warning. Sri gestured at Jabala. "Who would come at this hour, Jabie?"

Jabie shrugged. "No idea." She walked dutifully to the door and opened it a crack to see who would come to see the Queen at this late a time. Her voice was muffled as she made inquiries, and Sri could not make out the language. There were two masculine voices at the other side—that she could hear.

Sri asked, impatiently, "Jabie?"

Jabie said something to the men on the other side of the door, and then turned back to Sri. "It's Marici. He wants to come in and speak with you now?" Her eyebrows went high over her wide brown eyes as if to give Sri a secret message.

Sri nodded curtly. "Fine." She shook her head a few times, slightly impatient with her brother's strange behavior as of late. "Please let him in, and then you should get some rest."

Jabala opened the door and said something quietly to the men outside, and then Marici pushed passed and entered Sri's chamber. He was still in his red silks, and had obviously just come from the merriment underneath the golden dome.

"Your Highness." Jabala murmured while dipping into a curtsey. She turned to Sri and spoke in a more formal tone than the two used in private. "I shall take my leave, my mistress, as you commanded." With that, Jabala scurried off to her room adjacent to the Queen's chamber and closed the door.

Sri watched Jabala go, and waited to hear her door close before she focused her attention on Marici. Still standing by the bed, Sri was uncertain whether she should get under the blankets to hint that she wanted to sleep. "Do you need something, Marici?"

Marici smiled wryly, and stumbled a few paces into the bedroom. "I...missed you. Where did you disappear to?" The King found a seat at the end of Sri's bed.

Sri remained standing. "I was tired. It's been a long day."

Marici laughed heartily and slapped a hand on the bed with force. "Sri, tired? I have never heard of such things!" He stood and walked behind his sister so that his breath could be felt against her neck. "You, tired? The one who dances with Bali on the sand? The one who won't go on walks with me though I beg? Could you not have stayed by my side tonight if only to please me, sister?"

Sri turned to face Marici. She would not tolerate his drunken tantrums at this hour. "Marici, you have had too much wine, and you should go to your chambers—to bed."

Marici stepped in closer and closed the gap between the two twins. "Actually I..." Marici laughed again, in a slow whisper. "I was..." He then leaned in and whispered in Sri's ear. "...hoping you'd let me stay here tonight. Just to lie beside you? I missed you."

Sri pulled a blanket over her body, so her form was not vulnerable to Marici's piercing black eyes. "No. You will go to your own chamber, and you will sleep there."

The King made a pouting lip—but he was mocking his sister. "Awww," he said, in a long drawl. "Awww." He stumbled back to the bed and sat down once more. Marici looked up at his sister with a big grin. "All right. You win, Queen Sri." He patted a space next to him. "Come sit?"

Sri shook her head. She was losing patience, and thinking of other places in the palace where she and Jabie could sleep tonight.

"Well then, answer me this, Sri." Marici quickly lost his drunken demeanor and looked seriously at his sister. He leaned on the edge of the bed and narrowed his eyes to slits, while the red grew more dominant in his pupils. He stared for a moment, and then growled under his breath. "Answer me this, Sri. Where did you go tonight? You did not simply go to bed."

Inside, Sri felt fear. A nervous mixture of nausea and betrayal swam in her stomach, and promised to make haste if Sri did not use her mind to center herself. Did he know what she had done? Was he asking simply as a way to tell her that he knew? Surely not. Sri exhaled, and let her nervousness go into the air. "Marici." Sri began, centered. "I grew tired of a celebration of blood. I went to the gardens and took a walk. A long walk. I am allowed to do that."

"Without guards? Without telling me?" Marici's mood had mellowed slightly.

"I enjoy my privacy." Sri retorted quickly.

Marici stood from the bed, and walked with balance towards the door. He was suddenly more sober. Before exiting, he turned once to Sri and gave his command. "Do not walk alone again, sister." The King opened the door, and disappeared to the black marble hallway beyond the Queen's chamber.

~

On the other side of the door, Marici spoke quietly to his man. There was no passionate anger in the way he exited the room. But disappointment read clearly in his eyes. He looked at the dark assassin, who was dressed in modest black silks. "She lied to me, man."

Marici began the long walk to his chamber, at the other end of the black marble hallway. The footsteps of the two men echoed behind them. Marici had excused the guards for one hour, so that he may have a moment alone with his sister. He had made the hallway completely dark, save a few lit candles so he would not miss his steps. Vanilla candles—the light of his sweet sister.

The black clad man nodded silently, and awaited the questions from his King. He had vowed to keep Sri safe. This was his new code, and he was indebted to Marici for life. For sparing his life. He had obediently let his eyes remain fixated on the beautiful Queen, and had reported back to the King each night since the caravan had arrived at *Govandhara*.

The two men stopped midway between the Queen's chamber and the King's chamber. Marici put his arm around the shoulder of his man. "Tell me exactly what you saw, man." The King turned the black clad servant around to face him, to read his words beyond their shaped meaning.

The dark guard spoke simply. His voice was always humble now. It never rose above the whisper that only Marici's ears could hear. "I saw your Queen enter the sanctuary. She remained there while the moon shifted over the sea in the night. At that time, two figures walked out and escaped into the garden." The guard paused, and tried to find the next words carefully. To not accuse or assume anything about the Queen. "A few moments after that, she ran out of the sanctuary to the palace. Quickly. I followed her, until she went to her room."

Marici's eyes went red. "This, she did not tell me." He motioned to the black clad man to continue walking down the hallway. "Perhaps Sri finds peace in the sanctuary. But peace is not found in the company of two other people." He tightened his jaw and turned to his man. "You are to report to me twice a day now. Once at night, and once in the morning. I want you to watch her balcony and see what goes on while she sleeps. Always, if anything strange happens, you should come to me."

The dark guard bowed deeply before the King. "As you command, my master."

Marici nodded approvingly, and patted the assassin on the back. "You serve me well, man." The King opened the door to his chamber, and slipped into the comfort of his room.

Marici banged his head on the doors. He needed answers. Something was not right—he could feel her heart and it was no longer just his. Something else was inside it. Had he not satisfied her? He must do something. He was losing her. It was only a matter of time.

~

At dawn, Sri awoke with a feeling that she must leave the palace grounds for a short time. It was one of the few times that the girl rose before Jabala, with more energy than she had ever had. Sri kissed her nurse on the cheek, and dressed herself in a simple purple wrap, and walked the distance from her chamber to her brother's in the black marble hallway.

Each step was taken with a purpose, and without fear. Despite the warnings of the guards and men that the King was not awake just yet, Sri walked forward and opened the door of her brother's room. Marici had not slept. He sat on a green divan in the entrance room to his suite, still in his red silks from the previous night. His head was in his hands, and he smelled of Kasimian rum. Sri focused beyond the pathetic sight of her brother, and stated her request. She wanted to go to the temple of *Govandhara*, just one day's journey from the palace. She knew that Ajan would be making a journey there, starting this afternoon. She wished to go with him. Of course, she would take any guards and men he wished. And, Jabala would go with her.

Marici gave his blessing for this journey, feeling that time spent on scholarly pursuit of the gods was just what the Queen needed to bring her back to normal. It would be the first time Sri had left the palace since they came. Marici stood, and embraced his sister with a kind of desperation. He would miss her—he needed her. But, he understood that she needed time at Ajan's temple.

Sri nodded, and returned the embrace. She did not comment on the broken state of her brother nor did she pass judgment on him. She was going to the temple to release herself from him, if only for a few nights. She was not sure when she would return, but it should not be longer than one moon's time. Marici consented.

That afternoon, Sri and Jabala joined Ajan, and a team of guards for the journey to the temple of *Govandhara*. Marici arranged for the finest horses and swords to accompany the Queen on her path, but he did not come to the beach to bid her farewell. He was still in his room, with his head hanging in his hands, wearing the red silks from the previous night's feast.

Sri and Jabala dressed simply for the journey. Both in simple wraps instead saris or salwar-kameez, with no jewelry. Simple sandals, and loose hair. Sri's thick mane of black flowed next to Jabala's luxurious brown one. No adornments. Sri let her body be free under a loose covering that was meant for the comfort of riding. She would ride her own horse—and insisted on a black mare.

The court whispered as the Queen rode with Ajan and Jabala towards the temple, taking the path of Varuna's beach to the south. Bali's eyes shined to see such a change in the demure *rani*. Once a shadow of Marici, Sri's head was held high as the caravan departed. A smile was on her lips—she knew. Sri knew who she was, and was commanding the journey.

Ajan and Jabala rode a few paces behind the commanding Queen, so that they might secretly exchange glances and simple bits of conversation during the journey that would fall into the night hours. The change in Sri did not go unnoticed by the Grand Priest, who had raised and molded this child for sixteen years. He enjoyed the freedom and pride that she exhibited. Despite her great beauty, Sri had managed to rise above her limited station. It was no longer the delicate arch of her brow or the curving in of her lips that one would notice upon looking at her. It was the way Sri could prove herself a Queen without words.

Sri rode her horse with skill and speed down her grandfather's beach, taking little time to enjoy his beauty. She needed to find peace at the temple. This is where she would find answers. The sooner she could get her caravan there, the sooner she would find the path. It was comforting that the two people she loved, who had known her through everything, were riding right behind her.

At the rise of the moon, the caravan found itself turning from Ajan's forest to the path that would lead to the magnificent white temple. The reflecting pools were not as tended to since Sri left, and weeds had grown in some places around the borders. But, it was still grand and humbling. Sri paused her horse when the site of her childhood came into her eyes, and dismounted her horse.

She walked towards the temple, letting the beautiful white structure with etchings of the gods carved upon every crevice overwhelm her. Many emotions drifted in and out of her mind on revisiting this place again. And then she found what she felt. Safety. She was home. She had never felt this way when she was growing up—her days were so structured and rigid. But now, she was returning to her childhood temple having become what she was destined to be. And, she was taking control of that role. In this temple, Sri could breathe.

Ajan and Jabala let Sri walk alone to the grand marble structure. Jabala especially realized that something was going on inside the Queen, and the evolution that was claiming her soul would be complete upon this path. Ajan watched his ward, with love in his eyes. He had missed her dearly.

Sri collapsed at the steps to the temple, and held herself in her arms. She sobbed in tears of relief. She was home—and safe—and understood more now. Her body curled on the lower step that would lead to the central prayer room with such blinding white light.

Ohm. Shanti, Shanti, Shanti.

~

Ajan had taken Sri in his arms to bed, as he had so many nights when she was a girl. This morning, Jabala did not wake her with scoldings of laziness. Sri rose when the sun came into her eyes and persuaded her to rise. Jabala had simply laid out several silks, of simple quality, for Sri to choose from. She had left a tray of cha and bread for the Queen to nibble on. Jabala had granted Sri privacy, and independence.

Sri was not sure what she would do. Perhaps wander in the forest and along the beach of this great temple. She was not hungry, but drank a few sips of tea. She was not cold, but wore a honey yellow wrap—her favored one at fifteen. She chose no shoes. She had no idea where to wander to. It did not matter—no one was watching.

A few hours went by, and Sri had no idea where the time went. She had managed to step only from her room to the door of Ajan's office where she tapped lightly at the door with a carefully shaped nail. He would have to be listening for a knock to hear this feminine scratch from the other side of the room. Sri did not want to intrude.

A masculine voice called out from the study, "Enter."

Sri carefully opened the door, and presented herself to the Grand Priest. It had not changed. The bookshelves, which had been full before, were now flooded with novels. New shelves had been added towards the ceiling of the room, to create space for all the new reading material. Still, no light besides what candles would offer was available. "*A formula for secrecy*" rang in Sri's mind as she remembered. Red silk pillows, a bit older and more worn, were centered in the room. Still no chairs.

Sri smiled, and looked at Ajan. "Hello, old friend."

Ajan went to Sri with outstretched arms. "I knew it was you by that little tap. You're the only other who comes in my chamber." He placed his strong arms protectively around Sri. "It is so nice to have a moment with you, darling." He placed a kiss at the top of her head.

Sri held Ajan, and sighed against his chest. The warmth of his body, and the scent of vanilla that seemed to linger in his silks, made her feel welcome. "It is so nice to be with you, Ajan. Here, in this temple. Like the last moons have been a dream and this is what I wake to."

Ajan walked Sri to the pillows in the center of the room, and took a seat. The Grand Priest had taken to wearing black silks over red or white. Simple tunics and pants, with his ceremonial swords at his hip. He still looked noble in this somber attire—he was cut of the finest blood. He looked older, though. Ajan's chiseled features showed age around them. And his fantastic hood of black hair displayed more grey and silver.

Sri took a seat, and sat with her legs tucked at a diagonal to her body. She looked into the cerulean eyes of her mentor, and smiled sadly. "If you knew what I had done, Ajan, you would not see me the same way again."

"Nonsense, Sri. There is nothing you could do to change how much I love you." Ajan clucked his tongue, and swatted away this ridiculous banter.

Sri's eyes searched Ajan's carefully, her black pools moving quickly over the blue centers of Ajan's face. "Is this true, Ajan? Even if I betrayed my King?" Her voice was smooth and supported, without the nervousness of her crime.

Ajan gave Sri and incredulous look. He squinted. "You...would never betray your King..." Ajan blinked quickly and added, "Sri?"

Sri continued her questions. "What if I did something that was so against the laws of Kasimi, and yet was so in favor of the people? What if I did something that was against rules, but was in the name of compassion and mercy? Then what?"

Ajan scratched his forehead at the outpouring of questions. What if? What if? What then? Ajan shrugged and then looked at the child with a wrinkled brow. "How can something be in favor of the people, but against the rules? You do not make sense, Sri." Ajan looked down at his lap, and away from the Queen. "What do you speak of? Are you in trouble, Sri?"

Sri would not tell Ajan of her deed—he would have to find out on his own. The girl shook her head and fussed with the folds in her wrap. "No, I am not in trouble, Ajan. I am just trying to understand how your love for me works."

Ajan breathed out, loudly. Though he still suspected something was very wrong with his ward—something very wrong—he was reassured by the fact that she was not in trouble. Or at least that is what she was telling him, which he wanted so much to believe. Ajan had never thought about this before. This question of loyalty. If there were a situation where he must choose between Sri and his vow to Kasimi, who would he choose? That is ultimately the question that Sri asked. "Ah."

Sri frowned and placed her face against two waiting fists. She repeated softly, "I am just asking, Ajan. I am not in any trouble."

Ajan ran his slender fingers through his peppered hair, and thought about the question once more. *Would I choose Sri?* "I do love you, Sri..." Ajan said to begin his statement.

"But..." Sri interjected, from her face down position.

"But..." Ajan added gently. "But, I put my duty to Kasimi and to Kasimi's King above all else. Even if my heart were to break, I must obey my blood oath to serve as Grand Priest."

"Even if you knew that Kasimi's King was not acting in the name of *Brahma*?" Sri looked with widened eyes at Ajan, and moved her posture to direct herself at him. There was so much pending on this answer. She was testing Ajan's loyalty.

"Even if, Sri. I do not question my King." Ajan closed his eyes to emphasize the finality of his words. His voice was solid in the statement.

"Ajan...you said that you would not return to your warrior path, and now serve the gods. You told this to the King when you all but refused to work with Lord Ashok on a campaign against The Isles. Are you saying you would obey the King if he ordered you to be a warrior once more? Even though it is not what you wish to do?"

Ajan was growing irritated at this conversation. His voice rose in volume. "What exactly are you trying to do, Sri? Test my loyalty to Marici? What?" He shook his head and flared breath through his nostrils. "If Marici ordered me to be a warrior, then I would either have to obey him or cease my services to Kasimi. It does not mean I cannot protest the King, and offer him my counsel. But ultimately, Marici is law, and I will either obey or die."

"Die?" Sri asked gently, bringing her own arms around her torso to cradle herself.

Ajan softened at the sight of his crumpling ward. "Sri, darling," he began, softly. He put a hand on the girl's shoulder. "We can disagree with Marici. We can even voice our grievances. But He is law. If we do not agree with his choice of law for the mortal realm, we must slip from the mortal realm and answer to *Brahma*."

Sri nodded mildly. "I see." She took a few moments of shaking her head from side to side, and parting her lips to speak. But again, there was nothing she really could say. Ajan seemed—resolute. She understood him, and his loyalties, despite how much her heart ached. *I would go against Kasimi for you, Ajan. If it was in the name of mercy and compassion.*

After a long moment, Sri finally said. "I think I am going to go for a walk outside in the gardens."

Ajan gestured with his hand around the chamber. "You can always find me here, darling. I'll see you at the evening meal, then?"

"Absolutely." Sri said, as she rose from her place by the red pillow. She walked away from the circle, and exited through the door without looking back.

~

Sri found herself in a very different forest than she had remembered from just over a year ago. The trees and bushes had not been groomed as they once had been, and there did not appear to be as many servants around to tend to the grounds. Mango trees that used to be cared for each day, were left to run wild with their fruit that dripped off the branches to the ground. Leaves rustled in the wind, and escaped into the sky's breath when they were no longer strong enough to cling to the branches. Things were quiet in the forest. Sri thought it was more beautiful this way.

The path that was meant for walking was still tended to. The green underneath was kept to a certain height, and the stones were artfully placed on the perimeter. The hands of servants could be felt as Sri walked. But she no longer felt watched, or the need to make eye contact with the dozens of servants that would keep each acre. Sri could just wander. Even the guards had not questioned her desire for peace on her childhood walk.

She walked further in the forest, and realized that she was on the path towards the sanctuary. Sri slowed her steps, not wanting to have that place come into sight again. It had been where she had cried over her mother's name. *Rani*. It was no longer a place of meditation and peace for her. She walked slower, making the time pass with less space.

Though she did not want to look upon the sanctuary, she found herself in front of the structure in a few moments. That inadequate building of stones and weakly woven straw was just as she had remembered it. She did not like this memory. But, she knew she must walk further towards it to completely rid it from her mind and heart.

"*Namas Namas!*" came the jolly greeting of an old man as Sri walked towards the sanctuary. He waggled his bald brown head, and ran with his short legs towards the Queen. "*Namas Namas!*"

Sri looked behind her quickly for the source of the familiar voice. She leaned forward and looked at the short, old servant who was running her direction. Half heartedly she replied, "Namas Namas?" while trying to remember who this person was. And then the pieces of the memory fit together, and Sri realized that is was the old man who had helped her in the sanctuary. Who had been her friend. It was Brahma! She said again, with more energy, "Namas Namas!"

"*Viseet Brahma, man-y, man-y time!*" Brahma chuckled as he hopped the last step to greet his Queen. He put his arms around Sri and placed his bald head on her shoulder. "*Goot you see!*"

Sri held this sweet old Kasimian in her arms, and patted his head gently. "Oh Brahma, it's good to see you too!" She pushed away from him, but kept her arms around his forearms. "How are you?"

Brahma pointed above at the sun and said, "*Brahma ees hut hut hut!*" He laughed again, waggling his head in delight. "*Come, we seet there.*" The man pointed at a spot of shade under a banyan tree.

Sri chuckled, happy to be in the company of her old friend. "All right, Brahma." She walked arm in arm with the old man to the quiet spot by the shade.

"*Palace ees ver-y nice. Brahma hear. Fun times?*" Brahma beamed at Sri, while he made his comment about *Govandhara's* palace.

"Fun time?" Sri laughed, and took a comfortable seat under the tree. "I wouldn't exactly call it fun, Brahma. It is…interesting. My brother seems to be enjoying himself."

Brahma waggled his head more slowly. This was confusing to him. Being a Queen was not fun? He pointed to himself with his stubby fingers. "*Me,*" he said, "*if me rani, fun time for Brahma. Fun time!*" He slapped his knee and chuckled loudly for a few seconds. "*Why not Sri make for fun like Brahma do?*"

Sri watched the old man with delight, and smiled through his laughter. "Well, I don't really get to tell people what to do, Brahma, like you'd think. It's Marici's palace, his feast, his party. It's not mine."

Brahma thought about this with a serious expression on his always-smiling face. Though his silly gestures would belie this sadness, Brahma must spend a great deal of time thinking about where he came from. Before the temple.

Brahma raised one finger in the air. "*Problem ees, Sri afraid of King?*" He nodded and then smiled broadly. "*Yes thees ees problem!*" He bobbed his head towards the Queen. "*Man-y raja do for rani to make fun time for her. Unless rani ees afraid.*" Brahma's old eyes softened and he looked back at his young companion, who he had missed so much. "*Why rani Sri scared?*"

"I..." Sri stopped, and put a hand to her mouth. "I am scared, Brahma. So very scared, you have no idea." Sri sat back on her knees, and slumped in her position under the shade. "Marici is a very powerful King. It would be so unwise to do anything to anger him. You just can't disagree with him, Brahma."

Brahma laughed and waved his hands in front of his face. "*No, no!*" he managed to speak in between his bursts of laughter. His body swayed, and he shook his hands with his loud chuckles.

"What?" Sri said with amusement.

Brahma held his buckling tummy and caught his breath. He patted his bald head, and then looked at Sri with twinkling eyes. "*Problem ees, you don't treat raja like King of peepul. Treat raja like raja of gods. He ees not!*"

Sri threw her arms up in the air. "How am I supposed to treat him? He is the King, and he is a god, Brahma. I've seen his power! He is the sky, nothing can take that away!"

Brahma put a hand on Sri's shoulder, and brought the child close against him. "*Yes yes, powerful god, yes. But, gods for judging too. Gods and raja are for judging, too. You see?*" Brahma closed his eyes and tilted his head up towards the leaves of the tree. "*You see? Problem ees, Marici not judged by rani and this makes for no fun.*"

Sri sighed contentedly and rested her head on the old man's shoulder. His words were so simple—his language so broken. If she were like many of the nobles at her court, his words would not even be received in her heart. But it was the simplicity of his manners that touched her. That made her realize that his pain, and experience, filtered through such age and humility, was valuable to her. "How do I judge a King, Brahma?" Sri asked.

"*Rani Sri judge for raja by not being rani when he is not raja.*" Brahma bobbed his head forward and repeated this statement. "*Rani Sri judge for raja by not being rani when he is not raja.*"

It was the one truth that she already knew, but had refused to admit to herself. To not be the Queen anymore, when Marici would fail to be the King of Kasimi. And as her old friend had so wisely put it, she would guide her King by doing this. Sri needed time to figure out what she was going to do.

Brahma said quietly, "*Sri need to think here, in thees place.*" Brahma gently pushed Sri against him, so she could use his old body as a pillow for a long nap. "*And Brahma ees old and tired.*"

Sri turned her head so her black eyes could look at the gentle face of the old servant. "Yes Brahma, let's nap here." She placed herself against Brahma and let the gentle breezes drift in the hot air to her face and skin. She felt at peace, here. But it was only temporary. In the moments before sleep overcame her, Sri made decisions for the next few days. In one week's time, she would return to Marici's parlour and tell him exactly what she had done. She would make no apologies for her actions, and if her brother chose to punish her, she would accept it.

Sri remembered the magnificent whirl of water and wind that had emerged from the ocean as she and her brother danced through the night sky, and dove through the depths of the cold waves. She could not save him then. Marici had let his magic and anger claim him that evening, and Sri was helpless to his ethereal powers. But she knew in her heart what he was doing. And she knew that he felt alone and trapped when the anger unleashed itself in the sky.

She would return and face her King with pride and compassion. What she had done, she had done to save Him. She saved innocents that would have been sent mercilessly to the gods. She had been the King that he could not be.

17

Over the weeks that Sri was absent from the palace, and showed no signs of returning until the next moon, Marici ended the feast on *Govandhara*. He had his artists paint pictures of the Queen, and sculptors design statues of gold and emeralds in the shape of the beautiful Sri. The only music that would be played must have to do with the Queen, and her purity. Marici was lost without his sister, and not able to hold court or audiences without his jewel at his side. The proud smile that he wore when his sister's hand was in his, disappeared. There was no happiness at the palace without the Moon's Light.

At night, the guards listened to the King's cries and moans from his chamber. It was not a weak sobbing of longing for another. There was a pain in his stomach when Marici called out for "*Sri!*" in the long hours of the night. His bed went untouched. The King would sit in the entrance room of his suite, in a single green chair, and wait for Sri's return. Night after night. When the sun broke through the sky over Varuna's ocean, Marici would howl from his balcony for his lost sister.

The noblemen thought that the company of a woman may ease the King's pain. The more esteemed Northern nobles called for their unmarried daughters, cousins and sisters to come forward for an audience with Marici, to be examined for the position of concubine. Insulted and angry at the notion that he would need another woman besides Sri, Marici screamed for the nobles to leave his parlour. He did not want to create an heir without Sri in the palace. And when he did choose a concubine, she would have to be approved by the woman who was more pure than any other.

Finally after the third week, two letters arrived for Marici. His man delivered the sealed papers to him on a silver tray, and Marici took them in his hands with ginger care. He looked at both of them with equal weight, and noticed Ajan's seal on the first one. His hands trembled. It was word from the temple of *Govandhara*. Marici let the other letter slip to the floor, while he claimed the one that held the word of Sri. He brought the parched paper to his heart and opened it with a slow, ceremonial motion:

Your Excellency:
Your Queen will return with me to the Palace of Govandhara in three sunsets. We will arrive with the caravan, your men and your horses. We look forward to being in your presence once again. For Kasimi.
Your Humble Servant,
The Grand Priest of Kasimi

Marici closed his eyes slowly and breathed a sigh of relief. Finally, his Queen would return and he would be complete again. He re-read the letter with trembling hands. Three sunsets! It would hardly be enough time to prepare for her return. The artwork was not finished. Audiences needed to be scheduled that he could not attend to due to her absence. There was so much to do.

The King stood up, and paced around his chamber with a rapid step. He called for guards, people, men from whatever distance could hear. He needed people to help him prepare for this return.

Marici paced madly and rubbed his disheveled mop of black hair in the middle of his head. "The Queen returns!"

Marici ran into the black marble abyss outside his door and ran towards Sri's room. The guards all looked at the King with concern, but dared not question his behavior. Marici pressed his hands against the door, and dragged his fingertips down the length of the gold frame. "The Queen returns!"

Finally, the King's sobs began. Marici hit his head with power against the door, and he collapsed his body to the cold floor waiting by his feet. "The Queen..." he murmured softly through his heavy tears. "My Queen..." he tried again. "My Queen returns to me!"

~

The celebration of *Govandhara* began once more. On the day that the letter came, Marici put on his cobalt blue tunic and pajama pants and led a celebration and feast on Varuna's beach. The joy that had been asleep for three weeks had commenced once more. The King walked the length of the beach with a line of guards behind him, and painted the sand with glory. His Queen was returning to restore him to greatness once again.

He had a vision of how his sister would be welcomed back to the palace. On the third sunset, when the caravan rode up from the south on horses, the party would await her. It would be a re-creation of the night that he and his bride rode to the palace for the first time. His eyes swept over the sand, and saw the servants and nobles in the many colors that they would wear. He would want a rainbow of color in the silks and jewelry of the court to highlight the sun's rays on his grandfather's water. A tabla would play lightly in step to the Queen's walk. And Sri—Sri would float off of her horse with the help of a guard. Since she had been riding on a long journey, her black hair would be tied neatly back to free her view. Her sari, or salwar-kameez—perhaps a simple wrap for such a trip—would be white. Knowing his sister, she would wear no jewelry though he had sent many trinkets of gold to her at the temple.

She would walk towards him. And the swirl of nobles and servants would move to create a line from where her horse stood in the shallow water—to him. Marici would hold his hands out gently, and his sister would come forward. A few strands of hair would escape from her clasps, and be blown against her angelic face. Marici would restrain himself, and let Sri walk the length to his embrace. And then, finally, she would be his once more.

Marici's trance was shaken by the onslaught of servants who were beginning to get things in order. News had spread that Sri would return, and the court seemed to beam with the message. He could see the smiles on the nobles' faces grow brighter, and the picking of flowers by lords for their ladies. He best let arrangements be made, and so Marici walked from his grandfather's land to his parlour—where he could make more plans for his Queen's return.

Marici walked back to the palace, where he paused to look at its colors. The white marble that created his palace must be cleaned. It was not pure enough. He would tell his men to take brushes of horse hair and bring perfection to the palace, so that the carvings inside the crevices would be pronounced. The windows in all their shapes and sizes, and all the balconies disturbed him somehow. They were not uniform enough—at least there was order with each level. He loved the parlour's balcony, especially when he and Sri would hail the beach below. Marici could hear the gentle lapping of the fountains behind him, as he walked closer to his home. More water should flow, and more candles of the Queen's favorite vanilla should burn to lure her to her chamber. He would tell his man to get started. *My Queen returns to me.*

The King walked the stairs to his chamber, and seated himself in the same green chair that he had been in when the message from the temple had been delivered. He closed his eyes and recreated the moment when he opened Ajan's letter and read of Sri's return. The paper felt weathered, and was moistened from ocean spray on the messenger's journey. *Three sunsets.* It echoed in his mind.

Marici's eyes looked to the fallen letter by the side of his chair. *Yes, there had been two messages on the silver tray, hadn't there?* Perhaps a personal note from Sri. The King picked up the second letter and examined the seal on the outside. He didn't recognize the symbol. His long fingers broke the seal, and the King's black eyes with a ring of red around the pupils, went through the letter.

His hands tensed around the paper, and he was brought back to the rain in *Videha.* He could hear Vishal's evil words again, and they made his eyes burn with red.

I am leaving here, and with my departure go The Isles. We will have nothing to do with your new child King. We will have nothing to do with Kasimi. When I leave, I take my land with me.

He had failed as a King when he let that demon escape—and there was little time left. He must correct this. He must never fail his ancestors and his people again.

The king swallowed slowly, his saliva taking a long time to travel the length of his neck. He stood from the velvet cushions beneath him, and walked through the doorway to his bedroom.

His bedroom had changed drastically over the time he had come to the palace. Once decorated in rich tapestries, it was now a minimalistic womb of black and green marble. There were no windows in this inner chamber, though Marici liked the view of the night sky and the morning sun. Artists had created canvases of each image to place on the east and west walls of his room. There was no furniture. No one else but the King should be able to sleep here. It was his bedroom. His clothes were kept in a dressing chamber, so no bureaus were needed.

His bed was larger than Sri's. Raised off of the ground by a cherrywood frame, the luxurious quilts of cobalt silk spilled to the bare wooden floor. The King had exactly four pillows, to line the length of his bed. He wanted perfect order.

But today, Marici wished he had put a desk in his room. Or a table. Somewhere he could write. The King walked to his bed, and reached for the few sheets of paper that he kept underneath it, in case he thought of something in the middle of his dreams. He dug his hand further under the bed to retrieve his ink and pen.

He would need a hard surface upon which to write. The bed. Marici tried to lean the pen against the paper, but found the softness of his pillows to be too disruptive to his writing. The floor. The King knelt to the ground and placed his paper flat upon it. His hands traced the paper to make it smooth, and clean of wrinkles. His eyes focused upon the empty canvas, and then upon the ink that would aid him. Putting pen to paper, the King began...

~

Two sunsets later, Sri did arrive at the palace on *Govandhara* with the caravan. The Queen had felt an urgency, and gathered the guards, servants and Ajan to ride back to Marici a day earlier than planned. She needed to speak with him, and could no longer wait. There were no stops on the way back to her palace. Only Ajan managed to keep his horse's pace in time to Sri's, as the group moved quickly up the coast.

That morning, Sri rose an hour before dawn and took tremendous care with her appearance. She chose to wear her finest red salwar-kameez, and paint her face in many bright colors to accent her features. The gold jewels that had been sent by her brother to her were placed on her neck and wrists to show that she was the King's wife. Sri stared at herself in the mirror all morning, waiting for the sun to enter into her room and reveal her true face in the reflecting glass.

When dawn came, Sri spoke to Jabala and Ajan, and informed them that she intended to return to the palace that day with or without them. She would bring the guards, and so it was not necessary for the two to return immediately. But she would very much enjoy their company on the long but beautiful trip towards the north. It did not take long to get her Grand Priest and nurse to accompany her. Within one hour, Sri's group was assembled and rising with a fast pace towards the north.

Marici had not expected Sri home until three sunsets from when he received the message. But, they could clearly see a few miles down the beach. His Queen and men should be upon the palace's grounds within the hour, at the setting of the sun.

Marici bit his fingers rapidly. Many of the court's nobles were walking in the gardens or off on their own. He would not have time to gather them in the bright colors he had imagined and place them along the sand to form a bridge from the water to the King. Bringing Sri back to him. He shook his head. There must be something grand, to welcome the jewel back to *Govandhara*. But what? The gifts were not ready. The musicians were not gathered. The feast was not in place. Marici started to bite down on the edges of his nails.

His eyes widened. Marici threw open his door and walked to the guards in the center of the black marble hallway separating his room from His Queen's. He spoke very softly, to keep the surprise for Sri only known to those who must. He asked them to place all the paintings of the Queen that they could find, both finished and unfinished, in the parlour. And quickly. There was not much time. And—he asked them with pleading in his eyes—to show the Queen to the parlour as soon as she arrived. The moment she did.

Marici spread his hands before the guards and raised his head to examine them with his commanding red eyes. The guards were to bow to Sri, and then tell her that Marici requested her presence in the parlour. They were to allow her to walk first to the palace and then follow obediently behind her. He repeated these instructions to the guards quickly. He made them repeat his commands back to him—evidence that they had listened.

Marici went to his room, and called a man servant to attend to him immediately. He would want to wear something elegant, and ceremonial to reclaim his Queen back to the palace. It would take time, and he would not be ready when Sri arrived. And though he would want to run to his sister as her horse pounded the last bits of sand, he would take the time to present himself properly to her. To find the nicest garments and jewelry, and place his sword at his hip.

When Sri's horse arrived upon the palace's beach, a teem of guards raised their swords to the sky and kneeled before Sri as she dismounted her horse. The Queen, dressed beautifully in her reds and gold, bowed to the guards and consented to the King's wish. She walked with her chin held high up the sand and past the entrance walls, into the palace. She did not pause to greet the stay nobles that took walks along the beach, or to look back at Jabala and Ajan. She needed to speak to Marici.

She arrived in a room that was her heart and soul, stripped to the artist's palette. It was no longer a bare parlour that waited to be decorated. It was a chamber of images—of a lost Queen. Sri paused when the guards closed the door behind her, afraid to walk into this strange place. Everywhere she looked, the paintings stared back with those strange eyes of black with a red ring around the center.

The paintings had been placed lazily around the parlour, propped up against the walls or placed loosely on the floor. Some were finished in great detail, and captured Sri in moments of festivities and prayer. In these paintings, the face of the Queen stared blankly back at the onlooker. A beautiful image trapped in a canvas with no real purpose other than decoration. Some images were of Sri sitting quietly on the dais, or dancing with the noblewomen—the absence of a smile so poignantly captured on her young face.

A few of the paintings held magnificent color. The artists had captured the luxurious hues in her saris of cobalt and crimson, and the way the shades could vary dramatically according to the sunlight. Her jewelry, and the way her hands would idly place themselves along the gold in her nervous habit, seemed to capture the attention of certain artists. Someone had truly studied her—had spent time learning the way she would absently play with her fingers or let the corners of her mouth pull a smile down after an exchange of laughter in the court. One painting, which drew the Queen during a sunset walk on Varuna's beach, caught the way Sri would cry into the sky with no tears.

Scattered in between the completed and detailed paintings were unfinished ones in different sizes. In some, her face and body were complete but the color schemes had not been mastered. In one large painting in particular, the Queen was only half completed. Her tall form stretched the full length of the parlour wall in this work. She was dressed in a gold sari, and her neck was completed with an emerald choker. But her body and face were only half there—the other half was a blank canvas waiting for the other side of the Queen to join it. And yet the painting looked complete somehow. So much attention had been paid to the detail of her silks and the expression in her peculiar black eyes that the painting appeared to be done.

Another work which was sprawled on a silk swatch on the floor was of Sri—perhaps as she would look as an older woman. Sri walked closer to this work, and leaned on the floor to view it more closely. There was a gentle rounding to her face with the addition of health in the elder years. Soft lines groomed her smile and eyes, lighting her face with wisdom as only age could do. A sprinkling of silver dotted her raven hair. There was peace in her eyes. Maybe even joy. Sri stroked the silk and smoothed it free of the wrinkles so that she could look at the vision more closely. *Perhaps this is what my mother would have looked like?*

What have I fallen into? Sri looked carefully around her with widened, enlightened eyes. This was how they viewed her. The artist's eyes could always capture the truth that one had hidden so deeply.

The truth was simple. The artists of *Govandhara*'s palace had created a critical audience of Queens who were dressed in lovely silks and expensive jewels in the many moments a woman can have in this role. They had interpreted the high noble and judged her, before putting the paints so carefully onto the canvas. The eyes of these paintings searched the outside realm, and watched. The real painting in the parlour was Sri. The images created of color watched her, the masterpiece of Marici that was in a constant state of interpretation. While the artist's Queens were comfortable in their two-dimensional cages, Sri was trapped in the painting that Marici had designed for her.

With a hesitant step, Sri took her place by the fire, careful not to step on the newly-inked papers. Strange—the King writing poems? She looked over at Marici's exquisite handwriting, and began to read his cryptic essay...

18

Evil can fester within a society even in the presence of the gods. When blessed with the right of divinity in the mortal realm, it is a holy obligation to pursue that evil with a sword of might and to conquer it with no mercy. No blood must be spared in the creation of such a perfect state. No blood of birth, marriage nor death. The will of the gods must be rigid for generations to come. A will so grand that nothing can escape it. It will stand as the new model for Kasimian society and it will please the gods.

There will be a people who rule by divine will. The direct descendants of the gods and their consorts and children will be part of the divine class who will have supreme right over Kasimi as dictated by the will of Brahma. The Highest Rulers of the divine class are the God King and his consort, and no others. The eldest son of the King will be the Heir Apparent, but will not become the High Ruler until the God King passes to the next realm. The mother of the Heir Apparent will remain a spiritual head next to her son and his wife until she joins her husband. The other children of the King and Queen, and the offspring of these children, will be of the Brahman divine class, but not High Rulers. They will be able to serve in the reserved positions of a divine government, and in the priesthood. No one must question the King.

No one must question the Queen. No one must question a direct relative of either.

The lord nobles and warrior protectors will be in a class directly beneath the divine class of Brahma. They are the heart and soul of the Kasimian land since they will rule over the kingdoms. They must obey the divine class but will have direct claim over the land that they own. The nobles will be the rulers of the Kasimian noble class. The oldest son, and in some instances approved by the King and Queen, the oldest daughter, will inherit the land and title of his or her father. The other offspring may serve as warriors or advisors, directly under the King and Queen, but will not be the rulers of this class.

The other good people of the Northern and Southern Kingdoms who do not hold titles or noble blood will make up the common class. These people must answer first to the divine Brahman class, and then to the Kasimian noble class. The common people will be the merchants and soldiers that serve the Kingdoms faithfully, and make up the belly of Kasimi. Children of the common class will remain of this status.

All others who call themselves Kasimians will cease to hold free membership in this society. Those not of pure Kasimian blood or of the seceded portions of the Kasimian Kingdom will no longer be true members of this society, and will be subject to the rules and desires of the Brahman divine class, the Kasimian noble class, and the common class. Those who are placed in this untouchable class must not own property, and must relinquish any claim to material items to the local rulers of the land. Their purpose in this world is to pay penance for the misfortune of their births. Children of this untouchable class will remain of this status.

Wives will become the class of their husbands, while concubines will remain of their birth status but be welcomed into their lover's class. Thus, children will be the class of their mothers'. A woman of the Kasimian noble class who marries a member of the Brahman divine class will be Brahman, and her children will be Brahman. A woman of the Kasimian noble class who becomes a lover to a member of the Brahman divine will remain a Kasimian noble, and her children will be of her status. A woman of the divine class who marries a man of the common class will become a member of the common class, and her children will be common.

It is forbidden for members of the upper three classes to marry or consort with the untouchable class. Untouchables must only consort with untouchables. Transgression of this law will be punishable by execution. Any expression of romantic interest or intention from the upper three classes to the untouchable class will offend the gods, and damn both souls to eternal suffering.

The four-caste system did I generate
With categories of constituents and works;
Of this I am the doer, know thou this—
And yet I am the Changeless One
Who does not do or act.

I decree this as My Will and Law.
Marici, King and God of Kasimi.

19

Sri waited in front of the entrance for Marici to arrive. Her own eyes were now fully red, and she clasped papers tightly in her hand. So tightly that her fingers hurt, and the paper began to crumple inside her fist. Sri felt anger and betrayal, and a desperate need to save Marici from himself and from her people.

Marici opened the door with a bright smile on his full lips. He took a few steps into the parlour and presented himself before His Queen. Long, black hair had been sculpted into a tail, tied with a black string. He was dressed in a charcoal grey tunic of raw silk that was made black in the shadows. It lifted gently to touch upon his neck before shaping around his torso. His body had grown into a man's form during his stay at the palace. There was a firmness to his chest that had not existed before.

The rest of his body was claimed by black. Shiny black pants of some animal skin fashioned tightly around his legs, and his feet were claimed by black boots with a slight heel that shined against the flames of the fire. A traditional sword was sheathed by his left hip, but the handle was encrusted with onyx.

The King walked to Sri's side, and placed his strong fingers on her shoulders. He began to massage her muscles underneath the red silk of her sari blouse. He did not see the anger in her eyes.

Marici leaned in and inhaled the lingering vanilla and perfumed scent that seemed to taunt his senses. "Sri, I have missed you..." he said while beginning to kiss the soft skin at the nape of his sister's neck. "Darling..."

Sri did not return any of Marici's affection. Her shoulders remained fixed, and did not lean up to receive his fingers. Her head tensed, and did not tilt to feel her brother's lips. When he was done claiming her, Sri took a few steps back to truly look at the villain in grey and black. Her eyes had never felt so warm before, and the red was beginning to mix itself over the black pools. She breathed once, and prayed to *Brahma*. She breathed a second time, and asked for her mother's spirit to give her strength. She breathed a third time, and began.

"Did you write this out of anger, Marici?" she said, in a gentle calm that hid her true feelings.

Marici finished inhaling his sister's fragrance before responding, savoring the last bit of magic.

The King stepped forward, keeping the distance short between himself and Sri. He spoke in a cool whisper. "I wrote this so that there will be no more anger in Kasimi. I see you found it and read it without letting me explain how this came about. I had wanted to read it to you, explain it to you...but you've seen it now." Marici took one step forward and placed his hands on Sri's shoulders once more.

Sri took her hands, and removed the controlling grasp of her brother on her body. Her tone remained sweet and gentle, but her words were commanding. "You are mad, brother. You cannot do this. You will not do this." Sri walked to a far corner of the room, near the painting that showed only a half painted Queen.

Marici paused in his place and simply watched Sri. His eyes narrowed, and his lips moved up into an amused smirk. "Not even my artistic masters can capture your true beauty, Sri. You are more stunning than I remember."

"Do you even hear me, Marici? Do you?" Sri's tone was rising and she was beginning to show her anger in her voice and gestures. "Do you hear me? This edict, this law—You will not do this."

Marici rubbed his chin, and nodded quietly in contemplation of his sister's demands. He walked to the balcony entrance, stopping to observe a few of the paintings of Sri along the way. He looked through the balcony doors to the view of the beach below. "You must be tired after such a long journey, Sri. You've been gone for so long." Marici pivoted on his heals and looked at Sri carefully. "Promise me you won't go for so long again? *Acha?*"

Sri's eyes narrowed, and she screamed out at her brother's mindless words. He was mocking her. He would not hear her, but he was seeing her.

Marici's eyes moved over Sri's body and around the paintings in the room. He wanted to see his Queen in beauty. To watch the way her body would move, and her lips would smile.

Sri began a very deliberate walk to the fireplace with her red eyes focused on the bright flames. When she arrived, the Queen kneeled before the fire and she chanted a prayer to *Brahma* before holding her hand out to burn the papers that had created such an evil law. This, Marici would watch.

Marici's growled underneath his breath at the act of his sister, and he walked quickly to the fire to kneel beside her. His eyes moved from the burning trail of paper to his sister's red eyes. To burn his wishes was to burn Him. His hands, which only moments ago had been tender, were now the talons of a monster against Sri's body as he threw her down to the cold floor while simultaneously placing his body atop hers. He used his hands to hold Sri down, and he looked deeply into her eyes. His body pressed into hers, hip to hip, and his desire to make her obey him rose to his heart.

Sri's lips turned upward, just slightly, satisfied that she had finally made her brother see. She would not fear his power over her, nor would she respond to his threats. Her body lay still, and motionless underneath him.

"I am glad I burned it, Marici. I am glad I burned it! You cannot do this...I will not let you..." she whispered sharply.

In the low, rumbling tones of thunder, Marici spoke, "Let me?" A maniacal and low laugh ensued. "Burning my words does not take them from me. That law is burned in my heart. It can be easily done again." Pressing his hips further into Sri, Marici growled and said through his teeth. "Why do you disobey me, sister? Why? Answer me."

Sri shook her head as much as she could from underneath Marici. "Why? Why?" Her eyes fluttered open and closed. "Why?" Her chest heaved up for air under the pressure of her brother's body. "...I'll answer you..." She wriggled in place under him and sighed in the pain that followed her abrupt movement. But, she confessed her disobedience.

"You cannot rule the fate of people, Marici. You cannot place them into determined and sealed classes that clearly put some at an advantage and others at a disadvantage. Some are born to privilege, Marici...we both were...the people in our court were...and they carry it. But you cannot force people to be born to disadvantage..."

Marici closed his eyes and pushed his body even closer into Sri's form. He brought his head up to his sister's, so that his lips were pressed against her ear. "Wrong, Sri..." he growled into her ear. "Wrong. Do you not remember who I am? Who you are—and together who we are?" His tongue traced the length of her ear before his lips found a resting place on her lobe. "I am the son of

Varuna II, and you are his daughter. We are direct descendants of the sea god Varuna, and hold his divinity in our blood. It is our right to rule Kasimi. Decree fate? It is MY right and MY will and MY duty. Do not presume, sister, that I cannot do this. Do not presume that what I do is against the gods. It is for our ancestors that I do this. For *Brahma*! To preserve divine blood so that there is true order in our land! To ensure that nothing can ever hurt a divine creature! In this order, there is peace. There is p..."

"You are wrong, Marici! So wrong! Oh, brother!" Sri yelled over Marici. She had listened to his twisted logic, and slowly her anger had turned to fear and sympathy. Her brother was insane. There was little hope of bringing him back to her so all she could do was fight for what she knew was right. For Him.

"You are so wrong! Do you not think of all the innocent people in Goane and The Isles who will suffer because you blame them for our mother's death?"

Marici let his grip on Sri's body go on the invocation of their mother's name. For a moment, he lay helpless on top of her—in shock. His sister had been so cruel. So horribly cruel, and he had nowhere to hide or run. He just lay atop his mother's daughter with few breaths, before sitting up to look into the fire. Marici found calm in the way the flames had a rhythm of their own like the strikes of light that he could summon from the sky. Finally, he said, "Our mother should not have died."

As soon as Marici's body had released itself from hers, Sri rubbed her wrists to bring blood back into them. She sat up and breathed precious air into her lungs without lifting her black eyes to her brother's helpless body. When his words reached her ear, Sri paused her thoughts of the edict and prayed for her mother's soul. And her eyes wandered to that painting of the older Queen, as she imagined what her mother would look like now.

"No, our mother shouldn't have died. And neither should the mothers of The Isles and of Goane."

Marici shook his head and brought his face into waiting palms. His fingers stretched over his skin, and traced his bones. "Do you not think I hurt because of the women and children who will suffer from this law? But all good things come of pain, Sri." Marici then turned to look directly at Sri. "With this law, there will be a defined order to Kasimian society. Something like the rebellion in the Northern Kingdom could never happen again because there is a structure of the gods in place."

"Why? Why this way?" Sri asked, pleading for reason from her brother. "Why?"

Marici closed his eyes and brought a hand to his chest, and tapped his fingers in rhythm to his heart's beat. "Do you remember, Sri, what we created in the ocean that night? Do you remember, darling, what became of the sky? I do." His heart's rhythm grew faster, as did the beating of the Marici's fingers on his chest. "It was my might, and I thought it a simple way to bring The Isles back to order. The bad blood would be cleansed away at the end of the storm, and peace would be brought back to Kasimi and The Isles could once again join us—free of the evil they once possessed."

Marici ceased the tapping on his heart, and leaned forward on his legs to study his sister's face. "I received word, Sri, that the people of The Isles are safe now. Ships came and took them away—to Goane." He bit his lip and leaned back in his posture, closer to the heat of the fire. "I have little doubt that Devyn and Bali were involved. I know how they feel, and they will be punished accordingly. But because of their foolishness—what could have been a simple way to bring The Isles back—has failed. And now, no blood must be spared to bring order back to this land."

Sri let tears fall from her eyes before she permitted herself to look back at her brother. Her hands reached out and she brought her body close to his for a lasting embrace. "Oh Marici, how I love you, brother. But I am not as pure as you have had your artists paint me."

Marici held his sister to him and buried his face in her red silks and vanilla scented hair. "Sri, darling. You are my life..."

Sri continued to hold her brother so close to her body. "Marici. It was not Devyn nor Bali who brought the people of The Isles to Goane. It was me, your twin sister and Queen, who gave life to The Isles. I am not ashamed."

Marici tightened his arms around his sister, and squeezed so she could not speak more. His own tears fell into her hair, and his teeth clamped down on handfuls of raven tresses. "I don't believe you. A Queen never disobeys her King."

Sri pushed away from the embrace and sat back on her knees, creating a new distance between the twins. She was relieved to have confessed. She nodded her head twice. "Yes, a Queen never disobeys her King. I am no Queen, Marici." Sri closed her eyes and let water drip slowly, as her smile grew wide on her face. "I acted as a woman of the people, brother. I did what you could not."

Marici had already risen from his place by the fire and had started to pace in front of the balcony entrance with his head held in his hands, and water coming from his own eyes. Inside his body, his heart was broken. It was clear now. The times when his sister had felt distant, he should have done something. All that time, he must have not have loved her enough—for her to do something this evil. A woman so pure could never act so wickedly unless pushed by one so sinful. He blamed himself. He could not be angry at his sister. The King's black eyes darted around the room at the beautiful images of his sister that claimed the walls and floor. The image of such a beautiful woman dressed in the finest silks and jewels, dancing on the beach of Varuna—it was as it should be. But he realized that she should not be drawn alone. She should be beside her King. Always beside her King. And he had placed her in such isolation over the past few moons.

"Sri, I am so sorry."

Sri's eyes opened, and her heart started with a pounding of hope. "What?"

"I am sorry."

"Marici?"

"I drove you to this."

"To what?"

"To evil."

Sri's eyes closed, and her heart stopped in its place. It was over.

Marici began again, and walked close to his kneeling sister. He looked down at her with pity in his watery eyes. "I did not love you enough, or protect you enough. It is what drove you from me, to disobey me. It was my lack of focus on my Queen that drove her to evil. I forgive you. You were not acting of your own will."

Sri stood from her place, and began walking around the perimeter of the room. She examined the paintings of a woman who had been Queen next to her twin brother. They had painted her so beautifully, in her costumes of cobalt. She spoke softly, though her brother's ears would not receive her words. "I acted of my own will."

"I forgive you. Together, we will bring my order to Kasimi. We will please the gods with this order." Marici walked to Sri, to observe the paintings of the twins under the honey dome.

"I am leaving you, Marici."

"We will find our way to one another again, Sri." Marici was soon behind Sri with his hands upon her shoulders. He worked her delicate muscles with his fingers and continued his chant about the order of Kasimi. "I will make you so happy, Sri."

"I am leaving you, Marici."

He had heard her the first time, but had hoped that it would only take his touch to bring her back to him. He turned Sri around so that she was before him once more. He wanted his sister to look at the pain in his eyes, and see that she could not leave someone who loved her so much.

"Oh Sri, I love you so much." He traced his hands down her body, and kneeled before her. His head was buried in her stomach, and he pleaded for her presence. "You cannot leave your husband, Intended One. You were born to be my Queen, and to be a symbol for our people. You were born to be at my side, to guide me. It is what *Brahma* made you for! You are my better half. Where will you go, Queen? Your home is here."

"I am leaving you, Marici." Sri repeated. There was nothing left for her to say. Her hands remained at her side, though she ached to embrace her brother and tell him how much she loved him. A part of her wanted to remain by his side so that she could lead him back to the right path. But staying would only encourage his cruel ways. If she loved him, she would go. "I will go where I am needed. This is no longer my home."

Marici leaned his head back and looked up into the eyes that had mesmerized him on so many a night. "I will not let you leave. You took vows, Sri. You promised to be my wife, and to guide me. I will not let you leave!" His voice was weighted, and swallowed deep in his throat. "I beg you, please don't leave me!"

Sri brought two fingers to her lips and kissed them, and then placed that hand on her brother's head. "I will always love you, brother. I vowed to guide you, above all. Now, I guide you by leaving you." Sri left her kneeling brother in his place, and walked to the door that would lead her away. "I do this out of love for you." Her finely kept and jeweled hand turned the knob of the parlour's door, and she was gone.

Sri did not look back when she walked away. But her ears and heart carried the painful screams of the King that called out for her in the empty parlour.

~

In the dark, all that remained were the silhouettes of two lovers at peace after sharing their bodies in the night. She had asked him to come, begged him to come to her, with a note slipped under his door with the word "Me" scrawled on it in her own hand. He found a way to her chambers through a series of maneuvers and climbs because she asked him to. The moment he entered the chamber, her lips found his and the two lovers tumbled to the floor in a deliberate and passionate round of lovemaking that savored every touch and taste, and lasted until both bodies could no longer move.

Her hands moved hungrily against his body, but did not ravage him for just pleasure. She was remembering the way he felt. The way his muscles had only grown more beautiful with age. The way he would whisper promises into her ear. But tonight she whispered the promises back without hesitation, and the two bodies discovered a union they had never found before. Their flesh joined with excitement and devotion, and the rhythm that followed was the creation of love that only spiritual friends could share. She would miss him.

When it was done, Jabala stroked Ajan's hair as he slept on her bed. She pulled her naked body from over his, and grabbed a white wrap to pull over herself. Smoothing her long brown hair back, Jabala looked out towards the moon that would guide her with her Queen, and then let the light reflect on the sleeping body of her friend.

She watched Ajan for a long time, wishing it could have been different. But she would not have traded the many years of friendship and pleasure she had with him for the dignity of celibacy. They had found love in their own strange way. She kissed his forehead and smiled lightly over him. *I will miss you, my dearest companion.* It was time. Jabala stood and walked to the window without looking back.

~

The two old friends who shared nearly a lifetime of history walked along Varuna's beach under the moon. They held hands, and stopped to grip each other when their hearts were too heavy. The distances between their embraces grew shorter and shorter until they found themselves locked in each other's arms as the waves crashed around them. In the next realm, they mused, they would be together. There was never a time when she did not love him, nor he her.

She begged him to come with her, and he begged her to do what she must to save her life. But he could not go because his life was in *Mithila*, and he would always be the uncle of the Grand Priest. He could not shame his family by making such a visible statement. While he loved her deeply, and it broke his heart to know that this embrace could only last a few more moments, he must let her go. And he could not go with her.

Fate had stepped in heavily when Bali was only fourteen. She had loved Janaka, and had given herself to him without remorse. Janaka had fallen in love with the most beautiful woman in the north and had every intention of claiming her. But, she was promised to another and on her fifteenth birthday, Bali was wed. The love did not stop. The two people found ways to catch one another, and embrace—without Bali's husband knowing.

Now, they must break apart once more. Since the two nobles had their hearts broken so early in life, they were able to understand the pain. She would always be so beautiful to him. Janaka would always be the man who had owned her heart.

Bali broke off the embrace, with no tears in her eyes. Janaka stood in his place while the ice-cold water played at his ankles. She turned, and walked away as the wind whipped her glorious silver hair behind her while the man who would always love her watched her leave his life again.

~

Sri waited on the beach with the group of horses that would carry them away, to their next meeting point. All the arrangements had been made with the help of Janaka's powerful friends, and soon her followers would be away from the mainland. Marici had remained in the parlour, not answering to guards, and did not run after his sister to restrain her. Both sister and brother knew that it was over.

She had stopped crying when she walked past the reflecting pools of the palace, and through the entrance walls to be free on the sand. She was no longer His Queen, and her new role had yet to be defined. There was sadness in her heart. But, Sri was willing to face the consequences of her decision.

Devyn was there with her. He was a silent but tender presence during this long night. He would be joining the group that would leave *Govandhara*, for his people would need him. He could no longer serve a King that had, in his heart's opinion, betrayed the people of Kasimi. He would follow the leader that had been merciful and loving. He would follow the girl that he cared for.

Devyn made no attempt to speak to Sri while she waited for the group to assemble. He watched her with gentle and patient eyes, to make sure that she was fine in her own company. Even now, he would not shelter her from the reality of the hard path that was ahead. He would just be there for her. A soft arm went over Sri's shoulder, and the two friends stared out at the ocean and the way it could look only in *Govandhara*.

It was time to go.

Part IV

20

Sri massaged her back with one hand while holding a glass of coconut milk in the other. *How is it all possible?* She looked outside the window, at the gardens of her home, and sighed contentedly at the day. There was a gentle rain beating down on the palm trees, and there was no movement of birds or servants to cloud her view of the garden. Her hand moved in soft, circular motions on her lower back and her drink lingered at her lips to savor the sweetness. The time had passed too quickly, and so much had happened. This moment was peace.

Sri had made her home in Goane, in the village of Sura. Her life was modest compared to her days in *Govandhara*, and she preferred it that way. Her days were content in her gardens, picking and tending to herbs and fruit or taking care of the estate's animals. She would socialize with the people in the town's market when she went to purchase meat and spices to make the evening meals. She led the normal life of a Goanian woman, and it was good.

There were times when her old life would resurface to haunt her. There were still paintings of the King and Queen of Kasimi that were done on the sides of old buildings. But they were beginning to fade. There were Kasimians of pure blood who had made lives in Goane, who blamed her for the death of the Kasimian Kingdom. Sri blamed herself at times. Since her departure, it was rumored that *Govandhara* had gone into mourning. The court was sent away, and the King would receive no visitors. Kasimi was divided, and The Isles were deserted.

Her new life would also haunt her. The survivors of The Isles looked upon her as their goddess and Queen, and had erected statues and icons to honor her. And, the Goanians viewed Sri as their savior for returning the colony to an independent and free land. *Govandhara* did not pursue the colony, and Sri knew Marici would never touch it as long as she was there. She was still greeted with her title from time to time, though she took no formal position in the free Goane. "I am Sri..." is how she would respond.

Sri shook her head, trying to focus on the gentle rain falling on the garden. She started massaging her back again, and let out a heavier breath.

"From the sound of that sigh, may I assume you missed me?"

Sri chuckled, and took a taunting sip of her coconut milk. She smiled mischievously, "Why do you assume such things?"

"I have to make assumptions with such a beautiful woman, my Queen." A hand went to stroke Sri's cheek softly, while another went to take over the massaging of her back.

Sri purred softly and leaned in to the hand that would soothe her aching. "Oh, now. If you are my subject, why are you not kneeling before me?"

The subject kneeled and put his head against Sri's lower back while his hands continued to massage and soothe. "I kneel before you, O Beautiful Sri."

Sri chuckled, and placed her glass down on a nearby cherry-wood table that had been built just for that purpose. She turned around to face her subject and put his head into her abdomen. "And I love you, my dutiful subject."

Devyn raised his head, and looked up into Sri's eyes. "I love you, too. But...did I ever have a choice?" His hands went to smooth over Sri's tummy and his lips kissed her naval through the thin silk of a green wrap.

"Yes, I think you did have a choice..." Sri patted Devyn's head and laughed at her kneeling lover. "And you chose wisely." Sri dragged her hands around Devyn's white tunic and then tugged at his collar to bring him up to her height. "I thought you were going into town today to meet with Vishal? You're home early."

Devyn rose and placed his hands lazily over Sri's shoulders, to draw her into a warm embrace. He laughed as her bosom could no longer meet his chest, due to her growing form. "Vishal sent a messenger as I was leaving. He'll be coming for dinner instead." He kissed his lover's forehead. "Besides, he wants to see you."

Sri canted her head to the side, and looked out at the rain. "That would be nice." She had distance in her voice, suddenly.

Devyn brought one hand underneath Sri's chin, and lifted her head to look up into his eyes. He said softly, "Your thoughts, darling?"

Sri slipped away from Devyn's arms by walking a few steps backwards. She turned to face the garden on the other side of the window, and reclaimed her coconut drink from the side table. Making everything as it was before Devyn entered the room. She was, all at once, very far away from him.

Devyn was used to his companion's moodiness these days. Her distance did not stir him. He had come to expect these changes, and had been advised well by his five wise sisters, to let Sri have her space during this time. He remained in his place, and asked softly. "Do you not want Vishal to come for dinner? Why, Sri? He is our friend."

Sri continued to drink her coconut milk, and look out on the rain, pretending not to hear Devyn. If she were her usual self, she would turn to Devyn and tell him the truth. She loved Vishal, as Devyn did. He was a dear and close friend. His presence was always welcome in their home. But right now, Vishal wished to speak of politics and of Kasimi. It had been fifty moons, as Vishal said, and Sri's body was now changing things for Goane and The Isles. She carried the future of the kingdom now, and it included another's blood.

Vishal was their dearest friend, and would stand up for their child along with Sudha. He was also the most politically minded one of the quartet. Where Devyn and Sri wished to plan for the future of a free Goane, Vishal sought to communicate once again with *Govandhara* with the goal of peace in his heart. He knew that Sri was the only hope for this vision.

But, she was not her usual self. Though she understood why it was necessary to have Vishal over for dinner to both enjoy his company and to discuss things with Devyn and Sudha, she was not in the mood to deal with her birth role. She resented the council of priests always subtly bringing her brother's name into the conversation along with *Govandhara* while the sweets were being served. She knew that tonight, she would want to concentrate on the chocolate and almonds rather than on the subject of Marici.

Devyn had been speaking for a while, but Sri had tuned him out while she continued her introspection. As she began to focus once more on his words, she could tell that he was in his logical mode. The tone of his voice was flat—the tone he used when he wanted to persuade her to see things from an intelligent point of view. There were also few natural pauses in his words, confirming that he had these points lined up in his mind.

Sri quickly interrupted him. In a firm voice that hinted of annoyance, she replied, "I don't feel well, Devyn. I don't want to talk about politics. I don't want to have to listen to Vishal go on and on about how we can unite our land. I don't want to remember and relive *Govandhara* tonight, Devyn. I do not feel well!"

Devyn gave Sri an incredulous look and stared at her for a moment. "Um..." He inched closer to her, and grasped her forearm gently to coax her to turn towards him. He smiled and looked upon her with tender and understanding eyes. "I'll have dinner alone with Vishal, then?"

Sri retorted briskly, "So you two can talk behind my back?"

"No, so we can leave you in peace, Sri. Do you not love and trust me enough to socialize with my own friend without you present?" Devyn was trying to remain calm and reasonable though Sri was beginning to test his patience.

Sri bit her lip. She could begin to protest and to twist and turn Devyn's words to use against him. Or, she could concede and enjoy a pleasant afternoon with her lover. There were things happening in her body that made her desire and crave rage while her mind begged her for sanity. Here was the crucial point. Sri looked at Devyn with a blank expression that could paint anything in the next moment.

Devyn decided the outcome. He brought Sri's hand to his lips and kissed it, and then looked down her hand into her black pupils with the ring of red around the center. "I love you, Sri."

Sri melted immediately. There was no way she could contest the warm and pure affection of her lover. Her eyes softened, and she was trapped again by her own tenderness for Devyn. "I love you too, Devyn. But...I..."

"I have already asked Vishal to speak nothing of politics, Sri. He just wants to see how you are doing. All right?" Devyn strokes his fingers underneath the soft part of Sri's chin.

Sri bit her lip again, and her cheeks flushed with her embarrassment. Devyn had already predicted what she would protest, but she had not given him a chance to explain. She clamped her eyelids down and murmured, "Oh Devyn, forgive me. I...I am not myself these days. I...have little control over what I know I should do and what I know I should not do. I love Vishal. Why would I protest a dinner with him?"

Devyn wrapped his lover up into a gentle embrace and patted the back of her head. "There, there, darling..." His hand crept down to the small of her back, and commenced massaging the muscles that he knew ached. "How could I be anything but understanding with you when you carry something so precious for the both of us?" His strong hands worked their way around to the front of her abdomen where he moved his fingers in circular motions.

Sri leaned her head back, and her black hair fell smoothly against her hips. His touch was so warm, and expressed his love for her. In the years that they had spent in Sura, their love had grown into something so unconditionally forgiving and tempting that Sri was happy to deny her existence as a wife for the one of a lover. All it would take was the touch of his hand or the length of his gaze for Sri's heart to beat faster and her passion to grow stronger. She was called a whore by some, since she was wed to another. But in the embrace of her lover, she was free.

Sri's hands moved forward and danced down Devyn's chest, where she spent some time relearning the way his shoulders were so broad within his frame. His skin was so soft, taut against his mature body, and always cool to the touch. She was in love with him.

Devyn traced his hands from her abdomen around her hips, and then teasingly to her inner thigh before repeating the whole motion again in an unrushed pace. His lips sought a place on her neck that was made damp by the humidity. His kisses went to her collarbones, and his hands went to gently nudge the silk open so that he could caress her full bosom, and feel the gentle swell of her stomach.

Sri moved in the same unhurried pace as her companion, and began to unfasten the ties of his tunic with one hand, while playing thoughtfully with his skin with the other. Sri whispered in his ear as he kissed her neck. "The child kicked..." Sri bit on his ear playfully. "She knows you're there..."

Devyn chuckled as he continued to do away with his lover's wrap. "Or he knows I'm there..." Devyn pulled the silk away from Sri's arms and let it land on the ground.

Sri nuzzled Devyn's neck, and then went to rub her nose against his. "Do you want a male heir so badly, love?" She laughed, her breath tracing all the way to his ear where she began to pay attention to his lobe. Sri sighed in contentment, "I'll be happy with either." She went to pull the tunic off Devyn's body, letting it join her silks on the ground.

Devyn pressed his form to meet the fertile body of his partner. His hands slipped completely around her, before picking her up into his arms in a smooth motion. His lips locked possessively on Sri's, the motions growing more demanding. "I will be happy if our child is like you..." he whispered before changing the pace from gentle to passionate.

Devyn walked onto the covered part of his terrace, just beyond the window where they had lingered. He laid Sri down onto the cherrywood bench that was just outside the rain's reach. He took a moment to look at her body as it grew with child. He enjoyed the way she looked right now. The swell in her belly was a testament to their love. The beautiful curve of her stomach possessed him on sight, and filled Devyn with love for Sri and their child. His lips began to move up and down her abdomen, kissing slowly and tenderly.

Sri leaned back, and closed her eyes to enjoy the beginning of an afternoon of lovemaking as the rain beat around them. Her hand lazily traced her abdomen as Devyn kissed, exchanging gentle pats on her own belly with pats on her lover's head. Her hand soon found the ties of Devyn's breeches.

Devyn's body tightened at the first touch of Sri's hand on his manhood. He helped with the last part of removing his clothes, so that both man and woman were naked together in the garden. Devyn pushed Sri's legs apart and placed them upon his back while he turned to calmly collapse upon Sri's womb. He placed his arms beneath Sri, and began to madly kiss around their child's resting place and down to the fertile region that had conceived.

When Devyn's lips began to kiss her softly, she arched her back and squeezed her legs around Devyn's back. Their lovemaking was so easy and comfortable. She never felt any shame. Her lover made her feel more beautiful to be with his child. The climax was easily reached, and it would only be the first of many. Sri pulled at Devyn to steady his hips with hers.

Devyn was careful not to put pressure over Sri's tummy, especially at this point in her pregnancy. Lovemaking had to be done with care, to protect and love both her and the child. Devyn stood slightly over the bench, with Sri's legs wrapped around him. He focused his eyes on those beautiful onyx circles with red borders—those eyes maddened him—the way Sri could penetrate him with her gaze as he entered her. Devyn put his hands tenderly over Sri's womb, and entered the mother of his child.

Sri began to move slowly with Devyn, as they expressed love for one another and for their child. She grew lost in the rhythm, and the pleasure. She propped herself up on her elbows to look into Devyn's eyes as he penetrated her. Sri would never be ashamed of the love she shared with him. The child would never be a bastard with a father that loved it even in the womb.

The lovers continued as the rain began to hit the ground with more force. They reached a moment of ecstasy together, with Devyn inside Sri's body and Sri inside Devyn's mind. When the rhythm ceased, the two lovers went to lay their hands atop the growing life in the womb. Devyn covered Sri's vulnerable body from the rain and cold, and began to whisper in her ear.

21

The rain continued into the evening, as did their lovemaking. After they lost consciousness and awoke to the darkening sky, Devyn carried his lover to their simple bedroom and wrapped her up in a blanket so that she could sleep more comfortably. He watched her, until it was time to prepare dinner for Sudha and Vishal. It was hard for him to leave her.

Sri woke to the tempting smells of her favorite dish—spiced lamb. Things tasted different in Goane because of the way the people grew their herbs and blended their spices. The Goanians had mastered the sultry taste of spicy and sweet, often combining fruit in the meat dishes. Devyn, who had learned to cook from his five sisters, was able to masterfully blend apples and berries with his lamb.

The woman rose from her bed, and pulled a simple green wrap over her, so that she was presentable for her lover and friends. She dragged herself to the kitchen, and paused by the doorway to admire Devyn, and his skill in the kitchen. Everything was complete—he was just placing mint around the lamb, and mixing the rice with cinnamon and coconut milk. It was such a simple thing that Sri had never been able to appreciate, when servants took care of these things. In Devyn's home, servants went home to their families in the evenings, and the lovers prepared their own supper.

"When will Vishal and Sudha get here?" Sri said quietly from the doorway.

Devyn started. He was lost in his ritual of stirring and chopping. "Oh, Sri. I didn't hear you wake up. How do you feel?" Devyn added as he went back to stirring the rice. "They should be here soon. I think the rain has slowed them."

Sri stretched like a cat by the doorway before making her way beside Devyn. She slid her bare feet along the smooth, blackstone floor.

The kitchen was so simple, and it was the most comfortable place in their house. The room was small, and encased completely with grey and blue stone to keep the heat and fire within its boundaries—no windows. A deep fireplace was the cooking center, spanned the entire east wall. Near the fire was a worn, dark wood table meant for chopping and preparing. There was a constant feeling of either dawn or twilight in the room since the fire was the only source of light. On very bright days, the hint of sun would flow in through the window in the dining area just beyond the kitchen.

A few stools and blankets were placed in no particular order about the kitchen. It was the Goanian cooking that drew her, and lured her, to this place. There were always people gathered in this small room—drinking and laughing—sharing the tasks of the day. There was always something to taste and savor.

Sri rested her head on Devyn's shoulder while he stirred the rice. "Do you know if Jabie and Bali will be coming after dinner?" Sri plucked a bit of rice from the bowl to taste and then kissed Devyn's cheek. "They haven't been around in a while."

Devyn moved his head so that his lips could attempt contact with Sri's. "I don't know. I haven't seen those two. I would think they would come, especially Jabala." Devyn laughed slightly, and then stirred with more energy before placing the mixed rice aside. "I haven't seen those women in so long. What are they up to?"

Sri chewed rapidly, finishing a mouthful of berries that she had stolen from her side of the table. "Well, Bali is busy being Bali, and Jabie is being…Jabie. Bali is still a merchant at heart. The last thing I heard—she was pursuing business with the far northern lands. Jabie is back and forth, helping her. They come around during the day—you could stay and chat you know?"

Devyn knelt down before the fire to warm the lamb and fruit. "I don't think we'd mix well. Three women."

Sri shrugged. "Five sisters." She smiled, and continued, "I hope they come tonight, so we can all chat. I…am going to ask Jabie to stay with us once the child grows due. Is that all right?"

"It is your home, too, Sri. Jabie is your mother. Of course she's welcome here." Devyn wiped his hands on a cloth.

Sri nodded four or five times, and then went to sit on a stool near the fire while Devyn put the finishing touches on the dishes. She sat with her growing belly in between her divided legs, and rubbed her womb slowly. "I've missed Jabie. It seems like we've all gone our separate ways in the past few months. Do you think she'd want to come and stay with us?"

Devyn went to Sri's side, and knelt down before her by the fire in the kitchen. He poked at a few things within the flames—some bits of meat and other dishes that were warming—before taking the hands of his lover. "I think Jabala loves you, and thinks of this baby as her family too. Yes, she'll come to stay with you even though she doesn't have to."

Devyn interrupted before Sri could speak again. "I know what you think, Sri, and it's not true. Jabie loves you, and she's known that you have always thought of her as an equal. She has her own life here, yes. But you must never doubt the love you two had for each other when you were growing up. I was there, Sri. I remember the way she would love you when you were young..."

Sri smiled and patted Devyn's salted red hair. "You're a wise old man, aren't you?" She laughed and stretched her feet to feel the warmth of the fire.

She quickly changed the subject, "What do you think we'll talk about tonight?" This question had been the source of a tantrum earlier, and promised the same episode. But, it was at the front of Sri's mind because she knew the answer. She just wanted Devyn to acknowledge that this—this thing they had done since arriving on Goane—would end with the coming of her child.

Devyn sighed heavily, and looked away from Sri. He would not answer, because he knew it was an excuse for Sri to behave poorly. Instead, he stood up, and took a few of the prepared dishes from the hearth with him. "I'm going to get the table ready. Vishal and Sudha should be here in a few moments. You can either join us, or not. It's your choice."

It sometimes seemed like Devyn could turn his affection on and off when it came to her. In reality, his mindset was simply stable. She was the one playing games, and Devyn was avoiding them by maintaining his stance. He could be understanding up to a point. Devyn lingered by the doorway in the kitchen to say one last thing.

"We would all very much like to have you join us for dinner."

~

Vishal and Sudha arrived only seconds after Devyn left the kitchen. They entered without knocking and walked forward yelling out their friends' names. Devyn called back in a jolly tone, "You two! Over in the dining room..."

Vishal entered the uncomplicated room first and went to hug
Devyn who was placing dishes down on the low, round cherrywood
table. There were no chairs—just random and mismatched pillows.

This room maintained the concept of simplicity that pervaded
his home, and Goanian culture. Things that seemed to decorate
were really in the room for a purpose. Beauty was added to the
elements as an afterthought. The large window that extended the
span of a wall was the source of light, and the lace curtains could
shield the overwhelming amount of sunlight that seemed to flow
inside during mid-day. The sets of candles that were hung randomly against the wall—were for light during the night hours.
These had been lit earlier today since the rain did not allow the
sky to provide sufficient light.

"Devyn! Good to see you…" Vishal said while put down the
bottle of wine he had brought. He walked to his friend and placed
his arms easily over him. "Good to see you!"

Devyn inched away from Vishal's hug. "You're soaked,
Vishal. Didn't you wear a covering when you rode over here?"
He then patted Vishal's back to emphasize the man's wet clothes.
"Let me fetch you something dry." Devyn peered at Sudha,
"And you too."

Vishal waved Sudha in to the room, while they dripped water
on to the tapestry-like carpet below their feet. Devyn went past
both of them to fetch some blankets and clothes to replace their
now transparent pajama suits.

Both priests had aged, and had almost traded physical traits
over the years. Vishal, once powerfully built and intimidating in
form, was now rounder and softer with a sad look in his dark
eyes. Where once he would wear the colors of The Isles with
pride, he settled for very neutral styles of dress. His hair had gone
grey over time, and he began to look more like his dead father
with each year. Sudha, on the other hand, had lost some of the

roundness in his belly though his face had aged as Vishal's. Where once Sudha was jolly and carefree, he was quieter now.

Sudha was the only one of the three priests that had remained neutral over this incident. While he supported Sri with her decision in The Isles, he still had ties to a very loyal Southern Kingdom. Sudha had visited *Govandhara* over the years, once or twice. And, he maintained homes in the South and in Goane. Since Marici had closed the palace doors, Sudha did not have to make a choice.

Devyn returned with two long shirts and blankets and passed them to the already undressing men. "This should do it."

Vishal nodded in thanks and placed the comfortable shirt over his body. "Feels good to be dry again, *acha*?"

Sudha, watching Vishal for approval, repeated the action, and then sank into a pile of nearby pillows. A few starting dishes had been placed on the table which were eagerly met by his fingers. In between bites, he complimented Devyn on the yummies. He bobbed his head while going back for additional handfuls.

Vishal snickered at Sudha, still finding his predictable behavior amusing. He walked to the opposite side of Sudha and found a comfortable seat. He leaned back on his elbows and looked over at his two friends. "How is she?"

Devyn signed heavily and ran his hands through his hair. The answer was complicated. He bent his knees and fell into a resigned seat on the pillows between Sudha and Vishal. "She's in good health, due soon." He pressed his lips out into a conciliatory grin. "But she's not going to join us for dinner—I don't think."

Vishal pulled the blanket around him, and nodded slightly. "She doesn't understand, does she..."

Vishal motioned to Sudha to hand him the sack he had carried under his clothes. In between heavy handfuls, the Southerner tossed him the leather pouch which Vishal caught perfectly in waiting hands. With an apologetic nod to Devyn, Vishal reached inside the sack to retrieve a letter. Devyn already knew what was inside.

The letter contained the official seal of *Govandhara*. And it was in gold. Vishal had already read it—the gold emblem had been broken hours ago. "Marici's man has written a letter requesting Sri return after the baby is born so that she can raise it with the King."

Devyn covered his face with his hands. "Impossible."

Vishal continued. "Devyn, what choice do you have here? Once that child is born, everything changes. This...world...we have been living in for the past few years...is over. We've been left alone by that boy. Now that boy has something to fight for—his wife and her child."

Devyn clenched his jaw behind a covered face. "His wife and my child."

"Think, Devyn. Do you think Marici really cares that this is your child? He cares that it's Sri's child—and if it's her child—in his sick mind—it's his child. He will want to claim the baby as his own blood." Vishal's voice softened, and he leaned to put a steadying hand on his friend's shoulder. "Most importantly, we need to plan. If we don't—both Sri and the baby are in danger."

Devyn placed a hand over Vishal's and squeezed. "I know. You are a good friend to think of us now." He sighed once, and again, and looked over at Sudha. "Council me, friends. You no longer have to persuade me that I need to take action."

As Devyn spoke, Sri listened from the kitchen. Heavy with child, she pressed her ear against the wall closest to the room, and held her weight with spread hands. She would not go share dinner with these men—she did not want to face this reality tonight. But she wanted to hear what her friends and her lover had to say about her fate. More than anything, she wanted her child to be safe.

Devyn closed his eyes and nodded in disapproval at his circumstances. "Council me. Surely you have some plan that Sri and I should follow."

Vishal looked at Sudha to get silent approval from the man before speaking. The two had discussed alternatives earlier today when Sudha received the letter. He was the only one of the priests who was still on neutral terms with *Govandhara*.

Instead of Vishal leading this part of the discussion, Sudha wiped his face on a cloth, and bolted ahead with the discussion. With unusual poise for the subject, he looked over into Devyn's dark eyes, and spoke with confidence. "You have to determine your path. Peace or war with *Govandhara*. This is up to you and Sri. Peace: You and Sri go back to *Govandhara* and arrange something with Marici. War: You and Sri continue to live in Goane as mother and father to the child. Goane will have to face mainland Kasimi."

Devyn leaned forward with his elbows on the table. "You've thought about this a lot, haven't you, Sudha?"

In the kitchen, Sri sank to the floor while holding her rounded belly with protective arms. She pressed her face into the soft space between her thighs and her womb, exhausted by the responsibility of her child to Kasimi. *Marici will want his blood and will shed his people's to get it.*

Sudha shrugged. "I thought everyone had been thinking about it since it was obvious that Sri was with child." He picked up a handful of olives and began gnawing at one in particular with his teeth. "What did you think would happen?"

Devyn stood up and paced before the window that held the picture of the night's storm. He rubbed his chin with an idle hand, and felt his steps fully. "Why does Marici get away with this? He would kill his own people?" Devyn turned to face his friends and crossed his arms over his chest in judgement of the Kasimian King.

"He would kill his own. He ruined his sister's life, and now wants her child? How can he get away with this?"

Vishal broke the tension by standing up to be at Devyn's side. He gave Sudha a disapproving glance and a suggestion that the man should eat rather than speak. Vishal spoke gently to Devyn. "He's a King and a God to the people of Kasimi. That is the reality *Brahma* has given us. These messages are not always clear—and the decision is yours and Sri's to make. We will support you both no matter what you choose."

Sri raised her chin from her position of surrender and seriously questioned her circumstances. It had been a risk to take Devyn as her lover, but she could not deny her heart. Life had been so peaceful in Goane. But the truth was that she was hiding. Everyone who had followed her was hiding from a King they would not face. Why? Because he was given his position by the gods? Because he was the sky power? He had disappointed their ancestors. He had no right to her child. Sri stood up, energized by her defiance. She promised herself that she would not leave her child in the hands of a man who had betrayed her. If only she could speak to Ajan now. He would be able to help.

The men had settled down, aware that the conversation regarding *Govandhara's* Heir was over. Finally, laughter was interspersed between stories, and friends were sharing a meal. Devyn's voice would not be heard often, evidence of the heavy thoughts on his mind. But Vishal would tell him something or another to bring him back into the lighthearted banter.

~

Sri woke to the feeling of cold hands on her cheeks, and the sound of a cheerful alto voice. She started a bit before being lulled into a comfort by the "Shhh…" of a familiar woman.

"Jabie…" said Sri, while wiping the sleep away from her eyes. "I'm so glad you came. Where's Bali?"

Jabala laughed. "You haven't seen me in weeks, and you ask for Bali. How's that, Sri?" She added quickly, "Bali is in the dining room with Devyn and the others."

Jabala had aged gracefully over the past few years. She still looked the same: brown everything, gentle soul. But her eyes had lines around them, and ever-present dark circles, that made her look sad. She was happy in Goane, though. With Bali, she had worked as a merchant and made a home amongst the Goanian people. Sri did find it odd though, that Jabala never found a lover. She always returned to her bed, alone, at night.

Sri smiled, stretching in her bed. "I thought both of you would come tonight, that's all."

Jabala stroked through Sri's sleep-disheveled hair and kissed her forehead. "How do you feel these days, Sri?" She inclined her head and looked down tenderly at her friend. "You're growing bigger—you must be due soon."

Sri smiled and rubbed her belly, that seemed to get bigger with each nap. "I am due very soon. By the full moon for certain." Sri sat up as much as her body could afford on her bed. "Jabie?"

Jabala had turned around to retrieve a glass of water for Sri. She smiled, and returned a hand to Sri's head. "*Acha?*"

Sri picked at the blankets around her and arranged them in no particular way. She smiled again, nervously, and her lips began twitching. "Mmm…Jabie…I would like you to come help me as the baby grows more due." Sri put her hands over her stomach and looked down at the swell. "This child, is the most important thing to me and Devyn and I want everything to go just right. Everything will, if you are here…helping me."

Jabala grinned knowingly, and replaced the glass of water on a table next to her girl. "I brought a bag with my things, intending to stay with you for the next few months. I didn't know you had to ask me." She winked at Sri, and pulled the blankets around her.

"I...don't know what to say. How did you know I'd want that?"

"I didn't know if you wanted it, Sri. But I wanted it and I knew you wouldn't turn me away."

Sri stared at Jabala for a few moments before closing her eyes to drift off again for the evening. It was all settled, and the girl could now rest comfortably in her nurse's arms while the storm continued on outside.

~

Bali had gone straight for the dining room when she and Jabala had arrived at the house. Her visit, though social, had taken on a serious tone from the moment she set forth on her mare for Devyn's house.

Bali had lost something when she arrived in Goane, those few years ago. She seemed brokenhearted—missing a part of her spirit. She had left behind her legacy in Kasimi. After spending a lifetime building herself as a noble woman with a lord's hand, she spent her power on one decision. This, she did not regret. But the price of her decision was foremost on her mind, it seemed. Her light blue eyes always reflected the heavy choices she had made, keeping her lost in her memories. Bali was still Bali, but what she once was had been buried beneath her loss.

But Bali, like Vishal, was still aware of the political world that existed outside of Goane. Though Kasimi was quiet and *Govandhara* was nearly dead, it was only a matter of time before Marici changed his mind about things. She enjoyed her life, and was overjoyed at the life Sri had found on her own—but Bali knew exactly who Sri was before, and what part she had played in changing that role. It could not stay this way forever.

Bali placed her cloak away on the nearest chair, and nodded to Jabala as she went to Sri's bedroom. She then stepped into the dining room and found a place next to Devyn after smiling and nodding to the men. She poured some wine, and listened to their banter for a few moments before interrupting the conversation.

"Do you really think that Devyn and Sri have a choice? Perhaps Marici has already sent people to Goane to ensure that the proper decision is made."

Vishal, Devyn and Sudha froze in conversation. The men dared not breathe, or utter a response, to such a pointed comment.

Devyn's eyes darkened and he looked into the old woman's face. "What did you come to my home tonight to tell me?"

Bali consented to tell him what she knew with a polite incline of her head. "As you wish." She turned her body towards the Goanian, and put a hand on his shoulder. "How much longer do you have before the child is born?"

Devyn massaged the bridge of his nose with a thumb and forefinger and responded in a muffled voice. "Not much longer, at the full moon."

Bali sighed, not realizing that Sri was this far along. "We have less time than I thought."

Vishal piped up through his clenched jaw. "So what's the problem?"

Sudha remained silent and passive.

Bali did not turn to face Vishal. She continued facing Devyn. "I have sources—the same as Janaka—as I am a merchant."

"Janaka?" Devyn asked suddenly.

Bali nodded. "Yes. I do you know that message you received with the seal of *Govandhara*?"

"How did you know about that?" Vishal snapped.

Bali waved Vishal away with a gesture of her hand. "I just do—and do you really think the messenger of that letter has left or—"

Bali felt for her wine to take a large gulp for confidence before the next statement. "—or do you think he is still here…watching…waiting to see what the action is? Maybe Marici has sent more people to make sure of his plan."

Vishal spoke firmly. "I think you're paranoid. Marici would never put Sri in that position. He loves her! He hasn't declared war because of her. You're just a crazy old woman."

Bali dismissed the comment with a light chuckle. "I am old, Vishal. And Marici does love Sri. But, he has someone else to worry about now."

Vishal quieted and turned to Devyn to say something.

All Devyn did was nod to both Vishal and Bali. "I'll take care of it."

22

"Oh *Brahma*!" Sri screamed, while Jabala dabbed a wet cloth at her forehead. "*BRAHMA!*"

Jabala had been doing everything possible since the rising of the full moon. She had tried dabbing Sri's head with water-rinsed towels, and elevating her feet. She had tried pouring cold water over her body while the sun trespassed inside the bedroom. She had held Sri while she cursed the gods and the man who had loved her. There was nothing that quieted Sri in these hours. Jabala just comforted and worried about the girl. But, she knew everything would be fine.

Sri breathed heavily, until the pain passed. It had started earlier in the day with a slight twinge—the way she'd feel after eating too many sweets. But this twinge could be felt in her heart and right away she knew it was time. Without warning Devyn, Sri called for Jabala to help her in her bedroom. She let Devyn go hunting, not letting him know what was to pass.

"Oh *BRAHMA!*" Sri screamed again. "What is going on, Jabie?"

Jabie remained calm, pressing cool cloths all over Sri's hair. Jabala did not answer Sri. She had never been this close to a woman's event. She had only heard the faint screams from the servants' chambers during the time. She remembered holding her lower abdomen in sympathetic pain and going on with her chores.

Sri was sweating and had begun to shed her clothes during the last pains that occurred. It was so hot and sticky, and she had rolled her head to the left and right, trying to get some cool air inside her. She twitched her hips suddenly, when the pain overwhelmed her, and arched her lower back in towards her body. But the tightening of her muscles only exacerbated the pain. Even deep and quick breathing could not alleviate the moments of torment.

Jabala offered continuous and kind words during the moments of pain knowing that nothing could comfort Sri. The pains continued all day, and the house's servants found it strange that the lady seemed to cry in torment and not rise from her bed.

Bali was called for towards evening. She knew the reason why she was summoned as the messenger galloped towards her home, and went quickly to Sri's bedside.

Bali knew exactly what to do.

"Sri...lift up the sheet so I can see how you look." Bali said gently, while lighting the vanilla candles in the woman's room.

Sri held her abdomen and bedding protectively. "No!" she said firmly. She didn't know the reason for protesting, but the pain was unbearable.

Bali lifted up the sheet with conviction, while Sri started another episode of pain. She looked at the woman's swollen body and the flesh that appeared to be peeking between her limbs. She sighed, "You will be a mother soon."

Sri arched her back up in the air so her body was lifted up towards the ceiling. She screamed for *Brahma* again.

"Hold her down," said Bali, while she positioned Sri's legs into a wide straddle on the bed. "And prop her back up so she can push."

Jabala's eyebrows knit. "Push?"

Bali nodded vigorously. "It's coming." She reached between the sheets and placed a cupped hand to feel the arriving head of the baby. "Now push, Sri."

Sri just screamed as loud as she could, and hoped her body would take care of the delivery. She felt a burning sensation between her legs while a baby ripped at the delicate flesh that was usually treated with such care by Devyn. There was blood from the tearing that extended through the inside of her hips, and constant pain from her body's involuntary torture.

The orders that were barked at her were a blur during the final moments of the birth. Sri looked out the window to focus on the full moon that had promised a child. The pain met a point with her body where she had to surrender, and then release it. It was meant to move a child from her womb, to her arms. Sri separated her mind, but kept her heart with the pain, and waited.

And waited. Over the next hour, the pushing continued but the baby refused to come. But after one moment of excruciatingly sharp pain where the last bit of flesh was ripped and the last stream of blood flowed, a baby cried in Bali's waiting arms.

Sri felt her body at ease in the bed, and she looked desperately to find the face of her child. She could feel nothing at this point but her heart pounding in her throat, waiting to meet what she had grown.

Bali smiled, raising the baby to show Jabala and Sri. The darling creature had a mat of reddish brown hair—a combination of mother and father. The skin was a nice mocha like the mother. And the eyes were black with a thin layer of red around the pupils—like all the ancestors.

Sri held the child in her arms, searching the baby's innocent gaze. She then placed a long kiss on her daughter's forehead, and looked up with pride towards Bali and Jabala.

Sri knew that the baby she held in her arms was a destined symbol for the people, as she had been. But in this life, she wished that her daughter could truly lead the people to a greatness they had never seen before. But now was not a time to have such thoughts for a baby.

23

The black clad man kneeled down before his liege in the dark room. He bowed his head and awaited permission to speak on the day's events. His job was to watch and answer to his master.

The room was completely dark, save a few lit candles to show the way to the table in the center of the empty hut. There was no physical feeling to the space, as a room would have. No items or things or colors to define its boundaries. But what the hut did not have in the way of materials, it had in the way of presence. There was age in this room, and purpose. There was sadness and longing. There were two men, one sitting while the other hovered over him protectively. They could not be seen, but they could be felt. The men transcended the space they occupied.

The black clad man, kneeled down, without as much strength as his early years had once brought him. But in this dark room, he could hide from everything he had done before, and answer only to a man.

The assassin began to speak, a rattling of mucus against vocal chords, before a voice damaged from smoke began to tell the tale. "A girl-child was born tonight and both mother and daughter are in good health. The baby shows the blood of *Govandhara*."

A voice that sounded older than its true years responded back in the black of night. "What does she look like?"

The black clad man continued. "She is as her mother and father, showing signs of both houses. Red hair and a thin line of red around the eyes."

The same voice responded back. "Goanian and of *Govandhara*? Is it certain?"

The black clad man hung his head and nodded, responding back without words in affirmation.

At this moment, another man entered the hut with heavy, pronounced steps. He too was dressed in dark colors—his image indiscernible within these walls. The candlelight did reflect off the top of his head, representing the aged man's curse. His body generated much warmth in the otherwise cold room. He too knelt down before his liege, and bowed his head.

The heavy voice came again from nowhere. "I have been told a girl has been born to *Govandhara*. What more news can you bring me?"

A soft voice whispered the news back, careful to not let the words slip beyond a defined space. A secret. Perhaps this man was ashamed to speak. If he whispered, it would take away the sin. "Goane intends to raise the child without *Govandhara*. It is determined to be that way."

The liege's jaw tightened. It could not be seen but his silence reverberated in the night onto his two messengers. "It is not determined to be that way. *Govandhara* has not spoken yet. The child rightfully belongs to the gods."

The heavy-set man struggled on his knees and let emotion leak out in his whisper. "But what can *Govandhara* do now? Goane has spoken for the child. Unless war…"

The liege waved his hand through the blackness. The wind from the gesture made the candlelight dance angrily, before the motion of breath calmed the waves. "There will be no war. *Govandhara* has a quarrel with one man, not one thousand."

Age shows some wisdom and more danger. The rashness of youth was mellowed away for the keenness of mind. Directing the anger one has for an entire society against one man can be more dangerous than war. The voice continued, "I am certain you know what I am saying."

The black clad man brought his head up and said with conviction, "I will kill for you."

The liege shook his head mercifully. His eyes fixed upon his loyal servant with a strange tenderness. "You will not kill again, man. You have served me well and with loyalty. You have done your time and now your conscience is free. You will not kill again."

A new voice, coming from behind the master's chair, spoke softly, "I will kill for you."

The liege nodded once, and then twice. "Yes. You will kill for me. It has to be you. We have spoken and you know what you must do."

Someone swallowed nervously.

"There must be no hesitation in this room. What we do now, is for *Govandhara*. We must not think of the past or the consequences of the action in personal terms. We must think of *Govandhara* only, and of its heir. This is the only way."

There was silence in the darkness. This group of men thus pledged their loyalty and hearts to the soul of *Govandhara*, in the mind of their liege. A war had not been started this evening—but the passion of one man has been confirmed. There would be blood shed for *Govandhara*, but only of one man. Murder—like war—makes for tales of pain for many years to come. But murder—unlike war—cannot be blamed on the politics of a kingdom. It is not as easily forgiven, or forgotten.

~

Time passed in the hut as the hours of night went by. The liege remained in his seat but barely said a word after he had made his decision final. The other three men continued on in their dialogue and planning, to ensure that this mission was executed perfectly. There would not be many opportunities to do this.

Outside, the night was thick. Goane, unlike Kasimi, retained its moisture throughout the year. Even when water did not fall from the sky, the air promised a sweat on one's skin. The men did perspire this night, except for the liege. He sat—cold and calm—in the hut.

The black clad man was an expert in watching and finding patterns in a man's behavior. Over the past few weeks, he held a careful watch over the home and had taken note of the day-to-day goings on. The assassin had not only watched the Goanian, but had also watched over *Govandhara*. The times when she was alone would give more information than the moments when he was alone.

The first hour was spent in uncomfortable silence, interrupted only by sounds of confusion. Sighing was heavy and breathing could be heard. The pacing of the man who hovered over the liege could be felt by the way the candlelight moved from one side to the other. The men moved into their own corners of this odd-shaped hut, trying to find their thoughts—or escape them. But they did not leave the inner sanctum of their group. Outside was Goane.

Finally, the assassin spoke up in a rough voice. In the darkness, he stood from his sitting position and walked over to where the others stood and explained his thoughts. "It is hunting season, and Devyn rides every afternoon to the middle of the forest. It is a few hours ride from the house, and he usually goes alone...rides the black horse..."

Surprising—for a man to hunt alone. The man who was to kill responded, "Are you certain he goes alone? Does he not meet friends or companions when he rides?"

"No, he goes alone. I have watched a little. He goes to the same spot..."

"To hunt?"

"He has a sword, and his killed a few times. Sometimes, he just walks. He is always there...for a few hours. And returns home late for the evening meal. It is his habit." The assassin needlessly warmed his hands over the flames of the fire, though the heat of the night was sufficient.

Cerulean blue eyes gazed back at the assassin with an intent expression. "This is a pattern? He does this alone, has consistently done this alone?"

The black-clad man bowed his head. "Yes my lord. I am certain."

The soft bellied man called out from the southern corner of the hut. "I didn't know he did this—and he and I have been companions for some time now...I am not certain that..."

He was cut off by the priest. "If you are not aware of it, it makes it more real. People do not share their solitude with others." The King's protector was speaking of personal experience. His mind went to his clandestine walks to meet Jabala, and for a moment his heart stopped. That thought made the moment so close—his steadfast and unquestioning loyalty to *Govandhara* paused. Jabala—his dear and wonderful old friend. She had chosen her heart when she went with Sri and Devyn to Goane. She had broken his when she left.

The images of Jabala made his tender thoughts move to Sri. She had been the jewel of his life—and when she left, a part of him went with her. He had wished he had not the heart of a King's servant, but the heart of a man. Else he would have been the one to take her away, not Devyn. Instead, he chose his duty and lost his life's work. When she left, it was so easy to become the model of his position. Emotion was not an issue anymore.

But now, emotion was an issue. If he did what he had promised, he would hurt her and her child. But it was for her good—to bring her and the heir back home. If he refused, he would die for insolence. Ajan was not afraid to die—he was torn. What kept him loyal now, besides his vow to serve the King, was the heir to *Govandhara* and her mother. What he did now, he did for them.

"If we do this, it must look like the Goanian did not die—but left. He must look like a coward. Death will only chain Sri to this place. Her heart will lock here. But anger—and misunderstanding—will bring her home."

The Southerner's eyebrows lifted in surprise. "Should we not first take care of the physical details before we begin on subtleties?"

The liege spoke in an ice-calm voice that cooled the room with its timbre. "No no...the murder will be done easily. It is how we execute now that will make the difference. Continue, Ajan."

Ajan rubbed his eyes with his knuckles. "We will have to dispose of the body, in the ocean. There is a chance otherwise that it will be discovered and Sri will see the details. She'll know. She can see the truth when she sees the image...it will be painted on Devyn's face."

Sudha chimed in once again. "Gentlemen, are we sure? Is there nothing we can do other than to kill Devyn? He was once our friend..."

The liege let out a thick sigh that spread his minted breath towards Sudha. "I have made the decision." He let one minute pass, tapping a finger at the hollow wood table. "Devyn is no longer a friend of *Govandhara*. He is an enemy who deserves no part of my family. Understood?"

The bald man went silent in consent. He voiced a choked, "Understood..." to confirm.

Ajan paced more broadly across the room now, blood flowing through him with vigor. A part of the warrior had remained dormant—and his mind was working for both a purpose and reason. He had convinced his heart that this mission was for love. The two in unison brought back his blood from war. "The route through the forest will take us to the ocean. It is the way we came here without being detected...I remember it..."

The old assassin cocked his head to one side. "She will never know what happened then. But—what will we do after this event—to get to her?"

Ajan bit at his lip and rubbed his chin. This part would be more difficult. They could not leave right away because they would need to face her. To implore her to return to *Govandhara* with the child. But if they showed up at her home a short while after Devyn disappeared, she would know. She would sense it.

Sudha spoke in low tones while his stomach rumbled quietly. "We will wait. We will let his vanishing weigh on her and Goane. And I can play a role in this..."

Silence came again over the men in the room. This was one of the more important parts of the plan. To bring Sri's heart back to *Govandhara*. It was unlikely that Sudha would have the answer.

Sudha stood and walked over to join the black clad man and Ajan in this honest circle of men. They surrounded the liege at the table and looked into each other's eyes with resolution.

"I am a trusted member of the home, and I can use this. I can pretend to bring good news to the home—that *Govandhara* wanted to make peace—to meet or talk or something—politics. With careful words, Sri may grow to think that Devyn left her because of *Govandhara*."

Ajan shrugged, "Why would that be of consequence?"

Sudha shook his head and waggled his finger slowly. "But you see, over the years, Devyn has been shy of politics. He has not responded to them and sometimes even angers if Vishal or I brings up the topic. Especially about the child. It could be planted in her mind that he left because of politics. If done carefully, and over time."

Sudha shifted his weight nervously while he thought out his plan. "Vishal has been pressuring him about this very topic—what do with about the child—all the consequences. I could see how he might bend. I could paint him as a coward..."

Ajan nodded. He now understood. "Yes, that is brilliant. It is exactly what needs to be done. Each night we can craft what you will say and do so that every thought of Sri's will be anticipated. We will bring her to hate her lover for leaving...and to love *Govandhara* for offering peace...and she will come home."

Sudha bobbled his head energetically. "Exactly—exactly— carefully we will do it. But we must be patient. Wait...for the right moment. Wait for quite a time after the death before we approach her."

Ajan had compromised himself now, and did feel the pangs of guilt. It was one thing to carry out one act for the greater good of a society. But now, he was manipulating his child. Would the gods forgive him? Was there not another way to use the truth to persuade her? Not with the damage Devyn had done. The friend he had found in that Goanian was now his enemy. He would have to do this.

"We will sail from the coast in the north down to the main dock in two moons, and make it appear as if we have just traveled here from the mainland. Agreed?" The liege stood from his chair on this statement. He had grown tall and strong over the past few years, and now rivaled Ajan for build. His black silks stuck to him like water even as he took his proud posture. "I believe it is planned then."

As the King stood, the three servants kneeled. The plan had been made over the course of a night. They bowed their heads and waited.

"I want this done within four nights or else I will be disappointed."

The King walked to a recessed room in the back of the hut where he would sleep and wait. He left his men: assassin, warrior and traitor to make proper arrangements. His breathing grew less frequent and loud, until the silence intimated that the young liege had fallen asleep at this tail end of night.

The three men, not comfortable to speak near the King, went outside to escape his ears. The camp was hidden in the rolling hills of Goane, on the other side of Sura. What separated the two spaces was the forest, where Devyn found solace each day. One corner of the beach was behind the mountain, similar to the geography of *Govandhara*. The forest's trees again interrupted the sand before Sura's beaches took over the boundary.

It was not a well-liked space in Goane. Hidden from the rest of the land and without much vegetation or animals, the rolling hills were deemed unnecessary. They were beautiful, as one could stand atop them and see into the depths of the water. But no one adventured onto them. The Kasimians attacked Goane through the mountains when they colonized the land—they were a cursed place.

These hills were the perfect place for the caravan to wait and watch. The sea route from Kasimi was isolated and it would be most unlikely for any merchants to spy the ship. The men took a modest and unmarked boat, one that would not be easily recognized. They sailed up along the Northern part of the territory, to this deserted sight. No one encountered the men. They made certain of that.

Ajan breathed in the thick air of Goane, made cooler in the hills. He crossed his arms over his pounding heart to silence the beating, and looked up at the sky. "I never thought it would come to this…"

The assassin, usually quiet in the space of the Grand Priest, walked alongside the man and looked at him with tenderness. "You have never had to kill in cold blood, have you? Only in the name of war?" The black clad man put his hand over his own heart.

Ajan shook his head. "Is there a distinction? Killing is killing. I have done it before. I will do it again, for my kingdom."

"It is different this time, my lord." The assassin looked at the ground. "When I close my eyes, I can see each of my victims. I can remember the order to kill. I can relive each moment. In my youth, I actually enjoyed it." He walked off and continued his thoughts. "And now, as I grow old, I am haunted by it."

"I have been haunted in my time, too." Ajan said in a gruff voice. He rubbed his hands idly and paced away from the hut. "I killed without thought. I raped without regret. And now, I will kill a man who was my friend because he is my enemy. It's a simple thing."

"It might be simple, but it will hurt you more than him. He dies with a clean conscience." The assassin put one hand on Ajan's back and patted him reassuringly. "You serve your liege with loyalty. Take comfort in that."

From his place away from the assassin and Ajan, Sudha mouthed in a nervous tone, "I am not sure that I want to do this…"

Ajan snapped towards the Southerner, and walked briskly towards him. The wind helped the tall priest along, and brushed his jet black hair against his neck. "You have come too far to turn back."

"I believe in our Kingdom, yes. But I do not believe in killing a friend. We can do this another way. Don't you think Marici is being rash?"

Ajan put a strong hand on Sudha's shoulder and squeezed tightly. "You had plenty of time to break away, before we reached this point. It's too late."

Sudha winced, and put a thick hand atop Ajan's to gently push it away. But Ajan's hand remained on his shoulder. He struggled to gain a steady voice and asked, "It's not too late if we all…"

Ajan dug his strong and nimble fingers into Sudha's body. "Do not make me have to tell him. *Acha*?"

Sudha exhaled as the fingers were released from his body. He began to rub his shoulder, bringing blood back into this spot. "I'll go now."

Sudha had been warned. The large man walked off to a steady and distant part of the hill where he had left his horse. He would ride through the forest to his home, and contemplate the night's activities. He would hang his head in shame, and remember his duty.

Ajan watched Sudha go and tensed his hand up into a fist while grinding his teeth. He said into the air, "I don't trust him."

The assassin was close to Ajan suddenly. He put his old hands on Ajan's back and massaged the Grand Priest's muscles. "He won't betray us. He's too weak…I promise you he won't betray us. He is nothing to us."

The Grand Priest left the grip of the assassin, and walked forward to look at the forest that went beyond the hills of Goane. He let his angry eyes close in on themselves and his pounding heart die to a still beat. He breathed in the heavy air and pushed it away with a low roar. He would kill for his King. Even if it meant betraying himself.

24

Devyn arrived after the evening meal, as usual when he hunted. He had no idea he would return home to a house full of visitors who eagerly anticipated the viewing of a child—his daughter. When all the horses were parked outside his home, he was confused and hopeful. He pushed his stallion into the hands of a waiting servant and went quickly towards his bedroom to see if his wife was all right. He had no idea what awaited him.

Everyone was eating and laughing in the living room. The house was filled with joy, concentrated in the smiles of the visitors. Each person in his home, he knew well. All had the means to make it to his home quickly since they were neighbors. Vishal was there, raising a glass in celebration.

Devyn walked into his bedroom to find his lover asleep and also to find Jabala's back turned to the wall. Bali was asleep in a chair beside Sri. But Jabala turned around, holding a little girl wrapped in white blankets when she heard the man enter. She smiled and placed the baby in Devyn's arms.

Devyn looked at his little girl and his knees gave way until he found a seat at the edge of Sri's bed. "Mine?" he muttered.

Jabala nodded. "No other child."

Devyn grinned lazily, and turned his attention back to his little girl. She looked so much like Sri, and was definitely his child. He was immediately captured by the black eyes—with the thin line of red around the pupils. He had remembered so many evenings gazing into Sri's eyes, and loving her. He knew that these unique eyes were shared by other members of *Govandhara*, as well. Devyn melted as he studied the little nose and cheeks of his daughter. She would look exactly like Sri when she was grown. He would love her the same way he had loved Sri. There would be no other fathers.

Devyn looked up at Jabala with sad eyes. "When did she deliver? I had wanted to be there...she..."

Jabala sat beside Devyn, by Sri's hips on the bed. "Sri would never want you to see her in pain. It was a very hard birth for her. She just wanted to give you the gift at the end."

Devyn nodded. "Is she all right?"

Jabala put a comforting hand on Devyn's shoulder. "She's fine—just tired—she won't wake up for a while."

Devyn nodded and then pulled his body up alongside his sleeping lover with his daughter in his arms. He held these two women, and fell asleep quietly. Jabala watched over the family.

While drifting off to sleep, Devyn was filled with the love for his family and the fear of what was to come. The child had been born.

He would need to plan. Soon, the quiet period after the birth would be complete. Politics would follow—the ones that Bali and Vishal had been warning him of. He looked down at the little girl and ran a masculine finger over her new face. How could such an innocent be the symbol of so much? How could her life start out in such a complicated way? What could he do to make it simpler?

They could run. He had saved up the means to live a comfortable life, perhaps in the far northern lands, away from the warm waters of Goane. He had heard that the people from the far north were peaceful and honest, and welcoming to strangers. He could leave everything behind—take Sri and his child—and live in peace there.

But could they really run? The child was too young to take such a treacherous journey. And, he and Sri had already run from one Kingdom. To run from Marici once again was unspeakable. It just shouldn't be this way. Devyn's eyes swelled with tears and his mind filled with anger towards his kinsman. It was true, was it not? Marici was now his blood. Through the common love of Sri.

He could not run from his family. If Marici really loved Sri, he would not impose his will on her and the child. But what if Marici really thought of this little, tiny girl as his heir?

Devyn's fingers finished tracing the little girl's face, and with the last touch, he was filled with strength and resolution. He would not run away from the tyrant King. He would just live his life. If violence and anger were to be the things that Marici enforced on his family, he would face them. He could not shelter his daughter from who she was, or from where she came. He refused to. He could only set an example for her, by living his life without fear.

With his mind clear, Devyn was soon to drift off to sleep while his guests continued to celebrate in his home.

25

When dawn came, and the house was quiet, Devyn awoke to the sounds of the earliest birds. The steady and low humming nudged him from an already light slumber. He looked around the room to make sense of it. Jabala was asleep in a wooden chair next to his and Sri's bed. Devyn walked quickly and placed a heavy blanket over her. He was comforted that she was there for Sri, and his daughter.

Still dazed, Devyn sat on the edge of his bed, and fussed with the quilt. He was careful to not move his weight too much and to stir Sri. He ran his hardened hands over his red hair and rubbed his eyes to make them alert. He then looked around his bedroom at the fantastic sights of the morning. The sunlight was still pink, and whispering in the window. His lover looked peaceful, wrapped in several layers. And now, by the side of Sri, was life.

The cradle, a wooden structure that Bali had brought back from her journeys, held the infant with pride. Jabala and Sri had made simple blankets of cobalt blue, the color of the North, during the end of the pregnancy. Devyn recalled the sounds of laughter coming from the bedroom when the two women worked on the baby's things.

Devyn went to his newborn daughter's side and picked up the waking child with his large hands. He held her close to his heart and rocked her to lull her back to sleep. Fascinated by her face, Devyn leaned down to kiss her forehead and muss her red hair. The baby blinked a few times and then drifted back to sleep. *So peaceful for a newborn.*

He then turned to look at the center of his heart and life. His lover, his friend, his ward. Devyn crept by the side of the bed she favored and sat beside her. He freed a hand from the baby and ran it over Sri's head, savoring the touch of the black silk through his fingers. It seemed like ages since he had really felt her hair. Devyn leaned in towards her and inhaled her scent. There was nowhere Devyn would rather be. His lips found Sri's and he stayed there for moments.

Sri awoke to the kiss of her lover, and the pain of her birth. She moaned slightly and then bit Devyn's nose playfully. "Remind me to never let you touch me again..." She laughed weakly and then rolled over on the bed.

Devyn pulled the blankets down to admire the body of Sri. She wore only a very loose white covering over her body. Sri still had some of the puffiness in her abdomen that remained from the birth, but her body looked young again as he had remembered. She had been beautiful with child—she was beautiful now. He brought a hand over her body while the other cradled the sleeping infant.

"But aren't you happy I made you a mother?"

Sri turned around, a gentle smile on her lips, and leaned her head on Devyn's shoulder. She kissed his cheek, and sighed lightly, "I'm very happy to be a mother..." Sri reached her hand out and patted her daughter's little fingers. "But you have no idea of the pain." She laughed, and continued to brood over her child.

"Mmm…" Devyn hummed, enjoying the moment. "I could sit like this all day, but I have other plans for us." Devyn stood up to walk the child back to her cradle. "Are you too weak to ride?"

Sri's eyes lit up. "Ride? It's been months…months since I've been farther than our garden. I can ride."

Devyn looked with concern at his lover. "But you said you were in pain?"

Sri shook her head spoiled-child like. "No no no—not in too much pain to ride in the day…we can bring the baby, no?"

"We aren't going that far, I don't see why not. She looks well." Devyn grinned, "We'll go slowly, enjoy the day. I have something to show you—a surprise."

Sri's eyes grew bright like her daughter's. "Oh? Oh really?" She began to make motions to rise from the bed.

"Really."

Jabala snapped from her sleep, "Are you sure you two should be going out? The child is but a day old."

Devyn and Sri looked over at Jabie, smiling mischievously at her. Sri rejoined, "And shelter our daughter from our wicked ways? Never…it will be good for the baby to get in the sunshine, and I haven't been outside forever. I just have to, Jabie."

Jabala laughed, "You know, I would be happy to watch the little one while you two ride."

Sri cocked her head to one side to entertain the thought. It was quickly dismissed. "I don't want to leave the little one the day after I met her for the first time. She's strong enough to go for a little ride outside, don't you think?"

Jabie nodded with a grand smile. "Of course. Look who her parents are." Jabala got up to take the infant from Devyn's arms. "I'll get her dressed for the ride, so the sun doesn't get at her skin too much." She began to rock the waking child in her arms, and made a soft maternal expression as she exited the bedroom.

Devyn looked down at his lover, and patted her hair. "You sure you're up for this?"

Sri rolled her eyes, and then kissed Devyn's shoulder. "Very much so, Devyn. Let's get dressed and go."

He laughed, and stood up from the bed to retrieve both his and her clothes for the ride. Soft white cotton would be perfect for a warm day like today. Devyn took a pair of pajama pants and a loose white tunic, and found a white robe for Sri. He threw it playfully at her on the bed and said, jesting, "I hate to ask you this—but put some clothes on."

Sri caught the smooth, white robe, and retorted. "I want to wear pants."

"Not in your condition. You should ride to the side, not straight ahead. You can hold on to me."

"So—I don't even get my own horse? How boring!"

"Don't be spoiled, Sri." Devyn laughed, while he finished fastening his pants around his legs and hips. He pressed the creases out and walked to Sri. He placed a kiss on her nose, and then leered, "Do you need help putting on that robe?"

Sri dimmed her eyes and leaned back on the bed, having taken off her resting robe. She angled herself so that her swollen bosom was gently displayed before Devyn and said in sweet tones, "Oh, I definitely need help..."

Devyn purred, looking at the beautiful body of his lover still curvy from pregnancy. He ran his hands over her body, not able to control the hunger that stirred in his body. "Sri, you have no idea how happy I am, do you? No idea at all, do you?"

"I do, Devyn."

Those were the last words that were spoken before Jabala re-entered the bedroom. Devyn and Sri did not make love—it was too early after the birth. But Devyn did not place Sri's robe on her body right away, choosing to hold the bare form of his lover for a few moments. He could not let go. Finally, Sri stirred and kissed Devyn by his ear and whispered in her warm breath, "We should get ready to go, no?" He was jerked back to reality.

The two people, clad in white, met Jabala as she entered the bedroom with a carefully dressed child. The little girl was wearing a sky-blue dress that Bali had brought from the far north. It was a simple cotton gown, with silk trimming—perfect for a hot day. Jabala had spent time fussing with the newborn, making sure that the sleeves went down to the girl's tiny elbows, and the lines of the dress were perfect. She had then placed a white lamb's wool blanket over the baby's body and head to protect against the sun. "She needs the extra layers so soon after her arrival."

Sri nodded and accepted the baby into her arms while Devyn doted on the two. He squinted, and asked with a worried tone, "How will we keep her from falling if Sri had to hold on to me while we ride?"

Jabala shook her head. "Don't you have younger siblings, Devyn?" She laughed and handed Sri a carrier that would place the baby's body through it to snuggle near her bosom. A strap connected it over her head and around her back. "Sri—you'll just have to be careful to not press to hard against the child while riding. Go slowly—and be careful."

Jabala motioned with her hands, "Now go off, young family!"

Devyn laughed loudly at his being scolded, while Sri was careful to place the child against her bosom. He then took Sri by the hand, and hurried outside to the front of the house to where his favored horse would be waiting.

The wind blew against their faces as the three people opened the door. The morning was still not developed, and the sun's pink and red rays were gradually turning yellow through the cracks of the palm trees. The cool breeze was strong, making Sri pull her child to her, and Devyn pull Sri to him.

"It's a beautiful day, Sri. It will be a nice ride." Devyn beamed as he put an old, soft blanket over the back of his black stallion. He took a brush and worked over the body of the animal. This black horse was one of his favorites, and knew the path to the forest well. It was an older animal—which was better. He would not be frightened of having three creatures atop it, and would go slower and travel with more care.

Sri patted the mane of the horse and smiled, "It's been so long since I've been out. I'm so excited, Devyn!"

Devyn grinned, "This will not be the only thing, you know. I have a surprise for you in the forest...for you and the child."

Sri's eyes widened, and her brows arched upward, "A surprise?" She then settled her face back to a calmer position and whispered, "What kind of surprise? I remember last time when you took me to the forest we..."

Devyn cut Sri off by putting a finger to her lips. "Well, that's not the kind of surprise I was thinking of...though I am open to persuasions of your beautiful kind."

Devyn mounted the horse first, to ensure Sri would be steady when she climbed atop. A nearby servant was summoned with a hand gesture, and Devyn asked him to lift Sri to the horse so she could hold the child. With skill and little help, Sri mounted the horse to the side. She was able to position herself in front of Devyn holding the baby in her arms while side-mounted. Devyn took the reins of the horse and used his torso to cradle his wife and daughter.

"Ready?" Devyn asked with strength.

"Absolutely!" said Sri, with girlish excitement. "Go now!"

And off they went, into the forest while the morning came up around them. Devyn would steer the stallion on the path through the tamed palm trees and wild flowers that came in every color, before the lush forests of Goane overtook the path.

Sri looked up at these trees that she had seen for years, as if she had been away from them for a lifetime. The way the rising sun played in and out of the thick palms, and the texture of the trees fascinated her. After her eyes were satiated by those sights, Sri would gaze down at her little child and up at the sky that grew bright. It was almost too much for her senses to take in. The smells and sounds of this garden path, alongside the innocence of her daughter, made her heart surge. And then she was reminded of the man her hands touched, and the love for Devyn overwhelmed her.

The flowers that lined the path were new since Sri had been late in her pregnancy. The roses, which were usually lavender through the years, had a strikingly blue hue to them this season. If she closed her eyes, and put a hand on her child's head, she could smell the perfume.

The baby, not aware of what was going on, did fuss and cry out sometimes. But, she was easily soothed by the gentle rhythm of the horse and the voice of her mother. She was surprisingly good natured for such a young one, and easily hypnotized by the sounds of birds and the smell of flowers. Sometimes Devyn would hum a tune in a soft male voice to lull the baby back to sleep. She was easily convinced.

After what seemed like just minutes, the family arrived at the border of the garden to the forest. Larger trees of a darker green hovered over the line of palms, and welcomed the guests to use a covered path through it.

The scenery suddenly changed. The subtle sounds of birds and insects evolved to a slightly harsher sounds of stronger animals. There was more energy in this lush forest than on the gentle garden path, causing Sri to shiver in fear and delight. Everything was sharper. She could smell the leaves on the trees, and the scent of trapped water. One moment, Sri would see a curious brown monkey that ran quickly across the trees. In another moment, she would see a long and textured snake that slid dangerously close to their horse. Sri appreciated how the powerful and serene elements of the forest could exist together.

Devyn picked up the pace and ran the horse faster when they got more into the forest. They didn't move too quickly worrying that the child would wake or stir in this new environment. But Devyn wanted to reach this one area of the forest that he went to each day, as quickly as possible. He gripped Sri tighter with his body, and rode at this new pace until he reached the clearing where they could stop and rest for a moment.

Devyn paused his horse at a nearby tree, and dismounted to secure its reins. He patted the animal with affection, and gave it an apple to work on while he helped Sri and the baby dismount. Devyn kissed Sri's lips and pulled her close into his arms being careful not to crush the little one.

"Let's rest a while, Sri…" Devyn pointed to the clearing where a small pond stood amidst the dense trees. "Over there, we can sit for a while. You must be tired."

Sri smiled and kissed her lover on the cheek. "Where are you taking me?" She grinned and began to walk towards the water with Devyn.

Devyn reached a finger down to pat the baby's nose and smiled, "Will our daughter be as persistent as you?"

"If I teach her correctly, she will be more so." Sri laughed, and then went quiet. Her eyes went to look upon this part of the forest that she had never seen before. This magical clearing where colors and beauty came forth suddenly.

The trees stopped at the border of the pond, forming an imperfect circle. Their branches mingled above the water, but did not meet completely in the center. The sun was let in through these breaks, making the water shimmer like molten gold.

Colors overflowed around the pond. Flowers, similar to the ones on the garden path, had sprung up in between the trees in various colors and styles. They had formed a thick padding on the ground, and had lined the grass that led up to the pond. Sri and Devyn held hands as they approached.

Sri bent down to pick a few flowers of blue to place in her hair. She then wove the stems through the locks of the baby's soft red curls to match her own.

"Devyn...I didn't know this place existed in the forest..." Sri said, as she lowered herself down to sit near the pond.

Devyn laid back in the flowers, letting them fold around his body. He turned his head slightly to eye his lover. "I just found it a month ago, my darling. And when I saw it, I knew I had to take you here."

Sri smiled down at the baby, and opened her dress to feed her child at her swollen bosom. The quiet baby took her mother's breast in her mouth and began to feed, silently. Sri stroked the baby's hair, fixing the flowers, and looked over at Devyn. "She is very quiet for a baby. Should we be concerned?"

Devyn shook his head. "My sisters were all quiet as babies. I think it just runs in my family." He laughed and then plopped back in the flowers.

Sri boosted the child up to feed more easily, and smoothed her own hair back with her freed hand. She looked around, her black eyes absorbing the vivid colors. A heavy thought rolled too easily off her tongue, "Do you not think I worry about the baby?"

Devyn put a peace of grass in his mouth. "What do you mean?"

Sri held the child tighter to her. "Devyn, there is a lot we will have to worry about. You do realize."

Devyn sighed, and put his hands on his chest while his eyes closed out the sky above. "I do know, Sri." He rolled over on his side so he could look at her. Really look at her. His nervousness subsided at the sight of the nursing child, and his heart fell slightly. "Sri, I know the problems. I am determined to raise this child as my own. Is that a problem?"

Sri shook her head. "And I am determined as well...but it will be difficult. We will have to be strong, especially for her." She looked down at the baby, and traced her right hand over her daughter's head.

Sri continued to smile gently, and then looked up at the sun flowing in through the trees. She reached a hand out to Devyn's empty one and grasped it loosely in hers. They sat like this for a little while. No words were exchanged. Hands touched and caressed with no demands, in the strange flowers by the pond.

Finally, Devyn rolled up, half-dazed and smiled at his lover. "Let's go." He stood up, straightening his now slightly stained cotton pants, and helped Sri to her feet.

Sri chuckled, and sprung up with energy. She kissed playfully along Devyn's neck and ear and whispered to him while her eyes dimmed, "I love you..."

Devyn inhaled the scent of the flowers in her hair, and went weak in his knees for a moment. She had power over him. It was the look in those incredible black eyes. And now she was the mother of his child. And she loved him.

The family rode at a leisurely pace, running through the trails in the lush forest for another hour. Sri, exhausted from the nursing, fell asleep against Devyn's shoulder, leaving the man to ensure that the child did not shift in the ride. Soon, he would be near the place where he had visited every day over the last part of Sri's pregnancy. There was something there he had built for her.

During the hour that Sri napped, Devyn felt safe to let thoughts and worries surface. He knew that these troubles weighed on her heart and mind, more so than on his or Vishal's or Bali's. Though she resented the talk of the political reality surrounding her child,

Devyn would often find Sri staring with worried eyes into the garden. She was thinking—keeping her plans to herself. He had been rough on her only because he wanted her to talk to him—to stop keeping this inside. It was the one time he felt shut out by Sri.

Devyn leaned down into Sri's ear and whispered for her to wake up. This made her twitch as she was jolted from a deep sleep. The baby moved and made a few sounds which were quickly tended to by both parents.

Devyn put his head on his lover's shoulder and fixed his lips on her ear. His warm breath played along her skin while he kissed the soft flesh behind her earlobe for a while. Sri sighed at Devyn's touch and sank into his strong chest that cradled her. She surrendered to his touch, closing her eyes, and enjoying his lips.

"Oh Devyn…" she sighed softly in his ear.

Devyn smiled against her cheek, and ran his hands over her shoulders and arms. "Look around you, Sri…"

Sri opened her eyes fully, and absorbed the sight as instructed. The trees were thinner in this deep part of the forest. There were stretches of sky interlaced with the leaves, where birds could be more easily spotted and light could dance more freely inside. The gentle hills of Goane were within sight beyond the forest, their view skewed by the height of the trees.

The air was decidedly more moist here, perhaps because the ocean was closer. Or perhaps rainfall was more common in this part of Goane, than elsewhere. Sri squinted slightly, and looked up at the rich blue sky in confusion. For a moment, she remembered *Govandhara*.

"Devyn, I don't see anything unus…" Sri stopped as her black eyes, with a ring of red around the center, fell upon this one sight. Her mouth went open and her hands trembled around her daughter's body.

Devyn had been coming each day to build this sanctuary. It looked exactly like the one she remembered in *Govandhara*—the only place that had provided her with peace during her youth. It was made of different rocks, woven together from Devyn's scavenging trips in the forest. The roof was not symmetrical, made of thick layers of straw and also dried rose-petals. Inside, Devyn had written with his own hand, in cobalt-blue dye, the story of Kasimi, up to the third miracle of Sri and Marici. He had then written of the strength of Sri's journey, and the birth of their child. He had done this because it had to be done. There was no reason for his lover or their child to forget the past.

Devyn whispered this in her ear as Sri gazed upon this image of *Govandhara*. He told her why he had done this, and how much he loved her. Her eyes welled up with tears and her hands clasped their daughter with love.

"You...y...built this for me?"

"Not just for you—for both of you. You are in Goane, Sri...but both of you are daughters of *Govandhara*. With a real history. You should both never forget."

"You did this for us?"

Devyn nodded slowly, his own eyes welling up with tears. If he had to give a reason—"I love you, Sri."

Sri's chest raised to catch a breath. Her trembling hand went awkwardly to feel the skin on Devyn's face as best she could. She savored him, wanting to find a way to connect herself to him. Her mouth fell silently open, to say something.

Devyn let a tear fall down his cheek. In a voice that was heavy with emotion, he said, "I had to show you and the baby, today...how much I love you..." His hands went to move hurriedly over Sri's body as he searched to find words.

"I love you..." he said in a whisper met with more tears.

Sri turned around so her lips could meet Devyn's. She let her mouth fall slowly against his. She sighed and let her tears join his own. Their lips touched, and the pure kiss began in an unhurried way. Two lovers cradled each other in forgiveness, in a passion that overwhelmed both of them. Sri sobbed gently against Devyn's kiss, and he against hers.

Their bodies melted together—Sri's form swallowed up when Devyn took her in his arms. Two would fall together as one when the knife came from the beloved murderer. Ajan would not even know that the fragile mother stood behind his intended victim.

Devyn bled as a sword of mass pierced his back. A line of red flowed down his white clothes, and onto his stallion. His hands tried to stop the sword as it went through his body—to keep it from moving forward. But his lover was pressed so tightly against him that the sword pierced her flesh while her lips were warm against his. And her blood fell against her lover, while her eyes closed.

She jerked slightly and looked with horror into Devyn's eyes while he stared back at her. She gasped for breath while blood gurgled from both their mouths into the other's. They tried to speak and move, to discover what had happened.

Devyn stirred. "No! No!"

Devyn begged her not to go but those black eyes with the thin layer of red around the center had closed. Blood had seeped through her white dress to cake onto her body. Every way that she had touched him went limp. Her hands that held a child and touched his face lost their caress. Her lips mouthed quietly, "...love...you..." and then lost their movement against his. The warm breath that she shared with her lover was gone.

Devyn gasped quickly now as blood came through his mouth. "No...no...no...no...no...NO!" His chest heaved while his wounds gushed red from his back and stomach onto Sri's clothes.

His hands reached to their screaming child that was crushed against the mother's dead body. He turned his head to see what had been done.

Ajan, an image of darkness, stood watching from a distance behind the horse while his friend bled to death before his eyes. His cerulean gaze was cold and blank while he saw the man who had served in *Govandhara* with him whisper out the last bit of life. He had not intended for Devyn's eyes to meet his. For a moment—for just a moment—he felt sick while the wounds bled out.

Devyn choked at the sight of Ajan, and then turned back to his lover to die.

Ajan kneeled down to pray to *Brahma* for Devyn's soul, when he grew aware that something was very wrong. He heard the sound of a child screaming.

Ajan ran to the site of his dead friend, to find that he had taken away what he had intended to protect.

He had not seen a woman pressed against Devyn. He did not think that she came out here with him. He did not hear the sound of a woman's voice. He did not intend to hurt her. Why would she come? Why would she be there? He had wished only to take away Devyn. He did not know Sri was there. How could he have been so careless?

Ajan screamed out in terror, and took Sri's body off the horse and into his arms. "NO! What have I done!" He smoothed Sri's hair back with shaking hands and kissed her forehead. He rocked her back and forth in his arms while he screamed out. "Please please please please please be alive, Sri. Please…I love you, my darling. I didn't mean to. OH SRI!"

Ajan stood up with his dead and bleeding ward in his hands and walked through the trees while screaming out to *Brahma* in pain. He fell over in his tracks and began to call out at what he had done.

The black clad assassin rode forward on his horse to find Ajan. The group of men had been waiting a few paces back to await the results and take care of Devyn's body. When they heard Ajan scream, the assassin was sent forward. Instead, the old black clad man rode past the dead body of Devyn on the horse and a screaming child to find Ajan—holding the Queen in his arms. Dead.

The assassin showed no emotion, and spoke in a firm, commanding voice. "Give her body to me, Ajan."

Ajan shook his head. He did not want to give up the dead ward who he loved. Who he had killed. He wanted every drop of blood that would fall from Sri to drip on his skin so he could feel the last part of her soul against him.

The assassin jumped off his horse and claimed the dead woman from Ajan's unwilling arms. The black clad man did not know how it had happened—but he suspected. It did not matter now. They would have to deal with the outcome, and move forward. The goal was the protection of the heir.

The black clad man walked back to the place where Devyn's body lay, with Sri in his arms. He placed Sri down by the strange looking hut that appeared nearby, and then went to claim Devyn's form to place beside her.

As for the child—the goal had been attained. The men had been sent to ensure that the Heir to *Govandhara* return to the Kingdom. The black clad man took the baby girl in his arms, and looked on her with passive eyes. He would not need to tell his King what had happened.

Ajan had returned to the site, and was kneeling down beside the dead form of Sri with his head buried in Sri's bleeding abdomen. He continued to sob into her body, while his body rocked back and forth in disbelief.

Ajan flashed back to the demoness who had visited him after he delighted in the red haired youth. He had changed his life because of this creature, and the gods had gifted him with Sri. What his life was intended for—he had taken away in pursuit of the King's word. He had served his King faithfully, but had failed his gods.

The black clad man waited for Marici to arrive on bent knee with the child in his arms. Their liege would be soon to follow, to witness the death of Devyn.

Within moments, the King's black stallion came forward to look upon a clearing of blood. Marici's dark eyes, with a ring or red around the center, examined the ruby blood with curious eyes. Devyn must be dead. A sense of satisfaction passed through him. But he looked up at the sky, and it reminded him of *Govandhara*—and Sri—and his heart fell.

The King left his horse by Devyn's, and dismounted to walk to his kneeling servant who held the child. The King, wearing the black clothes of his caravan, looked down at the assassin with unfeeling eyes.

"What happened?" he asked, his eyes not traveling to the blood.

The assassin answered calmly, "An error was made and both of them are dead."

Marici followed the trail of blood to find the dead bodies of Sri and Devyn, side by side, outside of the hut. The King grabbed his heart for a moment while his eyes fell upon the dead image of his sister, and he felt a sensation of death over his own body. Marici dropped to one knee in pain, while he focused on the blood that had fallen on Sri's soaked dress. But, he let it pass.

"What else?" Marici asked, his voice choked.

The assassin kept his eyes down and responded in even tones. "Here is your heir."

Marici's dark eyes softened and his hands went trembling out to reach for the child. "This is the one?"

The assassin nodded once.

He took the little girl in his arms and stared at the face that he knew so well. Those eyes—black with the thin layer of red on the pupil—belonged only to his blood. Every wrong that Marici had done his sister could be righted in this little girl. Marici would love her, and give her everything. She would be his child.

Marici cleaned away Sri's blood from the baby's head and smoothed the blue flowers in her hair. He took her out of the blood soaked white blanket and wrapped her in the folds of his black tunic. His lips kissed her on the forehead, while he knelt with the child in his arms.

"I love you, little one...You are my heir. You are my Queen. I will call you Devi."

Afterword

When a person is dying, her voice goes into her mind; her mind into her breath; her breath into heat; the heat into the highest divinity.

That which is the finest essence—the whole world has that as her soul. That is Reality.

~Chandogya 6.8.6~

About the Author

Heir to Govandhara is Saira Ramasastry's debut novel. She holds a B.A. and M.S. from Stanford and an M.Phil. from Cambridge in England. She is currently working as an investment banker and living with her husband in Silicon Valley.

11116029R0

Made in the USA
Lexington, KY
11 September 2011